More Rave Reviews for Dave Duncan

★ "Excellent . . . brimming with wit and low-key charms; neither aficionados nor newcomers will be disappointed." —*Kirkus Reviews (*starred review) on *The Alchemist's Apprentice*

★ "Duncan is a superb storyteller! His fortieth novel is a totally enthralling romantic adventure. The characters seem to live and breathe, especially the charismatic hero. . . . He grabs your heartstrings on page one and doesn't let go until you discover his fate."

—*Romantic Times* (4½ stars) on *Ill Met in the Arena*

★ "Duncan's storytelling has never been better [than] in this superb fantasy. . . . How the children of Celebre reunite makes for a captivating, adventure-filled story."

—*Publishers Weekly* (starred review) on *Children of Chaos*

★ "Inventive, labyrinthine, witty, and thoroughly engaging: Duncan rarely disappoints, and here he outswashbuckles himself." —*Kirkus Reviews* (starred review) on *Paragon Lost*

★ "Should please not only Duncan's many loyal fans but also those who enjoy the work of Terry Goodkind and Jennifer Fallon."

—*Publishers Weekly* on *Mother of Lies*

★ "Duncan's outstanding third Venetian fantasy mystery . . . neatly blends a vision of magical Venice with an engrossing whodunit."

—*Publisher's Weekly* (starred review) *on The Alchemist's Pursuit*

BOOKS BY DAVE DUNCAN

THE BROTHERS MAGNUS
Speak to the Devil

"THE DODEC BOOKS"
Children of Chaos
Mother of Lies

THE ALCHEMIST
The Alchemist's Apprentice
The Alchemist's Code
The Alchemist's Pursuit

CHRONICLES OF THE KING'S BLADES
Paragon Lost
Impossible Odds
The Jaguar Knights

TALES OF THE KING'S BLADES
The Gilded Chain
Lord of Fire Lands
Sky of Swords

A MAN OF HIS WORD
Magic Casement
Faery Land Forlorn
Perilous Seas
Emperor and Clown

THE STARFOLK
King of Swords
Queen of Stars

A HANDFUL OF MEN
The Cutting Edge
Upland Outlaws
The Stricken Field
The Living God

THE GREAT GAME
Past Imerative
Present Tense
Future Indefinite

"THE OMAR BOOKS"
The Reaver Road
The Hunters' Haunt

THE SEVENTH SWORD
The Reluctant Swordsman
The Coming of Wisdom
The Destiny of the Sword
The Death of Nnanji

THE YEARS OF LONGDIRK
Demon Sword
Demon Rider
Demon Knight

STAND-ALONE NOVELS
West of January
The Cursed
A Rose-Red City
Shadow
Strings
Hero!
Ill Met in the Arena
Pock's World
Against the Light
Wildcatter
The Adventures of Ivor
The Eye of Strife
Irona 700

WRITING AS "SARAH B. FRANKLIN"
Daughter of Troy

Please see www.daveduncan.com for more information.

SPEAK TO THE DEVIL

DAVE DUNCAN

A TOM DOHERTY ASSOCIATES BOOK
NEW YORK

SPEAK TO THE DEVIL

Edited by Liz Gorinsky

A Tor Book
Published by Tom Doherty Associates
175 Fifth Avenue
New York, NY 10010

www.tor-forge.com

Tor® is a registered trademark of Macmillan Publishing Group, LLC.

ISBN 978-0-7653-6334-3

First Edition: May 2010
First Mass Market Edition: December 2016

Printed in the United States of America

0 9 8 7 6 5 4 3 2 1

Once upon a time, as the Age of Chilvary was ending, there lived in a little-known kingdom in Central Europe five brothers . . .

THE PLAYERS

THE BROTHERS

- Ottokar: thirteenth Baron Magnus of Dobkov, head of the family
- Vladislav: knight, a warrior currently held hostage in Bavaria
- Marek: a monk in the Benedictine monastery at Koupel
- Anton: recently enlisted in the Light Hussars
- Wulfgang: Anton's varlet

THE GOVERNMENT

- Konrad V: aging king of Jorgary
- Konrad: crown prince, his grandson
- Zdenek: cardinal, the king's first minister, known as the Scarlet Spider
- Svaty: archbishop of Jorgary

AT CARDICE

- Stepan: Count Bukovany of Cardice, lord of the march, keeper of Castle Gallant
- Edita: his countess
- Petr: knight, his son and heir
- Madlenka: the count's daughter
- Ugne: bishop of Cardice
- Giedre Jurbarkas: Madlenka's lady-in-waiting and best friend

- Ramunas Jurbarkas: seneschal of Castle Gallant, Giedre's father
- Karolis Kavarskas: knight, constable of Castle Gallant
- Dalibor Notivova: deputy constable

AT PELRELM

- Havel: Count Vranov of Pelrelm, lord of the march
- Marijus: knight, his tenth son
- Leonas: an imbecile, his fifteenth or sixteenth son
- Vilhelmas: a priest of the Greek Orthodox faith

IN POMERANIA

- Wartislaw: Duke of Pomerania, Lord of the Wends

SPEAK TO THE DEVIL

CHAPTER 1

In the darkest hour of the night, a troop of the Palace Guard came marching along the serpentine alleys of Mauvnik, capital city of Jorgary. Arriving at the home of Baron Radovan, they pounded the door knocker. When that produced no swift response, they thundered on the panels with the butts of their pikes and shouted abuse, making enough racket to silence the cats and start dogs barking. Nosy neighbors opened shutters. When at last a terrified servant peered out through the grille, their leader bellowed for all to hear that Lancer Anton Magnus was wanted at the palace at once. The guards continued to stamp and jingle and chatter in the roadway until the lanky youngster they sought came stumbling out, his hussar uniform awry and his eyes still blurred by sleep. They formed up around him and marched him away.

Anton was not told that he was under arrest. He was not required to surrender his saber. He was not even sure that the Palace Guard had authority to arrest a lancer of the Light Hussars, although these men seemed to think they did. They refused to say who had sent for him at this ungodly hour on a Sunday morning, or what his offense might be. He had been sinning, yes, but adultery was not a criminal matter. The slut's husband might call him out on a point of honor for it, but Anton was not worried about dueling a man who was currently far away in Bavaria, being held for ransom, and thirty years his senior anyway. If not lechery, then what? His conscience was unspotted otherwise.

A worse worry was that Anton Magnus had no idea how the palace guard had known where to find him. If the sergeants-at-arms had begun by seeking him in the verminous billet down in Lower Mauvnik that he shared with Wulfgang, his brother and varlet, then Wulf could have told them only that Anton was visiting a lady; he did not know which lady, and would not have told that even if he did. How had they known that he was sleeping the sleep of the exhausted in the bed of the luscious Baroness Nadezda Radovan?

At that point the lovely baroness—who was not as lovely as she must have been the year Anton was born, but still tried to behave as if she were—had become very unlovely indeed. She, who around midnight had been kind and fond to her "*Darling* Anton," praising both his privates and his prowess, had become shrill and abusive. To go from wearing nothing at all to the dress uniform of a hussar without a varlet's help was a long process—breechcloth, trunk hose, puffed shirt laced to the trunk hose, fancy slashed breeches, slashed and padded doublet, garters, socks over the hose, boots—with spurs, even at a ball—sword belt, sword, dagger, short cape, tall hat with narrow brim and tall plume; and all the time the harpy in the bed had been screaming that she was ruined, that the news would be all over Mauvnik and probably the entire kingdom by morning, that Anton Magnus was an evil young deviant preying on respectable women, and if he thought she was ever going to put in that good word to the minister of the army that she had promised last night, then he had the brains of a tadpole. And so on.

He had said nothing until he had his boots on and was heading for the door. Then he had dropped a copper *parvus* on her dressing table and told her exactly what he thought of her worn-out body and alley-cat morals, thus demonstrating that their relationship had been terminated by mutual consent.

Now the roofs and turrets of the palace stood inky black against the autumn stars. Only two windows showed light, both in the central tower where old King Konrad lay interminably dying. Anton's escorts were taking him to the south gate, to a part of the palace he did not know. And they still refused to say why.

Boots clumped on the miry cobbles. The air was warm; bats squeaked and swirled overhead. It was going to be another fine day, although perhaps not a fine day for Anton Magnus, the most junior recruit in the Light Hussars.

At the great gate, a bell was rung, a hatch opened, a password exchanged, and then the postern door swung open. Six boots marched across a yard reeking with a familiar smell of horses, and entered a dimly lit guard room.

As he stepped inside, Anton Magnus's anger and frustration turned to freezing terror, just for a moment. Then he relaxed, seeing that he had been mistaken. The man waiting for him in the gloom was innocent enough. Indeed, he was not even a man, for his face was smooth, and his head, though close-cropped, was not yet tonsured. His brown robe was that of a novice Franciscan. Franciscans were usually harmless. In his momentary, dazzled confusion, Anton had thought he was seeing a Dominican.

Dominicans were friars of a different color, and could represent the ultimate terror: suspicion of heresy or Satanism, interrogation, the Question, the stake. That was absurd in this case, of course! Anton Magnus never dabbled in such crimes, and had he not still been half asleep he would never have confused the two orders.

Yet suddenly his conscience no longer shone like a well-honed blade. On the royal hunt two days ago, he had pulled off an insanely reckless feat of horsemanship that had been witnessed by at least a hundred people. It had made him the talk of the court. It might have started suspicious tongues wagging, arousing whispers of Speaking. But it had certainly not been remarkable enough to expose him to a formal investigation by the Holy Office. A watch might be set on him in future; no more than that.

"Lancer Anton Magnus of Company D of the Royal Light Hussars?" The boy looked bored and sleepy, not frightened or malicious.

His throat too dry for speech, Anton just nodded.

The novice lifted a lantern and adjusted the wick. "If you would be so good as to follow me, lancer?" He led the way, sandals slapping softly on the flagstones.

For the next few minutes, Anton Magnus continued to reassure himself with positive thoughts. He still hadn't been relieved of his saber. Wherever he was being taken was no dungeon. The lantern's faint glow and that of the occasional sconce shone on mosaic floors, frescoes, and wide mirrors, then a staircase wide enough to admit a coach-and-four.

"May I ask who has summoned me here at this ungodly hour?"

The boy glanced around briefly and flashed an amused smile, but did not reply.

At the top of the stairs, he led the way across a wide hall, dark as a starlit night, with only twinkles reflected from mirrors, chandeliers, cornices, and gilt picture frames, hinting at its great size. Beyond that lay another chamber, even larger, and then a third, vaster still. By then Anton Magnus had guessed the answer to his question. Very few men in the kingdom would merit such splendor, and only one of them would still be active at this hour of the night. The third doorway had been guarded by four sergeants-at-arms, who evidently knew the boy, for they had let him lead Anton Magnus past them without a word, saber and all.

Although by day the third antechamber must teem with anxious petitioners, tonight it was almost deserted. Three lamps gleamed near the far-side door, their light faintly reflected in the polished marble floor. At a desk there sat a single elderly friar, reading, guarding a door, and probably also keeping an eye on two boys nearby, who were writing on slates. He was clearly a doorman, and Anton presumed that the novices were messengers, being kept properly busy at their studies during the quiet hours when their nimble feet were not required. His guess was confirmed as his guide went to join them.

The friar looked up and nodded at the sight of the visitor. He rose and glided to the door he guarded, which must certainly lead to the inner sanctum of the most powerful man in Jorgary, the king's first minister, Cardinal Zdenek.

Anton detoured to a convenient mirror for a hasty inspection. He straightened his plume and frowned at creases in his britches and scuff marks on his riding boots. Wulf had spent an hour polishing them last night, before Anton went off to the ball, but much had happened since then. No matter; they would have to do. Whatever had caused the cardinal to summon him in the middle of the night, it had not been to inspect smears of rouge on his collar. He twirled up his mustaches and turned back to his guide, who was waiting with the door open.

Zdenek's audience chamber was ablaze with light from four huge chandeliers, reflected in the high crystal mirrors and gilded paneling. Rich brocade drapes covered the windows. Just one of those chairs of velvet and gilt would cost as much as Anton would be paid in the next five years. He felt suitably humbled.

The great man sat on a chair that was very nearly a throne, head bent to study a single sheet of paper. He was flanked on one side by a writing stand with inkwells and shelves to hold papers and on the other by a small table bearing four leather-bound folios and a goblet containing about two mouthfuls of dark ruby wine. He did not look up as his visitor came to a halt before him. Having no choice, Anton Magnus waited to be acknowledged. The door closed softly behind him.

Behold a portrait of the king's faithful servant, laboring at all hours: Zdenek himself was elderly, shrunken inside his scarlet robes. The hand steadying the paper was skeletal and the color of lichen-spotted bone. His eyes were hidden by an uncomfortable-looking set of eyeglasses clamped to a beak nose; his beard and hair were silver, in stark contrast to the brilliant hue of his robes and broad-brimmed, tasseled hat, below which his eyebrows stuck out like two pale horns. He was a study in snowy white and the deep scarlet of clotted blood, like a winter battlefield.

No true churchman, Zdenek had probably never baptized a babe or buried a corpse in his life. Few laymen could read, so most clerks were clerics of some sort. Ability and diligence had raised him in the king's service, and some political favor for the pope had bought him a cardinal's hat. He ran the kingdom now as he had run it for a generation. He was reputed to need almost no sleep. His many enemies called him the Scarlet Spider.

So the mystery of how Anton Magnus had been located was solved. The Spider knew everything—everyone knew that. Whichever young man escorted the baroness to the ball would escort her to bed later; this was understood but did not explain why the king's chief minister had summoned the most junior recruit in the Light Hussars. They inhabited different worlds. Cardinal Zdenek should not even know that Lancer Anton Magnus existed.

And apparently he didn't, for Zdenek continued to read. Lancer Anton Magnus continued to stand at attention. He dearly wished that he had stopped at some doorway in the town to empty his bladder. After what seemed an age, the old man acknowledged his visitor by laying the paper on the writing stand and looking up. Lamplight blazed on his eyeglasses, masking his eyes so that his face was a skull lantern, a macabre decoration for All Hallows' Eve.

The hussar saluted. "Anton Magnus, Your Eminence." His uniform said everything else necessary.

The cardinal studied him without any expression whatever, as if he were a piece of statuary.

The hussar felt a welcome shiver of anger replacing his apprehension. This was a test of nerve. Captain Walangoin had tried the same sort of tricks on him when he was sworn in ten days ago, but the Magnuses of Dobkov had been famed for centuries for their suicidal courage. Zdenek must have better things to do with his time than Captain Walangoin ever could. So Anton Magnus must keep his own face immobile, staring unblinking at those glowing fiery disks until the bloodless lips below them indicated a smile.

They didn't. "I see now," the cardinal said in a dry whisper, "why the fair baroness enlisted you with a speed extraordinary even for her."

Anton felt a red tide flood his face. *I did not realize Your Eminence had summoned me to hear my confession.* But he did not say that. Silence was the best defense.

The cardinal held out his right hand. Anton knelt to kiss his ring.

As he rose, he caught a glimpse of a fading smile, worthy of the amusement with which a man might regard a cavorting puppy. "Welcome, lancer. Pour yourself a glass of wine over there."

Anton turned in the direction indicated and went to where a bottle and crystal goblets stood on a small sideboard. He was surprised to see that there was another man present, a friar at a desk; he was behind the door, which was why Anton had not seen him earlier. He was writing something and did not look up.

Anton poured a very small amount of wine into a glass, well aware that dawn must be close and he could not have slept more than an hour. He returned to the cardinal.

"A glass, I said; not a sip. You insult His Majesty's hospitality."

Anton Magnus went back to the sideboard and topped up the goblet. If this was an attempt to make him drunk, it would not work. He had stayed very sober at the ball, having been forewarned by his messmates of the exertions the dear baroness would require of him later.

As he straightened, glass in hand, the cardinal spoke again.

"And bring that chair."

The chair was solid oak, with arms and a high back. Was this a test of strength or good judgment? Make two trips so he could use both hands, or risk taking chair and glass both? Angry at this continuing childishness, Anton decided to risk one trip. He managed to lift the monster with his left hand alone and carry it back across the room without cracking his shins or spilling his wine. He set the chair on the floor and himself on the chair.

His host raised his own glass. "To the king and your service."

He did not stand, as one should to toast the king, so neither did Anton.

"God preserve His Majesty." The wine was richly spiced Hippocras from Smyrna, caressing the mouth like a woman's kiss. It had been a favorite of Anton's father, but such luxuries had been missing in Dobkov for the last two years.

So here he was, a penniless esquire owning a uniform, a suit of armor, and two horses—he had not even received the expected and hard-earned honorarium from the baroness—being treated as an honored guest by the most powerful man in the kingdom. The world had gone insane, or he had. Perhaps he had cracked his skull at the hunt and was imagining all this.

"Tell me about yourself," Zdenek murmured. His eyes were still hiding behind reflected lamplight.

Insanity! "Your Eminence, I am the fourth son of the late Baron Patredor Magnus of Dobkov. My ancestors have held—"

"Yourself, not your ancestors. The Magnuses of

Dobkov are famous in the history of Jorgary; you are not. Not yet, anyway. Start with your brothers."

"As it please Your Eminence. Male Magnuses come in two sizes. The large ones become soldiers, the small ones take holy orders. My eldest brother, Ottokar, is one of the largest. He succeeded our father five years ago." How much detail did Zdenek want? Why should he want any? Anton shivered, wondering if some family problem might lie behind this madness. "He is married and—"

"And ought to make his wife sleep in another room before her fertility bankrupts him. Next?"

"Sir Vladislav is even bigger, a knight banneret in His Majesty's Heavy Hussars. For the last two years he has been a prisoner in Bavaria."

Vlad, like Baron Radovan, had been captured at the Battle of the Boundary Stone. Jorgary's attempt to take advantage of a disputed succession in Bavaria had failed spectacularly. Court gossips disagreed on whether the cardinal had lost his touch at last or the featherbrained crown prince had talked his ailing grandfather into ordering the invasion against Zdenek's advice. The boundary itself was now a day's march closer to Mauvnik than it had been, and the kingdom was still bleeding gold to ransom its nobility. Two thousand commoners had bled to death on the field.

"Third is Marek, now Brother Marek of the Benedictine house in Koupel. And then me. His Majesty most graciously accepted my petition to enlist in his Light Hussars, and I arrived in Mauvnik about ten days ago. Of course it was Vladislav's reputation that won me this great privilege."

The cardinal was staring down at the paper again. It was completely covered in tiny, spidery writing, even along the margins. Anton could read, though he was badly out of practice, but not upside down. Was the friar behind him writing down everything he said?

"How long did it take you to ride from Dobkov to Mauvnik?" Zdenek inquired in his raspy voice.

Anton blinked. "Um . . . fifteen days, Your Eminence." Why ask that, for God's sake?

"Why so long?"

"It was a new experience for me, for I have never strayed far from—"

The skull's crystal eyes blazed. *"Never lie to me, boy!"*

He flinched. "Your Eminence's pardon . . . I had agreed to accompany a caravan of merchants who wanted protection on the road. Your Eminence must understand that my brother the baron is desperately trying to raise money to pay Vladislav's ransom." The nobility were all land rich and cash poor. "It was time that I sought my own way in the world, and I could not have afforded even to enlist in His Majesty's service had Vladislav not written to insist that I must be equipaged before his ransom be paid."

In his grandfather's day he would have become a knight errant, roaming Christendom in search of tourneys where he might win fame and fortune jousting. A knight unhorsed and captured in the tilting yard would forfeit his arms, armor, and horse, which the winner might then sell, often back to the original owner. A horseman as good as Anton could have made his fortune very rapidly. Nowadays chivalry was out of fashion and the miserable alternative was a career in the king's cavalry—working for *wages* like a journeyman wheelwright.

The cardinal sneered. "So you held your nose and

became a trader's hired guard for two weeks? You think I care a spit for your confounded petty honor? Or that I don't know how Ottokar will likely have to sell land to ransom that big idiot who got captured in Bavaria? Stay with the truth from now on! You have another brother."

"Wulfgang, Your Eminence. He is only seventeen." Anton Magnus risked a smile, which was not returned. "He's a family freak, being medium-sized. Lacking the usual clue, he seems unable to decide between the sword and the cross. Ottokar told him that if he did not soon make up his mind, he would be too old for a career with either. I brought him with me as my varlet. He is very good with horses, and fine company, in a quiet sort of—"

"Seventeen?"

"Yes, Your Eminence." *Oh, damnation!* "Just turned eighteen, I mean—last week."

The cardinal twisted around to the writing stand to make a minute note on the paper, then turned it face-down. He leaned back in his chair, put his fingertips together, and let Anton Magnus study the glowing eyeglasses for a while. He had already known everything Anton had just told him and probably a lot more beside.

He said, "Tell me exactly what happened at the hunt on Friday."

CHAPTER 2

Anton Magnus took a swallow of wine and was relieved to note that his hand did not shake.

"I made a fool of myself, Your Eminence."

No comment.

"I was assigned to guard the ladies and other guests. It is not a desirable duty, because it is . . . I am sure Your Eminence understands."

During a court hunt, the crown prince and his guests chased deer. Or rather the hounds chased deer and they followed the hounds. The huntsmen did the real work, locating the available stags, seeing that the bloodhounds found the scent and the greyhounds stayed on the trail; eventually gutting and skinning the meat. Meanwhile the ladies, children, and elderly guests picnicked on the grass in the royal forest. The guards watched out for dangers, of which there were virtually none worse than wasps—perhaps a wild boar or a rabid wolf, once every ten years or so.

So the hussars would spend a long day astride restive horses in the heat and the flies. They did get time off, alternating watches, but on their downtime they had to stay out of sight among the bushes with the horses and grooms. When mounted they must do nothing more than sit there and look romantic; flirting with the ladies was strictly forbidden. Regrettably, no one was assigned to guard the guards from the ladies. Some of the court jades, notably Baroness Nadezda, enjoyed taunting newcomers to make them blush.

Worse, there were innumerable opportunities for a man to make a fool of himself. His horse might tread on a child's foot. Or get bitten by a horsefly. Or scare away the deer. Or even take off after the quarry, because the hussars' mounts were all hunters and knew what the horn calls meant as well as the men did.

"We were gathered at Chestnut Hill, Your Eminence, the top of a steep meadow, with a beechwood at our backs. And the stag came right through the woods behind us. We could hear the horns and hounds growing closer and closer. The horses became very excited. Then the stag broke cover not fifty paces to our right and went racing down the hill towards the stream. To my shame, my horse ran away with me, Your Eminence. I was very lucky not to get killed. The hunt saw me in the vanguard and several men trying to follow took bad spills. By Our Lady's mercy, the crown prince had more sense! I have already been severely reprimanded by Captain Walangoin, and warned that I am now on probation. Any further offense at all and I will be cashiered."

The cardinal nodded and took a tiny sip of wine. "Seven men injured, two of them crippled for life. Four horses destroyed. What exactly was this ditch that caused such carnage?"

"It is a stream, Your Eminence, with tall hedges along either bank. The stag managed it, of course. The hounds went through the shrubbery, although it slowed them a lot. But my horse managed to jump the first hedge, find footing on the gravel, and gather himself enough to clear the second hedge also."

"So you were the first man on the spot to beat off the hounds and provide the mort."

"Yes, Your Eminence." Anton's hand patted the hilt of his saber in fond memory.

At last, Zdenek moved his head so that the fire died from his glasses and exposed his eyes. They were deep-set, shrouded in wrinkles, dark and unreadable.

"Well, that is the official story. That is what you told everybody. Now tell me what really happened."

"I raked my horse's flanks with my spurs."

"It was deliberate?"

"Yes, Your Eminence."

"You knew that you might very well be killed?"

"Yes, Your Eminence."

"And what did you hope to gain?"

"I was afraid that the stag might follow the water and the dogs would lose the scent. The stream was not obvious, but I had been watching the birds and knew it was there. I had noted where it might be jumped. My horse was fresh, the hunt's were not. I thought I might turn the stag or set the dogs on the right trail."

"The stag was none of your business."

"But I am new at court; I need to be noticed. I need money to help ransom my brother. Before the hunt I was a nothing. I had hope that a daring display of horsemanship might cause the crown prince to send for me later."

"The crown prince watched his best friend break his back. His Highness wanted to hang you from the nearest oak."

"So I heard, my lord." Even so, by the end of the day they had all been talking about the tall young lancer.

Now that the story had reached the ears of the king's chief minister the true payoff might be at hand. Fortune favored the bold.

The cardinal made an impatient noise. "Had the baroness promised you a turn in her bed?"

"Not in words, Your Eminence. I had been told of several ladies at court who could advance a man's career."

"Or give him the clap. Some think that Lancer Anton Magnus is a Speaker."

The old man's glasses were shining again. So, very likely, was Anton's forehead. Speakers were sinners who could talk to the devil. They could call on Satan for help.

"Dobkov has always been famous for both its horses and its horsemen, Your Eminence. One of the men following me managed to clear the stream as I did."

"His horse broke a leg, though. Did you pray as you rode down the hill?"

Anton could be damned saying either yes or no, for a man could pray to Satan. "I commended my soul to my Maker and asked His forgiveness." That happened to be the truth, but truth might not satisfy the tormentors.

"You have great confidence in your horsemanship, I see. Also ambition and fanatical courage."

"It runs in the blood. No Magnus has ever run away from anything." Most of them died young.

"They have also been noted for loyalty to the throne. If I sent you back to Dobkov with an urgent message, how soon could you get it there?"

Oh, this was a tricky one! What was emerging now? Was this it, at last? Anton sensed something moving in long grass.

"Urgent enough to kill horses?"

"Urgent enough to kill men."

He let the silence grow, holding the old man's gaze—his eyes were visible again. Yes, there was a challenge there, and no Magnus ever refused a challenge.

"My horsemanship is second to none, Your Eminence. If I cannot do what you need, then no man can."

That was absolute rubbish. Anton Magnus was very, very good, but the cardinal could call on hundreds of superb riders in the Hussars.

Zdenek nodded. "What do you know of the northern marches?"

"Nothing." Honesty had been called for.

"Do you recognize this?" The old man spread out a paper, an etching showing a fortress, a huge and dramatic fortress on a plateau. On three sides its curtain wall rimmed the edge of a sheer precipice dropping several hundred feet to a turbulent river. The back of the stronghold nestled against a high cliff face, and the only visible access was up a steep road clinging to the mountainside. Unless the artist had dreamt it, that was a castle to withstand almost anything.

"Recognize, no," Anton said. "But if I had to guess, I would say it must be Castle Gallant."

The cardinal's smile was skull-like. "Correct. Brother Daniel, show our guest the way."

Cued by a nod, Anton rose and walked over to the Franciscan, who stood up. He was tall, although not as tall as Anton, with a narrow, ascetic face and a black leather patch over his left eye. He was also young, with a dense hedge of red hair around his tonsure. He spread out a printed tract of about eight pages, right-way-round for Anton to read.

"An itinerary," Anton said, as if any fool knew about those and he was uncertain why was he being bothered with this one.

"Correct," the friar said in a scratchy voice. "From Mauvnik, east to Moravia. It lists towns, cities, villages, landmarks, noble houses where gentry may seek hospitality, monasteries for the rest of us, road quality, tollbooths, drinking water, fords, ferries, bridges for use in wet weather, and so on. Villages with inns and fairs are mentioned. Here is Dobkov and the ancestral home of the Magnuses. You probably followed an itinerary much like this one on your journey here . . . ?"

He waited for a reply. Was this a literacy test? Fortunately Anton's eye picked out a name he knew. "Putovat? Had a very fine church."

"St. Vaclav's?"

"Didn't get near enough to ask. I was shadowing a dangerous-looking bull. Is this relevant?"

The friar smiled bloodlessly. "Only inasmuch as Dobkov is shown as being ten days' journey from Mauvnik. More or less, of course. Itineraries' travel times are more faith than deed." He laid it aside and produced another. "Now, this one shows the way north from Mauvnik and on through Pomerania via the Silver Road. The last entry in Jorgary is Castle Gallant, in the county of Cardice, which happens to be shown exactly ten days away, as was Dobkov. May the Lord have mercy on all who travel."

"Bring that back here and sit down," the cardinal said from the far side of the room.

Anton obeyed, calculating that he could, if really motivated—meaning offered a hundred florins or more—ride home to Dobkov in less than a week. Three days, using post horses on dry roads. But this was late in the year. Weather would be critical. Daylight and moonlight . . . Even before he sat down, Zdenek began speaking again.

"Lords of the northern marches are charged with keeping out Wend raiders. If they can't keep them out, they are expected to retaliate—hunt them down on their own territory and make examples of them. It is a wild and bloody land."

Anton nodded. He knew that much. Several historical Magnuses were buried up there, having failed to live long enough to be anybody's ancestors.

"The northern marches comprise four counties. Pelrelm is by far the largest and Cardice the smallest. You may ignore Kipalban and Gistov, which are irrelevant in this instance. Pelrelm is so mountainous that it is good only for raising fighting men and cattle. The count of Pelrelm can muster about two thousand men-at-arms, and probably mount them after a fashion. Cardice is barely more than one fertile valley and a fortress, Castle Gallant. The only town of any size is Gallant itself.

"So Cardice is small, yes, but it owns a profitable lead mine and the fortress guards the Silver Road to the north. The keeper levies a toll on the traders passing through. He has few followers of his own, but he can hire mercenaries when necessary. Are you with me?"

"Yes, Your Eminence." Pelrelm's hill men might assemble much faster than Cardice could find mercenaries for hire, but a good mercenary force, well trained and made up of pikemen and mounted archers in roughly equal numbers, would be far more effective, man for man.

"Now it gets complicated." The cardinal spoke slowly, as if he found explaining things to hussars a painful exercise. "Castle Gallant belongs to the king, but the office of keeper has been held by members of the Bukovany family for so many generations that it has become virtually hereditary." The snowy beard writhed in disapproval of such careless mismanagement of a royal resource. "Admittedly, they have always been loyal and usually efficient. Last summer, Count Stepan sent his son, Petr Bukovany, here to court to ask for recognition as his father's heir. He made a good impression. The king knighted him and granted his petition."

Meaning that Zdenek had approved of him. The old king was past caring, from all accounts. He would sign anything the cardinal put in front of him.

"While he was here, we were able to advise him of some disquieting intelligence His Majesty has received concerning Pomerania. Duke Wartislaw, who claims the title of Lord of the Wends, has been buying ordnance from Sweden, heavy guns especially. He has been building up his army and we suspect that he has his eye on Jorgary. His Majesty directed Count Bukovany, via his son, to increase Cardice's garrison." He added with a hint of admiration, "Sir Petr negotiated a remittance of certain taxes to help allay the cost.

"I should not presume to instruct a soldier such as yourself, lancer, but if Duke Wartislaw wants to invade Jorgary, he will have to take Castle Gallant first. Driving herds or flocks over mountain passes is one thing, but a modern army needs tents, rations, fodder, cannon, powder, shot, women, and much else. At this time of year he must come by the Silver Road, and he must come before winter. Now, late September, would be about right. By the time His Majesty's forces can muster and march north, Wartislaw may have laid waste half the kingdom. Even if he does not, once he has taken Gallant itself, he will never give it up, and our border will never be secure again."

Anton nodded, perplexed. What in the world did the old villain want of him?

"Just yesterday, Saturday, His Majesty received an urgent and disturbing message from Cardice. The courier left there on the fifteenth, so he took eight days. He was half dead and had ridden several horses into the ground. You understand now why I sent for you?"

Anton guessed that he had been sent for because eight days would not do. "How soon does your reply have to be there, Your Eminence?"

The cardinal's eyes appeared and then vanished again behind their curtains of fire. "I hope that you will be my reply. If so, you have not an hour to waste."

Anton squared his shoulders. It had worked! Whatever the Scarlet Spider wanted, that insanity at the hunt had worked! "I am honored and eager to serve, Your Eminence."

"Don't be so hasty. You haven't heard the whole problem yet. The message was that, on the morning of the fifteenth, Count Bukovany had suffered a severe stroke, and the doctors held out no hope of his surviving. Sir Petr had gone deer hunting that morning and was charged by a boar at exactly the same hour his father was smitten. He was brought back on a litter, fatally gored. Are you still so eager, Lancer Magnus?"

Witchcraft! Not quite so eager. "You suspect Speaking, Your Eminence? Satanism?"

"I do. Answer my question."

Anton had thought he was to be asked to deliver a letter. Now the job description sounded like much more than that. Far more than anything he could handle, in truth.

"I am still very eager. Who sent the message?"

"Ah!" Long yellow fangs showed for a moment in the cardinal's beard. "You ask shrewd questions, young man—perhaps Our Lady has answered my prayers. The warning was sent by the castle seneschal and countersigned by Count Stepan's daughter, delivered by a juvenile son of the chief huntsman."

"I should have expected the constable, or whoever was the count's military deputy, to send it by a party of his lancers."

"So should I."

"Treachery?" Anton said with a shiver.

"It has the odor of treachery on it. The boy, Gintaras, is still barely coherent after his ordeal, but he confirms that the palace staff distrust the *landsknechte* presently reinforcing the garrison."

Mercenaries were notoriously ready to change sides when money changed hands. They could have intercepted the official message while the private one slipped by. Anton thumped his sleepy brain to make it think harder.

"What else do I need to know?" How much would he be paid? A hundred florins would sound downright scrimpy now. To think Ottokar warned him that he might find life dull in the Light Hussars!

"You must remember that it will take at least a month to bring any significant number of the king's men to the rescue. The only force that might be brought to Cardice's aid in short order would be the Pelrelm muster, but the present count of Pelrelm, Havel Vranov, is known as the Hound of the Hills. Vranov would make a good impression on the devil. His specialty is burning down houses with people inside. He undoubtedly hates Wends with a passion, as his career shows, but he is not above casting a covetous eye on Cardice. Petr Bukovany reported that Vranov had been urging Count Stepan to marry his daughter to one of Vranov's uncountable sons. The king refused to approve the match, and that was the answer Petr took home with him."

Anton could remember Ottokar and Vladislav discussing political and military messes like this one. He wished that he had paid more attention, but he doubted that any of their examples had ever been quite this bad.

"So the nearest ally may not be much better than the enemy?"

"You may indeed find yourself between the dogs and the wolves. This cannot be described as an easy mission, Lancer Magnus. If you arrive to find the Wends already in possession of Castle Gallant, then you will very likely die. If you arrive before that, you may still be overwhelmed despite the best that you or anyone could do."

And still no price had been mentioned. What would his father have said? That salty old campaigner had said many things that might be pertinent in this instance. Anton chose the most polite. "Then the prize must balance the risk."

"How much do you want?"

"Five florins and Your Eminence's favor."

The fiery eyes flashed. "Insolent young devil! If you won't haggle, then neither will I." The cardinal beckoned to Brother Daniel, who brought over a black leather satchel. Zdenek began to fish out its contents, laying them on the table for Anton to see. First came a sash of cloth-of-gold, as wide as a man's hand, bearing emblems of a crown and a cross embroidered in pearls. "The baldric of a companion in the Order of St. Vaclav—it gives you precedence immediately after the royal family." Next was a baton, decorated with bands of gold and jewels in colors like butterflies. "From recruit to marshal of the army in less than two weeks? You will be the talk of all Christendom."

Parchment scrolls followed, with royal seals dangling. "Your honorable discharge from the hussars . . . letters patent creating you Count Magnus of Cardice and lord of the marches . . . your commission, promoting you to marshal, and appointing you keeper of the fortress . . . and the king's warrant requiring all his subjects to aid you in your present mission." The cardinal chuckled dryly. "You should, of course, be dubbed knight in proper form, but a humble man of the cloth like me must not wield a sword. I shall send the crown prince to Cardice to do it next summer, after you have secured the border.

"And this edict says that you may, and will, marry Madlenka Bukovany, who is now an orphan child of one of His Majesty's tenants-in-chief, and thus a royal ward in chancery. Marriage will let you get your hands into the Bukovany money chests and that will make your brother's ransom seem like small change."

The cardinal raised his eyebrow horns. He was probably amused by Anton's state of shock. The lancer's mouth felt drier than mummy dust. *An earldom?* No Magnus had ever reached such heights; he was barely twenty years old and had never seen a battle. After a moment he looked across at the shining eyeglasses and found his voice. "You do know how to inspire a man, Your Eminence."

The old man sneered. "It is cheap trash to His Majesty—paper and wax, a ribbon, and a piece of wood? If you die, Anton Magnus, you will have lost what is most precious of all, life itself, while the king will have lost very little. If you succeed, you may become founder of one of the great families of the realm, the Magnuses of Cardice, and that will be a worthy reward. I am relying on you to maintain your family's long and splendid reputation for loyalty and service."

No, he wasn't. Anton wished that were the case, but he was sure that Zdenek was actually relying on the family's long and shameful record of producing Speakers. He did not want a courier, or even a warrior. Alexander the Great himself would not suffice. He wanted a Speaker. He wanted witchcraft. He thought Anton could call on the devil to help him reach Castle Gallant in record time and counter the Wendish Satanist who had cursed the Bukovanys.

But Anton Magnus *wasn't* a Speaker. He had called on neither saint or demon for aid in jumping the stream.

"Well?" Zdenek demanded. "I cannot promise much else: a few hundred hussars at most, and not for thirty or forty days, even if the weather holds. They have all gone home, you see—officers for the hunting and men for the grape harvest. You are the only card I have to play. Do you accept?"

"Certainly I accept."

The old man truly smiled, for the first time. It looked very much like a smile of relief. "You are insane, young man, but I salute you."

"Our family motto is *Omnia audere*, and I will not be unworthy of it."

The cardinal chuckled. "A humanist hussar? My, what is the world coming to? And how do you construe that apothegm, scholar? 'To risk everything'?"

"It means, 'I dare any odds!' "

"Close enough. Well, I doubt if any of your ancestors has even faced odds like these—one man against the devil and the entire Pomeranian army. Put your trust in God, my son, not mottoes. Brother Daniel, is it dawn yet?"

The friar peered behind a drape. "Half light, Eminence."

"Then you needs be on your way, Lord Magnus, to dare all. Any questions?"

"How old is my bride, Madlenka Bukovany?"

"Ah, how could I leave out the most important part? Seventeen. Petr called her both a hellion, which is a judgment not unexpected from a brother, but also a great beauty, which is." The old man jingled a leather bag. "Gold for your journey." He began repacking the satchel. "You may need this engraving. May Our Lord and all His angels preserve you. Your varlet can gather your possessions and return them to Dobkov."

"I shall need my . . . I shall take my brother with me," Anton said. He saw no reaction from the cardinal, but he realized at once that he had let his guard down too soon and stepped into a trap. He had betrayed Wulf's dread secret. Yet he could not help thinking that it might turn out for the best, later.

CHAPTER 3

The brothers' billet was an attic in the slum area, Lower Mauvnik. It was smelly and cramped and the roof leaked. It would be an icehouse in winter and an oven in summer, and Anton could not stand upright there, even without his hussar hat. The old couple who lived in the fourth-floor room below it feared and hated all soldiers, but the pittance the king paid them to billet two men in their loft was probably their only income. The open steps were almost as steep as a ladder and creaked monstrously, so Anton made no effort to be quiet when he entered, although the relics were still abed in the dark. He climbed through the trap at the top, closed it, and carefully set his hat on the solitary chair.

A bed too narrow for two, a rickety chest of drawers, and a small table completed the furnishings, and the plank floor was carpeted by the clothes and domestic litter of two young men unable to afford servants. Being a count in a great castle was going to be a big step up.

Wulf was standing in the dormer, having opened the shutter to let in the first rays of daylight. He was shirtless, but seemed unaware of the cold, and he was shaving, which he did every day, although he was too fair to show much in the way of stubble.

Anton flopped down on the bed. "Sorry I forgot your birthday last week, Wulf."

"You are forgiven. I forgot it too. It's not exactly a major festival."

"You feeling better today?"

"I'm well."

He had been tortured by a pounding headache yesterday morning. Possibly in the evening too; Anton had forgotten to ask. He still sounded upset. Commands from a lancer to his varlet would not work in the current situation. Careful negotiation was required.

"What's gnawing your ass, then?"

"Nothing."

"You're lying. I've got important news and we've got to hurry, so spit it out, sonny."

Wulf turned around, his face shining with the oil he used to lubricate the razor. "You don't know? Really?"

"Really."

"Just that the next time you try to commit suicide, don't expect me to stop you, all right? It's my soul you risk and my head you hurt. I hope your palace trollop was worth it, but from now on you can enlist your bawds by yourself."

Despite the bitterness in the words, he spoke them softly. No matter how far he was provoked, Wulf never raised his voice. On the rare occasions when he was pushed too far, the first warning was the impact of his fist on the offender's face.

"Your soul?" Anton protested. "I never asked you to Speak. I didn't know you *had* Spoken until you told me yesterday. I thought Morningstar and I did that jump all by ourselves."

"Truly?" Wulf's yellow eyes glinted. "There I was, comfortably sitting on wet grass eating some noble leftovers in the company of six ignorant churls and a million horseflies, making eyes at a young nursemaid just on principle, when I see you waving for me to come running. The which I then do, anxious lest you need your nose wiped, and you say only, 'Pray for me!' Straightaway, you spur your horse down the side of a cliff and into an impossible double jump."

"It wasn't impossible!"

"Yes it was. And you knew what sort of prayer you were asking for."

Anton sighed. "I suppose I did sort of hint. But I was going to try it anyway, and if my survival was your doing, or your saints' doing, then I'm very grateful. What did you actually do, by the way? After I left?"

"I fell on my knees and begged St. Victorinus to preserve you."

"Aloud?"

"It doesn't work otherwise."

Who else ever prayed to St. Victorinus? Who but Wulf had ever heard of St. Victorinus? Obviously Wulf's odd behavior had been noted and reported, so Zdenek had known all along that it was Anton's brother who was the Speaker. At the end, when the cardinal had tricked Anton into admitting that he would have to take Wulf along to Cardice, that had been mere confirmation.

"Perfectly natural behavior. You saw me careering downhill like that, so of course you appealed to Our Lady to save me. There was no one close enough to hear what you actually said."

"I just hope you're right," Wulf said skeptically and went back to shaving.

Anton decided that a little more sincerity was required.

"Wulf, I know it wasn't fair of me. It was an impulse. I saw a chance to catch the eye of people who matter in this kingdom. It was for both our sakes. And for Vlad, too, remember! This town swarms with fine horsemen, but riding's the only skill I have that could get me promoted."

"You told me that swiving would," Wulf said scornfully.

"It did."

"Really? She does have influence at court?"

"Well, let me show you!" Anton dug in the satchel. "The baldric of a companion in the Order of St. Vaclav . . . a marshal's baton . . . letters patent making me a count."

His brother hooted. "By the blood, you must be almost as good as you say you are! Better than good—you must be stupendous! So you humped your way into a singing role in the next court masque?" Still laughing, the kid turned his back to continue his ordeal with the razor. Now that he had blown off his anger, the incident was closed. He had never carried grudges, fortunately, despite innumerable excuses provided by four older brothers.

So far so good, except that Anton would now have to reopen the wound.

He said, "Listen. We must be quick. I've got Morningstar and Sparrow downstairs, all ready to go."

"Go where?"

Anton spread out the engraving. "Do you know where this is?"

Wulf glanced over his shoulder. "That's Castle Gallant. I've seen a print of it before."

"It's mine now," Anton said. He lowered his voice to a whisper. The antiquities below were both deaf and the floor was surprisingly solid and soundproof, but he was going to be revealing state secrets. "I've just come from a meeting with the Scarlet Spider himself. He's given me a job. Given *us* a job, I mean. There's bad trouble brewing in the north. The Wends are massing to invade and they've blindsided him, although he didn't admit that. He thinks Pomerania is about to attack Castle Gallant, which holds the Silver Road. Now the keeper is dead, murdered by witchcraft, and his son also. He's survived by—"

"You mean the army's mustering?" Wulf spun around, eyes bright. "We're riding north?"

"Not the army, just us. Stop leering, you idiot! I'm serious. These things are all genuine: baldric, marshal's baton . . . letters patent creating His Majesty's 'dear and right trusty' Anton Magnus—that's me, believe it!—Count Magnus of Cardice . . . Here's His Majesty's permission and requirement that I marry the daughter, Madlenka. So what do you think of that?"

Wulf snapped the razor closed and laid it down. He wiped his face with his rag. All the while his golden, lupine eyes stared hard at Anton. He stepped over some dirty dishes so that he was standing close, looking down.

"Just like the fairy tales? '. . . gave him the princess's hand in marriage and half the kingdom and they all lived happily ever after'? But nobody heard me Speak to my Voices? Pure coincidence. Happens all the time."

"All right!" Anton roared. "So I cheated a little. What matters is that it worked! The king needs us! Zdenek needs us!"

"You say 'us'? What exactly do *we* have to do?"

"We have to ride like the devil to Castle Gallant. I marry the girl, take command of the troops, clean out the traitors, and hold the fort in the king's name."

"Ride like the devil?" Wulf repeated in a soft whisper. He took up his shirt from the bed. "Why us? You swore an oath, Brother. The day the Dominicans took Marek away, Father made all of you swear on the hand of St. Ulric never to tell anyone that I could Speak too. You all swore not to reveal that secret by word or deed, by omission or commission. You pledged your immortal soul, Anton Magnus, Count Nothing."

"I have not revealed it, nor told anyone." Anton realized that Wulf might well be building up to a fight. It was almost a year since they'd last had a roughhouse, and Wulf had won that one.

The golden eyes did not blink and the voice stayed low, but that meant nothing. "So why did the Spider decide to send you, only you, of all the king's men? He asked you because of what happened at the hunt on Friday. Did he tell you to take me along?"

"No."

"Did you say you would?" Wulf said, tipping his head sideways.

Anton squirmed. He rarely won arguments with his young brother, and it would be useless to threaten him. Straight orders had been working since they signed up in the hussars, and a sharp cuff to the ear used to, but none of those would serve this time.

"Wulfgang, I am asking you very humbly to make an exception, just this once."

"No. You think I want to be locked up for the rest of my life? Or tortured? Burned at the—"

Grovel time. "But this is the most incredible chance for all of us, Wulf! I get a wife rich enough to ransom Vlad. Otto won't have to sell off any of the family lands. And you can have anything you have ever wanted, anything my wealth can buy. I swear! You can be my constable, or master of horse, or go to Vienna to study medicine, as you talked of last year. Or Padua, or Rome."

"Or a monastery cell with a bolt on the door. Or a dungeon with ropes and pulleys. No. I will not make another exception. I hold you to your oath, Anton Magnus. You can jump off cliffs alone from now on."

"You want to see those Wend bastards raping and pillaging across Jorgary?"

"Go and find your princess and your castle," Wulf said, even more softly. He straightened up and turned away. "I'm not stopping you. I'll give you all the help I can, except not the sort of help you want."

"Get my boots," Anton said, raising a leg. He needed time to think.

Wulf pulled his boots off for him. Anton stood up as straight as he could under the roof and set to work on his buttons. Inspiration was elusive.

"Well, I respect your decision," he said.

"You'll have to. I'm not changing it."

"The cardinal will want to know why I'm reneging. Help me think up a good excuse without mentioning yourself, please? I obviously have no more need for this uniform, not after this. I won't even get to keep the discharge, because they'll cashier me. We'll have to look for a mercenary company to sign with, I suppose. It's tough on Vlad and Otto, and I hate to think what's going to happen when I take that baton back to Cardinal Zdenek and tell him I can't do what I promised. Where did you put my clean trunk hose?" He looked around the heaped litter of the room.

"You're standing on it. Why don't you just stuff your pretty baton where it will give you more backbone?"

Unfortunately, Wulf's gentle manner hid an iron

stubbornness, an obstinacy high even by Magnus standards. Once he'd made his mind up, it was a frosty July before he ever changed it. Even Father had learned not to issue threats to his youngest son, because he would invariably be called on them.

Anton sighed. "The Wends will be happy. Zdenek told me I was the only card he had to play. Not that the old Spider can't lie, but he must be truly desperate to risk dabbling in Speaking. Or else he doesn't think a Speaker speaks to devils. Who was St. Victorinus, anyway? A real saint?" No answer. "And all those Wends, raping, burning, laying waste . . ."

After a moment, Wulf spoke in a whisper, not looking around, "Damn you to the lowest kiln of hell. All right. I'll do this much for you, just this once: I'll ask my Voices if I should go. If they really are demons, as the Church says, then they'll have a good chance to damn both of us."

Hope stirred. "I'm sure they're not demons, Wulf, or I wouldn't ask you. Of course I wouldn't. Zdenek wouldn't, either."

"The Church says they are. Now you're standing on my jerkin. You want me to help you into your armor?"

Yes, they would have to wear their armor. The proper way to transport armor was in barrels with oil and sand, so that the movement of the horse would keep it clean and shiny, but Anton owned no packhorse. Besides, although Jorgary was a reasonably peaceful and law-abiding land, most of it was dense forest and "reasonably" did not guarantee that two well-outfitted but unaccompanied gentlemen would never run into a gang of outlaws.

Anton's armor was custom-made and literally worth a fortune, being his younger-son inheritance. He was fanatically proud of it, from the toes of his sollerets to the crown of his barbutte—a newfangled Italian-style pot helmet with a T-shaped opening in the front. It was no trivial task for Wulf to clad him in so much steel. His gauntlets went into a saddlebag. There, too, went his hussar surcoat showing the royal emblem of a crowned bear, and Wulf tied on him the one it had replaced when they arrived in Mauvnik—the Magnus insignia of a mailed fist with the family motto, *Omnia audere*, and the mark of a martlet to designate a fourth son.

Wulf's own armor was simpler: leather boots and breeches, plus a plate cuirass worn over a chain-mail shirt. On his head he wore a light helmet, a sallet. By the time Wulf was ready, Anton had replaced the cardinal's treasures in the satchel, stuffed their unneeded clothes in a saddlebag, and was ready to go. They had arrived ten days ago with nothing more, and had acquired almost nothing since. He clumped forward to the hatch, then looked back expectantly at his mutinous brother, who was just standing there, hands on hips.

"You leave," Wulf said. "This will be a private conversation."

"I'll leave if you'll open this damned thing. You expect me to squat?"

"You're pretty good at stooping," Wulf said, but he came and lifted the hatch.

The old couple had not opened their shutter yet, and one of them was snoring. Anton started down the ladder; it creaked. When he reached the bottom, his brother tossed down the bags and then closed the trap on him. Anton was tempted to go back up again to listen, but he could not possibly do that without Wulf hearing him.

Not unexpectedly, the snoring had stopped. Without

speaking, he moved himself and the bags out to the corridor. He decided to wait there, rather than go down and have to explain the delay to the palace hostlers. They would be wanting their breakfast. So did he.

After about ten minutes he heard the ladder creak again. In a moment Wulf opened the door. He pulled a face at Anton, then turned to shout into the darkness behind him. "My brother and I are going on a journey. If we're not back by sunset, we won't be coming back, ever. Whatever we've left behind you can have. And thank you." He closed the door.

Anton took up the two smaller bags and led the way to the stairs. "Thank them for what?"

"Just for being, I suppose. And for not being as sorry for themselves as I am for them. That make sense?"

"Your Voices say you should help me?"

"No. But they didn't say I shouldn't, either. Now shut up, because talking with them has made my belly hurt already."

He was going to cooperate! Anton allowed himself a smirk, because his face wasn't visible. The bright side of Wulf's stubbornness was that he could be counted on to give a job whatever it needed. Once he started, he wouldn't stop until it was finished.

The palace hostlers had not enjoyed standing around in a cold and foul alley to please a very junior lancer, and wanted a slanging match to make up for it. Anton tried out his newly acquired hussar vocabulary on them, but lost badly. The foul-mouthed villains vaulted onto their mounts and rode off.

"You take Sparrow," Wulf said.

"Why, for mercy's sake?"

Sparrow was a rouncey, an ugly piebald. Morningstar was a courser, faster and larger, more fitting Anton's height. He was also a handsome roan with far better lines.

"Because Sparrow is nimbler. St. Helena warned me that you must stay very close. If we get separated I won't be able to find you again."

St. Helena was the mother of the Roman Emperor Constantine. Despite having died over a thousand years ago, she still talked to Wulf, according to Wulf. And he was serious about the horses, so Anton bit back his annoyance at this suddenly assertive young brother. He could be put back in his place some other time.

Wulf vaulted onto Morningstar's back and paused to raise the stirrups. "Remember to stay close," he said, and urged his mount into a run.

Prime was being rung in the distance to announce the new day, but the alley was still deserted, so Anton had no trouble following. Sparrow could keep up that pace all day. How long to Cardice as the devil rides? Suddenly Morningstar made a very sharp right turn into another alley. Fortunately Sparrow always led with his right foot so Anton could turn him to follow. He must have rounded the corner in the nick of time because, for a startling moment, there was no sign of Morningstar and Wulf, but then they somehow flickered into view about two lengths ahead.

Going faster. Anton nudged his mount to speed up, but Sparrow had realized that he was supposed to follow close. Even so, the alleys were narrow and a few pedestrians were appearing already. There would be accidents. Wulf must be made to slow down.

"Wulf! *Wulf!*" But the clamor of horseshoes on cobbles was echoing off the walls and drowning out his shouts. Moreover, Wulf was deep in conversation with someone on his right, nodding his head, gesturing with his free hand. Anton could see no one there, but his crazy brother must.

Faster still! The two horses raced flat-out, weaving and winding through a labyrinth of alleys until the walls seemed to fly by in a blur. No seeming: they were a blur, and a fog had rolled in. Pedestrians, mainly somberly clad matrons on their way to Mass, were vague and indistinct, like reflections on water. Sparrow and Morningstar could see the illusion too, for their screams of terror added to the roar of hooves on stone. Anton's job was easier, but Wulf was the best horseman in the family now and was keeping his terrified mount under perfect control, riding it full-out. A trio of brown-robed friars came into view, deep in holy discourse, and totally unaware as the nemesis rushed upon them.

Anton wailed and closed his eyes. When he opened them, the shadowy friars were just ambling away into the fog behind him, seemingly quite unaware of what had hurtled *through* them. "Ride like the devil," he had said, and he had been taken literally. The mouth of hell would open before him at any minute. He had never been so scared in his life.

Now the noise had faded to a terrifying, unearthly silence and the light had almost gone. Whatever had happened to the city wall, the gate? The horses' feet pounded on grass or mud, but the impacts were barely audible. They were running through a mirage of trees, a forest of beech and chestnuts, which should have been impenetrable but in practice put up no more resistance than trails of smoke. When Anton managed to bring Sparrow close enough, he caught fragments of Wulf's conversation. ". . . put him in danger?" ". . . how long can you . . . ?" ". . . but will the cardinal play fair later, if he . . . ?" Anton could hear no replies, but Wulf certainly seemed to. A couple of times he laughed as he would if his ghostly companions were making jokes.

Then reality returned with a rush; Anton felt he had wakened from a dream by falling out of bed. The horses whinnied in fright as they found their hooves thumping on hard brown pasture. The countryside had opened up to fields and vineyards, very fertile, all gilded by fall and deserted on a Sunday morning. Low sun shone on gentle hills, wreathed with distant smoke plumes from burning stubble. This did not look like the countryside around Mauvnik, nor could it be Cardice, for there were no mountains. Straight ahead of them stood a massive masonry wall with a high arched gateway.

And Wulf—who, according to family legend, would be capable of riding a horse up a tree if he wanted—flew out of the saddle, turned a somersault in midair, and crashed to the ground.

CHAPTER 4

"Mother! Mother! You must get up now! You must! Havel Vranov is at the gates. I need you!"

Lady Madlenka Bukovany was addressing Dowager Countess Edita. The poor lady had retreated to the far side of the mattress and, had it not been hard against the wall, would very likely have fallen out already. She had pulled a pillow over her head. For over a week now, ever since her husband was stricken, she would not eat or speak. She had taken to bed and refused even to attend his funeral three days later. She did take fluids, so the doctors had forbidden her water and prescribed goats' milk, just to keep her alive.

"Mother, please, as you love me?"

Nothing.

"Mother, I absolutely swear that I will never argue with you again!"

Madlenka felt very guilty. The two of them had been constantly at loggerheads for months now. Not about anything in particular, more about everything in particular. Petr had laughed at their battles and said it was time his sister was married off. Which was true—still not betrothed at seventeen, Madlenka was practically an old maid. Father had agreed, but had done no more about arranging a match for her than he had about buying guns for the castle, as Petr had wanted. Now both Father and Petr were gone, she and Mother should be supporting each other. This torpor was *so* incredibly unlike Countess Edita! She had always been a strong, active woman. Opinionated, too.

With a sigh, Madlenka closed the bed curtain and turned around to meet Giedre's sympathetic gaze. Giedre was the daughter of Sir Ramunas Jurbarkas, the castle seneschal. She was officially Madlenka's lady-in-waiting, but was in fact her best and lifelong friend, less than a day younger. Father had referred to Giedre as Madlenka's shadow, but if so she was a midday shadow, being plump and short, where Madlenka herself was tall and skinny, with a face all bone. Giedre was dark, Madlenka fair.

"Do not think harshly of her, my lady. Whatever evil witchcraft smote your father and brother has taken her wits also."

Bishop Ugne said the same—that the fault must lie not with the countess but with the Speaker who had cursed her. His own efforts to remove the curse had failed utterly. Madlenka was convinced that the Satanist had been either Count Havel Vranov, the Hound of the Hills, or someone in his employ. Now he was at the gates with an army, and the constable, Karolis Kavarskas, was going to let him in. Vranov just might recognize that the countess retained some vestige of her late husband's authority, but he would spurn any attempt by Madlenka to assert her rights. An underage female orphan had precious few rights anyway.

The count's bedchamber at Cardice was a large room by Cardice standards, and a luxurious one for Jorgary. It had glass in its windows, rugs from Syria, and chests made from the cedars of Lebanon. The wall tapestries were of Flemish weave, depicting mythical scenes, faded now. Here her father had slept and here he had died, ending his line. Women could not inherit titles. No woman could be lord of the marches.

So now Sir Karolis Kavarskas, that most hateful constable, claimed to rule in Count Bukovany's place, "until His Majesty appoints his successor."

Or until Havel Vranov decided to appoint himself. Why else was he riding up the Silver Road with hundreds of men at his back?

"How long now before they open the gate?" Madlenka demanded.

Giedre peered through a clear spot in the lozenge-paned window to see how far sunlight had descended Mount Naproti. "Very soon, I think."

Knuckles rapped on the door. "Madlenka, my child?"

Madlenka knew that sonorous and melodious voice. "Please enter, my lord bishop."

Both women curtseyed as Bishop Ugne strode . . . um . . . waddled into the room. His voice was the best part of him, and his appearance never failed to disappoint. Even when swathed in many layers of ecclesiastical vestments of blue and cloth-of-gold, he was too short and dumpy to impress, and his towering miter made him look top-heavy. His face was ruddy and chinless, so dominated by a massive curved nose that Madlenka was invariably reminded of a parrot she had once seen for sale in the spring fair. It had clung to the side of its cage very much the way the bishop's soft white hand clutched his tall crozier.

The castle women distrusted the bishop and the numerous female servants he had brought with him. There were whispers that his housekeeper was his mistress, her sister was another, and his two young nieces were actually his daughters. Ugne was of noble blood—son, brother, and uncle of dukes—and had no doubt paid a high price to purchase his office, and that was another grievous sin. Everyone knew that the Church was corrupt; the Jorgarian clergy were probably no better or worse than any others.

Surprisingly, Father had rather approved of Ugne, on the grounds that most of his predecessors had refused to reside in this bleak mountainous diocese and had preferred to delegate their duties to vicars. Petr had approved too, for the very different reason that he ranked Ugne as the third best horseman in the county. He was also an enthusiastic hunter and had, by God's mercy, been present to administer the last rites on the day Petr was gored.

He glanced meaningfully at the bed curtains.

Madlenka shook her head. "No better."

"As the Lord wills. Now, daughter, why do you summon me with such frantic claims of urgency on a Sunday morning? It is everyone else's day of rest, but to those of us who do the Lord's work, it is a busy one."

Her note had explained the problem. If he did not consider it important, what was he doing here in the castle in his full vestments?

"Count Vranov, that's why! He crossed the border with a small army last night. One of Father's vassals . . . one of the tenants from up near the forks of the Hlucny rode in after curfew last night to report that a sizable troop of Pelrelmians had ridden by his fief. He saddled up and trailed them, and watched them pitching camp at High Meadows, then came up to the gate to report. Father would have rewarded him handsomely! You could see their campfires from the wall. This morning the lookouts heard their bugles sounding reveille."

The bishop frowned. "And what size do you consider a small army?"

"About two hundred fighting men, he said, and that's not counting servants."

"Who said? I hope you were not out on the wall cavorting with sentinels in the dark, *unchaperoned*?"

"My lord bishop! Of course not!"

"Then how do you know all this?"

"Dali told me." Dali was Dalibor Notivova, Constable Karolis's deputy. "He came to see me, but I was certainly never *alone* with him. Later I sent for Sir Karolis, too. He condescended to come eventually, although he kept me waiting long enough. I asked him what he was going to do, and he said he would open the gate and let them in!"

Father had neither liked him nor trusted Count Vranov, the Hound of the Hills. Now Madlenka suspected that he had been behind the sorcery that had killed both Father and Petr, and she was convinced that the constable was in the Hound's pay.

Bishop Ugne was looking thunderous. "Was Dalibor also the one who told you that Sir Karolis had not reported your father's stroke to the king?"

"I promised that person I would not reveal his identity."

The bishop took that refusal as confirmation, which it was. "My daughter, has it occurred to you that Dalibor Notivova may be after Sir Karolis's job?"

"It would be an improvement."

"Or your late father's, even? He is a relative, is he not?"

She hadn't thought of that and she felt herself blushing. Dalibor was a widower. But the idea was absurd—she could neither inherit the title nor pass it on to her husband. "I've known Dali all my life. He taught me how to groom a horse. He is distantly related to me, yes—third or fourth cousin. He's the only surviving male relative I know of. Of course, his claim would be through the female line and wouldn't be valid . . . would it?"

"Possibly not," the bishop admitted. "Arturas the herald could tell you. But the direct male line is certainly extinct, which means that the king will have to appoint another lord of the Cardice marches. A local man and a distant relative, even on the distaff side, might have a chance. But Dalibor Notivova doesn't, because he is a commoner and His Majesty has certainly never heard of him." Ugne peered at her suspiciously. "Or did you mention his name when you sent the report to Mauvnik?"

"No. He . . . My informant made me promise not to. To mention his name, I mean! He refused to say why." The devious cleric was tying her in knots.

Now the parrot had a cracker. The bishop smiled. "Then I have been misjudging him, just as you may be misjudging Count Vranov. You had no prior word that he was coming? I mean, it is both normal and commendable for a neighbor to come and pay his condolences after such a tragedy."

"Not a word! The counts of Kipalban and Gistov both sent couriers with expressions of sorrow and promises to endow prayers for their souls, but not Vranov. Not a word. So why is he here with an army?"

"Your definition of an army may not agree with the constable's, Madlenka. But on my way here I encountered Captain Ekkehardt, who was heading to the barbican to discuss this very problem with the constable. So why don't we go there and see what our military experts have decided?"

God be thanked! Until this disaster of her father's and brother's deaths, Madlenka had never expected to feel grateful for the presence of the *landsknecht* mercenaries in the town. But if Constable Kavarskas was to prove false, the Germans might prove a counterweight to his treachery. Delighted at the thought of action, she darted across to one of the chests and began hauling out clothes, hurling them aside, burrowing ever lower, until she had found the winter robes. She kept her mother's sable for herself—she was in mourning, after all—and tossed a dark brown fox fur one to Giedre.

A glance at the mirror called for a sigh. Black was definitely not her color; it made her pale face look like a skull. And the fur was not quite the same shade of black as her hat. She lowered her veil, so no one could see her at all. "Quickly, then!" she said.

Bishop Ugne had already opened the door and beckoned for the countess's nurse, who had been sent out to wait in the dressing room.

Madlenka, Giedre, and Bishop Ugne left the keep by the upper door, and were saluted by the sentries. They crossed a drawbridge high above a street and then climbed some steps to the top of the curtain wall, where they were brutally assaulted by the torrent of wind that always blew there. The reverent bishop muttered something in the vulgar tongue and grabbed his miter just before it disappeared. His vestments billowed and flapped. Madlenka wondered if she dared offer to carry his crozier for him.

Heads bent into the gale, they hurried along the wide parapet with the black slate roofs of the town below them to their right. On their left, outside the battlements, the wall dropped sheer for thirty feet to a cliff about ten times as high, and below that lay the rocky bed of the foaming Ruzena River.

Had their eyes not been watering so hard, they would have seen the great valley ahead of them, widening southward until the embracing hills fell away and it merged with the forests of the Jorgary Plain, clad that day in fall gold. Fields and vineyards, villages both large and small, lay well concealed, for even high church spires failed to overtop the trees.

According to tradition, on his way to the Third Crusade the Emperor Barbarossa had acclaimed the shelf on which Castle Gallant stood as "designed by God to hold a fortress." The great rocky slab blocking the western half of the valley had held a castle even in Barbarossa's day, but in the three centuries since then, many successive rulers had worked hard to take advantage of the Lord's generosity. The entire top of the little plateau had been fortified, and its sides chiseled and shaped. With steep cliffs rising above it on the west and the foaming waters of Ruzena flanking its other three sides, Cardice was renowned as one of the most secure castles in Europe. It had fallen to treachery twice, but it had never been stormed or starved into submission.

The valley ended abruptly about a mile north of the castle, under the ramparts of the Vysoky Range, which straddled the boundary between Jorgary and lands that had recently become part of Pomerania. Northbound travelers, whether pilgrims, merchants, or fighting men, had no choice of route. They embarked on the Silver Road at High Meadows. From there the trail climbed steeply up the western side of the valley, crossing gullies on log bridges, negotiating hairpins, edging around steep spurs on cuts barely wide enough for a single oxcart. Very few places on the whole ascent would allow two carts to pass. Eventually the road arrived at Castle Gallant's southern barbican, with a sheer drop on one side and a vertical cliff on the other. There the count's men collected the tolls.

Anxious to reach a point where she could see what was happening at the gate, Madlenka set a very fast pace into the wind. Bishop Ugne would have had to trot just to stay level. He had to shout after her. "I doubt if your haste is wise, Madlenka. Ladies should arrive with dignity, not steaming like a horse."

Annoyed, she slowed to a walk. Giedre was staying back. The bishop took this brief privacy as a chance to do some more holy nagging.

"You say you 'sent for' Sir Karolis last night? Whose man is he?"

She blinked away wind tears to look at him. "Well, he was my father's man, of course."

"But now? God in His almighty wisdom has seen fit to gather your father and your brother to Him. Whom does the constable serve now? Every man must have a lord, Madlenka."

"I am my father's heir." But a woman. What a difference that made! Petr had been a year younger than she, just sixteen, but had he lived, the entire castle would be jumping to his bidding without question, obeying the least gesture of his little finger. But men never did that for a woman, for a woman was a frail and foolish creature interested only in frippery and finery and tantalizing men with lust to lead them to damnation.

She missed Petr even more than Father. Never at rest, ever dashing about, always laughing—it was impossible to accept that he was not just around a corner somewhere, or just about to ride in from the hills with some fresh venison. Nobody said so, but she suspected the whole county mourned the boy more than the man.

"Your mother is his relic," the bishop declaimed, "and will have a dower interest in his estate, after the king has claimed his heriot. You undoubtedly will inherit a rich portion of whatever is left, but not the castle, daughter! This is a royal fortress. It did not belong to your father."

"Then whom do you believe the constable serves, my lord bishop?" Not Madlenka Bukovany, certainly.

"As your father's deputy, he must serve the king himself until a new keeper is appointed. Yes, Sir Karolis's duty is to keep the fortress safe until His Majesty sends someone to replace your father, may he rest in peace. But Karolis Kavarskas is not your servant, my daughter. He is a proud man. He fought well in Italy and Austria. His men here generally approve of him, as your father did. He cannot take joyously to an underage, unmarried girl *sending for* him."

Pompous as a stuffed owl! She muttered an apology.

"Tell him so," the bishop said, "not me. These are indeed hard times, Madlenka. The people have been troubled ever since your father brought in the *landsknechte*. They fear that war is coming, and now that your father and Sir Petr are gone, they are even more frightened. You must come to Mass today, so that you can be seen."

Seen while totally swathed in sable and black lace?

"And be patient if they try to mob you outside the cathedral to express their sorrow."

"Yes, my lord bishop."

"You should likewise show respect for Count Vranov. I agree that he is an odious sinner, but he is a man of power in the land, and someday—perhaps quite soon—Cardice may need his help."

Madlenka choked back several possible rejoinders before she found a sufficiently respectful one. By then she had turned a corner and come to a place with a view of the south road. The invading force crawling up it was close enough now to make out details in the low sunlight. A liveried herald rode in the van, flanked by a standard-bearer, followed in turn by a party of eight or ten horsemen, and then a column of men-at-arms marching three abreast. The streaming banner was unreadable, but there was no doubt that this was the Hound's army.

She paused to peer through a crenel. "How many?"

"Two hundred?" Bishop Ugne said hesitantly. "About enough to fill the lady chapel. Not many are knights, though; mostly mounted archers."

"They can't do us any harm as long as the constable keeps the gates shut, can they?"

Ugne made a scoffing noise. "They couldn't break in if they had fifty times their number. Captain Ekkehardt alone has two or three times as many men."

But if the constable had turned traitor, what then?

As they approached the barbican, she heard the clanking of the chains raising the gate. So the deed was done. They were too late!

She drew back beside Giedre to let the bishop enter first and receive the sergeants-at-arms' salutes. At this level the tower was a single large room, dusty and echoing, lit dimly from the doorway by which she had just entered and narrow slits along the side walls. It was dominated by the gigantic gears and treadmills that raised the three successive gates that an enemy must pass to break into the city. Mercifully, the porters who had to work the system had almost finished their work on the outer gate, and in a moment the deafening racket ceased.

The boss threw on the brake, and the men could relax, puffing and sweating from their work.

In addition to the porters and the normal sergeants-at-arms, there were at least a dozen soldiers present, half of them Cardice men and the other half *landsknechte*. The two were easily distinguished, because the locals wore conventional half armor of mail shirt and cuirass.

The mercenaries, on the other hand, were big, bearded Germans or Swiss, who seemed even bigger in their heavily padded armor—velvet or velour doublets and hose decorated with pleats and piping, slashed to expose linings of contrasting bright colors. No man was ever foolish enough to laugh at those, or at the gold chains around their necks or their wide, floppy hats with trailing ostrich plumes. *Landsknechte* were elite fighting troops, respected and feared all over Europe.

Ekkehardt's band had been hired in the summer by Petr, when he visited Mauvnik. They had arrived about a month ago, six hundred fighting men complete with wagons, horses, wives, children, and the usual foul mob of loose women. The town, where nothing exciting ever happened, had been packed to the rafters since. There had been surprisingly few fights so far, but ill feeling rumbled like a mountain thunderstorm.

Only two men in the room mattered, and they were peering out through adjacent loopholes at the advancing troops. Constable Kavarskas was a lean timberwolf of a man, a seasoned warrior of around thirty, with a scar on his forehead, iron streaks in his hair, and deep furrows flanking his mouth. He had lost his left hand fighting in Italy, and a hook replaced it.

Ekkehardt, in all his glory of blue and yellow, was a thickset badger by comparison. If he was shorter, it was by very little, and the padding of his clothes merely emphasized the meaty bulk inside them. His beard and flowing mustaches were the color of ripe grain. Kavarskas turned away from his loophole just as Madlenka arrived behind him.

"Sir Karolis!"

He reversed his turn and looked down at her as if she were something underfoot. "My lady?"

"Do you still intend to let that *army* into the castle?"

"Of course not. Whatever gave you that idea?" He glanced at Ekkehardt with an expression of long-suffering bewilderment.

"The constable," the *landsknecht* said in his heavy Saxon voice, "would never be so foolish, my lady."

They were laughing at her.

"No doubt this is Count Vranov arriving in person to convey his respects to the countess," Kavarskas continued, explaining carefully. "And your gracious self, of course. Such would be normal neighborly courtesy after so great a tragedy. He may have brought his wife, or some other family members along. A bodyguard is only a sensible precaution in these troubled times."

"Sir Karolis," Ekkehardt said, "suggested an honor guard of twenty knights to be admitted. This was too much, I thought. We agree Vranov should be allowed a token escort of five knights."

"Once admitted," the constable said, "he will be a guest protected by the laws of chivalry. To refuse him entry would be a gross discourtesy . . . my lady." Karolis did not need to address her as if she were ten years old, but he always did. He was right, though, curse him. To refuse the Hound admission would be a serious insult.

Although Havel Vranov had never given her personal

reason to hate or fear him, her parents had never spoken well of him. They rarely spoke ill either, preferring to change the subject whenever he was mentioned. Petr, more forthcoming, had said he was a savage and a monster. Gossip called him a prodigious lecher and adulterer. In odd-numbered years the lord of Pelrelm visited Cardice for a week or so to hunt with his counterpart, and in even years Father had returned the compliment. Normally that was the extent of their socializing, but this was Vranov's third visit this year. He had come in the spring with a proposition that Madlenka marry one of his sons. Asked whether the one being exhibited was legitimate, he had pretended to be offended—not at the suggestion that he might have fathered children out of wedlock, but that he would honor his bastards with a noble marriage. He had also indicated that he had many sons and could, if legitimacy were not a problem, dig up others for Madlenka's inspection. Count Stepan had declined both offers.

In the summer, after his return from Mauvnik, Petr had ridden over to the Hound's den to pass on the news that the king expressly forbade any marriage connection between the two marches. Undeterred, Havel had returned to Cardice just a couple of weeks before the tragedy, offering yet another son. That time there had been words, and Father had sent him packing with threadbare courtesy.

But now Father was not there, and the Hound was.

"If we let him in, the rest of his men must go back down to the High Meadows!" Madlenka insisted.

Kavarskas sighed. "Arturas the herald has been so instructed and is down there now. Did you really believe that I would just throw open the gates to such a force?"

"You just did, didn't you?" she yelled.

He glanced at the bishop as if hoping for sympathy or support. "My lady, the outer gate is always opened at sunrise in times of peace. It would be offensive to leave it closed when a friend is approaching. However, if you will look at the second windlass, over there, you will see from the lack of chain wound around it that the inner gate is still closed. These hatches in the floor cover murther holes, through which we can rain missiles or boiling oil down on intruders. The castle is still secure against anything short of a siege train."

Madlenka felt her face flame behind her veil. She was virtually certain that last night he had told her that the gates would be opened "as usual." Perhaps he had not actually lied, but he had certainly misled her and tricked her into making a fool of herself, raising an alarm where none existed. No doubt this was her punishment for summoning him.

Bishop Ugne was listening, smiling flabbily, and saying nothing. The wind had turned him even redder than the stones of the castle walls.

Outside, the clatter of hooves died away and was replaced by a shrill silver fanfare.

"Now we shall see, my lady," the constable said. "If they accept the terms Arturas offers, he will signal us to raise the inner gate. Perhaps you should go and warn your lady mother so that she can make ready to receive the visitors." The constable knew very well that Edita was in no state to greet anyone.

Smarting with humiliation, dismissed like an infant, Madlenka turned to retrace her steps.

"Wait!" Bishop Ugne was addressing the two men, not her. "The last time Havel Vranov came to this castle, he was accompanied by a false priest, a Father Vilhelmas.

That man is a heretic, a schismatic. You will not allow him back in."

For a moment there was silence while Sir Karolis assessed this unexpected challenge. He glanced at the *landsknecht* captain and seemed to conclude that it was none of Ekkehardt's business. Ekkehardt did not look anxious to intervene anyway. So it was up to Karolis to respond. The old enmity between church and state was back again.

"I agree, my lord bishop, that you are charged with protecting the souls of the good Christians of Cardice and keeping them safely in the bosom of Rome, but if Count Vranov chooses to convert to the Eastern confession, that—"

"Pomerania bows the knee to the Greek patriarch, but King Konrad has decreed that Jorgary will follow the true Catholic faith. Suppression of heresy is my business, not yours, constable, and my authority comes from the Lord of All. I say that the man Vilhelmas must not be admitted."

The bishop was a proud man, accustomed to authority. So was the constable, and he must maintain his dignity before an audience made up of Ekkehardt's mercenaries and his own troops. "On the contrary, my lord bishop: in matters of this world, mine is the authority. Until His Majesty appoints a new keeper, I shall continue to do my duty as the late count wished me to. He allowed the priest in and so shall I."

Bishop Ugne's face was now redder than sunset. "He did, and see where it got him! Within a fortnight, he was dead, his son was dead, his wife distracted, and his ancient line extinguished."

Sir Karolis Kavarskas coughed down a laugh. "The

man has a crooked eye, I agree, but does that frighten you? You seriously think he is a Speaker because of that?"

The bishop spluttered. "I think he is a Speaker, yes, but not because of that. Those schismatics are in league with the Father of Evil. Havel was a professed Catholic until recently, when he sent his priest away. Now he is a puppet of the Wends."

"I think you should go and pray for peace, my lord bishop."

"You will not admit that heretic priest, Karolis, as you value your soul!" Now the Church's threat was blatant and the soldier backed down.

"As Your Reverence says." Kavarskas beckoned over one of the archers and sent him down to the herald at the gate.

"Thank you." Bishop Ugne turned his back on the constable. "Come, Madlenka, we must go to the cathedral. Nobody can pester you while you are attending Mass. Giedre, you should run and warn your father to arrange a reception for Havel Vranov—but I think it should be a very small one."

"Wait!" Madlenka shouted. "Constable, when the count and his escort have been admitted, close the gate."

Kavarskas reddened. Before he could speak, Ekkehardt growled, "This seems a wise precaution."

"I am the one who makes such decisions!" the constable bellowed.

"Well, I think I agree with the lady and the captain," the bishop said.

The constable gripped his sword hilt and glared at them all. It was a fine demonstration of how a castle without a keeper resembled a chicken without a head.

"Do it!" Madlenka snapped and headed for the door. The bishop went with her, and Giedre followed.

As they swept along the battlements with the wind at their backs, she said, "The constable has been bribed, hasn't he?"

"That is a very serious charge, Madlenka."

"I know. What do you think?"

"Bought, like Judas?" He sighed. "It could be. Or he may just be frightened of the responsibility thrust upon him and hoping to lean on Count Vranov."

"And the *landsknecht*?"

"Luitger Ekkehardt is a good Christian, for a soldier, and he obviously does not trust Karolis, but mercenaries usually serve the highest bidder. This fortress would be worth a great deal of money to the duke of Pomerania. We must pray that the Lord will have mercy on us and support his own."

CHAPTER 5

Wulfgang Magnus had not fallen off a horse since he was six years old, and would not have done so now had he not been seized by a sudden wrenching pain in his gut. He had been unhorsed in jousting often enough—although mainly by Vlad or Otto, only very rarely by Anton—and armor was designed to protect its wearer from just that mishap. In this case it saved him from minor cuts or bruises, but was no help at all right after the jarring impact, because he immediately needed to vomit. For several minutes, he could do nothing but writhe on the turf and retch, racked by appalling belly cramps. It was fortunate that he had not eaten anything that morning.

When he finally managed to lift his head and look, Morningstar was still cavorting around, bucking and kicking in every direction. Sparrow was behaving himself because Anton had refused to tolerate such nonsense. He was now trying to catch the stupid courser before he entangled his feet in the reins. More red hot coals in the stomach . . .

Anton rode up, leading Morningstar. "What's wrong?" He sounded more irritated than worried, because he thought a warrior must be wrought of steel. He never displayed weakness or sympathy, especially over other people's suffering.

"Belly cramps this time." More heaving.

"Why?"

"Pain is the price we must pay."

"Who says that?"

"St. Helena."

"Pay for what?"

The conversation was going nowhere. Wulf wiped his mouth with the back of his hand and tried to sit up. His gut twisted again, doubling him over. At about his third try, he succeeded and was able to inspect the scenery. The stone wall ahead, two stories high and windowless, without doubt belonged to a monastery. It was designed to shut out the lustful, sin-ridden world and protect the holy peace that must reign within. Five years poor Marek had spent in there already; there he would die and be buried.

"Have you any idea where we are?" Anton demanded.

"Koupel. I have to speak with Marek before I decide . . ." Wulf paused, bracing himself to deal with the pain that would come as soon as he tried to rise. "Before I decide." He struggled to his knees at the second try, except that he doubled over again. It was several more minutes before he managed to clamber aboard his horse with Anton's help; he certainly did not leap into the saddle as a good rider should. "I have to speak with Marek."

"Wulf, they won't let you! Vlad came by here two years ago, when he rode to the war. He tried to see Marek. He wasn't allowed in."

Monks had renounced the world. They did not, like friars, wander through it, doing the Lord's work, helping the poor and the lame. Monks lived segregated, communal lives devoted to praising God.

Wulf forced a smile. "But you will be. Don your pretty ribbon, my lord. Tuck your baton behind your ear. You are Count Magnus of Cardice. You are rich. You can pay for prayers for your predecessor's soul."

Anton chuckled at hearing his title. "At the moment I could afford to buy forgiveness for one lecherous wink, nothing more. But if you really must talk to him, it's worth a try. You're not scared that they'll lock you up, too?"

How stupid could a man be? Anton had told him a thousand times that courage wasn't absence of fear, it was refusing to give in to it. Vlad had not been allowed in; Wulf's trouble might be the exact opposite. Certainly some of his belly cramps came from sheer terror.

"Of course not. You need my help, and my Voices told me to come here and ask Marek's advice before I decide. Now start being a lord and act stupid. Should be easy."

Anton scowled, having no sense of humor where his own dignity was concerned. They set their horses walking along the dusty trail to the gate. This was Sunday. There would be no one working in the fields, and as few as possible tending livestock. The monks would be at prayer, denying the world, rejecting the flesh and the devil.

Anton must be frightened too, if for different reasons. This situation could only be strange and discomfiting for him. Many times in past generations the family had produced Speakers, able to hear Voices and exercise strange supernatural powers. The curse had struck daughters more often than sons, and most of them had been hastily packed off into nunneries before they lost their immortal souls or the neighbors began to gossip. Others had run away and never been heard from again.

Marek had insisted that his Voices were Heaven-sent, not Satanic, and had demanded a chance to keep his freedom, swearing he would never use his powers for evil. He *had* used them for good, but word had spread and he had been taken away when he was a month or two older than Wulf was now.

By then young Wulfgang, the baby of the family, had been hearing Voices too. Terrified, he had promised never to use his gift—or give in to his curse, whichever was the correct description. Father had decided that he also deserved a chance and had made the rest of the family swear to keep his secret. They had all held to their side of the bargain, though it had been hard on Wulf. The Voices might speak to him at any time without warning. Marek, before being taken away, had told him that he should run as fast as possible to the church and kneel before the altar, holding a crucifix and repeating Hail Marys until the Voices stopped. That always worked eventually, but Wulf had grown thick calluses on his knees through many long nights and days. In time he had learned enough control that others rarely noticed his distraction.

Father Czcibor must have suspected, but had turned a blind eye. Ottokar had asked about the problem once in a while, but Vladislav and Anton never mentioned it. Wulf had assumed that Anton had completely put it out of his mind until that whispered appeal at the hunt. Well, today was providing a rude introduction to Speaking for Anton. He expected to be in control in any dealings with his younger brother and now he wasn't. No doubt his jaw was very tightly clenched inside his bevor.

A monastery gate always faced west, to the sinful world, just as a church faced east, to the direction of sunrise and hope and the coming of the Kingdom. Hooves clattered on stone as the visitors passed under the arch into a covered passage. A man emerged from a doorway and bowed to the noble visitors. He was a lay servant, not a tonsured monk.

Wulf made a determined effort to control his nausea and do his duty as a squire would. Technically he wasn't a squire, because Anton had not yet been knighted, but no one else would know that.

"Count Magnus, companion in the Order of St. Vaclav, lord of the marches of Cardice, come in peace."

The man's eyebrows shot up like partridges. No doubt he was surprised by a count traveling with a retinue of less than a hundred. Nevertheless, he recognized gentlemen and bowed again. "His Lordship is welcome to Koupel. Does he come seeking hospitality, or healing, or a retreat from the turmoil of the world?" He spoke the common tongue with an accent even worse than Mauvnik's.

Anton glanced at Wulf's face, which was probably as green as the hills, and took over the negotiations. "I can tarry only briefly, turning aside from my path for a brief visit with my brother, who is one of the monks here."

The gatekeeper's face look on a wary expression. No commoner lightly refused a nobleman, especially one of Anton's exalted rank. "The rule of St. Benedict does not allow personal visitations, my lord."

"We shall see if an exception cannot be made in exceptional circumstances. I will speak with the abbot."

The gatekeeper's face indicated that he strongly doubted that, but he did not say so. The visitors were admitted to the court, which was the size of a smallish meadow, entirely enclosed by buildings, of which those nearest the gate were obviously stables. The skyline ahead was dominated by the church in the background, its two great towers and rose window looming over many lesser, lower buildings. Those nearest to it, or even attached to it, were housing for the monks, their hospital, library, scriptorium, and other study areas. Nearer the court would be workshops, storerooms, servants' quarters, and certainly the hostelry, for monasteries offered almost the only safe refuges for travelers. This grassy area was thus a halfway house between the cloister and the world. Only very favored guests would be allowed to proceed farther in, and no inmate would be allowed to venture farther out without special permission, rarely granted. Early on a Sunday morning, there was no one else in sight.

Anton and Wulf dismounted and turned in their weapons; a more senior layman was fetched. Wulf concentrated on controlling his belly spasms and left negotiations to his brother.

The long lad put on quite a show. After years of watching Father and then Ottokar, plus many noble visitors to Dobkov, he knew exactly how to act the lord. He twirled his mustache, he flaunted his baldric and his baton; he used his height to overawe the senior gatekeeper, two successive novices, and three monks of steadily increasing age and rotundity. Best of all, his overwhelming youthful arrogance must seem so insufferable to these persnickety holy recluses that none of his victims would notice the nausea-racked boy behind him.

It took time, though. They sat on a stone bench and watched servants crisscrossing the courtyard, attending to the minimal Sunday chores. Wulf's innards gradually settled themselves. The bench faced east and the sun bothered him, so he pulled his sallet down, leaving only a narrow gap between its brim and the bevor that protected his chin and mouth.

Anton said, "Why are you hiding?"

Because he felt safer, somehow, not showing his face. But he said, "Sun is bright. Here comes someone."

A monk in a black Benedictine habit came pacing across the grass to tell them that they would not be allowed to speak with Brother Marek. Knowing that a monk would be able to read, Anton dug in his satchel for one of his imposing warrants and negotiations continued.

Eventually, against all odds, instructions arrived to deliver the visitors for inspection by Abbot Bohdan. Clinking and clanking, they followed a disapproving, elderly monk through a cloister, whose pillars were fashioned of lovingly carved stone, then across an obsessively tended garden, until they reached the abbot's residence abutting the north side of the church.

The abbot was eating breakfast. The abbot did very well for himself. His board was liberally spread with dishes—two of fish, one of eggs, a bowl of frumenty, a basket of apples, a roast goose, and a boiled ox tongue. Apart from a servant who hovered behind him, ready to carve him another slice of goose, or refill his crystal wine cup, he was eating alone, seated at the far end of a table that would hold a dozen. It was furnished with gold candlesticks, the fireplace was carved marble, the walls hung with tapestries, and the mullioned windows shone with butterfly-bright images of saints and angels.

He beckoned with a plump hand for the visitors to approach. The monk who had brought them remained by the door.

As much as a man could swagger in armor, Anton advanced along the hall with his humble servant shuffling at his heels. Wulf's mouth tasted of vomit and he feared that he would soon start retching again. He left his sallet down and his face hidden. That still felt right, though he didn't know why.

Abbot Bohdan was undoubtedly the fattest man he had ever seen, swathed in acres of black Benedictine wool. His face hung in folds below eyes like finger holes in dough. His cowl was set back to reveal an almost bald skull and hairless face, both of them beaded with jewels of sweat. He was tearing strips of flesh off a goose drumstick and apparently swallowing them whole. His piggy stare never left the visitors as they advanced.

Anton halted and saluted. "My lord abbot."

The abbot reached for a gold chalice and took a drink. "What d'ju want with Brother Marek?"

"Oh, largely just a fraternal visit. It has been many years since we saw our good brother."

"Magnus has renounced the world. To remind him of his former life of sin would not help him in his devotions and dedication. It would be a distraction and an unkindness."

"There is more. May I speak in complete confidence?" Anton asked airily.

"Why is your companion hiding his face?"

"Because I told him to. He went on a disgusting debauch last night and is currently suffering the penalty. The sight of him is more than the rest of us should have to bear. About Brother Marek?"

Curtains of flesh seemed to sink even lower over the nasty little eyes. "I give you two minutes to explain why I should listen to you for a third."

"There was an incident back before Brother Marek entered the cloister. I am charged to find out if he remembers anything of it." Anton was making it up as he went along—Wulf recognized the tone. "I regret that I am forbidden to go into details, but . . ."

"Forbidden by whom?"

"By the man who gave me this baton."

The abbot shrugged his great shoulders and took a lengthy draft of wine. "Who is your companion? What is the real reason he refuses to show his face?"

"His name is Wulfgang Magnus. He is my squire and brother to both me and Marek. I told you why he is being disciplined. Father Abbot," Anton said sharply. "I am on a mission of great moment and did not come all this way out of my road to discuss family trivia. I have the honor to be a companion in the Order of St. Vaclav, which numbers among its members many distinguished men, including Cardinal Zdenek and Archbishop Svaty, Primate of Jorgary. I have a royal warrant I could show you, but to brandish that at you would seem like a threat. Come, surely a few minutes' talk with one of your holy flock cannot imperil his soul irredeemably? Is his faith so delicate? Must I report to my superiors that you were contumacious?"

"Show me your warrant, lad!"

"As you wish, monk, although were you a layman of rank I should call you out on your implications of distrust. Don't put your greasy fingers on it."

Anton spread out the scroll and held it up so that Bohdan could read it. He pouted, then licked his thick lips. "This house is dedicated to God. King Konrad's writ does not run here."

Anton bowed and tucked the scroll back in his satchel. "I shall so inform His Majesty. He was of a contrary opinion." He turned on his heel to go.

"Wait." The abbot belched.

"Good one," Anton remarked. "Anything else?"

"Have you broken your fast yet?"

"Now that you ask, no, my squire and I have not. Our business is too urgent for delays."

"Brother Cenek!"

The monk waiting by the door said, "Father Abbot?"

"Conduct Count Magnus and his squire to the guests' refectory and tell the hosteler to feed them. I shall send in Brother Marek as soon as prime is over."

"Your Reverence is most gracious," Anton murmured.

Wulf coughed admiringly as they headed for the door.

CHAPTER 6

The guests' refectory was a dank, cool room, so long and narrow as to seem more like a corridor than a hall, yet Wulf found it beautiful in a hard, austere way. The tall stained-glass windows were set high enough that no one could see out or in; ribbed arches supported the stone ceiling. Fixed benches stretched the length of each side, with freestanding tables fronting them. It was a fair bet that male and female guests were seated on opposing sides and that a monk stood at the ornate lectern in the center and read Scripture to them during meals.

Lay servants poured water for the visitors to wash their hands, laid trenchers of hard bread before them, and then brought a breakfast of lamprey pie, pike in a thick sauce, eggs, fresh grapes, crusty bread, a mountain of butter, four cheeses, and flagons of Tokay. The sight of food churned Wulf's stomach, and eating with his sallet down, almost touching his bevor, would be impossible. He raised the helmet briefly to take a swig of the wine, which was surprisingly sweet and seemed to soothe him, confirming that he was suffering from no ordinary colic. He tried not to watch as Anton heaped his trencher and set to work with knife and fingers like a ravening, um, abbot.

"They eat well," he mumbled around a mouthful.

"Food's the only excitement they're allowed."

"Suppose so. What're you going to ask Marek?"

"Won't know till I see him."

"It's been four years!"

"Five." Wulf decided to risk another swallow of the Tokay.

Anton shrugged and cut himself another generous wedge of pie.

Wulf said, "Here he is!"

A diminutive black-robed figure had entered by the main door and was pacing along the refectory with an in-toed gait that Wulf had forgotten but now recognized as painfully familiar; head lowered, hands tucked in sleeves. Vladislav had always referred to Marek as "Midge," but Vlad cared even less for other people's feelings than Anton did. If he seemed even smaller now than Wulf remembered, that was quite natural, because Wulf had been only thirteen when his favorite brother was taken away by two Dominican friars and a troop of lancers.

Anton and Wulf jumped up with cries of welcome. Anton stepped around the end of the table to embrace him, armor and all, but Marek blocked him by making the sign of the cross in blessing. Baffled, Anton stopped.

The monk set back his cowl. His face was thin, pinched, with lines around his eyes. His smile was bloodless, professional. "So it really is you! I couldn't believe it. My little brother Anton a count? And the sash of St. Vaclav? What are you now, twenty-one? No, twenty! You must have done mighty deeds for His Majesty. Or was it those dashing good looks? Did you catch the eye of Princess Laima? Cloth-of-gold suits you, Brother."

Baffled, Anton muttered, "Thank you." He shot Wulf an alarmed glance, looking to see what he thought, then returned to his seat. Had he not realized that five years' prayer and discipline would change the merry youth he had known?

The strangely austere Marek turned his inspection on Wulf, who kept his greeting to a respectful smile, but found it so restricted by the bevor that he sat down and raised his sallet. There was no one else in that great hall to see his face.

"And Wulfgang, too. My dear boy! So tall now!"

Marek was the only Magnus who would describe Wulf as tall. Wulf cast about for a tactful reply. "Just well-proportioned."

"But big for sixteen," Marek said softly.

Why was Marek saying that? He could not have forgotten the difference in their ages. He was hinting at something, but before Wulf could question, Anton's steel solleret banged against his boot in a needlessly painful warning. Wulf suppressed a wince.

"Someone else remarked on that to me just last night," Anton remarked, while still chewing.

Not his lady friend, certainly. Cardinal Zdenek, most likely, Wulf decided. He didn't understand why his age mattered, or why the king's first minister would care about it.

"Oh, you haven't finished?" Marek said. "Hurry up, because there are much more comfortable places to talk than here." He stayed on his feet opposite them and regarded Wulf thoughtfully across the narrow plank table. He had dark, shrewd eyes, but his hands were ingrained with dark lines, like a peasant's.

"What brings you here, Brother Wulfgang?"

Shrug, forced smile. "I am but an humble squire. I follow my lord."

"When did the humility grow in?" Marek murmured in a faint echo of his former humor. "You are not planning to stay here?"

"No!" Wulf said, with more emphasis than courtesy.

Marek sighed and glanced sideways. "So explain that sash, noble Lord Magnus." Then he went back to staring at Wulf.

"It's a long story, Brother Marek. It's the real thing, but I haven't exactly earned it yet, if you follow me. You heard that Father died?"

The monk nodded and made the sign of the cross. "When Otto's letter came, the abbot passed on the sad news, and mentioned him in our prayers that evening. How is Ottokar?"

Wulf took over the talking so that he needn't pretend to be eating. He told how well Ottokar ruled now as baron, how Branka kept giving him twins, and of course how Vlad had gone off to war and been taken prisoner at the Battle of the Boundary Stone. Then there was Anton's acceptance into the king's hussars.

All the time he was tortured by the realization that there was something horribly wrong, something he could not pin down. This somber Marek was not the same happy person he had loved as a child, the only one of his brothers who had ever had much time for him back then.

"Well, it is wonderful to hear that you are all safe in God's grace," the monk declared, making as if to leave. "Let us go to the scriptorium and talk there. It's above the kitchen, so it's warm."

Under the table, Anton's solleret again pushed against Wulf's boot, more gently than the last time. Whatever failings Anton might have, there was nothing wrong with his wits, so he, too, was seeing the change in Marek. He had known Marek better than Wulf had.

Wulf forced himself to cut a slice of cheese. "I haven't finished eating. I'm talking too much. Tell us about Koupel. Are you happy here?"

Marek smiled carefully. "Oh, yes, yes! At first there was talk of making me a Dominican friar, you know, and I think I should have found their rule much too strict. Ours is easier. We live very quietly, every day like the last, but better a quiet life and the Lord's grace than sin and eternal fires. I assist Brother Lodnicka in the herb garden now. Very interesting work, and most beneficial. Our apothecary prepares many potent medications from the herbs we cultivate. Ah! You are not eating. Ready to go now?"

"No," Wulf said firmly, determined to talk business here, where he was fairly confident of not being overheard, not wherever it was that Marek had been told to take them. He had come to consult Marek, and a lecture on emetics and purgatives was not what he needed. "A couple of days ago, Anton performed an incredible feat of horsemanship at the royal hunt."

The monk's face froze. "We always knew he was the best of us on a horse. Even Vlad—"

"I'm the best now," Wulf said. "But I would never dream of trying what he did. It was almost miraculous."

"Stop!" Marek whispered. His gaze raked the hall as if in search of listeners. "Not unless you've come here to stay."

Now that was more like it: a specific warning.

"So much so," Wulf persisted, "that a few hours ago he was summoned by Cardinal Zdenek and promoted to lord of one of the northern marches. The Pomeranians are about to invade, but there is a very slim chance that—"

"Please!" Marek squeaked. "Do not lay this burden on me!"

"I was told to lay it on you, Brother."

"Told by whom?"

"St. Helena and St. Victorinus."

The monk crossed himself. All the color had left his face. "Oh, please, please! You don't know what you are doing!" He stared down at the table, avoiding Wulf's gaze.

Wulf cut off Anton, who was about to interrupt. "Exactly. I don't know what I'm doing, but you do, and I want you to instruct me. It was not Anton who bespoke the miracle, it was I. Whose Voices did you hear, Brother?"

"Satan's!"

With a shiver, Wulf said, "How do you know? The Evil One introduced himself? Did you smell sulfur?"

"Of course not. The Voices told me they were St. Uriel and St. Methodius, but now I know they were demons sent from the pit to deceive me. Do not listen to your Voices, Wulfgang, oh, please do not! They are no saints. They will trap you. They will corrupt your immortal soul and drag you down."

That was what the Church taught. What else could a monk say?

"How can it be evil to do good? I saved Anton from breaking his neck."

"*You* saved him?" Marek was becoming agitated. "No, Satan saved him, at your request. And I mean no insult to you, Brother Anton, but we mortals cannot judge what is evil and what is for the best. Only the Lord can do that. Do you remember the boy Hans? He cut a blood vessel and was bleeding to death. But I laid a hand on the wound and called out a prayer to my saints—as I thought then—and the bleeding stopped! He lived. A blessed miracle, we all cried. We were wrong!

"Still, my folly was not entirely evil. That was how the Church learned of my peril, and came and brought me here and led me to repentance and salvation."

This was what he had been taught, anyway—for five endless years. Wulf wondered how Anton was taking it. Oh, where was that clever, cheerful, mischievous Marek they had once known? This sneaky, sanctimonious monk, who wanted to lead them to some place where his abbot could eavesdrop on their talk—this brother they had found was not the brother they had lost.

"I saved a dying boy! I felt so proud! Sinful pride. And his family were so grateful." Marek paused, glancing from Anton to Wulf and back again. "Whatever happened to Hans?"

Anton said, "I forget which Hans it was, there are so many churls called Hans around Dobkov."

"Hans the blacksmith's son," Wulf said glumly. "He raped a girl last spring. Ottokar hanged him for it. There is going to be a child."

Again the monk made the sign of the cross. "Did I not just warn you? Anything the Voices do for you will turn to evil eventually, however good it may seem at first. That rape now weighs against my soul. How I mourn for that poor girl and her unwanted child! I will ask for my penance to be increased."

"If you fast any more you'll disappear altogether," Anton snapped. "Do you have to give your portion to your abbot?"

Marek ignored him. "Wulfgang, Wulfgang! St. Bernard of Clairvaux taught us that hell is full of good intentions."

"Then what is Heaven full of?"

"Good deeds and faith. You think you are doing good, but you cannot tell how much evil may follow from your appeals to the Evil One. The Voices offer you anything you can possibly want, just as the Enemy led Our Lord up the mountain and showed him all the kingdoms of the world. Are you so strong that you can refuse temptation as he did, even after he had fasted forty days and forty nights?"

"There is a price," Wulf said angrily, meaning headaches and belly pains. He did not want to hear any more of this.

"The price of witchcraft is eternal damnation."

"You are speaking in circles. First you say that your miracle was good because it brought you here and saved your soul, then that it was evil because Hans sinned later. If I always do my best to use my talents for good, will those acts be held against me on Judgment Day?"

"I told you: asking for things becomes easier and easier. Soon you will stop trying to justify your requests. When did you first hear the Voices?"

"I don't remember exactly. As a child."

Marek nodded. "Your first sin was in hearing them at all. Did you understand what they were saying?"

"Not to begin with."

"No, but your second sin was in listening to them. When did you begin to understand what they were saying?"

"Not long before the Dominicans took you away," Wulf muttered.

"You were at the end of childhood, the age when we all start to lose our innocence. And when did you discover that they would grant your wishes? When did you first use a whispered little prayer to cheat at archery? To put a horse over a high jump? To make a girl kiss you?"

"Not that!" In truth, Wulf was scared of girls. Their smiles, their scent, their shape, all made him want to do forbidden things, and he believed the mind should rule the body, not the other way around. Until now he had succeeded so well that Father Czcibor seemed to disbelieve him when he made confession, cross-examining him until Wulf wondered if some of the servant girls had been making up stories about him, except he couldn't imagine why they would.

"Little things like archery," he admitted. "Yes, I cheated a bit, once or twice, to see if the Voices would help me. But only rabbits were hurt, not people. And I never let anyone see me." Wulf waited for Anton to say that he hadn't known Wulf could work miracles, as he had claimed earlier that morning. He didn't.

Marek sighed. "The girls will follow. 'It is love,' you will tell yourself, and you will ask your Voices to bring her to you, or even to make her willing. When did you first ask for a real miracle, something that couldn't have happened just by chance? Like when I healed the boy's leg?"

"Two days ago at the hunt."

"Ah. Tell me about the hunt."

"Anton spurred down a very steep hill into a diabolical double jump. The riders who tried to follow him were all undone."

"'Almost miraculous,' I think you said. So it was still deniable, if only just?"

"I suppose so."

"But today?" The monk smiled slyly. "Anton spoke to Cardinal Zdenek a few hours ago. That's what you said, didn't you? How did you get here so quickly? We are a long day's ride from Mauvnik here."

"I Spoke. I asked."

"So you rode through limbo from Mauvnik to Koupel? Two witnesses are all the Church needs now, Brother. One to testify at what hour you left the city and another to say when you arrived at the abbey door. Two witnesses and you will be condemned, both of you."

"And then what?" Anton barked. "Did you take your vows voluntarily? The Church does not compel men to enter the cloister."

The monk's bright little eyes shone with sincerity. "But I was guilty of Speaking, my lord count! If I did not confess and repent, I would be tried, and an investigation of Speaking allegations is most arduous, most unpleasant. Eventually, when the Speaker can endure no more, he will either admit his guilt or call out to the devil to rescue him. It was better to repent while I had the chance."

"And now? Will you betray us?"

Brother Marek clasped his hands as if to pray. He closed his eyes. "If I do not report this conversation to the abbot, I shall be asked at my next confession and be refused absolution unless I make amends." Then he looked sadly at Wulf. "Repent, Brother, while there is still time! Stay here with us. We can teach you how to resist the devil's lures. It is a hard road to walk, but I learned, with prayer and penance and the holy brothers' patience. They taught me how. Repent and stay!"

Wulf shook his head.

"And you are now proposing to ride through limbo to the northern marches?" Marek continued. "Is that what the cardinal wants: to block a war by sending two young men to roast in hell for all eternity?"

Wulf felt the walls of the abbey closing in on him. Possibly also on Anton, as an accomplice. The gates would be locked against them. But anything would be better than a lifetime shut up in a cloister, being turned into a worm like Marek, never running a horse over the hills, never dancing with fair maidens . . .

"Did it hurt?" the monk asked eagerly, eyes gleaming. "There is always pain, and undeniable witchcraft must have hurt severely."

"It hurt some," Wulf admitted, pushing his trencher away. His nausea did seem to be fading, so that he could almost admit that he was hungry. He poured himself more wine.

"And yet you think you can just race all the way from here to the Pomeranian border? I warn you, Brother, if you think you know what pain is now, you cannot imagine what that will cost you. It will last for days. You will go mad, or even die. Many Speakers have died from their torment, for it is far worse than anything that human torturers can inflict. Does this sound like holy miracle or demonic treachery?"

Brother Marek was ablaze now, leaning forward, spraying spit and thumping his fists on the board. "Even if you survive, you may well be beyond help already. I was a neophyte. I had done only one false miracle. An experienced Speaker cannot be taught control, as I was taught when I came here. A hardened practitioner of the black art is too dangerous to restrain. Stay your present course and soon the only way to stop you summoning the devil will be to burn out your tongue!"

"So you *are* going to report this conversation to Abbot Bohdan?" Anton asked. "Back at Dobkov, Father and Vlad and Ottokar stood by you. They would have run the troopers out of the county with their lances if the Dominicans had not been there to threaten them with a bishop's warrant of excommunication. You will now denounce Wulfgang as a Speaker?"

Marek covered his face with his hands. He did not seem to be praying, nor weeping either.

Wulf stood up, sick at heart. "Thank you for your advice, Brother Marek. I was instructed to come and consult you, and you have duly instructed me. I expected to learn from your advice, but I fear I have been warned by your mistakes. If you will show us the way back to the stables, we shall be on our way. We can saddle our mounts ourselves. We don't want to disturb your brothers' Sunday devotions, nor your servants', neither."

Anton rose also, watching Wulf, letting him lead. That was a first.

Marek sighed and straightened up. He was biting his lip, but now there was a repellent beaten-dog expression in his eyes. "Who," he murmured softly, "told you to hide your face, Brother?"

"It just felt like a good idea." Wulf pulled his sallet down again.

"A very good idea." Louder he added, "Let me show you my herb garden. Not mine, really; *our* herb garden. You can get from there to the stables, although it is not the most direct route."

"An excellent idea." Wulf glanced hopefully at Anton. "That is most kind of you."

"Are you suggesting," Anton demanded, "that the monks may try to prevent us leaving here?"

"Not you, my lord," Marek whispered. "But they might delay your companion . . . ask questions . . . demand to see his face, and so on. He may have trouble getting out of the monastery. Hurry! We must be quick."

CHAPTER 7

Three trumpets blared in unison to announce the arrival of Count Vranov before the gates of Castle Gallant. The one on the left was slightly out of tune, which made the fanfare especially unpleasant for Juozas, the count's herald, who was standing right in front of them. As soon as the noise ended, he marched forward a few paces and loudly proclaimed the name and rank of his master, come in peace. Out came Arturas, his Bukovany counterpart.

Juozas said he'd been told that the agreement was the old man, two sons, the priest, and twenty knights. Arturas said there had been a change: it was to be only five knights and no priest. The sons were still all right, but everyone else had to go back down to the High Meadows and wait there.

Juozas walked back to Count Vranov, who muttered something blasphemous about meddling *landsknechte*, but sent him back to report that the terms were acceptable. The count chose five men-at-arms to accompany him, then urged his horse forward and led the way into the ground-floor chamber of the barbican. The inner gate on the far side was still closed, but a sally port beside it stood open. Arturas led them through that, into a roadway that flanked the cliffs of the mountain called the Hogback, and then, at last, through another gate into the town. There they were welcomed by Constable Sir Karolis Kavarskas.

Huddling beside Giedre in St. Andrej's Cathedral, Madlenka Bukovany thought she had never known a Mass to last longer, yet she cherished every fleeting minute of it, because it was a calm before what might be a very bitter storm. Two weeks ago she had sat here in the family pew with Petr and her parents. Last Sunday Petr had been dead, and she had stayed home to watch over a dying father and a prostrate mother. Now she had only Giedre to keep her company.

She would have to be as stupid as the church gargoyles not to guess why the Hound had come to Castle Gallant yet again. She could not help knowing that she was a rich prize for any nobleman seeking a wife. She was too tall and too skinny to be a beauty, not plump and cuddlesome like Giedre, but her family tree was rooted back in the tenth century and she would bring her husband a very large dowry.

Now she was the only heir, so he would get it all. Vranov was the first of the ravens to land only because his nest was closest. Oh, how she needed her mother to send him packing! Yes, her legal guardian was King Konrad, far away in Mauvnik, but he could not even know yet that Count Bukovany was dead, and would probably not react for weeks. By that time, Count Vranov would have his claws firmly into Castle Gallant. Who could stop him? He had bought off that pernicious traitor, Constable Kavarskas. The German mercenaries would sell out to the highest bidder and likely already had. How much should she offer to buy them back? How much money did she have available?

"I must speak with your father!" she whispered to Giedre, who nodded.

St. Andrej's was large and ancient, but Petr had called it small and old-fashioned after he returned from Mauvnik. Arches now were round, not pointed, he had said, and modern churches had domes. But Gallant's other three churches were tiny and even older than the cathedral. All four were filled to capacity every Sunday, for anyone who missed Mass very often had soon been advised of Count Stepan's displeasure. The count's pew stood near the sanctuary and opposite the pulpit; from there he could keep an eye on the congregation just as well as the preacher could. Only the count and his family could sit in church; everyone else stood or knelt as the action required.

Bishop Ugne had almost reached the dismissal. Soon Madlenka would have to leave this precious sanctuary and face the world, the flesh, and the devil, with the flesh very likely being in the shape of one of Devil Vranov's odious sons. She had met three of them, and each had been worse than the last. What pressure would the Hound apply to force her consent? To be legal, her marriage must be approved by the king, but legality had never bothered Vranov before. Why start now?

Bishop Ugne announced an unexpected prayer. She lowered her face . . .

"My lady!"

She jumped at the whisper coming from the end of the pew. Three men stood there, but they were not yet Vranov's men come to get her. The speaker was Giedre's father, Ramunas Jurbarkas.

"My lady, please come with us now!"

She rose with Giedre at her back, and followed the seneschal out of the cathedral by the side door. His companions brought up the rear, moving quietly. Perhaps no one in the cathedral saw them leave—except the bishop, of course, who must have arranged the diversion and therefore must approve of whatever was happening.

Jurbarkas was a small man, stooped and prematurely gray, but soft-spoken and universally popular, rarely without a smile for everyone. He had married twice, and was old to have a daughter of Madlenka's age. But he had never disparaged Madlenka as a child and was unfailingly gracious to her now.

Just as Constable Kavarskas had been Father's military officer, so Seneschal Jurbarkas ran the finances of the county. But he did much more than that, distributing the count's alms, supervising the castle staff, arranging for road repairs, and many other things. If some tenant's son in an outlying holding had reached an age to need a job, then the keep would suddenly want another kitchen brat or stableboy. Few people in the county had not sought his help at some time or other, and every petition had been swiftly handled or brought to the count. He was honest and loyal. Madlenka could trust him.

But he was no longer the man he had been. Father had said so many times, and had been looking for a man to take over at least some of Jurbarkas's duties, but had failed to find one he considered honest enough before he himself had died. That blow had shaken the old seneschal more than almost anyone. He had found himself thrust into responsibilities he had never had to handle before, and he was looking older by the day.

In the cool winter sunshine, his companions were revealed as two hulking nephews. Madlenka had known them all her life and knew them to be sergeants in Kavarskas's garrison, although they were currently wearing civilian clothing and armed only with staves. What was the town coming to if the seneschal felt he needed protection in the streets?

He started walking in the direction of the palace and she went to his side—his right side, because that was his better ear. Giedre brought up the rear, and her two cousins moved out in front as vanguard.

The narrow alleyways were almost deserted that Sunday morning and the few townsfolk they met all bowed or curtseyed as Madlenka went by. She barely noticed, eager to make the most of what must be a very brief word with Ramunas Jurbarkas.

"You know that Count Vranov is here, my lady?"

"Yes. And I think I know why."

"You are ahead of me, then. I have left him and his entourage in the hall and provided a light repast. Your mother refuses to attend."

"Seneschal, can I buy him off?"

The little man looked startled. "Buy him off? I very much doubt it. Havel Vranov must be one of the largest landowners in the kingdom."

"But he wants to marry me to one of his sons to get hold of my inheritance, doesn't he?"

"Maybe. But I doubt you have enough money to bribe him, and paying tribute to bullies just encourages them to come back for more."

"But we might buy some time! I need time for the king to respond! Father told me we were rich."

The little man tut-tutted. "*He* was rich, yes. Had your brother succeeded, then he would have been rich also. But I don't know that you are. The tapestries in your bedroom are family heirlooms and now yours. But

Castle Gallant and its town belong to the king. Everything else is debatable. The tolls your father imposed on travelers were a royal tax, strictly speaking, so who owns the gold in the money chest? What's yours and what's the king's will have to be determined."

She felt a stab of despair: was nothing to be left to her? "Determined by the king, I suppose?"

They climbed a steep stairway between two houses, only just wide enough for two abreast. The distance from St. Andrej's to the keep was not far for a crow to fly, but she was no crow.

"His Majesty has officials called escheators to work the abacuses, but if he reveals in advance what sort of answer he wants, then that will be the answer he gets. As an orphaned daughter of one of the king's tenants-in-chief you are in the king's gift. He can marry you off to any man he wants. Of course you can refuse, but the results might be very unpleasant. You get a gold ring and your husband gets your dowry, carefully calculated, not a mite more."

"Is that unfair, or am I just biased?"

Jurbarkas sighed. "I quite understand your dislike of it, but it is the law. You have never wanted me to lie to you, my dear. The easiest and most practical solution, from everyone's point of view but yours, is to marry you off to a trusted and experienced soldier, who can be appointed lord of the marches in your father's place. That way he gets everything except the king's heriot and your mother's dowry, so it won't matter who owns what, and the Silver Road will be securely guarded again."

"Some fat, battle-scarred, foulmouthed forty-year-old with the manners of a rutting boar?"

The seneschal did not venture an opinion on that. "An experienced soldier is usually old enough to have been married at least once. You can refuse the king's choice, of course, but his second choice might be worse, and the terms harsher. The third suggestion will be a one-way visit to a nunnery."

"No choice could be much worse than any of Vranov's spawn."

"Perhaps not," the old man agreed sadly. They began to climb the wooden ramp to the door of the keep, which stood on the highest point in the town. "The townsfolk do not want Vranov as the next count of Cardice, but that is for His Majesty to decide."

"Can they do anything about it?" she asked, thinking of all those *landsknechte*, and wondering which side they would choose. At worst, Castle Gallant might be sacked by its own defenders.

"The townsfolk? No."

"How about the garrison?" she asked, eyeing the two broad backs ahead of her. The seneschal must trust his own nephews or he wouldn't have brought them to the cathedral. Dare she plot a counterrevolution to drive out the traitor?

"Well, they're hard to judge . . ."

"Tell me the numbers!"

Jurbarkas laughed gently. "Your father always said you would make a good warrior! The numbers that matter most are the *landsknechte*. Captain Ekkehardt's contract calls for three hundred lances, which means six hundred fighting men plus four or five hundred boys and other supporters. The constable has about five hundred, mostly archers, but that's only if you include the militia, some of whom may be away on their farms. And there must be a thousand or more able-bodied youths and young men in the town who can handle a pike, or a wood ax, or a scythe in a pinch."

At the base of the stairwell the nephews stepped aside, their duty done. Madlenka gave them a smile of thanks before she remembered she was wearing her mourning veil. The seneschal was too engrossed to notice them.

Havel Vranov had a couple of hundred men at the gates. How many more were standing ready to come running when he whistled? Her blood chilled at the thought of battle raging in the streets.

"Why did you say that the *landsknechte* were the ones who mattered?"

"Because they're trained warriors, my lady, and will obey their leader's orders. Vranov's hill men may be savage enough, and will certainly be loyal to their lord, but they cannot have the skill of mercenaries. Few of Kavarskas's men have had any field experience, and many may refuse to follow him if he betrays his king and the late count's daughter. The townsmen will be mowed like hay in any serious battle, but there are a lot of them. You see? Nobody can be certain who will come out on top if the swords leap out, but the *landsknechte* are the safest bet."

It was horrible.

They halted at the door to the hall, and now it was Giedre's turn to detach herself.

Standing with one hand on the handle, the seneschal said, "I will speak for you, with your permission, my lady."

That was about the worst idea she had heard yet. "No! I can speak for myself. If you feel I am making a mistake, you may call me aside for counsel or even speak up and contradict me." Better that than have her trying to interrupt him, like a badly trained child.

The old man shook his head. "I understand completely your concern about your future marriage, Madlenka, but that is not what the count came here to discuss. I spoke with him only briefly, but he never mentioned that subject. If it comes up, then of course you may speak. I hope you will pardon my saying so, but the worries he brings us are more urgent, and I think the constable will be doing most of the talking. After you, my lady."

CHAPTER 8

The keep was the stronghold, an ugly stone oblong around a central open bailey. Most of the rooms were cramped and drafty. The great hall was the largest room in Cardice after the nave of St. Andrej's, but when Petr came back from Mauvnik, he had laughed and said that he had seen privies there that were larger. It was a long, awkwardly narrow room, full of tables and benches, for it was where the castle staff and garrison ate their meals. A small dais at one end marked where the count held court and presided over major festivals; there was a fireplace in one corner. The door was in the center of one of the long sides; glazed windows opposite looked out into the bailey.

There were more people present than Madlenka had expected, because Count Vranov had brought his token bodyguard in with him. Five swordsmen in half armor sat on a bench at the end farthest from the hearth, their surcoats bearing blazons of a hound's head. Dogs required handlers, so they were flanked by six *landsknechte* and six archers of the garrison, led by Deputy Constable Dalibor Notivova. It was more worrisome evidence of the divisions in the town.

So much for the chorus. The principals were grouped

on two benches before the fire, and they began to rise to greet her as soon as they realized she had arrived. She was so intent on them that an unexpected voice behind her made her jump.

"Why're you hiding?" The speaker was down on his hands and knees inspecting a mouse hole.

"Leonas!" she said. "You startled me." She lifted her veil briefly.

The youth scrambled up and leered at her with the wet-lipped, slack-jawed gape of a simpleton. He was one of Vranov's sons, built like a lance, all height and no width, with a beardless face reddened by windburn and all-over freckles that were much the same shade as his untidy thatch of hair. The count had brought him along to Castle Gallant on both his previous visits, explaining merely that the lad got picked on if he was left behind, a thoughtfulness that belied Havel's ruthless reputation.

"I know you," Leonas said proudly.

"And I know you. You've grown since you were here last."

He chortled. "My da says I've got a spear I could take boar hunting!"

Um . . . yes. Unable to think of a suitable response and distressed at the thought of how the half-wit might start using that implement in a year or so, Madlenka just smiled and headed off toward the group by the fire, followed by the seneschal. She lowered her veil again.

There was Vranov, of course, and Constable Kavarskas—what treachery had he been plotting with the Hound? The odious walleyed priest, Father Vilhelmas, was not present. The third man she did not know, but she strongly suspected he must be another of Havel Vranov's army of sons. Another suitor, third time lucky?

He was a bulky man of around thirty, with a battered and scarred face.

The count limped forward to meet her, doffed his hat, and bowed. Despite his evil reputation, he was very ordinary-seeming, and had always been well-mannered when she was present, although Petr had referred to him as a foulmouthed blackguard. He seemed to have suffered no ill effects from a lifetime of raiding and rapine other than a twisted leg. His only concession to age was a beard, gray streaked with brown, and his most noteworthy feature a massive hooked nose. He wore sword and dagger, but not armor.

"Lady Madlenka, I grieve deeply for your tragic loss. Father and brother, and both of them noble men. I have ordered prayers said for them in all the churches in Pelrelm."

She nodded her thanks, grateful that her face was hidden, regretting that she did not trust the veil enough to stick out her tongue at him. At least Father Vilhelmas was not here, loudly declaiming prayers for her father, who had disliked the squinty priest as much as she did.

"Thank you, Lord Vranov."

"And today I hear that your lady mother has been taken by melancholy. It is a heavy burden you bear."

"Indeed it is," she said. "Personally I suspect that some Speaker has laid a curse on us."

"I could not agree more," he said solemnly.

"You *do*? I mean, you couldn't?" How dare he startle her like that!

"I believe it. Father Vilhelmas is of the same opinion. Pray, let us all sit down and discuss our mutual problems."

He offered his arm, curse him, and escorted her to the corner fire, where the benches had been arranged in a V, separated by a narrow gap. He put her on the left one and sat on the other, across the gap from her. The seneschal moved swiftly to sit on her left, and the others arranged themselves and sat down—Kavarskas and Ekkehardt beyond Jurbarkas, with Kavarskas at the end next the wall. The second Pelrelm man, sitting beyond Vranov, was not introduced, but their family resemblance was obvious.

"Constable," the seneschal said, "would you please advise Lady Madlenka on the present situation?"

The warrior's nod of agreement displayed impatience at having to report to a slip of a girl who put on airs and *sent for* him. "My lady, Count Vranov has brought news that the Wends are planning an imminent invasion of Jorgary."

"How imminent?" she asked, but it was an involuntary reaction, like a blink. Her mind was rummaging through memories of what Petr had said in the summer, when he returned from court. He had explained to her, summarizing what he had told Father, that the reason he had hired a troop of *landsknechte* to overwinter in Gallant was because Cardinal Zdenek had warned that Duke Wartislaw of Pomerania was mustering his army and Castle Gallant was his most likely target. So Havel Vranov might be telling the truth this time.

"Within days," the constable said. "He believes that his sources are trustworthy."

"It is almost winter!"

"Wars can be fought in winter," Vranov interjected. "I beg you to trust me in this, my lady. I have been fighting the Wends all my life. I have killed them with arrows and pikes and swords and roasted not a few of them. My spies insist that what is being planned now is no mere cattle raid. The Pomeranian army is moving down the Silver Road towards the border. Crews are strengthening bridges and repairing fords. Their vanguard may be here by Wednesday."

Madlenka lifted her veil and looked around the worried faces. "Castle Gallant is unvanquishable! It is well-garrisoned now, with Captain Ekkehardt and his men here to help."

"It has no guns worth the name," the *landsknecht* said loudly. "Castles all over Europe hitherto deemed impregnable are crumbling like eggshells. England, France, Italy, Spain—all their rulers have been investing in bombards to knock down castle walls. Unruly barons are being brought to heel, for only kings and some dukes can afford artillery trains. Fortresses that have stood for a thousand years are being breached, like Constantinople. Your father should have set guns in the barbicans. I told him. He said maybe. He said next year."

Kavarskas scowled at the interruption. "Our curtain wall *could* be badly damaged by guns, but it stands on the cliff edge, so no breech would be usable. But the barbicans are vulnerable. One shot can smash a gate to kindling."

It was Vranov's turn again. "This explains why the curse was laid upon your honored father and brother! The Wends' Speakers have cut off Cardice's head and left it leaderless."

And Madlenka had assumed that her marriage prospects were all that mattered. What a fool she must have seemed to the seneschal! It was true that Vranov had fought the Wends for years. She had no proof that Father Vilhelmas had cursed her family; some Wend Speaker could have been to blame just as easily. Cardinal Zdenek had warned Petr about the Wends. Despite her dislike and distrust of the count, Havel Vranov would be an indispensable ally in a war with Pomerania.

She glanced at the seneschal on her left, but he was deep in thought, staring at the floor. The door opened and closed, and Bishop Ugne came shuffling in. He had shed his formal vestments in favor of simple robes and a wide tasseled hat; he waved everyone down as they started to rise.

"Do not stop for me. Carry on." He came to a halt in the gap between Madlenka and Vranov. He was puffing as if he had been running, an unusual breach of dignity for him. "A quick update, please, and then carry on."

"Count Vranov," the constable said, "has intelligence that the Wends will attack us within days. Castle Gallant has withstood sieges for months in the past, but Duke Wartislaw has a cannon big enough to destroy our fortifications."

"Has the king been informed?"

"I sent all my news to Mauvnik three days ago, Lord Bishop," Vranov said. "But His Majesty cannot even give us an answer in time, let alone reinforcements. If we do nothing, his courier will find nothing left here except ruins and corpses."

"You exaggerate!"

"Not at all. Duke Wartislaw has obtained a bombard, a monstrous iron tube twice as long as a man. They call it the Dragon. It is not as enormous as some the Turks used to take Constantinople, but it is big enough. It shoots balls bigger than a man's head farther than our crossbows can send bolts. Once installed, it will demolish your barbican in a few hours."

"A cleric should not argue military matters, but surely the debris will block the entrance?"

"The barbican will collapse, the Wends will storm the breach over the rubble, and Gallant will be overrun."

"It is not quite hopeless," Kavarskas said. "They can only come by the Silver Road. They can move their Dragon by boat to the end of the lake, at Long Valley. The Ruzena rises there, but is not navigable, so from there the gun must be drawn by oxcart. There are half a dozen places where we may be able to block them if we move fast enough."

"Then why don't you?" Madlenka demanded. Why waste time just talking?

"I certainly shall, now that I have heard His Lordship's news," Kavarskas replied in a tone normally used only to address tiresome infants. "But the Wends know all this as well as we do. They may have scouts very close to us already, watching the road."

"You have an outpost at Long Valley, don't you? To watch the road?"

He rapped the wall beside him with his hook to indicate impatience. "And so far the patrols have ridden out and back undisturbed. But the Long Valley post could be bypassed. If I were the Wend leader, I would already have moved a sizable force around the outpost and brought it close enough to keep a watch on the gorge. If the defenders sent out a force larger than the usual patrol—a force large enough to start demolishing bridges, for instance—then I would ambush it and destroy it. We lack the manpower to afford suicide missions, my lady. They must outnumber us twenty to one."

He grew louder. "These are not our grandfathers' days! We can no longer skulk behind the walls as they did, waiting until the enemy starves and goes away. If the Pomeranians invade, we shall need an active defense, with frequent sorties against their gun emplacement. But we will take monstrous losses if we charge along the road into their volleys, and Captain Ekkehardt and I between us have less than a thousand men."

"You have guns!" the seneschal protested. "Captain Ekkehardt's contract requires him to supply fifty armed arquebusiers."

"Those I have," the *landsknecht* said, "armed and well trained. But personal firearms cannot throw a ball as far as a cannon can. The Wends can emplace their bombard far outside our range."

"And arquebuses are very slow to load," the constable added. "An archer can get off several bolts in the time an arquebusier needs to fire one ball. That suffices if you are firing from fortifications, but is close to useless in the field."

This was all so wrong! Madlenka and the seneschal should not be here at a council of war. It should be her father or Petr listening to the arguments and making decisions based on experience and training. These men did not care a spit for her opinions or her military judgment, and neither did she. Some vital words had not yet been spoken. She wanted to know the real reason she was here.

"Da!" Leonas shouted in his slurred voice. "Why does this horse got horns?" He was examining one of the tapestries.

"I'll tell you later," Vranov shouted back. "Now be quiet!"

"How soon can we expect aid from the king?" Bishop Ugne asked calmly.

The constable banged the wall angrily with his hook. "Weeks or months! He cannot yet have received my report of the count's death. Count Vranov's news about the Pomeranians will arrive a few days later. In another fortnight we may receive a note telling us that His Majesty expects us to fight to the last man. To muster the army, with all the food, equipment, and fodder it will need, will take months. Then it must march across moors, through forests, zigzag from ford to ford . . . When it eventually meets the Pomeranians, they may well be closer to Mauvnik than to Cardice."

And by then Castle Gallant would be only a memory. Fortresses that refused to surrender were sacked. The conventions of war allowed the successful besiegers three days of unlimited rape, murder, pillage, and atrocity.

The bishop cleared his throat. "We appreciate your coming in person to warn us, Havel. It is time you told us your terms."

Terms? But of course there would be terms.

Vranov looked up with a smile like a child caught stealing a cookie. "I offer an alliance. I can spare a hundred horses and a thousand men now, and twice that many as soon as I am sure that Wartislaw is not just feinting at Cardice to conceal a move on Pelrelm. I can also lend you a single cannon. It is nothing like his monster bombard, but if you can emplace your gun first, he will have to work much harder. I will supply a master gunner, fifty balls, and enough powder for them. If you can delay the Wends until the flux breaks out in their camp, or until winter strikes, or until King Konrad can bring up his army behind you, then you will have won. At least this time you will have won."

"And why are you doing this, my lord?" Kavarskas inquired.

"Because you are my first line of defense. I hate the Wends and they hate me. If they force the Silver Road and occupy northern Jorgary, they can squeeze Pelrelm from both sides."

Never mind Pelrelm! What of Castle Gallant? At best it would be besieged, meaning famine and suffering. No wonder Seneschal Jurbarkas was worried.

"But there is more," said Bishop Ugne at Madlenka's shoulder. "You want more than that."

The count nodded, watching the seneschal, not looking up at the bishop standing over him. "Cardice provides board for my men, of course. And their women, if they bring them. Those are worthwhile extras for you, to make the men fight. Plus a thousand florins for the munitions and the rent of my gun and gunner. We can hammer out the details later."

"Later is the time for action," Ugne insisted. "Now is the time for talk."

Madlenka had never had much respect for the bishop, but suddenly she was very grateful for his support. She could trust his motives in this crisis more than anyone else's. He would be the last person to sell out to the Orthodox Wends.

The Hound shrugged. "You are right, my lord bishop. No disrespect to the constable or Captain Ekkehardt, but the strongest ally commands, always. I want Marijus here to be acting keeper of Castle Gallant. Just during the emergency, of course. Sir Marijus is the finest warrior among all my sons, well qualified to direct the defense of the castle."

Marijus Vranov glanced around the group without speaking, nodding to each in turn; his eyes lingered longest on Madlenka. His nose was not as dominant as Havel's and had been badly broken at some time in the past, but it must originally have had the same hooked shape. He was an imposing man, somehow, although he had yet to open his mouth. If she were to be forced into marriage with a Vranov, this one at least looked better than the first two suitors the count had produced—scars and all.

"Marijus has fought in Italy and France," his father continued. "He is familiar with sieges and the use of guns. If he defends Castle Gallant against the coming attack, then he can reasonably petition the king for a permanent appointment. I will leave him behind as surety for my good faith while I rush home to make preparations."

"It seems strange to me," the bishop said, in his sonorous, trained voice, "to appoint a schismatic Orthodox commander to defend a Catholic country. You also want your pet priest to replace me as bishop, I assume?"

Religion could turn any discussion into a raging riot. Madlenka caught the seneschal's eye and knew that he shared her foreboding.

"Not at all, Lord Bishop," the count said calmly. "It is true that Father Vilhelmas is a friend of mine, but I remain a faithful son of Rome; my family likewise. You have my sacred word on it." He crossed himself in the Catholic fashion, left to right. Marijus did the same.

The bishop beamed. "That is indeed welcome news. But then why did you bring Vilhelmas with you today, and the last time you visited Cardice? Why do you consort with a heretic cleric at all?"

The Hound chuckled. His air of confident good humor was probably designed to raise the bishop's hackles. "Because he happens to be a relative of mine. A distant one, to be sure—about a third cousin, or so. My grandfather's sister was captured in a raid from what is now Pomerania and carried off, never to return. Even so, Father Vilhelmas, her grandson, was born in wedlock and is an authentic, ordained priest. And yes, I allow him a small chapel in Pelrelm. Your archbishop is well aware of this, as you must be yourself, my lord bishop. The frontier within the hills is not as clearly defined as one might like, and many residents of my county prefer their traditional form of worship. My bishop turns a blind eye. The border is hard enough to defend without having religious differences fomenting discord and disloyalty."

"And why do you bring him here, this Vilhelmas?"

The count's tone hardened. "Because you have secret Orthodox supporters in Gallant also, Lord Bishop. If you do not know that, you should. Vilhelmas has only to walk your streets and he will be invited indoors to hear confessions."

"Or celebrate mass?"

"*Please!*" The interruption came from Marijus Vranov, who had not previously spoken. "We are here to talk war, not religion."

"My son is right," the count said. "We must unite. The best strategy for all of us is to appoint him temporary keeper of Castle Gallant."

The resulting silence dragged on until Kavarskas said, "The terms are generous. I would serve under Sir Marijus on his terms."

Why shouldn't he approve those terms? He had probably helped negotiate them behind everyone else's back, and been well paid for it already. At least there had been no mention of anyone being married yet.

"That is all?" the seneschal said at last.

The Hound opened his mouth, but his son spoke first. "It is enough! We are both threatened by the barbarous, schismatic Wends, and we must unite."

Captain Ekkehardt had hardly spoken since Madlenka joined the meeting, but now he did. "It is not enough for me. Our contract is for overwintering and garrison duty, not enduring a siege."

Silence and shocked glances. Surely the *landsknechte* were essential for any hope of holding off a Pomeranian assault?

The seneschal smiled toothlessly. "I am familiar with the contract. There is provision for more money if you have to fight. If the Wends do appear, then Cardice will certainly honor the contract. We expect you to do likewise."

"Not enough more," the *landsknecht* growled.

"You are backing out?" The older man spluttered like a kettle suddenly coming to a boil. "This . . . this is treachery! And cowardice. No ruler in Europe will hire your troop after this, Captain."

The mercenary's face was too well hidden behind its bush of gold hair to show a change of color, but his eyes flashed and his beard bristled. "There is no contract! The signing was made by Petr Bukovany, who is dead. His father is dead. The contract has lapsed, and I will lead my men out tomorrow."

"The contract was signed by the keeper on behalf of King Konrad."

"I saw no royal writing, no royal seal. This castle is indefensible against guns. Here to be slaughtered we do not stay."

"He just wants more money," Marijus Vranov said. "How much is he being paid now?"

The seneschal said, "Ten florins a month now, rising to twenty as soon as an enemy appears."

"That is generous for three hundred lances. How much more do you want, Captain?"

Everyone looked to Ekkehardt, who said, "Forty, starting today."

"Forty total, I hope, not forty more? You would serve under me, as acting keeper?"

"Yes. We have met before."

Vranov's son smiled for the first time, showing an excellent and complete set of teeth. It was a surprisingly persuasive smile. "In opposition. I prefer to have you at my side than in my face." He could be charming when he wanted, seemingly.

"And I you."

Madlenka wanted to heave a sigh of relief that the crisis seemed to have been resolved. If the news was bad, it was not as bad as it had seemed at first. So why did she have a nasty feeling that there was worse to come? Who were they waiting for? Well, if nobody else would say it, she would.

"There is one small problem, my lord count." Her voice trembled only very slightly. "I mean no offense, but we have only your word for it that the Wends are planning to attack."

Vranov turned his head to smirk at her. "I was wondering who would have the courage to say that. Marijus was there to hear the spies' reports, weren't you, Marijus? My troops can start arriving in three or four days. By then, the constable will have sent out scouts to survey the road, won't you have, Sir Karolis? The only other thing I can suggest is that we give you our most solemn oaths that we believe what I have told you to be true. You have some holy relic on which we may swear, my lord bishop?"

"We have a toe bone of St. Andrej in the cathedral," Ugne said.

Who would trust Havel or his smashed-nose son if they swore on a whole churchyard of holy relics?

Then the *landsknecht* loosed another volley. "We will need payment in coin, mostly silver."

The Hound frowned. "As will I, if I am to meet expenses."

Seneschal Jurbarkas was wringing his hands. "I cannot provide such amounts without royal authority."

The meeting exploded in shouts of disbelief. Madlenka was suddenly convinced that the whole discussion, ever since she arrived, had been rehearsed and staged in advance, like a passion play, and the true quarry was her father's gold—her gold, now. But she could not believe that the seneschal, Giedre's father, who had been like an uncle to her all her life, would have been part of such a conspiracy. Nor, and everyone else seemed to agree on this, could she believe that he would withhold the money needed to defend the castle against the Wends. That would make no sense at all.

The seneschal cowered away from the shouts. He seemed distressed and almost bewildered by the anger. "We do not have chests of coin hidden away. Our income comes from the tolls we gather from travelers, and few of them pay us in gold. The largest part comes from the big trader caravans that pass through here four times a year, two northbound and two southbound. They prefer not to carry bullion, so they pay in bills of exchange drawn on the Fugger Bank of Augsburg or the Medici Bank of Florence. Much of that scrip goes south to Mauvnik twice a year, as the king's share. Both of this year's remittances have already gone. As I was explaining to Lady Madlenka on our way here, I do not know how much of our substance belongs to the king and how much to her. I cannot in good conscience loot either the royal share or her inheritance until I am absolutely convinced that the threat is real and that there is no alternative. Not without the king's authority."

"Pig guts!" shouted the constable. "My men collect the merchants' tolls, and we know how they are paid. Large caravans pay in bank drafts, yes, but none of the other travelers do. You pay the king his share with the drafts, because scrip is safer to transport than coin, but the real money goes into the count's coffers. You must have millions of florins buried in the cellars."

Marijus rose to his feet, taller and larger that Madlenka had expected.

"This is absurd," he said. "By the time the Wends appear on your doorstep, it will be far too late to summon the Pelrelm levy, and Captain Ekkehardt and his *landsknechte* will be in Spain or Cathay. Are we children," he demanded in a tone that echoed through the hall, "to squabble while the Dragon creeps ever closer? Let us go to the cathedral and bind ourselves in common cause against the foe. My father and I will swear to the truth of what we reported. I will swear to defend the castle to my last breath, if necessary, and to relinquish my command as soon as we succeed or the threat turns out to be a false alarm. Of course it should be Count Bukovany negotiating for Cardice, but he and his son were the first casualties of this war. Do any of you believe their deaths were mere coincidence? The rest of you—Lady Madlenka, Captain Ekkehardt, Constable Kavarskas, Seneschal Jurbarkas, and especially you, Bishop Ugne—represent him. You also represent the common folk of Gallant, who cannot defend themselves. You must swear to recognize me as acting keeper until the king or events dismiss me.

"And as for payment . . ." he said, smiling, "I am sure we can find all the gold we need, even if we have to melt down St. Andrej's altar vessels."

CHAPTER 9

Brother Marek led the way along the refectory toward the kitchen entrance, moving with his previous solemn pace, toes in and head down, face hidden inside his cowl. Bringing up the rear, Wulf marveled again at how small he was, head and shoulders shorter than Anton. His lack of stature somehow emphasized his vulnerability to Abbot Bohdan's anger and punishment. There was more to *omnia audere* than suicidal charges against phalanxes of spears.

He did not enter the kitchen itself, but turned aside through an iron-bound door, which led out to a green yard studded with small wooden crosses. Here, under the leering watch of the church's gargoyles, brethren of bygone ages slumbered until the last trump should summon them.

Marek turned again and followed a path to a gate set in a high stone wall. He smiled as he selected the key he wanted from a bundle on a leather thong.

"We keep this gate locked because the herb garden is overlooked by the dormitory reserved for lady visitors. We mustn't tempt the novices! There are no visitors at the moment. Later in the day, perhaps . . ."

The key turned with a groan. "More seriously, the

first garden contains many herbs that can be dangerous, even just to touch. Many herbs with therapeutic properties can be poisonous in large doses, you know. Mandrake and cowbane and monkshood, for instances. This is a lesson to us that good and evil may walk hand in hand."

"Can too much good ever be evil?" Wulf asked.

The monk glanced up at him with a twinkling smile, looking for a moment much like the old Marek of their childhood. "That is what I was preaching! Almost any good thing can be evil in excess—water can drown you, air can freeze you. It is meritorious to give alms, but suppose you gave everyone in the kingdom a thousand florins? They would all want to be lords! No one would work, the farmers would stop growing food, and we should all starve."

After leading them into a large, walled enclosure and locking the gate behind them, he threw back his cowl. "Follow, and remember not to touch." He set off along the path at a much faster pace, almost a run.

Narrower paths divided the whole garden into small rectangular plots, like a giant's tiles. Each plot contained no more than one type of plant, although some types seemed to occupy several plots. Marek paused to lecture.

"This shrub is called Blessed Thistle. Very efficacious against the pestilence. And this is oregano—useful for treating cramps and dropsy. They say that the smoke from burning twigs of oregano keeps the devil away. Much used by the Inquisition."

The path led to another gate, another key, another brief lecture. "Of course not all our materials come from herbs. Willow bark, oak gall, and others we harvest from trees. Koupel has a great reputation for healing."

The next enclosure was larger, and included some

shade trees. Marek paused under a sturdy oak that still held most of its foliage. Wulf noted that they could not be overlooked, even from upstairs windows. He raised his sallet.

Marek stared hard at him. "Good to see you as a man, little brother. I am glad you came, but now you must depart. If you go through that gate over there, you will be back in the west courtyard, where the stables are. Greatly overrated brutes, horses."

Aha! "You think so?" Wulf asked. He glanced at Anton, but he had not caught the hint yet.

"Well, I do think so now," Marek said wistfully. "I shall go and meditate in the church for a while." He raised his hand to bless them.

Wulf said, "Wait! You could come with us, you know. We'll help you escape."

The monk shook his head fondly. "They would hunt me to the ends of the earth—and they would find me. I assure you, they *would* find me! God bless." He turned and minced away, his habit swirling around his ankles.

The other two stood and watched their brother go.

"Well, it was a good idea," Anton said grumpily. "At least he came to his senses eventually. At the beginning I really thought he was going to rat on you. You had better disappear. Cross the border as soon as you can and sign on with the best mercenary troop you can find."

In other words, run away. It was obvious that he desperately wanted and needed Wulf's help, but he wasn't going to come right out and ask for it again, not so soon after hearing what happened to apprehended Speakers. The next step would normally be to shame him into volunteering by hinting at cowardice. That had worked when they were children and Anton still hadn't quite adjusted to the fact that his little brother had grown up and could see through his ploys. In fact, Wulf had seen through them years ago and had always been too proud or unsure of himself to refuse the challenges.

"You're giving up?" he said innocently. Provoking Anton to pomposity was still one of his favorite pastimes.

"Of course not. I'll have to ride north by conventional methods. I'll almost certainly arrive too late and find Cardice in the hands of the Wends. Whether I do or don't, you really can't help me without using your, um, special abilities. I don't expect you to expose yourself to the ghastly tortures Marek described, or the penalties the Church would impose on you. You'd better leave the country fast."

"Wait," Wulf said, stopping. He knelt beside the tree and clasped his hands. "Most holy Saints Helena and Victorinus, I, Wulfgang Magnus of Dobkov, a sinner, beseech your aid, in the name of the Father, the Son, and the Holy Spirit."

For a moment nothing happened, and he wondered whether Anton had stayed to listen or fled in terror. Then, through closed eyelids, he saw the Light. The Light always came just before the Voices, as if Heaven had opened a window, but apparently only Wulf ever saw it. It was of no color that he ever met anywhere else, and it seemed to embrace him in a luminous mist, cutting him off from the rest of the world. It helped him sense, in a no doubt blasphemous way, why painters depicted saints with haloes. Usually there was a scent of apple blossom, but not this time.

Victorinus:—*The path you tread now leads into darkness.* As always, he sounded as if he were somewhere to Wulf's right.

"I have just been warned that you are the devil."

Helena:—*Why summon us if you believe so, than*

rather being silent? Were we or were we not, wherefore would we not deny?

"I do not believe very much of what my brother told me, my lady."

Victorinus again:—*Believe some of it, for bit and bridle, rein and hobble await you here.*

"Was it true what my brother hinted, that we don't need the horses?"

—*It is true.*

"Then please will you guide Anton and myself to Cardice?"

Victorinus:—*Will you accept the pain?*

"You mean pain that may kill me, as Marek said? Worse than anything human torturers can inflict?" Headache, then belly cramps. What worse horror lay in store?

—*Who seeks the prize must choose the price.*

The danger of a few hours or even days of agony was less terrifying than that of being turned into another Marek for the rest of his life. Wulf drew a deep breath. "How long will it take to get to Cardice?"

—*Time dwells not on the road you take, for it knows no sun or moon.*

"Then I will pay the price."

Helena:—*You we shall guide. Your brother you must lead.*

The Light faded and was gone.

He muttered his thanks before opening his eyes to look up at Anton, who was staring down at him with mingled horror and hope.

"You heard that," Wulf said as cheerfully as he could manage. "No, you didn't . . . We mustn't go to the stables. We can leave the swords and the horses."

Anton backed off a pace. "You mean Marek betrayed you after all?"

"They guessed . . . or could tell. We're a marked family, remember. Perhaps I was stupid to keep my face covered, perhaps it made them suspicious. It felt right, though." He scrambled to his feet.

"You're going through with this even after what Marek said?"

Wulf chuckled, although it wasn't easy. "You always told me that no Magnus ever refused a dare. I've just been dared by two saints."

To his surprise, Anton argued. He must be starting to grow a conscience. "That was childhood games. No one counts odds in battle, but burning out your tongue, locking you up in a place like this . . . That's different."

Wulf felt an unexpected surge of anger. If he must choose between lifelong captivity and extreme torment, then the sooner he got the torment over with, the better. "It is *not* different! Damn your eyes, Brother! You think courage is confined to soldiers? A thousand times you dared me and I never refused. Twice I broke a leg, thanks to you. At least once I got a concussion. Cuts and bruises galore. I seem to recall Father beating the lights out of you a few times for taunting me. I *never* refused, never! I was true to the family motto. It doesn't just apply to armored trolls. I'm a Magnus as much as you are. Now let me take your hand—unless you're scared, I mean."

Anton faked a punch at his nose. "Well done! I knew I could count on you."

"So you didn't believe what you were saying?"

"I wanted you to be certain."

"Even remembering what Marek said about anything the Voices do for me turning to evil eventually?"

Anton grinned down at him. "Who's daring who now?"

"Give me your hand, then."

"I think I left the itinerary in my saddlebag!"

"I don't think I need an itinerary. I have to lead you and I don't know what may happen if we get separated. I don't know how long it will take. It may seem like hours or only minutes. If I start squealing or groaning, don't pay any attention. Ready?"

"Thank you for this. I'll never ask you again, I promise."

Wulf hauled Anton into a run. Running in armor was part of their training, although running several hundred miles in it was not. They never reached the end of the herb garden. In moments the air began to glisten with the sort of silvery fog seen on windless winter mornings. The trees faded to ghosts. The brothers ran through the wall, and then out into fields beyond. Soon there was no scenery, no sky, no sun; not even grayness. Nothing. Limbo, Marek had called it. Their armor had become weightless.

"How do you know which way is north, Wulf?" Anton asked in a thin, strained voice. His courage was being tested, too.

"I don't. My Voices do."

For a while they ran in silence, Anton trimming his stride to match Wulf's. Then he stumbled, but caught his balance before he pulled them both down. "Sorry . . . Hard to run when you're not running on anything." His voice seemed to reverberate, as if he was speaking in a huge enclosed space, like a cathedral.

Wulf looked down and stumbled at once, because the ground he could feel under his feet wasn't visible. Only Anton was truly solid. A ghostly house appeared ahead, then more houses, then wraiths of villagers parading to church. The brothers ran right through them, through their houses, and back into misty forest. Had any of the peasants noticed the specters of two transient visitors? Were they even now running to their priest in terror?

An orchard. Cattle. A town. Mostly forest and no road. The images were moving much faster now, flashing by at arrow speed. A river underfoot was gone before the thought could register. No one could ever travel this fast in reality. This was what a falcon must see as it swooped down on its prey. At this rate they would be in Cardice in no time, which was what St. Helena had promised. There was no sound except their hard breathing. Wulf's heart was pounding, his mouth dry, yet he did not seem to be sweating at all.

He stumbled again at a sudden cramp in his right calf.

Anton grabbed Wulf's wrist with his free hand. "What's wrong? You're limping."

"Nothing. But you'd better keep holding on to me, in case I let go by mistake." He released his own grip.

"Better you slow down."

"No. The faster we go, the sooner we'll get there. Go faster!"

He almost cried out as the big muscle in his left thigh knotted, leaving him limping on both legs. He was developing a stitch, too, a monstrous, crippling, stitch. If his experiences after the hunt and on the ride to Koupel were a guide, then the pain would be even worse after he reached Cardice. "Ouch!"

"What's wrong?" Anton panted. "Take a rest?"

"No. Sooner we get . . . there, the . . . better. You lead. Fast . . . as you can."

They ran on, but Wulf was stumbling often now, and could not suppress his cries. Cramps ran through his arms and chest. This was hell, truly hell. He was meddling with the devil and the devil was enjoying torturing him, waiting to see how much he could endure.

Maybe the only way to find relief was to give up and admit that he was beaten. Perhaps then he would be given what he wanted. But even if that was the game, the fact was that he couldn't stand more. Every muscle in his body seemed to have taken on a life of its own, knotting, twisting. He could barely stay upright, staggering along as Anton hauled him.

Trees were flashing by, moving faster than fall leaves in a full gale.

"Stop! Please, stop!"

Anton slackened the pace. "We're about there?"

"No. I need a rest."

"No, we must keep going. You told me to ignore your whimpers." Anton speeded up again. "We must be almost there. I can see you're in pain, Wulf, and I am grateful for what you're doing, but there's no point suffering as much as this and then giving up and losing the prize."

Wulf's legs knotted up completely. He slid to his knees and then sprawled full length, leaving Anton almost running backward, hauling him like an ox pulling a plow. Fortunately the invisible surface under them seemed to be perfectly smooth.

Wulf was incapable of enduring such torment. He screamed aloud. "*Sweet Jesus!* Stop! Stop!"

"Just a little longer!"

"No! Stop! Holy St. Helena, please stop!"

Reality returned with a crack like thunder. He slid to a stop, sprawled facedown in grass and thistles, which filled his bare hands with prickles and narrowly missed his eyes. Anton pitched headlong, but with his usual luck avoided the thistles. The air was chill. A herd of sheep fled, bleating in unison.

Wulf screamed as every muscle in his body cramped simultaneously. It was worse! Worse, worse, worse.

"You all right?" Anton muttered. His face swam into view and then was drowned in tears of pain. "By the blood, you don't look it."

Wulf could hardly find breath enough to live, let alone speak. He writhed uncontrollably, every movement setting off more spasms. He thought he was about to die and that would be a very good idea.

"We must be close, Wulfie. We've come a long way. I can see mountains with snow on them. If I carry you, can you do the, er, miracle?"

Wulf swallowed the blood in his mouth and croaked, "Try."

Anton's clumsy attempts to lift him made his arms and legs thrash.

"Pox on you! If you can't help, why don't you at least stay still?"

"Can't," Wulf gasped.

Anton was big and superbly fit, but to lift another man onto his shoulders when both were wearing armor was a feat of note. Wulf's spasms of agony did not help him, but after four or five attempts he succeeded, bent almost double by the load.

"Walk . . ."

"Easy for you to say." Anton began staggering forward over the pasture. A few steps were enough to resume the Satanic journey, and he went shuffling through limbo while the mortal world, reduced to shadows on mist, rushed silently past.

CHAPTER 10

"Troubles never come singly, it seems," Marijus Vranov remarked. "The bad news we have brought must seem especially cruel to you, so soon after your bereavements and in your mother's melancholy."

So it's piety time now, is it? Madlenka pulled a face at him behind her veil.

"We must pray for strength to bear what the Lord sends," she agreed. And we must wonder how many of the afflictions were sent by Havel, not Heaven. She had hoped for a private talk with Giedre on the way to the cathedral, but Marijus Vranov was waiting for her at the door as she prepared to leave the keep. He offered his arm and she could not refuse it without giving insult. They walked down the ramp together, following an honor guard led by the constable. The Hound and Leonas came next, with the boy happily chattering nonsense, then Seneschal Jurbarkas and Giedre. Captain Ekkehardt and some *landsknechte* brought up the rear. Bishop Ugne had gone on ahead. A surprisingly large crowd of townsfolk stood around in the little square, watching with worried eyes. They neither cheered nor booed, and their silence chilled the air like a dark cloud.

"Indeed we must. And I want to reassure you on one

point. I know that in the summer my father was trying to contrive a marriage between you and one of my brothers, so I can guess that you suspect him of trying to foist me on you now."

"Honored as I should—"

He chuckled. "Don't say it. Of course marriage must be the farthest thing from your mind at the moment, even if King Konrad had not flatly forbidden any union between our two houses. I would not mention this at all except to reassure you. I am in a similar position to yourself. My wife died last week, giving birth to a stillborn son."

"Oh, no!" She stammered, trying to find words while she wondered whether to believe him.

"Oh, yes. So I also mourn and we are partners in grief. The Lord gives and the Lord takes away. Nor am I hinting that I am now free to marry someone else. I mean that there are times for joy and there are times for memories, and joy is very far away just now."

"Have you children already?"

"Two girls. I would dearly love to be with them at this time, but Duke Wartislaw has decreed otherwise. Although my father does not say so, I suspect he has never been so worried in his life. If the Wends can take Castle Gallant, they will have turned his flank. I mean they will be able to circle around and attack Pelrelm from the plain."

"Yes." Did he think she was a simpleton like Leonas?

"The townsfolk are frightened. Understandably so. May I suggest that you lift your veil and show them that you are not?"

"I am, you know. Terrified." But she obeyed.

"You truly do not show it. Perhaps I should wear it instead. It may be my face that is scaring them."

"You jest, my lord!" Despite his demolished nose, Marijus was the most impressive Vranov she had met yet. She had always known that she would have little say in the choice of her husband, and now that Cardinal Zdenek would be making the decision, her thoughts on the matter would count for nothing at all. One day she would be told whom she was to marry, and that would be that. She could only hope that he would make as good a first impression as this latest member of the Hound's pack. He had shown up well at that meeting, carefully staying silent until he could sum it all up and take charge.

"Are you really planning to melt down the altar vessels?"

He chuckled. "No. But I would if I had to. I am sure that the seneschal can find all the money we need."

"But will he? I do not know why he is being so difficult."

"Is he, by any chance, honest?" Marijus inquired with a smile.

"Of course! Absolutely."

"Not 'of course,' my lady. In fact he must be almost unique, and that helps explain his fear. You see, the next keeper, whoever he is, will march in and demand a close accounting of all the books to find out how rich he is. And then he will put the seneschal to torture to make him reveal where he has hidden the rest of it."

"No!" she cried. The thought of anyone torturing Giedre's father was intolerable. That kindly old man?

"It happens all the time, my lady. And if he has spent your father's money all his life only as your father directed, he is not about to start throwing it around now without orders from somebody in authority. He would be asking for trouble, you see?" He laughed. "Who would ever think that we should have to begin by fighting honesty? Altar vessels, here we come!"

It occurred to Madlenka that Marijus was likely to be around Gallant for some weeks or even months to come. She might be seeing quite a lot of him.

Most houses in Gallant were three stories high, with the bottom level being used for storage, workshops, or livestock. The streets were made even narrower by innumerable stone staircases leading up to the domestic floors, and these made natural galleries for spectators. As more and more townsfolk appeared to watch the informal parade, they stood on those stairs or packed back between them to let the nobility pass, so that Madlenka felt she was walking along a two-story canyon of people. More faces peered out of every window. Some stared angrily and showed their teeth, but she was sure that their anger was not directed against her but at the infamous count, the Hound who burned cottages with families inside.

As she and Marijus passed through the cathedral door, an argument broke out behind them, Leonas screaming that he wanted to come in, his father insisting that he stay outside with some of the guards.

Marijus looked around with annoyance. "Leonas gets frightened in churches. I think he's scared by the echoes. Come, we need not wait for the others."

Why not? Why was she here at all? Either her escort was lying about her marriage potential or he had some other use in mind for her. Was even the seneschal capable of betraying her? Of course he was, if he could be persuaded that it was for her own good, or in the king's service. She went up the steps with Marijus and entered the dimness.

Somehow the cathedral seemed both smaller and

grander when it was empty. She and Marijus led the procession along the nave toward where Bishop Ugne was already standing on the steps of the sanctuary, clad again in his vestments. She let her companion decide when to halt, and the rest of her companions spread out in a line on either side of them. The troopers—garrison, Pelrelm honor guard, and *landsknechte*—halted a few steps back. The cathedral did not fall completely silent, though, and when Madlenka glanced around, she saw many people pouring in the west doors, anxious to witness whatever was going to happen. As if doubting their right to spy on their betters, they were staying back and close to the walls, so newcomers had no choice but to move farther forward.

Bishop Ugne frowned at the unexpected audience, but he could hardly order the people out of the house of God. He announced a prayer for divine guidance and protection, but the quiet shuffling noises at the back resumed as soon as it was over. This public meeting was a serious error, Madlenka decided, but to terminate it now would be a worse one.

The bishop went to the altar and fetched the precious jeweled reliquary that held the bone of St. Andrej.

"Havel, my son, you have a statement to make?" he asked softly.

The Hound stepped forward. "I do, my lord bishop." But then he unexpectedly raised his voice and made a proclamation instead. "I employ men to spy on what is happening across the border in Pomerania. Last week three of them independently told me that they had seen Duke Wartislaw's army moving south along the Silver Road. He has fifteen or twenty thousand men and is bringing a very big bombard and some other artillery, and he seems to be heading for Cardice."

Sounds carried well in the old church, and moans of dismay announced that the townsfolk had learned of their peril. The bishop frowned angrily. Wondering if that was what Vranov had wanted all along, Madlenka glanced at Marijus, but his expression told her nothing.

Havel repeated his offer of aid, conditional on payment.

The bishop waited a moment to be sure he had finished, then held out the reliquary. "Place your right hand on this. Do you solemnly swear . . . ?"

The Hound swore as he hoped for salvation that what he had just said was the truth.

Then Marijus stepped forward and swore he would faithfully defend the fortress if he were acknowledged as acting keeper. He, too, spoke out loudly. People were entering by the side doors also now, and the tidings of war and allies had the cathedral humming like a summer beehive.

For a moment it did seem that an agreement had been reached.

Then everything collapsed.

Captain Ekkehardt was not as loud as the Pelrelmians had been, but he did not whisper either. He repeated that he was quite willing to fight for forty florins a month, but again he stipulated that he must be paid in coin. Again Vranov said so must he. Again the seneschal said he could not provide such funds without royal approval, and everyone tried to speak at once. Even the bishop was raising his voice now. The congregation groaned. There was no shyness now—people were pushing forward to hear.

Stupid, *stupid* old man! How could the seneschal not see that by hoarding the king's money, he was putting the king's fortress in peril? In fact he was risking the entire kingdom.

Madlenka realized that she was about to lose her temper. It was a bad habit of hers, as her mother had told her many times. Indeed, they had often had screaming matches about it. She always promised never to do it again, and she hadn't done it for . . . a while. Not seriously, anyway. She discovered that she did not care what the cost might be. She wanted to explode like a bombard, so she strode forward three steps to join the men in front of the bishop.

"Stop it! *STOP IT!* Seneschal Jurbarkas, if you will not spend the king's money, then I will spend mine. You must have far more than two thousand florins put away for my dowry. I know you do. Father told me. So I will lend that money to defend the castle."

More uproar, with the townsfolk joining in, cheering her. Crimson-faced, Bishop Ugne was trying to restore order in the Lord's house. Eventually he got silence.

"That money is not yours, Madlenka," he said. "You are not of age, and besides, it would belong to your husband. Stand back!"

She did not budge. She had foreseen that argument. She knew the seneschal, and how he had never done anything without her father's permission. What he needed now was an excuse to help her. She tried to argue and had to shout over the others' voices. Probably all that they heard were her final words: ". . . read the banns!"

"What?" They all spoke in chorus.

The question seemed to echo outward in circles like ripples on a pond.

"Read the banns for me to marry Marijus Vranov, of course." She looked around at the appalled faces. "I'm not saying to *marry* us! Banns just ask if anyone knows of an objection to us getting married, that's all. We know there is because the king has forbidden it, but nobody else does."

Judging by the bishop's expression, he had not been informed of that royal edict. Madlenka plunged ahead with what was already beginning to feel like a serious mistake.

"A marriage wouldn't be valid, and I certainly couldn't get married so soon after . . . after . . . while I am still in mourning. But once you have read the banns the first time, then Seneschal Ramunas can advance money to my betrothed, can't you, Uncle?"

Bishop Ugne looked ready to explode. "You would have me profane this house by making a proclamation I know to be false?"

"It isn't false!" Madlenka stamped her foot. "Banns are just a question if anyone knows of a reason why there can't be a marriage. Uncle, will it work?" She hadn't called the seneschal that since she was a child.

They were all looking at her as if she still was. Had she made a fool of herself in front of half the town?

Worse—had she fallen into a carefully prepared trap? Why was Vranov smiling?

"Yes, it would," the Hound said.

"I suppose it would," Sir Jurbarkas conceded, accepting this fig leaf of authority. "I may still get hanged for grand larceny, but I could do that."

"Then stand back, all of you," Bishop Ugne said. He wheeled around and strode back to the altar, to replace the reliquary. Then he returned to his vantage point on the steps. The nave was full and the transepts were filling up also.

He addressed the congregation. "As you heard, we

fear an attack by soldiers from Pomerania, but Count Vranov of Pelrelm is going to provide men and guns to help us. I have one brief announcement to make and then we will offer our prayers to the Lord for his aid and comfort."

"That was the fastest courtship I ever heard of," Marijus whispered, grinning at Madlenka.

She wished she had lowered her veil, but it might burst into flames if she did, her face was burning so. "A diplomatic marriage," she whispered. Reaction was setting in and she was trembling. She must have gone crazy. Shouting down a bishop in his own cathedral? Whatever would Mother say when she heard?

Bishop Ugne came down to stand directly in front of her and Marijus, so that he could keep the announcement private.

"Marijus Vranov, widower," Marijus said. "Parish of St. Juozapas, Woda."

The bishop nodded and glanced at the seneschal to make certain that he was listening. Lowering his voice, clearly anxious not to provoke any objections from the hundreds of witnesses, he said very quickly and quietly, "I publish the banns of marriage between Marijus Vranov, widower, of the parish of St. Juozapas in Woda in the county of Pelrelm, and Madlenka Bukovany, spinster, of this parish. If any of you know cause or just impediment why these persons should not be joined together in Holy Matrimony, you are to declare it. This is for the first time of asking." Finishing his quiet declaration, Bishop Ugne looked up to address the congregation, raising his hands and his voice. "Let us—"

"I so declare!" roared a voice, rousing the echoes.

Heads whipped around to find the speaker.

CHAPTER 11

Wulf uttered a last, gurgling scream and went limp, toppling both brothers out of limbo. Anton landed on a patch of dirty wet sand, with Wulf slamming down on top of him. Had he not been wearing armor, the impact might have broken his back, and it did knock all the breath out of him, but he still managed to rip off a barrage of oaths as he struggled free. They had landed on a roughly made trail, most of which was heavily rutted and surfaced with sharp rocks. A small freshet from a recent rainstorm had spread out a patch of silt and fine debris, and it was the only flat place in sight. Either Wulf or his saints had chosen the target carefully.

"Wulf? *Wulf!*"

No response. Anton rolled him over and stared in horror. The kid's face was all swollen and discolored as if he'd been worked over by a whole team of prizefighters. How could that happen inside his armor? His lips were swollen and bleeding, and he had probably bitten his tongue, for he began to choke on the blood. Anton hastily rolled him facedown again and felt for the pulse at his wrist. He found it eventually, but it was faint and much too fast. The boy needed help, and soon.

Anton was not in the best of shape himself, but he

struggled to his feet and looked around. The track was bounded on one side by a near-vertical bank of moss and boulders, tufted with a few grimly clinging shrubs, and on the other by a steep drop; he could hear a river grumbling down there. The valley was about a mile wide but it widened southward into a forested plain. The far wall was a mixture of rocky and thick forest, too steep to be any use, and dusted with recent snow higher up. The near side seemed no more cooperative. The trail on which he stood had been hacked out of the cliff by hand and was barely wide enough for a single wagon.

A sizable company of men had walked over the mud not very long ago, going downhill. A mile or so away, he thought he could make out a settlement, not a village, but a military camp for three or four hundred people, perhaps. Uphill . . .

Uphill his view was blocked by a slight bend in the road. He clumped over to the far edge and found himself looking up at a magnificent fortress, the original for the engraving the cardinal had given him, and not a hundred yards away. *Done it!* He had managed to arrive at Castle Gallant, his castle for as long as he might live. He ran back to make a quick check on Wulf, and then set off to fetch help.

The high curtain wall of reddish stone stood on top of a matching cliff, curving away out of sight. He could see how Castle Gallant had come by its reputation of impregnability. Certainly it could not be undermined, and no ladder ever built could reach from the valley floor to the top of the walls. Old-style siege engines—trebuchets and mangonels—were too inefficient to do much good unless a large number of them could be brought to bear, and here there was simply no room to site them.

Yet, however secure that formidable barbican must have been in its day, now it would be vulnerable to modern gunnery. The bend in the road would be a godsend for attackers, who could work outward from its shelter, building a redoubt of stonework to block the defenders' archery and shelter the gunners as they dug in their bombards. They would have a clear shot at the gates. Fortunately, this wasn't Spain or Italy. Large-scale artillery hadn't arrived in Jorgary yet.

This was certainly the Jorgary side of the fortress, and the Wends would be coming from the north. It was Anton Magnus's job to keep the Wends out.

The gate was closed, which was an unwelcome surprise. That implied a state of war, and perhaps even that the castle had already been seized by the Wends—why else close the gate on the Jorgarian side? It also meant that the garrison would be keeping a lookout, so he would have been seen already. He unlaced his satchel to find his baldric and baton. More than hard exercise was making his heart pound now. The castle was farther away than he had thought, uphill was uphill, and armor was damned heavy.

Last night he had imagined himself riding in on Morningstar's back, a gallant, handsome young nobleman sent by the king to take charge. In reality he was arriving as a sweating, breathless vagrant, muddy, bedraggled, and without as much as a sword. Wulf had slobbered blood down the left side of his surcoat. Still, Anton's appearances would matter very little if the porters were Duke Wartislaw's men and not King Konrad's.

The gate was a portcullis that could probably be closed in an instant, tons of ironbound timber falling free. Gasping for breath, Anton arrived at a grilled window off to one side and stared at a stubbled face framed by a mail coif. A closed gate and men-at-arms instead of porters definitely indicated a state of war.

"Declare yourself!" The words were garbled by a guttural Northern accent.

"I . . ." Anton paused to think. Had Count Bukovany died? If he hadn't, Anton must not announce himself as the new lord of the marches. He would have to be Marshal Magnus, come to direct the defense of the fortress, and his other documents would have to remain out of sight. If Bukovany was dead, then why was the new count arriving alone and on foot instead of with a train of at least a hundred knights?

"Open in the . . . name of the . . . king!"

He held up one of his scrolls to let the sergeant see the royal bear and the king's seal.

It worked. The man's eyes widened in astonishment. They took in the seal, his youth, the baton he held in his other hand, the golden baldric. He saluted.

"Master Sergeant Jachym, your servant, my lord. Open the sally port!"

Bars and bolts thumped, hinges creaked. The narrow sally port door swung open and Anton stepped through to face half a dozen grinning guards.

"There is a man . . ." He pointed. "Just around the corner. Badly hurt. Um, had a bad fall. Horse dragged him. Have him brought in and cared for. *Well* cared for! He is my brother!" he added menacingly. "See to that first, Master Sergeant. *Now!*"

Jachym barked. A trooper ran into the castle.

Everyone was waiting for more orders. Anton tucked his baton under his left arm and twirled his mustache with his right hand. "The count?"

The sergeant's first reaction was to cross himself, which answered the question even before his mumbled prayer for Bukovany's soul.

"Amen. Then I need someone . . . lead me to . . ." To whom? Cardinal Zdenek had warned him against the constable. If Anton dropped in on him he might find himself bouncing straight on into a dungeon— ". . . the countess." She was the least likely to be involved in the treason that Cardinal Zdenek had suggested.

Jachym frowned. He was a bull-necked man with a ruddy face and hard, searching eyes. So far he was reacting well to this sudden emergency. "Countess Edita is reported to be grave afflicted, my lord. Lady Madlenka, her daughter? Seneschal Jurbarkas? Or . . . of course . . . Constable Kavarskas . . . ?"

His mouth said that. His face, his stance, his phrasing were all screaming, "*Not Constable Kavarskas!*" And yet Kavarskas was his superior! His other men's expressions flickered, but there were too many for Anton to read individually. He registered only that even the garrison had doubts about their commander.

Four men came running out and sped off down the hill, two of them carrying blankets and poles to rig a stretcher. Anton had done as much as he could for Wulf. Meanwhile he must make a choice. Lady Madlenka was certainly tempting, but he would have to delay the pleasure of that meeting.

". . . to the seneschal," he said. It was he who had sent the report to Cardinal Zdenek.

At least a dozen more Cardice troopers had appeared in the barbican, while in the shadowy background lurked a trio of very different warriors, resplendent in the spectacular garb of *landsknechte*. Otto and Vlad often entertained *landsknecht* friends at Dobkov. These three were observing, not participating. Their leader would want his own reports on anything that happened at the gate.

"Llywelyn!" the sergeant said. "Take your squad and escort His Lordship to the keep and find the seneschal for him. You are under his orders."

Llywelyn was a man of around fifty, with a lethal, case-hardened look to him. He lined up his squad behind him with a few sharp words in another accent altogether, then indicated that Anton should head toward the far side of the barbican. He had enormous arms and shoulders; no doubt his armor was hiding a twisted spine.

"You're no crossbowman," Anton said. "The English longbow's your weapon."

Llywelyn beamed at this display of expertise. "It used to be, my lord."

Baroness Pavla had died when Wulf was born, so all Anton's life the table talk at Dobkov had been of military matters—from Father and his guests, and later from Ottokar and Vladislav. Anton had known an arquebus from a halberd and a ravelin from a *trace Italienne* before he wore his first pair of shoes. It couldn't hurt now to demonstrate that he was wise for his years.

"Can't manage a hundred-and-fifty-pound pull now?"

"No, my lord. I plays with crossbows now, see. Like toys, they are."

"Tell me what's happened since Sir Petr was killed by the boar."

Llywelyn drew a deep breath and spewed out a torrent of singsong that sounded somewhat like, "That was Saturday see and the count may God have mercy on his soul died on Monday see so they were buried side by side on Tuesday see and the Heavens wept for it and they say the poor woman hasn't stopped lamenting ever since and this morning the count of Pelrelm him they call the Hound of the Hills came a-calling and there's rumors that he's brought a son to marry the child Madlenka see and be the next keeper begging your pardon my lord."

"Good report, Sergeant." So Havel Vranov was—

"Sarge?" said one of the bodyguards at Anton's back. "I heard just now that they're gone to St. Andrej's."

Anton spun around, walking backward so he could look at the rest of the men. "Any of the rest of you heard that?"

"Aye," said two.

"A church?"

"The cathedral, my lord."

Anton completed his rotation. "To St. Andrej's, Sergeant. At the double."

CHAPTER 12

A sort of universal gasp of dismay filled the cathedral and then was instantly suppressed. Even the bishop stood slack-jawed and speechless. Madlenka and her companions spun around to locate the speaker. The congregation—which now filled the rear two-thirds of the nave—parted to clear a passage for him as he casually strolled forward, spurs jingling and sollerets tapping like hammers on the flagstones. He was smiling, evidently enjoying the sensation he had caused.

He was bareheaded, with curly dark hair, a pretty-boy face, and a stringy mustache, but the first thing Madlenka noticed was how tall he was, because he was clearly visible over the crowd. As the last of the congregation moved out of his way, she saw that he was wearing full armor, carrying his helmet under one arm. His surcoat was emblazoned with a clenched gauntlet, and he wore a golden baldric slanted across it, crossed by a leather strap supporting a satchel. He bore no sword, but there were streaks of blood on his shoulder and chest. He came striding forward in a clank of metal shoes and a jingle of spurs. How far back had he been standing? He must have very sharp ears to have heard the banns, or very quick wits to have guessed what the bishop was doing.

At first sight he might be just any man-at-arms with his rations in the bag on his shoulder. At second glance he certainly wasn't. His armor was superb, tailor-made. He was nobility. The jeweled baton he carried said so and the sash of honor across his chest shouted it. Most of all, though, it was utterly beyond belief that any commoner in Christendom could match that youthful haughtiness, or the impregnable arrogance of his mustache, twirled up like a water buffalo's horns.

Kavarskas and Dalibor Notivova moved as if to block him. He handed his helmet to Kavarskas as he might to a varlet and the assurance in that gesture was enough to make the constable fall back out of his way all by itself.

The newcomer bypassed the principals to reach the bishop, dropped briefly to one knee to kiss his ring, and bounced up again. From his bag he took a scroll bearing a red wax seal the size of a man's palm, which he handed to Ugne.

"If you would be so kind as to read this out, my lord bishop?"

The townsfolk were whispering like wind in a forest. That was no ordinary wax seal. Count Stepan had not used a seal near that size.

Madlenka tore her eyes away for a second to look at her companions. Marijus had flushed a deep red color; his father's face was pale with fury, and she felt a surge of relief that stole her breath away. Whatever scheme the Pelrelmians had been plotting had not included this intruder, this slender youth with the boar's-tusks mustache. Whoever or whatever he was, he was not a Vranov imposter.

Bishop Ugne glanced at the seal and looked up with shock. "Of course I shall . . . my lord?"

The newcomer smiled. "Just read it." He watched as the bishop strode over to the steps, where people would see him better.

Then the boy turned his smile on Madlenka. He beckoned her to him, so she went. "Your brother," he whispered, "told the king that you were both a hellion and a great beauty. I think he was guilty of two counts of criminal understatement."

Oh!

She gaped at him like a landed fish. He came from the king?

Already? But how . . . ?

"This is a proclamation," Bishop Ugne proclaimed, "issued by our beloved sovereign, King Konrad the Fifth, may God preserve him."

The congregation responded automatically: "Amen!"

He read it out in Latin, then translated it into the vernacular. Everyone was staring at the newcomer, and he was looking down at Madlenka. He winked. She hastily lowered her veil to hide her blushes. Better a boy sent by the king than any son of Havel Vranov, but she had not expected anyone like this.

". . . royal command . . . the said Madlenka Bukovany . . . in holy matrimony . . ."

Anton Magnus, a count, a companion in the Order of St. Vaclav, no less! And she was to marry him, by the king's command.

". . . under our hand in our capital of Mauvnik, this eighteenth day of September in the year of Our . . ."

Madlenka Magnus? Countess Madlenka.

What had she expected? Love? Like a princess in a troubadour's romance? He was little older than herself, she judged; handsome, she supposed; perhaps witty, or even charming, judging by his first two sentences to her.

"And now two more, if you please, my lord bishop." Magnus handed the bishop another scroll.

He was to be the new keeper, lord of the marches. She would not be heading south to anywhere. She would be staying in Cardice for the rest of her life, if the Wends did not raze the castle next week, and that wasn't going to happen if Count Magnus had arrived with an army at his back. He had arrived in time to save them.

What did the blood on his surcoat imply? Again she looked at Marijus, then at his father, farther along the row. They were both very pale now. What of the two hundred men they had left down at High Meadows? Had Magnus come with an army to fight the Wends and cleaned out the Pelrelmians in passing?

Bishop Ugne returned the third scroll, looking both shaken and overjoyed. "Now a brief prayer of thanksgiving, my lord?"

"Not yet," Magnus said. "I think you had better recite those banns again with the proper names." He offered Madlenka his hand.

She hesitated, then took it.

"Sorry I didn't have time to clean up," he murmured. "I hope you weren't in love with that whoever he is?"

She shook her head. He was tall, but not *too* tall. She was tall, too, although she felt small at the moment.

"What parish, my lord?" the bishop asked.

"St. Ulric, in Dobkov."

Where in the world was Dobkov?

"Very good. I publish the banns of marriage between . . ." He had to shout at the end, as the congregation began to cheer. If he still wanted to lead them in prayer he was again blocked by Magnus, who blithely turned his back on both priest and altar and raised mailed arms for silence.

"Thank you, good people of Cardice." He frowned impatiently at another cheer. "There are a couple of things we must do right away. You, I believe, are Count Vranov of Pelrelm?"

Havel surged forward, beard drawn back to show snarling yellow teeth. "I am, and I would like to know how you brought those papers from the capital in less—"

"I ask the questions here!" Magnus roared.

The royal proclamations had been dated on September eighteenth, which had been the day of the funerals. Young Gintaras was a superb rider, but he could not possibly have ridden from Gallant to the capital in just three days, not even in midsummer.

The new count was not about to discuss that, evidently. "You have no doubt expressed your condolences to the countess and my future wife, so your business here is complete. Constable Kavarskas?"

Looking considerably worried, the constable saluted.

"See that Count Vranov and all his companions are escorted to the gate they came in by. Make sure it is locked behind them. But you stay here."

Kavarskas saluted again and passed the order on to Dalibor with a nod.

"You will regret this when the Wends get here!" Vranov bellowed.

"They will be an improvement. May the Lord be with you, Havel." Magnus twirled up his mustache and glanced down at Madlenka. "Vice versa would be another improvement," he whispered. She choked back what might well have become a highly improper snigger. Her husband-to-be was nothing if not sure of himself.

No, he was good at seeming so. She was close enough to him to see the sparkles of sweat on his forehead; he was not as confident as he was pretending.

Count Vranov glared for a moment, then turned on his heel and stormed off along the nave, limping at the gallop, followed by Marijus and their knights. Dalibor took two men and followed. The *landsknechte* all stayed. Perhaps they no longer saw the Pelrelmians as a threat.

"Anton, my son . . ."

"My humble pardon, my lord bishop, but there are two more very urgent things I must attend to right now, vital for His Majesty's business. Constable Kavarskas, are you willing to swear fealty to me as count of Cardice and lord of the marches?"

Kavarskas was looking far from pleased, but he said, "Certainly, my lord. Bishop Ugne has testified to your right." If he hoped the bishop would now change his mind, he was disappointed.

"And who," Magnus demanded, "held your loyalty ten minutes ago?"

The constable's eyes narrowed. "The king, my lord. Who else?" His hook was steadying the scabbard of his sword.

"You did not, perchance, see Havel Vranov as your temporary lord, in the absence of a count of Cardice?"

Kavarskas looked for support to the seneschal, the bishop, even Madlenka, but could not seem to find it. "He was the senior nobleman within reach, my lord, so of course I was required to give weight to his counsel." He drew a deep breath. "And I think we all need an answer to the question he just asked you. How did you get here from Mauvnik so soon? Perhaps the reverend Bishop Ugne is wondering also."

There was a clear accusation of Speaking there. Surely not! Madlenka shivered. But there and back again in eight days? They hadn't expected Gintaras to reach Mauvnik in less than a week. She resisted an urge to edge away from her designated fiancé.

"If the reverend bishop wishes to ask me such questions," the count said cheerfully, "I shall give him answers. You are not the bishop and I am asking the questions. When was Count Stepan smitten?"

"On Saturday the fifteenth, my lord. A week ago yesterday."

"And when did you send your dispatch to His Majesty?"

"When the count died. I saw no point in rousing alarm unnecessarily if—"

"What date?"

"He died late on Monday, so the courier left at first light on Tuesday. That was the eighteenth."

"But not the first courier?" Magnus glanced at the much-reduced party in the front rank. "You are the seneschal?"

The old man smiled and bowed. "Ramunas Jurbarkas, your most humble servant, my lord."

"Humility doesn't impress me too much," Count Magnus said airily. "Honesty does. When did you send your report to the king?"

"The fifteenth, my lord."

"And why did you do so? It should have been the constable's job."

The old man looked sadly at Kavarskas. Then he said, "Because I was informed by a reliable source that, although a messenger had been sent right away, he did not take the south road. He was observed riding west."

Magnus must know that Madlenka had countersigned

Jurbarkas's report. He couldn't know that it had been her idea and she had bullied the old man into sending it. The count did not bring her into the discussion, though. Instead he raised his voice to a bellow.

"Llywelyn!"

There was movement at the back of the church.

"Wait!" the bishop cried, striding forward. "This is the Lord's House—"

"Suffer me in this, my lord bishop. I'm not going to lay hands on him. Ah, there you are." A burly archer had emerged from the crowd, with others behind him. When they arrived at the transept—"Llywelyn, you may accept the constable's sword if he wishes to give it up. If he doesn't, no matter. Here he is in holy sanctuary, and he may remain here forty days if he so wishes. You will post guards to watch over him day and night, and the moment he sets foot outside, you will arrest him and see he is secured in a dungeon. He is not to be maltreated otherwise. You act in my name in this and I hold you responsible for his safety and confinement. You may call on as many men from the garrison as you require."

"Then what?" Kavarskas shouted, hand on sword.

"Then you will be charged with high treason and given a fair trial. Will you go peacefully?"

Showing a dignity Madlenka would not have expected from him, Kavarskas handed the count's helmet to the archer, then drew his sword and passed it over also. He made reverence to the host, and turned to go.

Anton let out a soft sigh of relief that only Madlenka and the bishop could have heard. "One more to go," he murmured. "The name of the *landsknecht* captain?"

"Luitger Ekkehardt," she said.

"Captain Ekkehardt!"

The big man in his butterfly glory paused an insolent

moment before saluting the new count, no expression escaping through his barley-colored beard.

"You are under contract to the lord of the marches, an office I now have the honor to bear. I have your loyalty?"

The big man did not look impressed by this elongated youth. "We contracted for garrison duty, not siege work."

Anton fingered his mustaches again. "You mean you were hired just to look pretty, not to fight at all? I never heard of mercenaries actually having that written into their contracts, even if that was how they interpreted their duties afterward."

"The Pomeranians are coming."

"That's why the king sent me. Where have you fought?"

"In France against the English, in Moravia, under Casali on the Milan campaign, at Pisa, in Bavaria . . ."

"The Milan campaign—wasn't that Alberto Casali's troop? Fifteen years ago? Was that where you learned your trade? Casali looked like a rat and fought like a mouse. My brother Vladislav met him in Bavaria two years ago. Did you meet Louis Macquer at Milan? His men called him Basilisk Mouth—if he just breathed on walls they collapsed. Or Herman Maier? Now, there was a fighter, until he tried to field a cannonball outside Linz. You know Sigmund Geismeyer?"

Ekkehardt seemed more suspicious than impressed. "You know these men?"

"I've met most of them. Geismeyer collects the most gorgeous young squires. But we can talk shop later, Captain. Meanwhile, until I learn my way around here, I want you to be acting constable for me. Just a few days. I'll read over your contract and see if I think the price needs boosting. Any problems with this? Good. Lord bishop, your prayers would be very welcome now, for only God Himself knows how much I need His aid and support. Thank you for your sufferance."

Magnus took Madlenka's hand and led her over to the ornate ancestral pew. Between his armor and his height, he had trouble folding himself up enough to kneel in it as the bishop called for prayer.

Whisper: "Madlenka?"

"My lord?" she asked, shocked. Her father had never whispered when he was supposed to be praying.

"I was quite worried when I was told that I would have to marry a woman I had never met, but now that I have seen you, I have no worries at all."

"My lord is kind to say so. And I am likewise greatly relieved."

He frowned as if puzzled, then shrugged. "All women have that problem. I think you are very beautiful, which is what matters. I also enjoy women with spirit, and I came in just as you were throwing a tantrum at the bishop to read the banns. Right now you must promise me something."

"What's that?"

"You can't dig me in the ribs, but please do something drastic if I start snoring. I had almost no sleep last night and I can barely keep my eyes open."

"Riding hard?" she asked sympathetically.

"Well . . ." he murmured. "Yes, you could say that."

CHAPTER 13

He had done it! With his betrothed on his arm, Anton followed the bishop out of the cathedral. It was less than twelve hours since Cardinal Zdenek had given him an impossible job and he had already completed it. Well, most of it. He had traveled to Cardice faster than anyone had ever done, and his claim to the earldom had been accepted by the bishop, whose lead everyone else would follow. He had booted the Hound back to his kennel and arrested an obvious traitor who could be given a fair trial and then hanged as an example. The Pomeranian problem would have to wait for a day or two, but he could probably talk Wulfgang into dealing with the Wends for him. Which reminded him: he had better check on Wulfie and see if he had recovered yet.

It was nice to be cheered. He could hear the tumult building outside before he even reached the cathedral door. News of the new count must be all over the town already.

And he had acquired a bride who was tall enough to match his height but did not look freakish. He glanced down, she looked up. "Lift your veil," he said. "I know you're in mourning, but this is a moment for celebration."

He gave her his best boyish grin. "And try to look as if you feel as happy as I am."

"I am much happier, my lord."

"You mustn't argue with your future husband. The moment we're alone, I shall give you some intense kissing lessons."

"I look forward to learning."

Once she had plumped up after marriage, as women did, she would be a feast. Her eyes were purest blue and the glimpses he had caught of her hair indicated that she was a golden blonde. He admired her pale hands, with their long, supple fingers; the thought of them exploring his body in the near future was very enticing. If she came on in bed half as strong as she had in the cathedral when she shouted at the bishop, then she was going to be a hellcat to romp with. Until then he would have to behave himself, unfortunately, for he mustn't risk scandal so early in his reign. Tomorrow he would explain why early marriage was a political necessity.

"What was Hound Vranov up to?" he asked.

"I don't know, my lord. He arrived this morning with two hundred men-at-arms and claimed that the Wends are about to attack and we must accept his son Marijus as keeper of the castle."

"I see. And whose idea was it to throw your dowry into the pot?"

"Mine," she confessed, and explained how the seneschal was frightened to spend the king's money.

"He told you so?"

"Um. No. Marijus did."

"Then I think I arrived just in time."

"I believe you. What do you think they were up to?"

"Just guessing, I'd say the money was to buy off the

landsknechte and send them packing. Then you would have found the town and castle full of Pelrelmian troops."

"Yes," she murmured. "We were all deceived. And when the Wends came?"

"He was probably making up the Wend story," Anton assured her.

"But both he and Marijus swore on the bone of holy St.—"

"Oaths mean nothing to such men." Cardinal Zdenek had thought the Wends were a threat, but he needn't bother her with that news. "If Duke Wartislaw did invade, Vranov might have sold him Castle Gallant for cash and a guarantee that his own county would not be harmed. It doesn't matter now. Don't worry about it."

The streets were too narrow for a true parade, but the stairs along both sides provided handy grandstands for the cheering crowds. The people of Cardice were no longer orphans. They had a count again, a nobleman to defend them and tell them what to do. The king himself had sent him! Men doffed their hats and shouted blessings as he passed. Women curtseyed or even knelt. Gallant was an ants' nest of tightly packed houses, a firetrap. He would have to do something about that if the Wends did show up.

His first impression of the keep was rank disappointment. It was a fortress, of course, but a fortress did not have to look like an oversized grave marker. The only windows were mere loopholes, so the inside would be dark and probably cramped. His childhood home at Dobkov was a fortress, too, but it stood in rolling green countryside.

Of course the entire castle staff was already lined up at the door to cheer the new count. Once inside, Anton demanded his valet, who turned out to be named Kaspar and old enough to be Cardinal Zdenek's father. Washing water, Anton demanded, and it must be hot. He ordered the seneschal to organize the exchange of oaths, which he was told would be held in the great hall. He could remember his father having to put up with such ceremonies—cursing them in private before and after, but being invariably courteous and patient during. Count Magnus must practice courteous and patient.

He did not think much of the great hall, which was too narrow for its length, but it did have proper glazed windows, looking out into a central bailey, and from them he could see many other windows. So the keep was hollow, not the solid block he had thought at first glance. His place for the fealty ceremony would be on the big chair at the fireplace end. There was a smaller chair beside it, but he was not going to share the honors with Madlenka just yet. There must be no question that he had been appointed by the king and would rule in his own right, not as her husband.

He kissed her fingers. "Everyone has to come and meet me," he whispered. "They know you already, so there is no need to bore you with unnecessary introductions to people who have known you all your life. I expect you will need to rest for a little while after all the excitement in the cathedral."

"As my lord pleases," she said, blushing. Few things roused him as fast as a girl's blushes, although he usually saw them in more intimate surroundings.

The seneschal himself began the proceedings, first reading out the king's edicts, then kneeling on the cushion to put his hands between Anton's and swear to be his man, of life and limb, and so on. Since there was no constable present, the steward came after him, followed by all the rest in strict order of precedence. Each had to swear allegiance, then be granted protection and a few kind words. This was how the barons of Dobkov did it, so the count of Cardice must do the same, pretending not to be bored to distraction. Thinking lascivious thoughts about his future bride might help.

And where was Wulf? Wulf was important. Anton would need Wulf and his saintly friends to deal with the Wends. How to find him? The answer appeared when the butler withdrew and the next flunky to come hobbling forward was presented as Radim, the count's secretary. Radim was young, slight, and leaned on a cane because he had a clubfoot, which explained why he had been taught to wield a pen instead of a pitchfork. Ottokar employed a secretary, as had Father before him. Anton knew how a secretary was used.

"How long were you Count Stepan's secretary?"

"Half a year, my lord. Clerk for a year before that."

"You write a fair hand?"

The youth nodded, licked his lips, and said, "His Lordship said I did, my lord. And so does the bishop."

"Good. How many messengers can you call on?"

"Five or six, my lord. Not so many today, unless you give me time to—"

"One or maybe two will suffice." Anton explained about Wulf.

Radim nodded vigorously, touched his forehead in salute, and limped off to be useful. Anton sat back to receive an oath of allegiance from the castle apothecary.

By the time the parade ended, the boy was back, hovering within sight, but not intruding. He had the answer. "Sir Wulfgang is being cared for in the infirmary, my lord. He has been bled and is under sedation."

Anton had to be content with that alarming news

until he had made a brief speech, promising not to change anything in the ways his predecessor had done things, except to wipe the Wends' faces in the mud. He accepted three cheers.

Having informed the seneschal that he would like to dine shortly—with the lady Madlenka, if she would be so kind—and would need clothes so he could shed his accursed armor and temporary quarters for himself and Wulf, Anton told Radim to lead him to the infirmary, which meant downstairs, outside, and down the ramp. The crowd had dispersed, although a few knots of people still stood around the little square, all gaping in awe at their new count.

Problems buzzed in Anton's mind like midges. He had made a good start, but he had not earned his Vaclav sash yet. The Wends were one threat, Havel Vranov was another, and if they were in league, then they could come at Cardice from opposite sides. Had the castle ever had to withstand a two-pronged attack before? And why, in the name of God, had his predecessor ever let all these houses be built inside what was supposed to be a fortress? More immediate and personal was the dangerous question of timing. The common folk would simply be grateful that the king's man had appeared to take over, but the bishop and other gentry would wonder how the new count had traveled so swiftly. Were there any other gentry? This was border country, thinly inhabited.

Quite apart from having a bad leg, Radim did not even come up to Anton's shoulder, so Anton was continually having to rein himself and let the boy catch up. The streets were lined along both sides with outdoor staircases. Radim stopped at one that looked just like all the others, but he was clearly waiting to follow the count up it, so up Anton went—ten steps into hell.

The infirmary was a single room containing eight beds with barely enough space to move between them. It was dim, cold, and rank with the lingering stench of sickness and death. The doctor in charge was stooped and ancient; either he or his physician's robe stank abominably. Possibly both did, but the robe likely carried most of the blame, being encrusted with a lifetime's supply of blood, phlegm, and pus to show how practiced its wearer was. All the beds were occupied. Two of the patients were mumbling in agony or delirium, three others coughed continually.

For a moment Anton did not recognize the face on the pillow, only the tangle of flaxen hair. Wulf's eyes and lips were hugely swollen and turning purple. He had been drooling blood. He looked even worse than he had when he was lying unconscious on the hillside trail. Some of his armor was stacked beside the bed, but some wasn't and had probably been stolen already.

"Wulf? Wulfgang!"

The puffed eyelids flickered and opened to slits. " 'Nt'n?"

"Yes, I'm here."

"You . . . whoreson . . . Ge'me outa this plague pit."

"Yes, I will. Sorry, Wulf."

"He's confused!" the doctor said petulantly. "Severe trauma, but no bones broken, so far as I can tell under the swelling. I drew twelve ounces of blood and prescribed henbane, hemlock, and laudanum for the pain."

Anton drew himself up to his full height and glared down at the obnoxious leech.

"My father used to say he had watched twenty-four men die and twenty-two of them were killed by doctors."

"My lord!"

"Yes, I am, and don't you forget it. You will not go

near this man again, is that clear? I want him moved to the keep instantly. Radim, can you arrange that?"

The youth turned a horrified stare into a grin. "Certainly, my lord. The infirmary must have a stretcher. I'll find some strong arms." He hobbled two steps to the door and peered out, then started shouting names.

CHAPTER 14

Madlenka stormed into her bedroom. As the door closed behind her, she whirled around. "That *popinjay*! That upstart! That freakishly oversized, ditch-born son of a sow. Did you *hear* him?"

Giedre said, "Yes." That did not dam the torrent.

"Go and lie down, he said! Rest my poor little self! Too much excitement? What sort of a *child* does he think I am?" Madlenka grabbed up a painted vase and took aim at the fireplace. "Who does he think he is?"

Giedre removed the missile just before her mistress's throwing hand began to move. "He's the king's man. He's the count of Cardice. He's your betrothed and future husband."

"He's a snake! *He sent me to my room!* He wants everyone to see him as lord of Cardice and forget that it's marriage to me that gives him his place."

"It was the king who put him there, not you."

"You too? You also think I'm just part of the furniture? A serf tied to the land?" Madlenka caught a glimpse of herself in the mirror. Her face was redder than strawberries and all her teeth were showing. Oh, horrors!

"Well, you are a sort of serf," Giedre said. "Tied to

his bed by royal decree. Arturas says that the fancy sash he wears means that he's a trusted friend of the king!"

Madlenka forced herself to sit down on the stool and fold her hands on her lap. "I knew it! I *knew* it! No soldier, just a courtier. The arrogance of the man! I have never met such an overblown, self-important prig. We need a warrior and they send somebody's juvenile son that they don't know what else to do with. Probably escaping from a paternity problem involving triplets. He can't know which end of a pike is the handle."

The problem was that she had expected an older man, a mature man. Someone not unlike Father, in fact, just a little younger. Calm, fond, deliberate, soothing. This Anton didn't seem much older that Petr had been, and he was anything but soothing. The way he looked at her . . .

Worse, perhaps, was that she had no idea what to expect after the inevitable wedding ceremony. Nobody would even talk about that. No one ever explained. She knew that all women were instruments of the devil, sent to entrap men in sins of lust and vice, but she had no idea how she was expected to go about it. She knew what dogs did with bitches and ganders with geese, but visions of her squatting on the floor with her arms spread out and Anton standing on her back while gripping her neck failed to convince, somehow.

The way he looked at her, Anton knew exactly what she was expected to do and would want her to do it right away.

Giedre moved in close and began to dismantle Madlenka's headgear—hat, veil, and coif.

"I thought he handled the *landsknecht* in the church very well, didn't you?" she asked serenely. "He obviously knew what he was talking about, because he impressed that hairy German troll. And just this morning you were moaning that the king would send you a warrior. Foulmouthed, fat, and forty, I think you said, with the manners of a rutting boar." She took up a hairbrush and began to wield it.

Which was very annoying of her, because having her hair brushed never failed to bring Madlenka out of her tantrums.

"The manners fit. You think sixteen and thin as rope is an improvement?"

"Oh, yes! He's a lot older than sixteen. And if what they say about tall men is true, his . . . feelings will be a lot deeper than most husbands'."

Madlenka thought of stallions. "Stop it! I'm nervous enough already."

Her friend smiled smugly. "What I think is that if your Count Magnus hadn't turned up just when he did, the Vranovs would be shipping your inheritance out the gate on a mule train about now. And you with it. Which one of them would you want to be married to, if you had your choice?"

"Leonas. I've always liked hair that color and he does what he's told. What am I going to wear? I'm bereaved and betrothed, both. Half black and half white?"

"The purple velvet. It suits you. His eyes will pop."

"They already pop too much." But, yes, neither mourning nor too festive. The purple was somber but the gown itself full and rich, with short bodice, clutched-up skirt trimmed with ermine; a neckline low enough to be interesting and a bucket-shaped hat with dangling white lace. That would do. Her hair down, of course. Soon she would be married and wearing it up. "Oh, Giedre! What would happen if I refused him?"

The hairbrush began moving faster. "Don't even dream

of it! You'd be tossed into a convent, I expect. What's wrong with him? He's conceited, maybe, but he has a lot to be conceited about—young, handsome, trusted friend of the king, one of the leading peers of the realm, a lord of the marches. Most women settle for much less."

"I suppose so," Madlenka sighed. A convent would feel like a very safe place about now. "It's just that . . . I had always hoped that one day I'd meet the man I was going to marry and . . . lightning would flash in our eyes and angels blow on silver trumpets."

Her friend made a noise perilously close to a snort. "You have been listening to far too many troubadours. It doesn't work that way. You say the words, he does what he does, and the next night he does it again, and by the end of the week you're begging for it. My mother told me. And my grandmother. And your father's grandson will rule in Castle Gallant long after long Anton Magnus is gone."

Madlenka laughed. "That's true! Whatever would I do without you to keep my feet on the ground?"

"You are favored, what of me? Where is the even-more-handsome brother I was promised?"

That had always been their private joke—that when Madlenka was sent off somewhere to be the wife of some handsome young noble, Giedre would go with her to be her mistress of the robes, and would then marry the theoretical duke's theoretical younger brother. Who would, of course, be either almost as handsome or even more handsome, depending on which of them was spinning the fantasy.

"I expect he stayed home to feed the hounds," Madlenka countered. "Or he may have a few years' growing up to do yet. Be patient! Now I must dress. We'll have to find somewhere for the count to sleep until . . . And we have to get Mother out of the baronial bedchamber before . . . Oh, Lord! The wedding night! Although I don't suppose she'd notice if we joined her there. And what sort of an army did he bring? Have the Pelrelmians gone from High Meadows, or did he wipe them out on his way in? Single-handed, I expect. He thinks he's capable of it. And he didn't bring any baggage, did he? He'll need clothes made."

"Petr was tall. Would any of his things do?"

"No. Magnus is a hand taller, at least, and half as wide. If I am not to be wooed by a man permanently clad in armor, we'd better send for every tailor in town, Sunday or not."

An hour later, Madlenka was sitting in the solar, sharing some bread and honey with Giedre. They ate eagerly, for it was well past noon and they had not yet broken their fast. The ceremony in the hall had ended, but Anton Magnus had gone out of the keep without a word of explanation to his betrothed. Madlenka could not even complain about this insult, because she knew that he was in no way required to report his movements to her. She had three tailors waiting down in the kitchens. Dinner was late, for the Sunday repast required the presence of the count to say grace. He might not be aware of that custom, of course.

Count Vranov and his escort had been evicted from the south gate. His men were packing up their tents in High Meadows. That much she knew. There was no sign of a Jorgarian army approaching. Just how Magnus had materialized in the cathedral remained a mystery, and Vranov's hints of Speaking refused to be banished from her mind. If witchcraft could move a man unseen into a church, it could probably counterfeit the royal seal, too. Mustn't think about such things.

The door opened; in walked the count.

"Ah, there you are. My, that looks good. Come, I have someone you must meet."

The women had risen, of course. Madlenka said, "Dinner, my lord—"

"In a minute. This won't take long." He offered his arm and she had to accept.

Even indoors he walked too fast for her, clanking and jingling. "My brother Wulfgang is my squire. He came with me, and I've just rescued him from the infirmary."

"Oh, no! Not that awful place?"

"Yes. I'll do something about 'that awful place' as soon as I get the chance. I can't understand . . . Well, no matter." He was hinting that her father should have done something about it. Which was probably true, a pox on him!

He had brought her to the stairs, and was climbing at a more reasonable pace than he walked. "Wulf took a fall, a bad one. Fortunately he was wearing armor, but he's one all-over bruise, and that idiot doctor has been drugging him with sewage. I want you to look after him for me, will you?"

"Of course, my lord!" She felt absurdly surprised that he was going to trust her to handle even that sort of trivial task.

"Keep doctors away from him, understand? Wulf's tougher than boiled leather. He'll be on his feet again in a couple of days." Anton leered down at her. "At the moment he looks like sausage meat, so don't say I didn't warn you."

He swung open the door to the Orchard Room—

named for its murals, not its view, for it overlooked the bailey, like most other rooms in the keep. He let Madlenka precede him.

"Wulf! Wulfie, I brought you a beautiful nurse to speed your recovery."

The face on the pillow looked as if it had been thoroughly beaten with an ax handle, and all the rest of him was under the blankets, except for a tangle of honey-colored hair on the pillow. His eyes flickered but did not open. Both they and his lips were grossly swollen.

"He's been doped," Anton said with disgust. "But he should be better tomorrow."

Behind his back, Giedre was wearing a half-witted expression, her eyes turned upward and a hand cupped to her ear. Giedre was signaling that she had found the handsome younger brother who had been promised her and she could hear the angelic silver trumpets.

Which was annoying, because Madlenka already—in those first few instants—suspected that Somebody had Made a Terrible Mistake.

CHAPTER 15

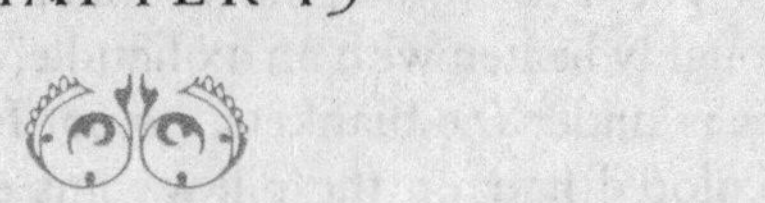

All his life, Anton had heard alarming stories about the perils of fatigue and how men did stupid things when overtired. He had never really understood this until that evening. Then the excitement and novelty which had sustained him all day suddenly drained away. All the previous night he had entertained Baroness Nadezda. For much of the night before his hard drinking messmates had feted the rookie for his triumphant near-suicide at the hunt. Now, close to sunset, his head pounded; the whole world seemed blurry and unsteady. He abandoned thoughts of persuading his betrothed to admit him to her bed without waiting for formalities. Tomorrow would be time enough for that.

Feeling as if he were carrying his horse, he climbed the steep and narrow spiral staircase in the watchtower at the top of the keep, stumbling several times on the worn steps. He had ordered two people to meet him up there. The moment he had completed his business with them, he would fall into bed and sleep. Sleep until Christmas.

As he emerged in the lookout, a chill wind spat raindrops in his face, but even that could not lift the deadening hand of fatigue. The walls were extra-high merlons topped with a conical roof, and the icy gale off the mountains whistled straight through the crenels between them. He registered that Dalibor Notivova was already there, saluting him. Luitger Ekkehardt had not arrived yet. Good. He wanted to deal with them one at a time.

He acknowledged the salute with a nod and began walking carefully all the way around, seeing his domain properly for the first time. The view was remarkable: a treeless moor flooring an upland valley cupped on three sides by rocky walls, close to vertical in many places. Behind that, to the north, stood ice-capped peaks. The Ruzena came foaming out of a gorge just north of the castle, curving around it almost directly below the tower where he stood, then surging and frothing off to the south.

The steep cliff that formed a backdrop to the west of the town was gouged by several vertical gullies that must hold running water from springs. An army at one gate could not reach around to threaten the other, so the defenders should never lack for food, either. At least three people had quoted Barbarossa's judgment of the site to him, but that doughty old warrior would not have approved of what else Anton was seeing. As he moved around to the west, he was looking down on even more slate than he had feared. The entire space within the curtain wall was paved with roofs.

He reached Notivova. The youth saluted again. He wasn't really a youth, though, probably a few years older than Anton himself. The chain-mail coif enclosing his head concealed everything except eyes, nose, and lips, but he seemed steady enough, showing only a trace of nervousness—which was quite natural when his superior was in a cell, awaiting trial for treason.

"Tell me about September fifteenth," Anton said.

"Aye, my lord. The Feast of Our Lady of Sorrows. I had spent the night at my mother's house, three miles from here. I had leave." He waited for the count's nod, then continued. "As I was coming back, across High Meadows, I saw a man riding very fast to the west, towards the Hlucny. That's a tributary of the Ruzena that marks the boundary between Pelrelm and Cardice. I recognized trooper Tomas and I knew he was supposed to be on gate duty that morning. I wondered what he was doing."

Again Anton nodded, struggling to make his weary brain concentrate. Men-at-arms despised men who betrayed their commanding officers, yet Notivova was impressing him.

"Did he see you?"

"I don't think so, my lord. The wind was behind me and blowing rain, so it would have been right in his face. I couldn't see him well—in fact, I only knew he was Tomas because I recognized his horse and his boots . . . he has red boots he's very proud of. But when I rode in I was told right away that the count had been stricken, and Sir Petr had just been brought in, dead, may God grant them both peace. I asked the constable if word had been sent to the king, and he said it was too early to alarm Mauvnik; he was going to wait a day or so to see if the count would recover."

"So you asked about this Tomas man?"

Notivova avoided his eye. "I didn't ask Sir Karolis. I asked some of the others and was told he was on a mission for the constable."

Then he had ratted. Good for him!

"Then what did you do?"

"I went and told the lady Madlenka, my lord. And she told me to keep my suspicions to myself, but she would take care of it. An hour or so later I saw young Gintaras riding out on one of the count's own horses . . . my lord."

Anton sighed and turned to lean his hands on the bottom sill of a crenel and stare out at the mountains glowing in their sunset finery. Weariness made him ache all over. "Young Gintaras did a fine job for his king." He dared not be more specific, because the timing of events must be kept muddy.

"He's a fine young horseman."

"Has Tomas returned?"

"Not that I've heard, my lord." A careful answer. A careful man.

Zdenek had backdated the king's edicts, so he had foreseen the timing problem. No doubt Gintaras had been suitably bribed to keep him in Mauvnik. Or he could be in a cell, of course. The Scarlet Spider left no holes in his webs.

"And no other courier was sent to Mauvnik until the eighteenth?"

"Not that I know of."

Tired or not, Anton must now determine how he was going to proceed. He was too exhausted to make major decisions, and this one might determine the success or failure of his efforts to defend Castle Gallant against the Wends. He could release Kavarskas and confirm him as constable; his hours in a cell would serve as a warning of who was in charge. Keep him there overnight, though, and his loyalty could never be trusted again.

Which meant that Anton didn't trust him now, so he had already made his decision.

He turned to look at Notivova. "You would repeat under oath what you just told me?"

"Yes, my lord."

"Then I will have to hang Kavarskas."

The man compressed his lips, staring down at the floor. After a moment he said, "Yes, my lord. I hope you won't promote me in his place, my lord. I mean, it would look bad."

"I'll decide that later. If the facts were as you say, then you made the correct decision in a very difficult situation."

"Thank you, my lord."

"For the moment, keep taking your orders from the German. Tell me about the road from Pomerania."

Notivova led him around to the north side of the tower so he could point. "As you can see, the trail from the barbican hugs the hillside to the mouth of the gorge, my lord. That's about half a mile, uphill slightly, but we have it in clear sight all the way. Any enemy approaching is walking on a killing ground. After you get past the bend it twists a lot going through the gorge. There are four bridges and three fords. About five miles up you get to Long Valley, on the other side of this mountain, which we call the Hogback. There the country spreads out. The Wends say the border's at our Long Valley outpost. We say it's about a mile farther on, at their landing stage. We don't fight over that mile."

"And you—I mean, we—keep a garrison at Long Valley?"

He nodded. "We send out a troop of six every morning. They spend two nights, then ride back, so we always have a dozen men there, enough so they can spare a couple to bring back warnings if needed. Usually all they do is report on what caravans are coming. Very few, this late in the year."

He knew his job.

Pause.

It must be Anton's turn to say something.

"This's an odd stronghold. Usually the value of a fortress is that an invader daren't bypass it and leave a foe in his rear. So the enemy has to shed a chunk of his army to besiege it. But everyone insists that there's no way to bypass Cardice."

"A nimble man could, in summer," Notivova said. "But he'll find himself on the wrong side of the Ruzena, and it's twenty miles down to the first ford. There are ways over the mountains west of us, but then he comes down in Pelrelm."

But if Pelrelm and Pomerania were to join forces, Cardice would be caught in a vise.

"I want you to lead the Long Valley patrol, not tomorrow, but the next day. I'll come with you."

Notivova was surprised, but approving. "Yes, my lord."

"Good. Don't discuss our talk tonight with anyone. Dismissed."

As the man's boot steps faded, Anton drooped against a merlon. He was shaking with weariness, but if he sat down in a crenel he would go to sleep and topple out backward, and it was a long way down. Where was Ekkehardt? And why was it he had asked the man to come up here?

More steps. He turned to watch the *landsknecht* captain emerge through the trapdoor, massive in his padded linen armor, shrewd eyes glittering above a bush of yellow beard.

Anton straightened up. "Good evening to you, *Kommandant*."

"And to you, Count." The big man scowled through his hayfield. Looking up to other men must be a rarity for him.

"Come over here." Anton led him over to the town side. "Barbarossa said this was a perfect place for a fortress, so I'm told."

"Maybe it was—then."

"How could Count Stepan have been so incredibly stupid as to let it fill up with houses like this? Even with slate roofs, the place is one big firetrap." There should be houses for the garrison, yes, but most of the land inside the curtain wall ought to be open space.

Ekkehardt grunted, perhaps surprised that this weedy youth had worked that out. "Pestilence."

"Explain."

"I mean, it's fifty years since pestilence last came through here to weed it out. The townsfolk breed like mice. The counts didn't notice, or weren't hardhearted enough to send them away. Who cares, in peacetime?"

That made sense, but it had been a terrible mistake, and Anton Magnus was going to have a hellish struggle to put it right before the Wends arrived and started sending fire arrows over the walls.

Now to more urgent business . . . "I haven't had time to read over your contract, *Kommandant*, but I'm sure we can agree on some increase. What I want right now is your views on how to defend that north road when—"

The heavy guttural voice cut him off. "My advice you can have for free, my lord. But all the money in Jorgary will not keep me and my lads here. We're packing now and will be gone at dawn."

After a moment, Anton decided that he had heard that correctly. "Why?" he croaked.

"One of our women is sick. She's an archer's wife, so he says, but she takes on others and he gets a cut."

"All armies have those."

"But she's sick, and now she's showing black lumps

in her armpits. We are leaving. No argument. I didn't want to blurt it out in the church and start a panic."

"Thank you," Anton muttered. It was more than a century since the Great Pestilence had devastated Christendom, but local outbursts of plague still happened from time to time, reaping a dreadful harvest. Some wretches suffered for days, but a man in perfect health could find spots on his chest and be dead in a few hours. Livid spots on the skin or lumps in groin or armpit warned of imminent death. The invalids in the infirmary were probably approaching the final stages of the fever. Likely Wulf had caught it from them while he was there. Anton himself might have caught it, and that brainless doctor who had not yet diagnosed the problem was doomed.

When you think things cannot get worse, they always do. All his dreams of glory came tinkling down like icicles in sunshine.

Wulf would tell him that that's what he got for accepting help from the devil.

CHAPTER 16

Madlenka knocked. In a moment Radim peered out, then emerged and closed the door behind him. He was red-eyed and unshaven, having missed half a night's sleep. He would not sleep on duty: Father would never have promoted him to secretary had he not been diligent to a fault.

"He's awake, my lady. He tries not to show it, but I think he's still in a lot of pain."

"Well done. We'll take over now. Go and catch some rest. The count is not up yet."

As Radim limped off along the corridor, she opened the door and stood aside to let Giedre carry in the tray. The window shutters and the bed curtains were open. Squire Wulfgang turned his head on the pillow to see who had arrived. His face was still swollen and multicolored.

But his eyes were golden!

"Good morning, Squire Wulfgang. I am Madlenka Bukovany. How are you feeling this morning?"

He licked his puffed lips. "Puzzled."

"Puzzled by what?"

"I hurt so much that this must be purgatory. Why am I seeing angels?"

"I think he's better," Giedre said, fussing with the food on the tray.

"Usually I'm much better than that, my lady. Sometimes even witty."

Madlenka caught herself smiling. "May I present my companion and best friend, Giedre Jurbarkas? Are you hungry? We brought you some beef soup." She caught up a spare pillow. "Can you raise yourself, or would you rather we lifted you?"

He tried to move and winced.

She said, "Giedre, you go that side."

Giedre shot her a disapproving look. She would be able to reach him while standing beside the bed, but Madlenka would have to climb up and kneel beside him. Why not? Nothing ventured, nothing won. She lifted her skirts knee-high and went ahead. Ah, if Mother were to make a miracle recovery and walk in to find her daughter in this compromising position? Or, the count? Much worse!

But no one did. The squire pulled up his arms to lever himself, the women took hold of him to help, and Madlenka could see that he was at least half naked. The situation grew more interesting—and incriminating—all the time. Even slight movements seemed to hurt him. He grimaced, but did not complain, and the three of them together lifted him enough to prop him in a reclining position. Despite the discolored swellings, his arms and shoulders were thick, all hard, firm muscle so unlike her own soft flesh. He smelled nice.

Madlenka scrambled off the bed and reached the soup before Giedre did. "Bring that stool!" she commanded and went around to the other side of the bed so she could sit close to him. She was much amused by Giedre's expression, but unrepentant. Her lord and master, the count, had ordered her to look after his brother.

Wulfgang needed his face shaved and his hair brushed. She might see to those personally. She popped a spoonful of soup in his mouth.

"Too hot? Too cold?"

"Perfect," he sighed, but it wasn't clear from the way he was staring at her whether he meant the soup or her. "Tell me what happened yesterday, when Anton arrived."

So she fed him soup and information. He drank some watered wine but refused anything that needed chewing.

She decided that shaving him would be a little too personal and might cause Giedre to have apoplexy, so she sent for the castle barber. While he was attending to her patient, she went off to check on Mother, who was still curled up like a frightened caterpillar and about as responsive.

When she returned to the squire, she found Anton there. He kissed her on the lips, which was brazen of him in public, but she managed to smile after it was over.

"Your patient is obviously thriving under your care, my lady," he said.

"I think he's being very brave."

"Oh, all we Magnuses are tough. I'm going to go exploring the town. Will you be my guide?"

"I'd love to, but I shall have to go and change first."

He shrugged, losing interest. "It's raining, and I know how women hate to get their hair wet. This afternoon, perhaps?" Then he left.

Giedre rolled her eyes. Wulf was frowning.

"Well, at least he's not in armor now," she said, going around to the stool beside him. "Do you need anything, squire?"

"I need you to call me Wulf. I also need to stare admiringly at you for about two hours. It is very beneficial for me."

"Very embarrassing for me, though."

"Nonsense. You should find it flattering, because I've never done it before with anyone." He had a wonderful smile. "And you mustn't make fun of my brother's armor. He's very proud of it. Did he show you the dent?"

"No," she said, intrigued. Was her husband-to-be a war hero after all? "Does it record a narrow escape?"

"Very narrow," Wulf said solemnly. "The mail was specially made for him—that's traditional, and in his case it had to be, because of his height. Designed in Milan, made in Augsburg; the best. Good armorers prove their work by firing an arquebus at it to show that the ball will not penetrate. Then they engrave a testimonial around the dent. I told him he ought to make doubly sure by proving it again while he was wearing it, and standing closer. That was the narrow escape."

"He did it?"

"I was afraid he was going to. It took me two hours to talk him out of it."

Giedre sniggered in the background. Madlenka laughed, then Wulf did too. She suspected there might be a grain of truth in that story, or at least in stories like that—about Anton. Not about Wulfgang.

"What do you do for amusement, here at Castle Gallant?" he asked.

"Hunt," she said.

"Falconry?"

"Yes, and venery—deer, and mountain goats. Plus boar, hares, badgers, wolves and so on. Very rarely a bear."

"It sounds like heaven, but too strenuous at the moment. Sing to me."

Yes, she would enjoy doing that. "Giedre, go fetch my lute, please."

Giedre rose and went to pull the bell rope. When a page responded, she told him to fetch Madlenka's lute. Then she sat down and made a face like a gargoyle. Really! Admittedly Madlenka and Squire Wulfgang had been indulging in a little playful flirting. What possible harm could there be in that?

CHAPTER 17

Wulf was feeling much better by afternoon—due, of course, to the superb nursing he was receiving. Madlenka fussed over him like a cat with one kitten. Now she was cutting up roast duck, which smelled delicious.

"Your brother says that you are tougher than boiled leather," she remarked, popping a piece into the invalid's mouth.

She must have iron fingers, for it was hot enough to hurt his wounded tongue. He swallowed it quickly. If she fed him molten lead, he would never complain about the service.

"All thanks to him. With four older brothers, I had to be tough to survive. And he was the worst. The best teacher, I mean."

He was rewarded with another smile, albeit a small one. That made twenty-two on this visit.

"Our herald says that the sash he wears means that he's a personal friend of the king."

Wulf urgently needed to confer with Anton and find out what stories he was telling. "If he can defend Castle Gallant from the Wends, he will be the best and dearest friend the king ever had. If he can't, he will qualify for a state funeral. Probably in two boxes."

Lady Madlenka raised golden eyebrows. "The smaller one for his head?"

"The larger one for his head."

Now her smile was a fanfare of trumpets. Count that one twice! She was, without question, the most beautiful woman in the world, with hair like autumn wheat and eyes of summer sky. She was tall and graceful, light on her feet. Her companion Giedre sat silently knitting in the corner of the bedroom, chaperoning her mistress. Although she might be lovely enough on her own, in a dimply, cuddlesome sort of way, she disappeared completely when Madlenka was present.

"Tell me about the other brothers."

"Why? I'm the only one of the five who's interesting."

"Tell me about you, then."

He tried to shrug and winced instead. "I am popular with dogs, horses, falcons, and honest people. I'm not mean enough to be a soldier, devout enough to be a cleric, or smart enough to be a scholar. I realize that you don't have failings, so I'll let you share some of mine."

He was leaning back against a pile of cushions, being fed like an infant, and it was heavenly. It was true that he still hurt from head to toe, but he could grit his teeth and move if he had to. He didn't need to be made of boiled leather to do that. And he could not take his eyes away from Madlenka Bukovany. The troubadours had it right about love at first sight. Faster than a thunderbolt. He had never fallen in love before and was already certain that he never would again, which must be a very bad sign.

The strange, wonderful, unbelievable, historical, sensational, exhilarating thing was that the lady Madlenka seemed just as fascinated by him as he was by her. Her eyes kept wandering to his arms, lying on the cover. Granted, they were a spectacular sunset medley of yellow, purple, and green, but she must have seen a man's arms before. Lately the covers had slipped a little lower on his chest and her gaze kept flickering there now. He suspected that he might be displaying a few golden chest hairs. By the mercy of God, the top cover was a quilt thick enough to hide a terrible bulge that would have shown up through any mere rug or blanket.

"Failings?" Madlenka murmured. "I don't think I need any failings. Do I have failings, Giedre?"

Giedre said, "I have known you to spend hours raving about young men with honey-colored hair and eyes as yellow as wolves'."

"I did not call them yellow!" Madlenka bellowed, and then blushed crimson, staring at Wulf in horror.

"Golden, then," Giedre said, not looking up. "You also went into raptures over muscular arms, as I recall."

Wulf knew he was blushing also, but perhaps that wouldn't show through the bruises. "It's true my arms are yellow," he said, "and also purple. My legs, now, are red with green stripes, if you'd like a peek. And I think you are the most beautiful lady I have ever set eyes on."

"That is *enough*!" Giedre said, jumping to her feet. "Out, my lady! This can only lead to trouble."

"No, it can't," Wulf said. "You are affianced to my brother by royal command. I would never try to steal you away from Anton, even if I thought I could. I'm loyal to him and loyal to the king and now I'm loyal to you, too, because you have been kind to me and I won't return hurt for kindness. I'm sure you would be true to your promise to him anyway. Nothing is going to happen, except that in a week or so, when I'm healed, I'll jump on a horse and ride away. He doesn't need me here. Meanwhile, what harm if I stare at you longingly now and again? I will never meet a more beautiful woman."

He meant every word of this speech, but if he asked St. Helena or St. Victorinus to arrange matters for him, anything might be possible. Marek had warned him about that temptation.

"Where's the spoon?" Madlenka said briskly, turning away. "I brought some suet pudding with honey. Can you manage it by yourself, do you think?"

"I am much restored by the excellent duck." Wulf heaved himself a little higher yet on the pillow and pulled the cover up to conceal any dangerous chest hairs.

Madlenka thrust a bowl of sodden pudding at him and moved her chair several feet away from the edge of the bed. Wulf winked at her.

"I saw that," Giedre said.

"You were meant to. Smile, goddess."

Madlenka folded her arms and glared at him. "Your brother wants us to be handfasted."

Pudding turned to mud in his mouth. "So that he can cohabit with you without having to wait for formal marriage? Nobody does that anymore! What did you tell him?" *No! Please make it "No"!*

"I said no. I said that I didn't want there to be any arguments about the legitimacy of the stalwart male twins I plan to give him nine months and two days after our wedding night."

"Make it three days to be safe. I think that was a wise decision. What does your priest say?"

"I haven't asked him. It's none of his business. Count Magnus is going to ride out with the Long Valley patrol tomorrow."

Why did she mention that?

"He needs to become familiar with the terrain," Wulf said. "If he is to repel an attack by the Wends, I mean."

"How can he possibly do that? He spurned Vranov's offer of help and sent him packing. The *landsknechte* all left this morning. We're worse off than we were twenty-four hours ago, when he turned up in the cathedral."

"Don't underestimate Anton," Wulf said defensively. "He's as proud as a peacock and smart as a jackdaw."

Before Madlenka could comment, the door flew open and the count himself strode in, ducking under the lintel. He nodded to the women, then added a smile as an afterthought. He obviously had something serious on his mind.

"How are you now?" he asked curtly.

"Much the same as I was this morning," Wulf said.

Madlenka curtseyed. "Pardon us, my lord."

She left, holding the door for Giedre, who carried the dinner tray. The moment the door closed, Anton strode over to the window and stared out at the bailey.

"I just sentenced a man to death."

Wulf winced. "Not a pleasant duty, I'm sure. But a necessary one. You are a lord of the high justice." Getting no reply, he added. "I've watched Ottokar doing it."

Otto did it very rarely, though, and didn't enjoy it either. The last criminal he had executed had been Hans the blacksmith's son, who had raped a girl while he was drunk and she wasn't. If Marek's Voices hadn't saved Hans's life when he was a child, it wouldn't have happened. But if Wulf's Voices hadn't brought Anton here to Cardice . . . Did Wulf bear some guilt too?

"I did it exactly the way Ottokar does it," Anton told the window. "He's talking with a priest now, and they're rigging up a noose down there in the bailey. They're harnessing a horse to a cart."

"For the constable?"

Anton nodded. "Karolis Kavarskas. He admitted that when Havel Vranov was here in August, Kavarskas took his money to let him know right away 'if anything important happened in Cardice.'"

"So he's hinting that Vranov knew that Stepan and Petr were going to die?"

Anton turned around with a sneer on his face. "He testified that Vranov *expected* that something serious was going to happen, but couldn't or wouldn't say what. Kavarskas also promised that if I spared his life now, he would testify against Vranov if the king ever wants to put him on trial. But there's not a moth's chance in hell that Vranov could ever be brought into a courtroom, or that anyone would take Kavarskas's word against his anyway."

"So Kavarskas confessed?" Trust Anton to get an easy decision on his first capital case!

"He didn't have much choice by then. He tried to bribe his way out of jail. I had him stripped and he had twenty gold florins in a money belt."

Wulf tried to whistle, but that hurt. "Does he have a family? Children?"

"That's irrelevant," Anton said irritably. "If he does, he should have thought of them before he took money from a man other than his lord."

"I suppose so. I hope you rewarded the garrison handsomely before you put its commander on trial?"

He was recalling one of their father's stories, and Anton flashed a momentary smile. "I reminded them that we are on war footing and doubled their pay."

"Smart man. Why did the *landsknechte* leave?"

"Must go. They're bringing him out." Anton headed

for the door. "Because Ekkehardt thinks the Wends are going to set up their big gun and blow us all to bits."

"Wait!" Wulf snapped. "What story are you telling? How do you explain the timing?"

Anton dismissed the problem with a wave of his hand. "My papers are all backdated to the eighteenth, so you and I are in the clear. We rode here from Mauvnik like the wind and at first we had a moon to help us. The question is how His Majesty, may God preserve him, learned of the emergency so quickly. That is a state secret. I have dropped a few hints to the bishop about the courier being intercepted, and carrier pigeons. Get it?"

"Got it."

Anton took hold of the handle and then looked around. "How soon will you be fit to ride, Wulf?"

Oh, that was what he'd come to ask? "Next year, maybe. I may go on pilgrimage to Jerusalem first."

"Seriously. Wulf, I need your help."

"You promised you would never ask again."

"Yes, but—"

Wulf pushed down the covers to show the colors. "Look. Every muscle in my body cramped up so hard it bruised. Every accursed one, and many times, not just once. I did what you asked and you promised never to ask me again. You think I'm ever going to accept this torture willingly now that I know what it involves? I'd rather be racked till I'm taller than you are. Dream not, Brother. I shall Speak no more."

Anton sighed and left, mumbling about having to give the signal to move the cart.

CHAPTER 18

In Tuesday's chill gray dawn, Count Magnus rode out as a member of the Long Valley patrol. His escort wore a motley collection of mismatched hand-me-down mail, both plate and chain, so they had little in common except their Cardice surcoats and the crossbows slung on their backs. His own fine armor marked him as a nobleman, as did his mount, a splendid gray courser named Avalanche that had been a favorite of the late Count Bukovany.

Just because Jorgarian troops continued to man the post at Long Valley did not mean that Duke Wartislaw was not slipping patrols past it, keeping a watch on Castle Gallant. If that were the case, then Anton would make a wonderful target of opportunity. He would be safer riding a nag and wearing the same nondescript gear as the troopers—assuming he could find any to fit him—but it did not become a nobleman to hide his rank like that. Well, if the worst happened, he would certainly not be the first Magnus to be nailed into his cuirass by a crossbow bolt.

The mountains were wrapped in fleece and the valleys blurred by something too heavy for mist and too light to be rain. The first half mile or so was easy enough, with cliff-up on the left and cliff-down on the right. The surface was in need of repair, but not bad enough to hinder an invading army. He had seen this part from the tower. The two roads, the north and south approaches to Gallant, were almost as impressive as the castle itself.

He thought about pestilence. He had thought of little else since the word was mentioned. The stricken *landsknecht* woman had died before Ekkehardt led his men out, and he had reluctantly accepted a bribe of a thousand florins to take the body away with him and bury it in the graveyard at High Meadows.

So far Ekkehardt had been the only one to mention plague. He might have been bribed to invent it. He might have made a mistake, for other diseases could produce buboes. Even that senile, half-witted doctor in the infirmary ought to have recognized the symptoms of pestilence if he had seen them. Anton clung desperately to the hope that there was no pestilence.

Plague might scare away the Wends, of course, even if he had to drive a thousand plague victims out the north gate to do it. Except that the townsfolk would just disobey him and hide their sick dear ones. Would the bishop forbid it as mortal sin, and if so how much would it cost to buy him off? Counts who quarreled with bishops usually lost. Plague would ruin everything. It was unthinkable.

He had troubles enough without it. He had set the seneschal to work building up food stores against a siege, but the cowards fleeing town were mouths that need not be fed. He would have to start cutting firebreaks through that maze of houses as soon as the enemy appeared, which would not raise his popularity much.

A leader must not be seen to brood. He turned to his new constable, Dalibor Notivova, riding alongside him in the van. Anton had already learned that the man was Cardice-born and had served abroad as a mercenary for a few years before coming home to find a wife and raise a family. Probably that story would turn out to be fairly typical of the whole garrison, but asking questions was the only way to learn. So Father had always said: nobles could learn even from commoners if they cared to make the effort.

"How far up the Silver Road have you traveled?" he asked.

"Only as far as the lake, my lord."

The trail rounded a spur into the gorge, dank and noisy, with the Ruzena rushing and foaming far below them. The roadway rose steadily, but before long it passed a roaring waterfall, appropriately named Thunder Falls. Beyond that the track and the river were more or less level. Then they came to the first bridge, spanning a small tributary.

Anton dismounted to inspect it. It was built of undressed tree trunks and disappointingly sturdy, able to carry a team of oxen quite safely. Whether it would also hold up under the weight of the great bombard called the Dragon remained to be seen. He sprang into the saddle again, and chose another companion to question.

The gorge was growing wider, the river calmer, the rain heavier. He changed companions again after inspecting another bridge over a tributary. Eventually they came to a point where they must ford the Ruzena itself, at a place where islands of coarse shingle divided it into many smaller streams.

"River's not very deep, my lord," remarked Big Herkus, his current companion. Big Herkus was about Marek's size; Little Herkus must be a giant.

The water barely came up to the horses' hocks, but

the shingle was a welcome sight, because moving an extra-heavy load over that would tax even Duke Wartislaw's resources. Wheels might jam, axles break, oxen balk at the footing.

Better still, the next bridge was a long timber span, carrying the road back across the Ruzena. It was in poor condition and a gang of sappers should be able to dismantle most of it in a couple of hours. They would need archers and lancers to guard them while they worked, of course, and Anton resolved to organize that expedition for tomorrow. He was starting to feel more comfortable, hoping that the Dragon would never arrive. It might just be a Vranov invention, like the rumor of pestilence.

Less encouraging was his discovery that his army was largely made up of rookies. Only two of his five companions had battle experience; the other three were local-born and locally trained. They might suffice if all they had to do was stand on the battlements and shoot arrows, but would they stand firm when the balls and bolts started coming the other way?

The valley steadily widened; the river wandered off, out of sight of the road. The rain stopped; a slight breeze arose. The lower reaches of the mountains were gentle and painted with grass or lichen; certainly some grass, because a herd of white specks—goats or sheep—was grazing the slope to the north. The floor of the valley was marshy, with ponds showing between stretches of moss and reeds, but there were enough stands of spindly aspens to restrict the view to no more than a hundred yards in any direction. In summer the air would be a fog of mosquitoes. At best, the road was muddy: the worst parts had been patched with corduroy topped with a layer of clay, but some of the tree trunks were rotting. The horses became skittish, testing their footing with every step. Oxen might not care as much, but a duke who planned to bring a monster bombard along here had not listened to valid advice. Or else he had Speakers to help him.

A faster splatter of hooves at his back and Notivova rode up alongside. "My lord!" He looked worried.

"Constable?"

"We should have met the returning squad before now, my lord. They're supposed to wait at the post until their relief arrives, but they never do. They all want to get home early."

Anton raised a hand to signal a halt. "You told anyone that I would be making a personal inspection today?" The post garrison might even now be standing in rows, ready to salute their new commander and impress him with their incredible devotion to duty.

"Not a soul, my lord." If the same image had occurred to the trooper, he did a fine job of keeping a straight face.

"How far to Long Valley?"

"We're in it. Half a mile or so to the border post. If Your Lordship can see those tall firs? They grow on a small mound in the marsh, the only really dry land hereabout. The post is there. Then there's another mile or so of this muck on the way to the lake head and the Wends' landing stage, where the ferry barges come. The lake's ten or twelve miles long."

Anton glanced around the scenery. "God made this place to stage ambushes."

"He certainly did, my lord!" Notivova showed relief that his commander had enough sense to see that.

For the new count to take fright and run away before he had reached his objective would just be good sense. It would also be rank cowardice by chivalric standards. Yet to charge ahead and be mown down would throw away the lives of his five companions, and worthy leaders did not do such things. Anton had no choice. If there was one thing a brainless Magnus colt like him could not tolerate it was a challenge like this. *Omnia audere!* Other men might call him an idiot, but success would make him a hero in the eyes of the garrison, and he would need true loyalty when the attack began.

"Then let's see if we can turn the tables. I'll be bait. Wait behind these trees. Stand still and make no noise. If I come back with the wolves on my heels, try to shoot them and not me, all right?"

"My lord!"

"You have your orders." Anton wanted no argument that might weaken his resolve. His heartbeat was disgracefully fast already.

He reached for the crossbow slung on his back and tore off the cover. It was designed for use on horseback, being small and spanned with a goat's foot lever. Now it was already spanned, and he loaded a bolt in the groove. The chances of hitting a target were remote, but just holding a weapon was a comfort. A lance would be even better.

He reminded himself that Caesar, Hector, Alexander—all great leaders—had been men of suicidal courage. If the city shaver sent by the king could prove that he had real balls, then the garrison would follow him to a man. There would be no more sad muttering about Count Stepan and Sir Petr.

Prodded into motion, Avalanche leaped forward, glad of the chance to show his paces. The big fellow was a hunter, able to choose his path, and he swerved around the corduroy patches, preferring to take his chances in the muck.

The trail wound like a snake between ponds and

swamp and the little aspen groves. The dark firs were farther off than Anton had guessed, and the ambushers, if they existed, might already have closed the road behind him. His excitement now was as intense as sex. His groin burned with it. *Omnia audere!* This was what a Magnus did. He had felt some of this battle lust going down the hill at the hunt, but here he had no Wulf to save him. This was his legend, live or die. Ancestors, behold! Even Vladislav might approve of him now.

Where was the enemy? What a fool he would look if he arrived at Long Valley to find the guards drawn up in rows, saluting their count.

Thirty yards off to the right, a man emerged from cover, running toward him as fast as he could struggle through the mud.

Some brainless Wend sounded a hunting horn, three long blasts to mean that the dogs were on a good trail. The woodland hatched about a hundred horsemen, like dragon teeth, a dozen riding out from behind a copse before him, more from trees behind him, on both sides. Some distant, some close. How could he possibly have missed seeing so many?

He swung Avalanche like a sword and headed for the running man. It was the Englishman, Llywelyn, bloodied and clutching a wounded arm to his chest with his free hand. Two enemy men-at-arms were converging on him and seemed likely to cut him down before Anton could arrive.

Assail a wounded man, would they? Anton spurred Avalanche cruelly. He dropped the reins, guiding his mount with his knees and using both hands for the bow. He must hold his aim until he could be sure of hitting the foe and not Llywelyn, but on horseback that might be forever. At the last possible moment, when the nearer

Wend had his saber raised to strike, Llywelyn threw himself flat. The bow cracked, and must have sent the bolt right through the hussar, for he toppled back, dropping his saber and unbalancing his horse. Anton had no time to reload. He dropped the bow and drew his sword.

The second attacker veered away from Llywelyn to meet the danger. He was a small man who would not match Anton in brute strength, so Anton ducked low and swung upward. Their sabers rang as the horses passed, and he managed to continue his parry into a backhand riposte at the enemy horse's rump. That would make it unresponsive for a while. He reined in Avalanche alongside Llywelyn, who was upright again, white eyes staring out of a muddy mask. Llywelyn grabbed for the saddle with his good hand, Anton reached down to grip his cuirass strap, and they both heaved.

With the wounded bowman draped over his withers, Avalanche made a game effort to run, but he was grievously overloaded and the footing was treacherous. Help was coming, though. Horn sounding, Notivova was leading his gallant band to the rescue. By luck or inspiration, he and his four riders had spread out and the aspens made it hard to judge how many they were. The Wends were fewer than they had seemed at first sight, maybe thirty or forty, but now half of them were between Anton and his rescuers.

"The odds are good," he shouted cheerily. "Good for a good fight, I mean."

Llywelyn was whimpering with pain, probably because his wounded arm was trapped underneath him and he needed his other hand to hold the saddle, lest he slide off, headfirst or feetfirst.

"Very grateful, my lord."

"I'm only doing my duty like you were. Hang on."

Two Wends were converging on Avalanche, timing their approach so they could strike simultaneously. Anton prepared to take the one on his right, a big, ugly, hairy brute.

It wasn't going to work, though. He had no shield, nothing to parry the other attack with except his vambrace, so he might well come away from this encounter with a broken arm. He might even lose a hand.

Shock!

He wheeled Avalanche to meet the other assailant, but his sword had disappeared. Blood was trickling out of a round hole in his right rerebrace. And also from a matching hole on the other side of it. He had apparently taken a quarrel through his upper arm. It was strange that he could feel no pain. He was spouting blood. He might lose his arm. He was thinking in patches. What should he do now?

Finding his way blocked, Avalanche had stopped, puffing hard and flickering his ears at the stench of blood. Llywelyn uttered a groan and slid to the ground. He tried to land on his feet, but collapsed in a heap among the reeds.

"Yield, my lord?"

A ring of mounted Wends surrounded them, with a dozen spanned crossbows aimed at Anton Magnus's heart. Not a likely-looking nobleman among them. Yield to a commoner? If he had a sword he could try to take one of the vermin with him. But black mist was starting to swirl around him, and even Vlad had yielded at the Battle of the Boundary Stone.

"I yield."

"Wise of you, Count Magnus." The new voice came from his left, and apparently from a priest, since he wore a jeweled pectoral cross and bore no arms or armor. He was clad in black robes and an odd pot-shaped hat; even his horse was black. Above a black pillow of beard his right eye was watching Anton with amusement and contempt; his left was studying the mountains.

"I don't yield to priests."

"You will yield to *death* very shortly if you don't get down and let us attend to your arm."

His accent sounded like pottery in a waterwheel, but what he was saying was probably true, and descending voluntarily would be more dignified than falling off in a faint. Anton kicked out of his stirrups and leaned forward to pull his right leg over. From habit he put weight on his right arm. That brought on the missing pain. He screamed, fell off Avalanche, and landed on top of Llywelyn.

He could not have been unconscious very long, but long enough for his captors to strip off his spaulder, vambrace, and rerebrace to expose the wound. A soldier who looked like a swineherd and smelled like the swine was stitching one of the wounds with a needle and gut. Another man was holding the other hole shut until it could be treated. There was no lack of pain now, murderous thunderclaps of agony.

Close by, Notivova and Big Herkus were tending Llywelyn.

"If you live," remarked the priest, watching from horseback, "then you will have some loss of strength in that arm. But a wound like that is very likely to lead to lockjaw or gangrene or just severe wound fever. You had better speak with your confessor as soon as you get back to Gallant, my lord."

"You are sending me back?"

The priest laughed. His age was hard to assess under that beard—mid-thirties, perhaps. "We don't have a jail handy, and you do more good for our cause botching up the defense of Castle Gallant than you would rotting in a cell in Pomerania. Who would bother to ransom you, Anton? We shall empty the Bukovany coffers soon enough without selling carrion to the castle."

"Who are you and why is a priest leading a band of raider scum—*Yeaew*!"

"Beg pardon, my lord," said the surgeon cheerfully. "Did I pull on that too hard?"

The priest was still smiling. "I am merely a humble servant of the Lord, Anton, doing good works in His name. Do not mock, my son. I just saved your life. My unkind companions wanted to leave you there, bleeding to death."

The surgeon tied the last knot and trimmed the ends of the blood-soaked string with a dagger. Another man wrapped the arm with a strip of Anton's shirt.

"His own men can dress him," the priest said. "Let us be on our way home to report a successful day's work. Tomorrow morning, Anton, you must send a party under flag of truce to collect your dead. After that, any Jorgarian found near here will be put to death. Go with God, my son. I suggest you leave warfare to grown men in future."

He made the sign of the cross, but he did it from right to left, backward.

CHAPTER 19

The rain had stopped. The afternoon was sunny and not far off being warm. Wulf insisted that he was well enough to get dressed and go outside. Madlenka insisted that he was not.

"I'm as good as I ever get," he retorted. "Or do you mean I should go outside *before* I get dressed?"

It was very childish humor, but one of the surest ways to recognize lovers was how easily they laughed at each other's jokes. What he felt for Madlenka Bukovany went far beyond mere attraction. It was more than lust or admiration or friendship. It was the best thing that had ever happened to him. It was an all-consuming, once-in-a-lifetime passion. Nothing else in the world mattered. He would do anything to win her or please her, and he was certain that she felt the same about him. Neither had mentioned it. They did not need to, and must not. It was a forbidden, impossible match, and perhaps that was the very reason the madness had come upon them so quickly. Giedre knew all this as well as they did, and scowled disapprovingly in the background.

So, wearing clothes that had belonged to Petr Bukovany and trying not to show how every movement hurt somewhere, Wulf emerged on the curtain wall battlements, escorted by the future countess and her lady-in-waiting. The air was cool and sweet, the sun warm, the snowy mountains both menacing and beautiful. A steady trickle of families was heading down the road to High Meadows, but Anton would not be displeased to see those extra mouths depart, even if he lost some strong men in the process. His edict putting the town on a war footing had roused the warlike and scared the peaceable.

Down in the bailey a hundred more-or-less able-bodied men were being outfitted from a heap of all the arms and armor that a thorough ransacking of the attics of Cardice had turned up. Wulf ought to be down there, helping. Tomorrow, perhaps.

"This is a very beautiful place," he said, studying the scenery as he strolled along the battlements with his love at his side. The urge to offer his arm or take her hand was a torment, but they were visible to half the town, and Giedre was walking close behind, so it must be resisted.

Madlenka said, "Ha! It's cold and bleak. All my life I have dreamt of living in a gentler land, in a big city with gaiety, with music and dancing."

He looked at her quizzically. She was as tall as he was and in other shoes might even be taller. That would not have bothered him, had things been different. And it certainly did not matter now, since the king had decreed that she marry Anton. "Vienna? Florence? Rome?"

"Mauvnik, probably."

"Mauvnik doesn't compare with those."

"You've seen them?"

Anton would say of course he had, and describe them, quoting stories he'd heard.

"I've seen Mauvnik. It's much bigger than Gallant, I admit."

"Father always talked of marrying me into some noble family with influence at court. He almost never went to court himself, because his duty was here. A voice near the king's ear was important, he said."

"Near the crown prince's ear might matter more now." Or Cardinal Zdenek's, although nobody knew how long the Scarlet Spider would remain as first minister when the crown changed heads.

"But now the king has sent a personal friend to marry me, instead," Madlenka said wistfully. "So I must forget my dream duke in Mauvnik. I must live and die here in Cardice. Still, I should not complain. Your brother is young and handsome. I could have done very much worse."

Or very much better, Wulf thought sadly. And never as well as she deserved. No man was that good.

"And Giedre," she continued, "has refused a hundred suitors here because she planned to come with me when I went away to marry my dream duke. She was to be mistress of the robes."

The wind was at their backs now, blowing up the valley, and Giedre would not be able to overhear.

"She's very pretty," Wulf said. "But I would never call her beautiful. I have only ever met one girl I would call truly, breathtakingly beautiful, like a dream of angels."

Madlenka ignored that. "The rest of our plan was that Giedre would marry the duke's younger brother, who would be even handsomer."

"Well that part came true. Being handsomer, I mean. And if she fancies a serf's cottage in Dobkov, then marriage might be negotiated. But staying with you would not be on the table. I am going away in a couple of days." It was that or go crazy.

The lady bit her lip. "That's probably a good idea. And one of us must go indoors now. Not because I don't enjoy your company, Squire Wulfgang, but because we have been seen together long enough. You are my fiancé's brother, after all."

"I am. And I love you."

He hadn't expected to say that.

Madlenka walked on, staring at the ground. The wind had reddened her cheeks. "You must not say that."

"I swear as I hope for salvation that I never said it to any woman before, but I do love you. I don't know how it happened—I think it was the first moment I saw you. Oh, I must sound like a fool! I'm sorry."

"Keeping talking, fool," she said quietly, so the wind snatched away her words. Would it spread them everywhere?

"You too?"

She nodded.

She loved him! He didn't know if he should turn cartwheels or jump off the battlements. "Truly? You love me also? Say it, please, just once."

"I love you. I wish it were you I am to marry, not your brother. But it is madness! We must not even dream of it. The king has decreed that I will marry Anton."

Who cared nothing for her, who would cheerfully marry Medusa herself if she brought him an earldom. Wulf had not asked his Voices to make Madlenka love him. He would not ask them to interfere at all. He *must* not! Anton was his brother. Anton was a wealthy noble, outranking Otto and probably much wealthier, while Wulf was a penniless younger son, a mere esquire.

Marek had warned him: the girls will follow. "It is

love," you will tell yourself, and you will ask your Voices to bring her to you, or even to make her willing. Had any prophecy ever been fulfilled faster?

No, he must not think about it. No more Speaking!

But were she promised to any other man than Anton . . .

"Squire!" Giedre shouted, running closer. "My lady! Look! Coming down the north road. Only four of them? Isn't that your brother on the white horse, squire?"

Yes it was, and two of the others were riding close on either side, as if they had to hold him in the saddle.

"He's been hurt!" Madlenka said. "Run! Ring the bell."

Giedre hoisted her skirts and took off at a very unladylike sprint toward the north barbican, but the watchers there had seen the newcomers and the alarm bell began to toll.

"Go to him," Wulf said. "I'll follow as fast as I can."

Following would be a mistake. He did not go down to the city gate, nor even to the bailey. Anton would not slump on a horse that way unless he was seriously hurt, and he would never let them take him to that pesthole infirmary. So Wulf made his painful way back to the keep and started looking for whatever bedroom Anton was using until he could evict the ailing dowager countess from the master suite.

The keep, which from the outside seemed like a simple hollow box, had been built in many stages at many times, and was a labyrinth on the inside. Stairs led to passages and more stairs; levels changed; corridors ended without warning. Fortunately he had no trouble obtaining help. The new count was the talk of the town and everyone must have heard of his mysterious brother, who had been injured. All he had to do was find a page, explain who he was, and demand to be led to the destination he wanted. It was, not unexpectedly, the room formerly used by Sir Petr.

There Wulf made himself as comfortable as possible on the stool by the dressing board. He clasped his hands and bowed his head. Whispering did not work, but speaking softly did. "Most holy Saints Helena and Victorinus, hear my prayer."

For a nerve-racking moment there was no reply. Then came the Light and Victorinus spoke at his shoulder.

—*Say what it is you need, Wulfgang.*

"How badly is my brother injured?"

—*He took a quarrel through the arm and lost much blood.*

"Will he recover?"

—No. *He is too weak now to amputate the arm. Even if you can stop the bleeding the flesh will rot in a few days.*

For a few minutes Wulf prayed in silence to greater authorities than his Voices. Then he spoke aloud again. "If I ask you, will you heal my brother's wound?"

St. Helena said,—*Of course. But you are still very weak from the last miracle. The pain would kill you.*

There always had to be a catch. God did not dispense miracles without a price—why should Wulfgang Magnus be favored beyond all mortals? He was not a great sinner, but he was a sinner. All men were sinners. His lust for Madlenka was a sin.

"You are telling me that to save Anton I must die?"

Silence. The Light was still shining through his eyelids, so the Voices had not gone away. He had asked a forbidden question, or asked it the wrong way.

"Why do you answer some questions and not others? Why do I have to suffer pain at all? How am I special that you perform miracles for me when other people are not so blessed? Are they holy miracles or the diabolical false miracles that Marek said?"

Still no answer. Yet the Light remained, as if the Voices were waiting for him to issue them orders or ask a sensible question. Saints could be extraordinarily annoying at times. Thinking back to Father Czcibor's hagiology lessons, he decided that this was probably their dominant characteristic.

"Do I have some great destiny, for good or evil? Am I fated to write my name in history? A prophet? A teacher? A conqueror?"

Again silence. They would never prophesy.

"Would you restore me to health if I asked?"

Helena said,—*You* chose *that price.*

"Oh? Had I refused the pain, what other price could I have paid? Should I have asked what the alternative was?" Eternal hellfire?

One of the voices sighed, probably Helena, but it was Victorinus who said,—*Danger. All pain is a warning of danger. Pain teaches you not to touch hot dishes or break the law. The alternative to pain is danger and possibly worse pain later.*

Worse pain than what Wulf had endured recently was almost beyond imagining, but perhaps not beyond experience in the afterlife. "What sort of danger?"

Silence.

Wulf had told Anton that he would never again call upon his Voices' help, but now that help was needed to save his brother's life. Marek had warned him that asking became easier and easier. Marek had also warned that the trial for Speaking was "most arduous" and he had talked of tongues being burnt out. But Anton was about to die, and if Wulf let that happen he would always wonder if he had done so because he wanted Madlenka for himself.

He could. He could let Anton die and then declare himself count, as his brother's heir, marry Madlenka, explain to the king later. He could have everything he could ever want: *the devil took him to a very high mountain and showed him all the kingdoms of the world and their glory.*

But in this case the devil was tempting him *not* to ask his Voices for help. How did that work?

He could hear voices, mortal voices, approaching along the corridor.

"I chose pain as the price for bringing my brother here. Can I change my mind now?"

—*Yes.*

"Then, most holy Saints Victorinus and Helena, I beg you to cure my bruises. I will risk whatever danger this brings. But please leave the marks on my face to heal normally."

—*Oh, Wulfgang, Wulfgang!* Helena said sorrowfully. —*You are going too fast, far too fast! You are blundering into a wilderness, alone, untrained, and unprepared. You do not know the perils that await you.*

"Then teach me."

—*We cannot.*

"Then do as I say and I accept the price, whatever it is."

—*If that be your wish, then be it so.*

"Thank you."

The pain had gone. He had forgotten how pleasant life could be without it. The Light faded. He opened his eyes and folded his arms. A glance in the mirror made him chuckle. His eyes were so ringed with dark bruises that he looked like a badger.

Suddenly the room was crowded—four troopers bearing Anton on a stretcher, Madlenka and Giedre, the odious doctor from the infirmary, plus several more that Wulf did not know. Anton was laid on the bed and everyone else packed around. Deciding that it was time to intervene, Wulf muscled his way in until he reached the bedside. Anton was ready for laying-out already: face bone white, lips blue, eyes closed. His right arm was bare, with a bloody bandage around the upper part; his armor was bloody.

Wulf bellowed. "*Quiet!* That's better. You! Yes you, Doctor! Go away." He bent close. "Anton! Brother, it's Wulf. Who else do you want here?"

Without opening his eyes, Anton mumbled. "You . . . Radim, Kaspar . . . Constable Notivova."

Wulf straightened and repeated those names. "Everyone else leave. Now." He waited, interested to see who stayed.

Madlenka, on the far side of the bed, was giving him puzzled looks, surprised by his sudden return to health. Nobody else should notice that, except possibly the drunken old leech of a doctor, but he likely wasn't capable of counting to three, let alone putting two and two together.

Madlenka was the last one out, leaving a rakish-looking young man in mail—who must be the constable—plus an elderly man and a youth leaning on a cane.

"Who first, Brother?"

"Kaspar . . ."

The old man stepped forward. "My lord?"

"Hot water. Towels. And wine."

Wulf added, "And good water to drink."

Kaspar hurried out, moving as if his feet hurt. He must be the count's body servant, and old enough to have been Barbarossa's.

"You look as if you came off worst," Wulf said cheerfully, stepping closer. Any more worse and he would be dead already.

Anton ignored him. "Constable?" He licked his lips.

"My lord?" said the man in armor.

"Send out funeral party tomorrow. No troopers."

"No guards?" Notivova looked puzzled.

Anton mumbled something incoherent, but it was obvious enough.

Wulf explained. "We can't afford to lose more men, and the Wends can. They probably won't harm civilians, but you'd better pay them danger money. Get Bishop Ugne to assign a priest or two. How many men did you lose, by the way?"

Cold eyes stared at him out of the steel coif. "You are His Lordship's brother?"

"I am. Squire Wulfgang. You must be Constable Notivova. I'm not giving you orders; I just know how the count's mind works. He'll overrule me if I'm wrong. How many men did you lose?"

"Fourteen, squire."

Hellfire! "Bad! Surprise attack, I suppose?"

"So the only survivor told us."

"Butchers! Any more orders for him, Brother?" Wulf had to bend right down to hear the reply.

"Double guards. Full war footing. 'Ware surprise attack."

Kaspar scurried in, bringing a bottle of wine and an armful of towels. Knowing that Anton must be parched by his loss of blood, Wulf raised his brother's head and put the bottle to his lips. The constable left. A servant brought a steaming pitcher of water. Another brought a flagon of cold, and Wulf sweetened it with wine before letting Anton drink any.

He realized that the youth with the cane was still there, clutching a waxed wooden tablet and looking half dead with worry.

"You are Radim?"

"Yes, squire."

"You want to dictate a letter, Brother?"

Anton murmured something about the king, but he was barely conscious now. He might be about to die.

"I think you'd better rest for a while first. Radim, why don't you find out exactly what happened and draft a report from the count to His Majesty? I'm sure you can put it in proper form better than he can. Bring it back here when you're ready."

Having disposed of everyone except himself, Wulf got down to the horrible job of removing his brother's blood-caked bandage.

He would have known that Anton was dying even without the Voices' prophecy. The bolt seemed to have missed the bone, but internal bleeding had made his arm swell up like a sack of melons below the bandage, all the way to his fingers. Using great care, Wulf managed to cut the knot with his dagger and unwind the sodden cloth. Both the entry and exit wounds had been very clumsily sewn shut, but they still oozed and the flesh was so puffed up around them that he could barely see the stitches, let alone remove them.

"Am I going to lose my arm?" Anton whispered, eyes closed.

"Not if my Voices will help. Try a few prayers of your own."

Wulf washed his bloody hands as well as he could in

the scarlet water. He then went over to the fireplace and knelt to pray, ignoring the slurred and incoherent mumble in the bed.

"Most holy Saints Helena and Victorinus, I humbly beg that you will restore my brother Anton to health."

Light shone through his eyelids.

—*You are too far away, Wulfgang,* Helena said. —*Go closer. Lay your hands on him.*

Surprised, he obeyed, and took the wounded arm in both hands. Anton did not react to his touch. He had stopped praying. Without a miracle he would slide quietly into death.

Then Wulf would have it all: earldom, wealth, and—best of all—Madlenka. He need only send for that ancient doctor and leave the patient in his murderous hands. In an hour the cathedral bell would toll. *The count is dead, long live the count!* Wulfgang, second Count Magnus of Cardice.

"Holy Saints Helena and Victorinus, I pray you to restore this man, my brother, to perfect health."

—*Do you accept the price?*

"If you mean pain, then no. But I accept any risk. *Omnia audere.*"

Helena:—*Oh, Wulfgang, child, you will regret this.*

Victorinus:—*Courage becomes you. Look for the fire, my son, the flame.*

Wulf peered around . . . Where? "I don't see any fire!"

—*Do not be too hasty. Search within.*

He searched: the arm; Anton's corpse-pale face; the rest of him, stretched out on the bed like a ribbon of steel . . . Ah! Now he made out a faint and ghostly glow—behind those lifeless eyes, inside his brother's head or superimposed on it—as if Wulf were seeing Anton with one eye and this vision with the other. It was like the worms of heat that crawled on embers and gave birth to butterflies of flame when you blew on them.

"I see, I think. What must I do?" Blow?"

—*Stamp it out!* Victorinus said. —*It is his soul, seeking to escape. If it bursts into flame and departs, he will be gone. Do not let him go! Picture it on your mind. Will it! Use your hands, for the heat cannot hurt you.*

Wulf tried to imagine his hands tearing a fire apart, scattering the coals; then switched the image to his feet stamping, grinding. That worked better, and in his fancy the illusional lumination crumbled to sparks, died, and was extinguished.

—*It is done,* Helena said. —*He will live, for a little span.*

The Light faded as he watched the miracle happen. An obscene sausage shrank to become a man's arm again. Bloat became muscle. Skin turned from fish-belly white to tan. Anton stared up at him from the pillow.

"What happened? How did I . . . ?" His gaze raked the room, the furniture, the bed curtains, and came back to Wulf. Suddenly he was fully conscious, and visibly terrified in a way Wulf had never seen before.

"You cured my wound?"

"My Voices did. Welcome back." Wulf stood up and looked down on him fondly. "We almost lost you, you know."

No regrets. Even Madlenka. Love could not be bought at the price of a life of shame. He could feel proud that he had passed a test.

"Who are you?" Anton whispered. "More to the point, *what* are you?"

"I wish I knew," Wulf said humbly. "The Voices will not explain. I am just . . . their protégé, I suppose. I do not understand. I am certainly not a saint." Saints did not think the things he caught himself thinking about Madlenka. "I must try to use their gifts to do good." *Not to steal Madlenka away from you, for instance. I still can. It would be so easy and feel so good.* "Let's get that armor off you, and tuck you in like the invalid everyone expects to see."

Anton slid out of bed, fully restored, and in minutes they had made a heap of all his mail.

"Bed!" Wulf insisted. "And listen. Everyone will guess that I have just used witchcraft. The bishop will ask questions that we cannot answer. I must leave Cardice at once—that's obvious. And you *must* play invalid for at least a day, or they will accuse you of being in league with the devil, too. You are in danger also. Promise me?"

"Of course."

"Let me bandage your arm, then. No one must see it."

The wounds had disappeared completely, without a scar.

"Go where?" Anton grumbled. "By my faith, I need you here, Wulf! Not just your Voices. You! You can do some things much better than I can."

"You didn't tell me you'd taken a head wound."

"I don't think I did."

"Well, you've never paid me compliments before."

Anton growled and tried to rise.

Wulf pushed him back down, not gently. "Invalid, remember! Now, what did you want your secretary for?"

"To tell the king the Wends have invaded, of course." He glared up angrily. Half naked and bloodstained, yet he still resented being babied by his kid brother.

"That's an excellent excuse for me to leave. I'll deliver your letter to the Spider."

It was time for Squire Wulfgang and Cardinal Zdenek

to discuss the division of spoils. Not fair that one brother should do all the work and get none of the rewards! This could be explained to Anton later.

"Wulf! I need you, I tell you!" Anton looked unusually sincere, and extraordinarily worried. "I need someone here I can trust. I have no real experience, just what I've picked up listening to Father and Otto and Vlad. I'm not qualified to be a marshal, leading the country's defense against odds of a hundred to one. I can't handle this by myself." His eyes brightened. "The man I really need is Vladislav! He's doing no good rotting in captivity in Bavaria. I told the seneschal I needed to pay a ransom for my brother. He wasn't very happy, but he admitted that it could be done. He mumbled something about letters to a bank. I didn't understand, but it can be done!" He twirled up his mustache in delight.

Wulf shook his head. "At this time of year, with a new moon coming, I'd allow ten days for the ride to Mauvnik and probably another ten to reach wherever Vlad is in Bavaria. Then twenty for him to ride back here. Forty days. Your war will be all over in less than forty days."

"But you could do it in less than an hour."

"No. No! *No!* The Voices are warning me that every time they help me, they increase my danger." Hinting that, anyway.

"Danger of what?"

"Of the Church catching me, I think. It may be something worse. Less than a week ago you asked me to pray for you as you tried to break your neck, and now you have me dragging you out of the grave. I'll carry your report to Mauvnik and I'll take Vlad's ransom along if you like—at least you can trust me not to steal it. But this latest miracle or magic is too obvious. I have to get out of here, Long One, before I end up like Marek with a life sentence of pulling weeds all day long." Or playing the torch in a torchlight parade, like Joan of Arc.

Anton scowled, but then he nodded. "That's fair. I can't thank you enough, and I mustn't endanger you any more. See how Radim is doing, will you? And see the seneschal about the ransom. I am the count and the money is mine to spend."

Wulf gathered the bloodstained clothes and armor into a heap, then arranged the bed curtains so that Anton was in deep shadow, visible only through a narrow slit. "Remember that you're at death's door," he said, as he tugged the bell rope to summon some servants.

CHAPTER 20

He found Madlenka and Giedre in the solar, counting their rosaries—praying for Anton's recovery, Wulf assumed, although Madlenka must have considered what might happen if Anton died, just as he had.

"He's going to be all right."

They looked up disbelievingly.

"Really. He lost a lot of blood, but the bleeding has stopped and he's resting."

"Our Lady be praised!" Madlenka said. She closed her eyes for another silent prayer. Was she asking forgiveness for certain evil thoughts? "Aren't you going to sit down?"

"I'm on my way to the stable . . . Mistress Giedre, I have something to tell Madlenka. Would you please give us a moment alone? Leave the door open if you wish."

The women exchanged glances. Madlenka nodded. "Just for a minute."

Disapproving, Giedre left. Wulf did not sit.

Madlenka rose and faced him warily. "She won't eavesdrop. What is this dark secret, Squire Wulfgang?" She was pale. She had guessed.

"I am leaving Castle Gallant, my lady. Within the hour."

She flinched. "You are recovered enough to ride a horse?"

"I bruise easily, but we Magnuses are very fast healers."

Anton or Vlad would have accepted the statement as either plain fact or macho bragging, but Madlenka did not miss the other possibilities. Her eyes narrowed.

"Tough as boiled leather, I was told."

"Tougher. But please make sure that my brother rests for the next day or two. Lock him in, or tie him down, if you can. Madlenka . . ."

Now what to say? He must not implicate her in his Satanism, if that was what it was, and he must not raise her hopes in vain.

"I have . . . a favor . . . I want your promise . . . It is possible that I will not be . . ." He was stammering. He stopped and started again. "But, in case I do . . . if I do . . ."

She smiled. "You are not making a great deal of sense, squire."

"How can I make sense when I am crazed by love? I just want you to promise not to marry him until you are sure I am not coming back!"

Now she stared at him as if he was a foaming maniac—and who could blame her? "You are going to ride down to Mauvnik and ask King Konrad to change his edict? To order me to marry you instead of Anton?"

"More or less."

"You truly are insane!"

"Almost, but not quite. It is not impossible! Listen . . . no, don't. There are things I cannot tell you. It is a slim hope, but I just may return with such a document."

"So the sash does not lie? You really are personal friends of the king?"

"My lady, it is no secret in Mauvnik that the king barely knows day from night anymore. Please, trust me. Wait for me!"

"Wait how long?" She was bewildered, naturally.

"Forty days," he said, because that was what he had told Anton. "Just don't go and marry him before then!"

"Marry? Now? With an enemy at the gates, my father and brother hardly cold in their graves, my mother blighted? There can be no wedding for me, squire, not for a year or more."

"Your mother?" Someone had mentioned a mother. "What is her ailment?"

"She was seized by melancholy when my father was stricken, and has refused to leave her bed since."

"Smitten by the same curse, you think? This is evil incarnate."

She said, "Yes," but her eyes were questioning. She was a clever girl, dangerously clever.

"I must go. I love you." He hadn't been aware of moving, but they were very close.

"And I you." She smiled sadly. "You were so badly hurt, and so brave."

"You were so kind." He had always dreamed that the mother he had never known had been like her—tall and gentle and caring. There were no pictures of her. He had always assumed that she had been blond like him, not dark like Anton, but he had never dared ask. He had killed her, being born.

Madlenka's smiles would raise the dead. She said, "A little flirting seemed harmless when there could be no future in it. Knowing we had nothing to gain, we thought we had nothing to lose."

"How wrong we were!" He put his arms around her and drew her close, but she turned away from his attempt to kiss her.

"You haven't told me everything, have you?"

"No, my lady. I dare not. Whatever you suspect, I beg you not to share your thoughts with anyone."

"Is it possible that Cardinal Zdenek was fighting fire with fire?"

Clever! "I have never met that eminent gentleman, and he would never admit to such unchristian behavior."

Then he tried again to kiss her and this time she did not refuse. He thought she would break it off very quickly, but she didn't and he had no desire to have it end—not ever.

"Father!" Giedre said, in a voice somewhat louder than normal. "What brings you here?"

The kiss ended. Madlenka strode over to the door and out into the corridor. Her voice drifted back. "No, it isn't there. I must have left it . . . Seneschal?"

"My lady, I am looking for Squire Wulfgang. The count told me to see him."

"He looked in here a few minutes ago, to tell us that Lord Magnus was much recovered. It was kind of him. Did he say where he was going, Giedre?"

"To the stable, I think, my lady."

The voices died away and Wulf started breathing again.

He must go. The sooner he went, the sooner he could come back and try to do something about the Wends. They would need some time to muster their forces. So Anton would be all right. Madlenka would survive. He wished he could leave her a present, a token of how he felt, or just a reminder of him until he returned. Or something to ease her burdens? Then the answer was obvious. If his voices could cure Anton, they could surely help her mother's despair. But how? A countess beset by melancholy would not be left unattended. An unknown young man would never be allowed into her quarters anyway.

"Most holy saints, how can I cure . . . I mean, how can I Speak for the countess without anyone knowing?"

The Light came.

—*There is a way, my son,* Helena said. —*Go.*

He stepped out into the corridor. Corridors in Castle Gallant were on the outside and dim, lit only by the loopholes in the outer wall. The rooms were on the bailey side, so they could have windows.

—*Left*, Victorinus said. —*Upstairs. Right.*

The corridor ended in darkness where discarded furniture had been left to molder. Wulf proceeded cautiously through the clutter of broken chairs, dismantled bedframes, and other litter until he reached a blank wall, whose stonework had been left rough and unfinished, a later addition to the original structure.

—*Stand in the right-hand corner. The lady's bed is on the other side of the wall. Now ask.*

"Holy saints, is there a curse upon Countess Edita?"

—*Yes.*

"I beg you to remove that curse and restore her wits."

The Light faded. Wulf headed back the way he came, wiping off dust and cobwebs. What next? Miracle or witchcraft, he refused to believe that healing people was evil.

He went looking for the seneschal, but the keep must be buzzing with more hunters than hunted, for he was cornered by young Radim. He had shed the wax tablet, but still bore his cane and his worried expression. Perhaps he always did.

"Squire, may I ask a question? I was talking with Dali—Constable Notivova, I mean—as you suggested, and he said that the Wend soldiers seemed to be led by a priest. A schismatic priest, of the Orthodox Rite."

Not sure what reaction was expected of him, Wulf said only, "Shocking!"

"The constable says he knows him," Radim added eagerly. "It was Father Vilhelmas, squire! He accompanied Count Vranov when he visited here last month, and he was with Vranov at the gate on Sunday, when the bishop insisted he not be admitted."

"Yes. If you could lead me to wherever I might find the seneschal, we could talk on the way."

"Oh. He wanders around a lot. He will most likely be in the counting room, squire. Down here."

Matching his pace to Radim's awkward hobble, Wulf said, "So what about Father Vilhelmas?"

"He was at Long Valley this morning! How did he do that?"

"I don't know the country. How *could* he do that?"

"Well, he could have doubled back through Castle Gallant, but he wasn't supposed to be admitted. Or he could ride west to the Hlucny and over Hlucny Pass, but all that rain we had here would be snow up there, and it's rarely open this late in the year, and it would take him at least three days anyway. At *least* three days!"

Secretary Radim was a sharp lad, clearly.

"Sunday? This is Tuesday. So it would just be humanly possible if the pass is still open?"

"I meant three days in summer," Radim said stubbornly. "The constable doesn't think it's possible."

"You're suggesting that Father Vilhelmas Speaks to the devil?"

They were going downstairs again, Radim moving even more awkwardly. He looked abashed at having his conclusions put into words. "It could be, couldn't it? Dali thinks so. Would the count want me to put that in his report, squire?"

"I don't think he would like you talking about it in Gallant. We don't want people to think there are Speakers around, do we?"

Radim shivered. "Oh, *no*, squire! The whole town would panic."

"Exactly! But I do think my brother will want to tell the king this news, so I'm glad you mentioned it. With other enemies, His Majesty would complain to the pope and ask him to excommunicate them for having dealings with the devil; he can't do that against Duke Wartislaw, because the Wends are already Orthodox heretics. Yes, the king should be told. How long until you'll have a draft ready for the count to approve?"

"Just a few minutes to write that bit in, squire. The counting room is along there."

"Excellent," Wulf said.

The counting room was a cramped and dim little office on the ground floor. Stout bars protected the windows, the door was sturdy, and there was probably a secret fireproof money vault carved into the rock under the rug. The fussy-looking man seated behind a well-littered desk agreed that he was Seneschal Jurbarkas, although he seemed more suited to being Giedre's grandfather than father. He marked his place in a ledger with one finger and regarded his visitor with distaste, conspicuously not inviting him to be seated.

"Squire! At last! I was looking all over for you to give you . . . where did I put them? Yes, those . . . three documents, and a purse of coins for your journey. On the count's instructions. Make your mark on this paper to attest that you have received them."

Wulf sat down, took up a pen, and signed *Wulfgang Magnus, Esquire* in a fair hand, adding the date. He unfolded the thickest of the papers.

"That's written in Latin," the old man said impatiently.

"So I see. I've known beehives with less wax, too. Hmm . . . The two gentlemen with the Italian names, on behalf of the Medici Bank of Florence, witness that the aforesaid bank will tender to the gentleman with the German name or his heirs and successors the sum of twelve hundred florins on the return of this document. Signed and sealed. Then he, the first party of the second part, instructs the parties of the first part to tender instead to a gentleman with a French name, and they add two more seals. He's from Bruges, so I suppose this went north with the spice trade and came back with wool? Then four others. And lastly my dear brother's seal and signature, witnessed by the bishop, no less, tells the bank to tender the loot to Baron Ottokar Magnus of Dobkov. It gets around, doesn't it? A harlot of a document!"

He folded it up. "It should have been made out to Baron Emilian of Castle Orel, in Bavaria."

"The count could not recall that name."

Typical! Wulf reached for the other two and glanced at them. "This one is for six hundred florins and this one for two hundred. The total must be very close to two thousand florins, mustn't it?"

Jurbarkas was watching him with some effort to seem amused. "My apologies, squire! I underestimated your talents."

Wulf grinned. "You were judging me by my brother, perhaps?"

"Certainly not!" But the seneschal turned noticeably pink. "Just by a lifetime of dealing with squires. Is there anything else I can do to assist? Anything you want?"

"There's one thing you can do," Wulf said, rising, "but it won't be easy."

"Anything!" The seneschal stood up also.

"Find a suitor worthy of that beautiful and charming daughter of yours." He bowed his farewell. One of Anton's first jobs should be to find and train a replacement seneschal.

Since he was already down at ground level, he went next to the stable, where he chose a fine chestnut courser named Copper and ordered that he be saddled for a journey. He had no luggage to pack. He browbeat the armorers into giving him a sword, donating the remains of his armor to the Castle Gallant militia in exchange. Realizing then that he was starving, he tracked a scent to the kitchen and told a couple of pretty girls to pack a roast ox for him to take on his journey.

He ran back upstairs to say his farewells.

CHAPTER 21

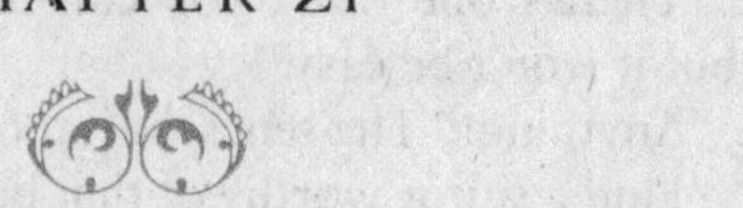

Count Magnus of Cardice was aware that he did have some shortcomings and that sitting still was one of them. He could sit a horse as well as any man alive—even keep up with Wulfgang, four times out of nine—but sitting in bed leaning against a pile of pillows and listening to Madlenka Bukovany reading from Wolfram von Eschenbach's *Parzival* was sheer torture. He tried to look interested, struggling with the antique high German and taking his cue on when to smile or seem sad from the inevitably present Giedre.

He had work to do, organizing the defense of Castle Gallant, and he couldn't do it in bed while pretending to be recovering from a major loss of blood. The bedroom setting was making him increasingly aware that it was two days since he parted from the overwhelming, oversexed, overripe Baroness Nadezda. Another night of abstinence would make concentration utterly impossible. Even now he was hard put not to ogle his future wife too openly.

Madlenka had spurned his suggestion that they get on with the meaningful part of the marriage and take their time to plan the ceremonial part for next year. For the life of him he could not see the objection to this. By the king's command they must marry and kings' commands should be obeyed promptly. A sheltered damsel like Madlenka could not understand the severe suffering that celibacy imposed on a healthy young man. He must get rid of her busybody chaperone and explain that if she did not consent to handfasting, the alternative was that he take a mistress.

Or should he get rid of Madlenka and explain this to Giedre?

Madlenka was not the type he would have chosen for his countess. She was striking enough in a classical way, but she had the coloring of a corpse and even her shapeless mourning garments could not hide her skinniness. What sort of midget babies could she push through those hips? What sort of pathetic tits would she offer her husband to play with? Giedre, now, was plump and blessed with the sultry Mediterranean look that could square a man's shoulders, puff out his chest, and so on.

A tap on the door announced the arrival of Radim with ink, wax, and the fair copy of the report. The boy had done a fine job with the drafting. Anton had ordered only enough changes to make his own actions sound more like a breathtaking feat of rescuing a wounded subordinate and less like attempted suicide while of unsound mind.

He had that part read to him again to make sure the amendments were satisfactory, then signed his name at the bottom: *Cardice*. He gazed at that proudly for a moment and then—with a sense of sheer wonder—added *CStV*. No Magnus before him had ever been appointed to the Order of St. Vaclav.

As Radim departed, in wandered Wulf, his normally affable expression distorted by facial bruises into ogreish menace. He looked even worse when he smiled.

"I'm away," he said. "I hope this is not goodbye, Your Countship."

But it could be. Anyone going on a long journey might disappear and never be heard from again.

"I wish you godspeed, Brother. Here's my report to His Majesty. It is late to be starting out. The sun will set in an hour. You sure you won't stay over and leave at dawn?"

"No." He came around to the side of the bed to give Anton a farewell hug. "God bless," he said, "and may He grant you good fortune. You'll need it," he added softly.

"You don't have to do this. I have lots of good horsemen here in Cardice who could carry my dispatch south." In the next month or so, miracles would rank very high among Castle Gallant's requirements.

Wulf chuckled. "When did you ever know me to change my mind? Except when I used to promise to kill you, I mean, and that was only after Father begged me."

"Never. But I'm going to need your help, Wulf." He meant miracles, but mustn't say so.

Wulf understood, because he shook his head very slightly. "I do intend to make it back here safe and sound. Don't slaughter all the Wends before I can get my share." He turned to Madlenka. "And the pulchritudinous countess designate? Farewell, my lady. You were most exceeding kind to the wounded sparrow who took refuge on your windowsill."

"Farewell to you, squire. I am distressed that you cannot stay longer with us."

Wulf lifted her hand to kiss her fingers. "Maid, in thy prayers be all my sins remembered."

She blushed.

Blushed?

"And just what does that mean?" Anton barked.

"Nothing," Wulf said hastily. "Farewell to you, too, my lady Giedre, and my thanks for your kindness also." He vanished out the door and closed it.

Madlenka opened the book again. "More *Parzival*, my lord?"

Sod Parzival, and his horse, too! "No. First I would like to know why you should be remembering my brother's sins in your prayers?'

She stared at him with a very good imitation of blank innocence. "It is only an expression, my lord, a politeness."

"Not, perhaps, because they were your sins, also? That you were sinning together?"

Now she sprang to her feet, slapping the book shut. "My lord, that is a vicious insinuation! You asked me to see that your brother was well cared for, and I tended him myself. But we were never alone together. Always Giedre or others were present. Your remarks were unworthy of your rank and my honor. You owe me an apology."

Anton's temper surged up like bile, almost choking him. If he were free to jump to his feet and storm around the room he might be able to deal with this conspiracy, but his lower half was not presentable and must remain under the covers.

"Oh, do I? I remind you that you owe me fidelity and chastity. And you, Mistress Giedre? What exactly were the kindnesses that my brother remembered to thank you for so graciously? Did you perhaps take invigorating little walks when you were supposed to be chaperoning my betrothed?"

Giedre recoiled and looked to her mistress in panic, guilt written all over her face.

"Aha! Will you swear on a Bible that you never left her alone with my brother, not once?"

"Once . . . but only for a moment, my lord. I mean, not long enough for . . . anything improper to happen."

"And you know how long those improper things take? By experience, you know, or just from old wives' tales? It is customary on a wedding night, Lady Madlenka, for the bedsheet to be passed out so the guests can see the bloodstain that proves the bride was a virgin. I trust that you are prepared to meet this standard?"

Lady Madlenka hurled *Parzival* across the room at him like a stone from a ballista. It would have brained him had he not ducked.

"How dare you?" they roared simultaneously.

The perfectly penned but ponderous volume impacted a priceless carafe of Venetian glass, which shattered against the stone wall.

"Upstart!"

"Hussy!"

"Interloper!"

Someone rapped on the door.

"Whore!"

"Murdering incompetent narcissistic foulmouthed blackguard!"

"Hellcat!"

"Am I interrupting something?" inquired a new voice. Into the room swept a woman of impressive dimensions, clad all in black from toes to bonnet; even her hands were hidden by lace cuffs, but her veil was raised to reveal a face like a glacier. She moved with the somber majesty of a funeral procession. "Count Magnus!" She curtseyed to him.

"Mother!" Madlenka cried, hurling herself into the

arms of—who else but?—Dowager Countess Edita. "Oh, Mother, you're better!"

The countess endured the impact with no perceptible wobble, then detached her now-sobbing daughter. "While bathing and dressing me, my women have made me informed of all that has transpired since I was cast down by grief. As His Majesty's chosen, you are welcome to Castle Gallant, my lord."

"And I congratulate you on your recovery, my lady."

"It was about time," she conceded. "A mere hour ago I felt my prayers being answered, and the blessed Virgin sent me the strength to accept God's will and rise from my bed."

An hour ago? Anton glared at his wife-to-be, who caught his eye and turned away quickly to be comforted by Giedre. Had Wulfgang taken to selling his miracles now? The timing alone was almost proof. That sneaky young serpent, with his sanctimonious preaching about keeping himself pure for some future bride! His cozy little fireside chats with the devil had certainly cleaned up those ambitions in short order.

"Your arrival is most opportune, Lady Edita. I have just had occasion to censure your daughter, who is my betrothed by royal decree. Of course I must make some allowance for Castle Gallant's isolation, but it is customary among nobility dwelling in less rustic surroundings to have young ladies chaperoned by older women, and never less than two."

The iceberg turned to scorch Madlenka with a cold blaze of outrage. "*Madlenka!* Have you given Lord Anton cause to question your virtue?"

"No! No! No!"

"Yes she has," Anton said. "I do wish my brother had

stayed longer, so we could hear his version of events. He left Gallant very hurriedly not an hour ago." He enjoyed the dowager lady's depiction of utter horror. "Furthermore," he added, "if she expects to continue her tantrums of throwing books at me and shouting down the bishop in his cathedral, then after our marriage I shall be forced to discipline her severely."

"By your leave, my lord," Countess Edita said, taking a firm grip of her daughter's arm, "we shall investigate these matters further. I shall inform you of the results of my inquiries shortly."

"You are most kind, my lady."

The moment the door boomed shut behind the three women, Anton hauled on the bell rope. The page on duty arrived in moments.

"Find Arturas," the count snapped. "I want him right away." Then he jumped from the bed—as much as anyone could jump out of a feather mattress—and started looking for trunk hose. He was respectable and brushing his hair by the time the herald answered his summons.

"I need Bishop Ugne. Does he come to me or do I go to him?"

Arturas wore a brightly splotched smock and had a streak of green on his nose, so he must have been painting the new count's arms on something. "Oh, you never *summon* a bishop, my lord! But in view of your recent injury, a discreet intimation that a courtesy call would be timely . . ."

"Then let him know that I need to speak with him."

If the countess reported that her daughter was not a virgin, all marriage preparations must stop. Madlenka would be hustled off to a nunnery, the king would withdraw his edict of marriage, and Anton could continue to enjoy bachelorhood for a few years longer, assuming that he could keep the Wends from the door. If she still was—and admittedly, as his first flash of temper cooled, he found it hard to imagine Wulf being such a rat as to deflower his brother's fiancée—then the union had better be sealed as soon as possible. Mourning period be damned. The king had commanded it. There was a war on. Wulf's healing had restored the count to the prime of health. In his case, healthy also meant horny.

CHAPTER 22

Copper was a fine steed, swift and steady, needing no guidance. As soon as they had left the castle, Wulf let him run, trusting him to know the road and find the best footing. He unpacked his lunch one-handed and started gnawing on a goose leg while he thought about the Voices.

Were they saints or demons? Why would they never explain or answer questions? There had to be a reason for that reticence. The prospect of another ride through limbo was daunting, and if the price was to be the same as before, he would refuse to pay it. Yet now he had healed Anton, and perhaps the unseen countess, and had suffered no pain for it.

He tossed away the bone and took a drink from his wine flagon. An excellent wine—the kitchen staff had done well by the count's brother. He started in on a thick slice of salted ham.

It was all very well to brag to Madlenka about changing the government's mind. A Speaker, however inexperienced and untrained, might hope to manipulate a senile, maundering king, but the calculative Cardinal Zdenek had ruled Jorgary with a steel fist since before Wulf learned how to breathe. And if the Spider could stoop to using Speakers, then so could other statesmen—the Church obviously did. So Zdenek would certainly have built defenses against Satanism into his web. He would deny it, of course, but any attempt to bewitch him must lead straight to toasted Wulfgang. Merely delivering Anton's letter at any time short of eight days from now would be an admission of Satanism. Zdenek, in short, was a necessary ally, but a highly dangerous one.

The advisor Wulf needed was Baron Magnus of Dobkov. Even if Anton had not assigned the two thousand florins to Otto instead of Baron Emilian, Wulfgang would have headed first to Otto.

He licked his fingers, took another drink, and then laced up his saddlebag. Copper had slowed to an easy pace, happy to run over the moorland road with a competent rider. They were too far from Castle Gallant for a magical disappearance to be noted, and the only person in sight was a shepherd about a mile ahead, driving his sheep down to lower pasture for the winter. The sun was very close to the horizon. Time to go.

"Holy Saints Helena and Victorinus, hear my prayer."

Copper decided he was not being addressed. He obviously did not notice the Light that dawned all around him.

Helena: —*We are here, my son.*

"My lady, if I ask you to take me home to Dobkov, what price will you demand?"

—*We do not demand any price. You decide what it shall be, but it is not paid to us.*

Talking with disembodied Voices was never simple. "What choices do I have?"

Victorinus, harshly: —*Agony, or madness, or death.*

Helena, more gently: —*All of us must meet with death eventually.*

Victorinus again: —*Our help puts you in greater danger every time you ask for it.*

They sounded just like Anton daring him to put his first pony over a ditch. "Can I refuse the pain and accept the danger?"

—*You can refuse immediate pain, but the danger you accept may be of greater pain deferred or death advanced. We cannot foretell the end.*

"Burning at the stake, for example?"

—*That is one possibility.*

Wulf decided that life must offer more profitable enterprises than trying to make sense of this. "Then know that from now on I refuse immediate pain and accept any future peril. Can you take me to . . . where is Ottokar, my brother?" Otto owned many estates and spent much of his life traveling between them.

Copper shied violently, making Wulf grab for the saddle pommel, and the world seemed to jar sideways and blur. He saw words, written on vellum, only about two of them legible, and then another two in their place. The vellum vanished and there was a man's face . . . another man's face . . . a tapestry . . .

"Whoa! Steady, Copper. Steady, fellow!"

A sudden breath of wind, or a rising partridge?

He calmed the shivering horse, wondering which of them had scared the other. His reaction to that flickering vision might have startled Copper, or the horse's fright might have jarred him out of a Voice-inspired daydream. The Light was still there. He had not had time to read the writing and had not recognized the two faces. But he knew the tapestry. It hung in Otto's counting room in Dobkov.

"Was that a warning you just sent me?"

Helena chuckled. *—You spurn our warnings. Your brother is at Dobkov and you should go there at once.*

"What? Why?"

Victorinus's voice came then, harsher and more commanding. *—Because great rejoicing awaits you there now, but later will bring great sorrow.*

"You've never given me such advice before." He should not be arguing.

—You stand higher now.

What did that mean? "Please take me to Dobkov as fast as possible."

The moor shimmered and grew misty. Copper whinnied in alarm and bolted. Wulf gave him his head. Soon the familiar pearly haze of limbo closed about them and the sound of the wind and beat of hooves died away. Trees and buildings flew by, flickering light and shadow.

He stood higher now? What did that mean? It might be a saint's-eye view of a man that Marek had called "a hardened practitioner of the black art." Marek had spoken of a first sin and a second sin. St. Helena had said he was not ready for another "step." A step could be another view of a sin in this instance. He could summon miracles without pain now, so he was progressing. To what? How many steps could there be? What was he becoming, saint or devil? Had he imagined that glimpse of Dobkov, or was he becoming a seer now?

Was he blessed beyond other men, or already damned?

The world was shimmering back into reality. Copper neighed in fright, but his hooves beat on dirt again. The high roofs and tall chimneys of Castle Dobkov showed against the sky ahead, making Wulf's eyelids prickle with nostalgia. He knew this road through the coppice like the nails on his fingers. It was not quite a month since he and Anton left home, and it felt like years. Even their arrival in Gallant last Sunday seemed an age ago. He let Copper have his head to run off his fear. The big lad had a fine turn of speed.

Soon the road emerged from the trees onto open pasture, and then he could view the whole castle, ancient and mossy, with sunset blazing red on its windows. No mountains here, only a few gentle hills, but the castle stood on an island in the river, half a mile or so upstream from the village. The channel was wide enough to need a true bridge on pillars with a drawbridge at the island end. Copper slackened his pace at the sight of the change ahead. He tried to veer to the right, then to the left, and Wulf would allow neither, so he slowed to a cautious walk, flickering his ears as the timbers boomed under his hooves. A bored porter on the gate sprang to life.

"Wolfcub! Squire, I mean! You're back! Chief, it's the Cub!"

Wulf shouted a greeting and carried on through the archway into the bailey, which occupied most of the area enclosed by the curtain wall. Part was grassy, part cobbled, and there the local residents and their herds could take refuge in time of war. Near the gatehouse stood the forge, stables, granary, and castle ovens. Most important for him was the house at the far side of the bailey, which still felt like home. He reined in at the main door.

As his feet hit the ground, a tumultuous torrent of house dogs came racing out to greet him. Even the hunting hounds in their pen caught the excitement and set up a chorus of baying. Voices called his name. Achim, former childhood playmate and now a junior hostler, came running, with several others in hot pursuit. For a moment Wulf thought they were all going to mob him in a group hug, but they remembered their station in time. They stopped and saluted.

And last, but never least, old Whitetail, who had been his constant childhood companion, came shuffling out to greet him, now lame and almost blind, but tail wagging furiously.

"Welcome back, squire!" Achim grinned, showing missing teeth. "We missed you. Place didn't seem the same."

He had noticed Wulf's bruised eyes, of course, as everyone would. He should have had the Voices cure them.

"I should hope not!" Wulf was detaching his saddlebag with the fortune in it. "But I was homesick for all your cheerful faces." It was also good to hear someone speaking properly. The strange dialects started just a few miles from home and grew steadily worse the farther one wandered. "Where is everyone?"

"All inside. Got some visiting gentry. And Sir Anton?"

"He's . . . fine. Doing very well, in fact, but I must tell the baron the news first. This is Copper. He will be your friend if you give him a rubdown and a handful of oats. And tell him how pretty he is."

He greeted the other smiling faces quickly, then ran up the steps into the lesser hall. He had already seen those visiting gentry and he could guess what their business was.

Castle Dobkov, although imposing when seen from the outside, was much smaller than Castle Gallant. A lot of it was solid masonry. The living quarters were cramped, and "lesser hall" was a grand name for a staff dining room, capable of feeding about forty people, so that every meal had to be held twice.

Who should be crossing it, though, weighed down by

a huge basket of clean laundry, but the baroness herself. Branka was a large and perpetually jolly woman, with rosy cheeks and golden hair, the sort of woman ancient pagans would have worshiped as an embodiment of the Earth Mother. In five years of marriage she had presented Otto with three sets of twins, and promised to continue doing so. She was her own housekeeper, as shown by the big bundle of keys dangling at her waist, and had even been known to dabble in cooking very successfully.

If Branka was not included in the current entertainment of gentry, then the men were talking business, which was exactly what Wulf feared.

She stared at him with eyes wide and mouth agape. "Wulfgang! What brings—"

He pecked her cheek by hugging her, basket and all, then took her burden away. "Just my ghost, but I died bravely. Tell me quick, who are the visiting gentry?"

She pouted. "Not real gentry. Count Dalnice's steward, a banker, and a notary. What happened to your—"

"Otto is selling off land?"

"He has to, Wulf. The west vineyards."

"No, he doesn't have to! I've got Vlad's ransom right here in this bag. All of it. Run and fetch Otto out of there quick, but don't say why I need to see him and don't tell the others who I am! Quick, quick, quick!"

Branka could be a human monolith when necessary, but she was very levelheaded and knew when not to argue. She took off like Copper. For a lady of girth, she could move with astonishing speed, spiraling up the stairs two at a time. Wulf ran after her, clutching the laundry as a handicap. At the top he judged that he had narrowed her lead, so he could claim to have won the race, if only barely. Branka headed left, to the counting room.

He turned right and threw open the door of the room he had shared with Anton all his life. It had always been cramped, but walls four feet thick had kept monsters out.

The big bed had been replaced by two child-sized cribs. For a moment he stared in shock, and then in bittersweet nostalgia. He should have expected this! A new generation had taken possession. Dobkov was no longer his home; he was a man of the world now, a journeyman Satanist.

He dumped the laundry on a cot, and then knelt to get his face thoroughly washed by Whitetail, who had laboriously followed him upstairs.

And then he saw Otto. Even Vlad would concede that Otto was big. He was twice Wulf's age and went to war no more, although in his time he had campaigned in France, Austria, and Lithuania. He had been as great a warrior as Father, probably better than Vlad would ever be, because he was smarter. He was still fit, able to vault into the saddle of a sixteen-hand stallion while wearing full armor. Normally he was the most amiable of men, but he had a jaw like a plowshare, which let him look as menacing as basilisks on the rare occasions when he wanted to. This was one of the occasions. He came sweeping along the corridor like a mad bull, dark eyes blazing.

"Wulf? What's the matter? Why're you here? Interrupting me!"

Wulf waved him inside and shut the door. "Would I interrupt you if I didn't have good reason? You haven't signed yet?"

"I'm just about to. Had ink on the nib."

Wulf pulled the papers out of the saddlebag. "This is worth twelve hundred florins. This makes eighteen hundred, and this one rounds out the full two thousand."

He grinned at his oldest brother's stunned expression. It was a shame Anton could not be there to enjoy the moment.

"Where did you get this?"

"It's a gift from Anton to Vlad. From his wife's dowry. See this bit? *Antonius Magnus Comes Cardici*—your little brother is now Count of Cardice, lord of the marches, keeper of Castle Gallant. Also a companion in the Order of St. Vaclav. He already shines brighter than any Magnus has ever done, Baron."

"Anton, married? Count?" Otto clenched a fist the size of a loaf of bread. "If this is a joke . . ."

"I swear it is the truth."

"Then I don't need to sell the land!" Jubilation swiftly turned to horror. "I shook hands on it, Wulf!"

Selling land was about the worst thing a nobleman could do. It was failure, a betrayal of both ancestors and descendants. The fact that the staggering debt owed to the Bavarian, Baron Emilian, had been incurred by Vlad, not Otto, did nothing to relieve the sense of shame.

Going back on his word would be even worse, though.

"Wait!" Wulf said. "Let me think . . ." He would never claim that his modest share of Magnus brawn might be offset by having the best brain in the family. That didn't mean he couldn't believe it in private, of course. "Circumstances have just changed dramatically, Brother."

The big man snorted. "You mean the fact that I don't need the money now? In no way can that justify reneging on an agreement. I needed it when I shook hands."

"No, I mean that Jorgary is at war. Pomerania has invaded. No one knows what will happen. King Konrad needs all his best warriors back, so he may pay off all the ransoms. The Wends may come this way. Anything is possible." Only Anton could stop disaster, but he was irrelevant at the moment.

Otto seemed to grow even larger. His face darkened. "Who told you that?"

"I'll explain later. Right now you just have to trust me. You don't even need to tell them what the serious news is. It's a state secret, so you couldn't tell it even if you knew it. Take my word for it, and give them your own. Tell them the deal is off and their master, Count Whatever, will not want to go through with it anyway when he hears the news."

Vlad notoriously could not tell a nod from a wink, and Anton wasn't much better. Marek was a scholar and shrewd, but even he stood in Otto's shadow when it came to understanding people. Otto could detect a lie at three hundred paces. And he knew Wulf wouldn't lie to him anyway.

He beamed. "Welcome, then! Make yourself at home. I'll go and tell them. By the way, who redecorated your face?"

"I did. It's a long story."

CHAPTER 23

Some battles are better lost than won. Madlenka should have remembered that, because—Heaven knew—recently the battles between her and her mother had outnumbered the stars. Few with Petr and even fewer with Father, but Mother! At the slightest provocation, they went at it like Crusaders and Saracens.

No! Madlenka refused to undress to be inspected. She was a virgin, she would be a virgin on her wedding night, and she would prove it with the traditional blood spot. Until then, Dowager Countess Edita would have to take her word for it and so would the despicable, insufferable Anton Magnus. She knew instinctively that in his brother's place, Wulfgang would not care whether she was a virgin or not. It would never occur to him to ask. Admittedly she would very likely have jumped into bed with him that morning if he had suggested such a thing, but he hadn't, so it was nobody else's business.

The countess insisted, loudly. Madlenka threatened to tear her eyes out if she tried. The countess threatened to call for help from Neomi and Ivana, her closest cronies. Madlenka swore she would tear their eyes out also, and if they jointly overpowered her now she would excecate all three of them later, two eyeballs at a time.

Moreover, she would take the first opportunity to dispose of the hymenal evidence so that the outrage would do them no good in the long run. The countess slapped her. Madlenka slapped her right back.

It was regrettable that Anton had mentioned Wulfgang, because he had to be discussed and described. *Only three days* Madlenka had known him? And she thought she was in love? Absurd! The countess poured scorn. Love within three days was mere infantile delusion. Love was something that grew and ripened within a marriage, not a passing fit of juvenile lust. As for falling for a penniless younger son . . . A man of eighteen was barely out of swaddling clothes. No rank, no lands, no prospects? Not even a squire, a varlet? An esquire, practically a serf! Madlenka struck her mother again.

At the end of an hour, a truce was declared. Both parties were exhausted and disheveled, but Edita accepted her daughter's oath, sworn on the Holy Bible, that she was still a virgin. Also, that her contact with the despicable debaucher, Wulfgang, had been limited to one brief kiss, with their mouths closed.

"We didn't know it could be done otherwise," Madlenka said sadly, and that almost started the battle again.

She had won it, though, which turned out to be a mistake. Having recovered their poise, they went in search of the count to reassure him on the vital question of his betrothed's virtue. He was closeted with Bishop Ugne, so they were refused admittance. They spent another hour in the solar, glaring at each other in silence.

When they were at last conducted to Petr's room, the new count's temporary chamber, they found him still resting on the bed but looking ominously pleased with himself.

"I am relieved to inform you, my lord," Edita proclaimed, "that your suspicions about my daughter were baseless. Not that I ever feared otherwise, not for a moment."

"I am delighted to hear it, my lady. And I have good news for both of you. The lord bishop and I discussed this unusual situation at length over some wine. We agreed that it would be unseemly and irreverent to hold a formal wedding so soon after the funerals. On the other hand, the king's command makes no mention of delay. His Reverence agrees with me, therefore, that a discreet handfasting would satisfy the spirit of the royal edict, as he put it, without disrespect to the letter. As long as we say suitable vows before witnesses, we shall be married in the eyes of Mother Church. Her formal, public blessing can follow at a more appropriate time."

Madlenka muttered, "Oh, no!"

"Oh, yes," the count said, beaming. "We must all do our duty and be true to our allegiance, no matter how it may conflict with our personal desires."

"I entirely agree!" said the countess.

That was when Madlenka realized that winning the battle had lost her the war. Handfasting was an antique, obsolescent custom that hung on only in remote areas where a priest might not be available in time to bless an imminent union in time for it to be holy matrimony instead of sinful fornication. It was unheard of among the nobility, and the countess would normally have rejected the suggestion with outrage. But a formal wedding during double mourning would be even more scandalous. A private handfasting would solve the Madlenka problem admirably.

Count and dowager countess waited expectantly for Madlenka to comment.

She had no defense left. She had promised Wulf that she would wait for him for forty days, but to mention that would make matters much, much worse. To hint that she suspected him of having supernatural powers would be calamitous. To protest that she had known Anton for barely three days would just prompt her mother to remark yet again that *she* had first met her future husband on the day before their wedding. To defy the king, her legal guardian, would result in a one-way trip along Sprosty Street to the Poor Claires' convent, there to await His Majesty's pleasure.

She could not defy the king, the cardinal, the bishop, the count, and her mother all at once. *Oh, Wulf, Wulf! I tried!*

"As it pleases my lord," she whispered. "But your wound, my lord? Should you not be resting?"

Anton beamed. "I assure you I have never felt better. I have completely recovered my strength. Now, the bishop suggested suitable words. Who shall we call in as witnesses, Lady Edita?"

"Now?" Madlenka said. "You mean to do this awful thing right away?"

That was exactly what he meant.

There followed a brief ceremony of joining hands and swearing fidelity, a quiet supper for two, and, right after that, Anton solved her virginity problem.

CHAPTER 24

Wulf's first problem was clothes. He was still wearing remnants of Petr Bukovany's wardrobe, which were annoyingly long in the legs and sleeves and flatteringly tight across the chest and shoulders. He had assumed that some of the castoffs he had left behind at Dobkov a month ago would still be around, but they had all gone to the servants or been reassembled as something else. Branka skillfully measured him in all directions and organized a make-do sewing session among the female staff who normally made the family's clothes. The kitchen was happy to provide the second half of a meal he had started some hundreds of miles away, and about fifty adults and children had to mob him and make him welcome.

They all wanted to know where Anton was, what had happened to Wulf's face, why he had come back, if he was going to stay long. The adult servants were too respectful to ask outright, and quickly hushed the children who did. Father Czcibor, the cadaverous but kindly castle chaplain, was content to wait and hear it in private. Truth be told, it felt very good to be home and to be somebody again after being nobody in Mauvnik.

But after an hour or so, when Otto had managed to

dispose of the steward and his helpers, there came the tricky moment. Wulf had to explain that he would very much prefer to tell his story to Otto alone. Branka raised her painted eyebrows very high at that. Father Czcibor lowered his feathery ones, and a winter chill descended, but Otto backed him up.

So shutters were closed, candles lit, and the two brothers settled down in the familiar old solar with a crackling fire and two flagons of Dobkov's best vintage. Their only companion, Whitetail, curled up at his master's feet and went to sleep as Wulf began to talk. In the long years of Father's last illness, Otto had naturally taken over as head of the family. Otto was completely loyal. He would support Wulf even against the Church's wrath, if he had to.

It was very late and the candles were low when Wulf finished, having revealed everything except his broken heart, which was the crux of the problem. That tragedy was too painful and too hopeless to discuss. He feared that even Otto, who had accepted his claims of miracles without a blink, would not believe that a man could find the love of his life at first glance. Both Dante and Petrarch had done so, but they weren't around to help with any heartrending verses. And Wulf was no poet.

"That's all?"

Wulf laughed ruefully and refilled his cup. "Isn't it enough?"

"No. Who are these Voices? Angels or devils? Who are you that they Speak to you? And what else can we do to help Anton? More wine?"

The answers took the best part of an hour. At the end of it, Otto took up the wine flagon again, but then just sat back, holding it and staring into the fire, thinking. One of the candles flickered and went out. The shadows moved in. Suddenly he said, "Throw another log on," and filled Wulf's cup. "So, in effect, you can do anything you want?"

"No!" Wulf said uneasily. "I have to ask. I have to ask aloud. Seems that in anything involving other people, I have to be close to them. I had to be close to Anton before they would heal his wound." He had not mentioned the curious glimpse he had been given of Otto negotiating in his counting room.

"Mm," Otto said. "Can you force people to obey you? Or change their minds for them?"

Wulf pulled a face. "I don't know. Don't want to know."

"Remember Great-aunt Kristina, the abbess?"

"No."

"Of course. I was very young the last time she came visiting. You wouldn't even have been born. In his last months, Father told me many stories he wanted recorded in the family chronicle, things that it would have been dangerous to write earlier. Kristina was a Speaker. She entered a convent voluntarily and, so far as Father knew, the Church never learned of her powers. She certainly kept them quiet. But she strongly believed that the Voices came from Heaven."

He sipped wine for a moment, pondering. "Some years ago, in France, there was a girl known as La Pucelle. Ever heard of her?"

"Vaguely."

"*La Pucelle* just means 'the Maid.' Her name was Joan, usually known as Joan of Arc. She was an illiterate shepherd girl who heard Voices. War had turned France into a desert. You can't imagine how bad the situation was. Branka's grandsire was there, fighting for the Burgundians, and saw it all. People were starving, living under hedges, resorting to cannibalism. It wasn't just the English, although no one could resist their bowmen. The duke of Burgundy was making war too, because he wanted the throne, and the rightful heir, called the Dauphin, couldn't get himself crowned because the duke held Rheims, where coronations were always held. Every time there was a battle, the French lost. The countryside had been ravaged so often and so many cities sacked that the Dauphin didn't even have the tax income to pay an army. By 1428 or so, he was at the end of his rope. He controlled no more than fragments of the country, with enemies closing in all around. The English were besieging the city of Orleans, and if that fell he would have almost nothing left.

"Enter this ignorant, uneducated girl, aged about seventeen. She gets herself to where the Dauphin is and says her Voices have sent her to take command of the French army. He thinks that sounds like a good idea and appoints her. You believe that?"

Wulf laughed. "No. I don't believe she would be allowed within two bowshots of a crown prince in the middle of a war."

Otto smiled at the crackling logs. "Yet it happened. He received her, listened, and believed. He had her examined by a panel of clerics, but in the end he gave her the army. It sounds to me as if that young lady had all the powers you have and was unscrupulous enough, or desperate enough, to use them to change a few men's minds. She turned out to be one of the greatest generals since Caesar. She remade the army—no camp followers, no swearing or cursing, lots of hymn-singing. The army was transformed, inspired. It raised the siege of Orleans. Every time it met the English now, it won. But then Joan was captured by the Burgundians, who sold her to the

English. The English put her on trial and convicted her of heresy."

That made no sense at all. "How?" Wulf said. "Why didn't her Voices rescue her from jail?"

"I don't know. That's something you must try to find out. Why didn't they rescue her when the English tied her to a stake? The English burned her, then burned her remains twice more and threw the ashes in the river."

"The first time would be the worst," Wulf grumbled, reaching for the wine flagon.

"But I heard recently that the Holy Father reopened the case and decided that her conviction had been an error. That didn't do her much good in this world, I grant you, but the Church did admit that it had made a mistake. Now listen! According to Father, Great-aunt Kristina used to hint that the Church doesn't want saints, not live ones. Dead ones can't argue, and people collect bits of them as holy souvenirs, but living saints who go around performing miracles could be embarrassing or even dangerous. Suppose they disagree with official doctrine and preach heresy? What if they call the pope names and denounce the Church as corrupt? Which it is, of course. Saints can perform miracles and the pope can't, so which one would you believe?"

Wulf had never heard Otto speak like this before. "There already is a St. Wolfgang. One is plenty."

Another candle went out.

"I'm serious, chaffhead," Otto said. "You told me that your Voices have warned you of danger and won't tell you what it is."

"They never answer questions like that."

"I just answered it for you. The Church doesn't want miracles, so it calls what you're doing witchcraft, acts of Satan. It's all about power, Wulf, worldly power. You are a threat to the authority of the pope and the bishops. But if Cardinal Zdenek believed that you were an agent of Satan, he would never have dared use you. It wasn't *Anton* the Spider wanted, it was you."

Wulf nodded. "He had to take Anton because I'm only a kid."

"You're not a kid anymore."

"But Anton's ten feet tall, ruts like a goat, and beats men's brains out with his mustache."

"So he's your puppet. You are the one the cardinal really hired."

Wulf sniggered. He knew that Otto had been deliberately plying him with wine, and he was also very weary. "I don't fancy telling Anton that!"

But Otto had struck to the heart of the problem, as usual, and now it was time to explain to him that Zdenek had not divided the rewards fairly. Yet Wulf still could not bring himself to talk about his love for Madlenka.

After waiting a moment, Otto sighed. "Back in the year Father died, a month or so after Marek was taken away, the Hartmannovas had a knighting celebration for Cousin Hans. Remember?"

"No." That year Wulf had been twelve and fighting his own problems—strange noises and lights and the gnawing terror that he was growing up to be a Speaker like Marek.

"I went in Father's stead, because he was too ill to travel. On the first night they held a ball and the first dance was a saltarello. There was a girl . . . every time we passed, our eyes met. When the dance was over I dragged my host through the crowd to her and had him introduce us. That was the end of the ball for both of us. We just sat in a corner and talked. Her name was Branka."

Wulf swallowed a lump in his throat. "Am I so childishly obvious?"

His brother laughed. "Your eyes melted when you mentioned the beautiful heiress, but after that one time you ignored her, except to say that you think you healed her mother. Tell me about her."

"There are no words. Her name is Madlenka. She's glorious. Out of this world. Angelic. Clever, witty, feisty, mischievous . . ."

"Did you tell her that you love her?"

"And she loves me! I never knew it could happen so fast."

Otto snapped his fingers. "Like that! I spoke with Branka's parents the next day and when we got around to talking about dowry, I accepted their first offer. Branka and I have never regretted our marriage for a minute. But it doesn't always have a happy ending, Wulf. Does Anton know?"

"*No!*" Wulf soaked in his misery for a few minutes, and finally said, "Anton wouldn't *care*! If it has two legs and no crotch bulge, then he doesn't *care* what face it wears."

"Like Vlad—two nights is a long-term relationship. You're like me, lad; you don't keep your heart in your codpiece. I'm sure Anton would happily let you have her if she was any ordinary wench. But she isn't, Wulf. She's the key to his castle, a ward of the king, and any nonsense will land you in more trouble than you can imagine."

"I know that, thank you. Not that I care about me. Only her."

"Her, too. Oh, saints! You've really been hit hard, haven't you? Cupid's filled you plumb full of arrows. I'm sorry, Wulf, I really am. So tomorrow you plan to hand Anton's letter to the cardinal, in person, and tell him you want the girl as your share?"

Wulf nodded. Coming from Otto it sounded even crazier than it had seemed before: suicide, self-immolation. Before he could say so, the last candle smoked and died, leaving only firelight. Otto heaved himself to his feet.

"Time to go. I am enormously proud of what you and Anton have done, Wulf. I'm humbled, honestly. No Magnus in three centuries has come close. One day your exploits will be added to the family chronicle in letters of gold, I promise you. And tomorrow, we'll decide how I can best help you both."

He took a new candle from the box on the mantel and lit it. He put it in a candlestick and handed it to Wulf, giving him a clap on the shoulder. "You're half asleep. To bed. Sleep well, Sir Wulfgang."

"There has been a mistake, my lord. I am Wulfgang Magnus, esquire."

"You have proved yourself worthy of knighthood. Battle honors are no less worthy if they must be kept secret. Come along."

Alerted by some guardian instinct, Whitetail awoke, heaved himself to his paws, and led the way to the door.

Wulf was to sleep in the main guest room, which was large by castle standards, but cold and musty. Many great lords and even royalty had slept there over the centuries, and the walls bore frescoes of their arms, some crude, some crafted in exact detail, some old and faded or even overlapped by newer work. A single candle flame did little to flatter them. He blew it out and set the candlestick on the table by the bed. Shivering, he stripped and slid in under the quilts. If one believed Otto's flattery, he was not unworthy of his surroundings.

CHAPTER 25

Neither armored foe nor the dawn screams of roosters could penetrate the walls of Castle Dobkov. Flunkies out in the bailey could stoke ovens, thresh rye, or crank the windlass on the well without being heard inside.

Regrettably, female servants slept in the attics. They arose with the roosters and the ancient floor beams creaked. Ottokar angrily pulled the quilt over his ear, trying to will himself back to sleep. Warm, soft arms embraced him. The tendency for occupants to collect in the middle was both the joy and the curse of a feather bed.

"You're awake," Branka murmured.

He said, "No."

"So what's the news that kept you tossing and turning all night?"

He abandoned hope of more sleep and rolled over to join in the hugging. "As far as the staff is concerned, Anton is betrothed to the only daughter of the late Count Bukovany and the first installment of her dowry will pay Vlad's ransom—Wulf delivered it. That happens to be true, which is useful. Father Czcibor can arrange a thanksgiving Mass for Sunday."

She said, "Mmph. No more?"

"Not for Father Czcibor."

He felt her mood change instantly. "Wulf's started Speaking?"

"How did you know about that? I never told you about it."

She chuckled and squeezed him tighter. "No, you didn't, but the senior servants all know. I arrived just after Marek was taken, remember, and they knew that something would trouble young Wulf at times, and he would run off to the church to pray, all by himself. A few of them even remembered one of your father's aunts being 'strange.' Father Czcibor remarked to me once, just after we were married, that as long as Speakers didn't answer the Voices they heard, then they were resisting temptation and were good Christians. I guessed that he meant Wulf."

"It's your brains that make me love you."

"This is a recent change."

"After the Dominicans took Marek away, Father made us all swear not to tell anyone about Wulf. So I couldn't tell you, and I didn't want to burden you, anyway. You'll forgive me?"

"Of course. You were right. I didn't know; I was just guessing. But now he's started?"

Otto had always feared that Wulf wouldn't be able to resist Speaking once he escaped out into the world. Damn Anton for tricking him into it, just to impress the court! That was typical of Anton. Had the positions been reversed and Wulf had tried something like that on Anton—not that Wulf ever would—Anton would have turned his back and let him go ahead and break his stupid neck.

"I'm afraid so. It was Anton's fault."

"And they've quarreled?"

Otto took time to consider. "I don't think so, not yet. But they may, and we mustn't let it happen. They've done amazing things, but they're in way over their heads, deeper than hell's cellar." He hesitated and then mentioned the other problem because he never willingly kept secrets from Branka. "Wulf got injured on the journey somehow, although his Voices cured him later. Cardinal Zdenek had ordered Anton to marry the late count's daughter. That would be fine by Anton, confirm his claim to the coronet. Stupidly, though, he ordered her to care for Wulf while he was disabled."

"Oh, no! Not Wulfgang! He didn't!"

"It isn't a matter of doing, I'm sure. But it is a matter of wanting to. On both sides, apparently. Of course it would never have occurred to Anton that those two were both in highly stressed situations. Wulf is terrified that he's sold his soul to the devil, she had just lost her father, mother, and brother and was ordered to marry a man she's never even heard of. When you think about it, what happened was almost inevitable. They grabbed at each other like drowning sailors."

"So you think you're going to ride off and help them?"

"My love, I have no choice. This is for no one but you, understand?"

"I swear."

"It's war! The Wends' vanguard has crossed the border. Anton was wounded and would have died if Wulf's Voices had not saved him—for the second time in three days. The main army is sure to follow. Jorgarian forces are weeks or months away and the only defense Jorgary has at the moment is a castle under the command of Anton Magnus, twenty years old and never seen a battle."

Branka whispered a Hail Mary. Otto said, "Amen."

She sighed. "When will you leave?" She was a worthy warrior's wife.

"This morning Wulf and I'll go on a brotherly outing, visit a few of the tenants. Hint that he has been having thoughts about a certain girl, if you must. We should be back before nightfall. After that . . . I don't know. For as long as I'm needed."

"You have time to say goodbye, big bull."

Otto found his brother in the lesser hall, again being mobbed by the staff and giving every indication of enjoying it, which he probably wasn't. The jabber died away as the baron approached. He announced the limited story about Sir Vladislav's ransom, which was loudly cheered. He added that he and Wulf were going to go riding that morning. He glanced across the table.

"We'll leave as soon as we can, Wulf?"

Wulf nodded with a smile that did not quite reach his wolfish eyes.

The brothers had no chance for a private chat before they rode out across the drawbridge together, Wulf on Copper and Otto astride his old favorite, Balaam, who was past any serious exertion but steady enough not to panic when Wulf started Speaking miracles. The sun was bright on golden leaves and warm for late September.

They left a lot of puzzled retainers behind them. When the baron went hunting, he took a retinue of beaters, hawkers, huntsmen, foresters, and kennel men. Going visiting, he would never venture forth without a train of at least forty men-at-arms. If he and his brother were merely planning an amble around the environs of the castle, why did they need to take such fat bundles with them, and why had they insisted that the baggage be attached to their horses' saddles, instead of loaded on a packhorse? He was behaving very oddly.

Wulf was puzzled, too. "What's the plan, Brother Baron?" he asked as they crossed the bridge. "What's in the bags?"

"My court clothes, mostly. And if anything goes wrong, I'll have to journey home the hard way."

The kid frowned. "Nothing should go wrong."

"Good. First you miracle us to Mauvnik. How long will that take?"

Wulf pointed to a hawk spiraling down out of the sky. His finger tracked it down until it vanished in weeds at the edge of the pasture and some anonymous rodent died. "About that long."

"Oh!" Otto wondered if he had overestimated Balaam's impassivity. "Secondly, we redeem the scrip for gold. The Medici agent there knows me. If Vlad tried to turn it into cash in Bavaria, it would take months."

Wulf chuckled. "We never thought of that! Old Jurbarkas should have warned us. He's Anton's seneschal, decent but doddery. Then what? We call on the cardinal?"

His tone of voice suggested he was ready to argue. Wulf had changed. He was not the same boy who had ridden away with Anton a month ago, two youths going forth to seek their fortunes. Anton must have changed also. They would not be human otherwise, after what they had been through already. And Wulf must guard his secret very closely now. If the cardinal decided that his Speaker helper had served his purpose and become a potential cause for scandal, he would betray him. The Bible said, "Put not your trust in princes."

The horses entered the coppice, where the air was

cooler. With no one overlooking them, this would be a good setting for a miracle.

"It would be safer if I called on the cardinal instead of you," Otto said. "You are vulnerable. I met Zdenek once, years ago. Father presented me to him. He wasn't a cardinal then. He won't remember me, but my title should get me in to see him." The Magnus name alone should, under present circumstances.

"While I take two thousand florins south to Bavaria?"

"Yes. And bring back Vlad."

They rode on for a moment. Then calculating golden eyes turned on Otto again. "I don't have to tell him that Anton is now a count, do I? Please?"

Otto laughed aloud. "Brother, I have sorely missed you this last month! I'd suggest you chain him down first."

Wulf grinned. "I'll let you tell him. His face should be worth every florin. Ready for me to Speak?"

Otto dug in his knees and shortened the reins. "Go ahead."

"You must stay close to me. That's vital." Wulf turned his head the other way and addressed empty air, "Holy Saints Helena and Victorinus, hear my prayer." Pause. "First, would you heal the bruises on my face, please, so I don't look so gruesome? Thank you." He glanced around to enjoy Otto's reaction when he saw that the black-eye bruises had gone. "And now, dear Saints, would you please move us directly through limbo to Mauvnik?"

The world became a silent, silvery mist. Balaam screamed in terror and reared. Otto grabbed the pommel of his saddle and clung tight with his thighs. Balaam bolted along the foggy trail, and now nothing was solid except Wulf and Copper, racing along at their side.

Balaam skidded to a halt and tried bucking again like a two-year-old. Eventually the old courser steadied, more from exhaustion than his rider's direction, but for a few moments it had been Wulf's horsemanship that had kept the two mounts close together, not Otto's.

He said, "Sorry! I was a little too sudden with that." He looked very innocent, but there was a devilish gleam in his eye. The world hadn't beaten all the boy out of him yet.

"When in Mauvnik, stay at the Bacchus" had been a family motto for generations. Otto was greeted with joyful deference and polite inquiries about "the hardships of my lord's journey." Wulf was welcomed back, having spent one night there a month ago.

If all went well, there would be no need to overnight in Mauvnik, but Otto needed a place to change. With Vlad's ransom in hand at last, he was freed from the penny-pinching of the last two years, so he demanded a private room, no sharing, with two beds if possible—most travelers were happy to sleep three or four to a bed. He also wanted a boy to guard the baggage when he and Wulf were absent, hay and fresh straw for the horses, and the room to be cleaned and ready within twenty minutes. The landlord promised everything he asked.

With Wulf playing valet, Otto shed his traveling clothes and changed into city wear. Leaving their room guarded by the grubby-faced youth they had hired, the brothers reclaimed their mounts and rode off up the hill to Upper Mauvnik. Even in the capital, they did not venture out without their sabers.

The local Medici agent did his business in his home

near the palace in a street so grand that it was both paved and wide enough for two wagons to pass. It was also less fouled with garbage and horse dung than most. Servants came running to take the horses and escort the noble baron indoors to meet the illustrious bankers. An effort was made to store Wulfgang in the basement with the menials while the oily Italian gentlemen discussed money upstairs with Otto, but Otto insisted that he attend. This gave the lad an hour's instruction in how little he would enjoy a career in banking, watching shiny coins being weighed and tallied, and listening to shop talk about the grape harvest. Otto wondered if his brother was noticing how skillfully the bankers questioned him. They would forward the information they gained to Medici headquarters in Florence, to add to the vast store of intelligence that the bank amassed from all over Christendom.

Vladislav had been given quarter, which meant that his captor must be reimbursed for two years' food and board. Otto had brought a pouch containing another sixty florins to add to Anton's two thousand. He did not explain why the money was needed and nobody was crass enough to ask.

It was close to terce before the brothers emerged in the stable yard, Otto carrying a stout leather bag containing sixteen pounds of gold. Not wanting to try vaulting into the saddle with this burden, he handed it up to Wulf, who whistled at the weight.

"I could stun a robber with this."

"Don't lose it. Come to think of it, I must be crazy, entrusting it to you. You used to be very good at losing things."

"I hadn't been gone a month when I lost my heart."

But not his virginity, Otto guessed. The small talk died, and the brothers smiled uneasily. The moment of double peril had come and they must part.

"I'd best hurry and find a comfortable chair in the Spider's web," Otto said, "in case I have to spend the rest of the day there. You remember where Baron Emilian lives?"

"Castle Orel."

"Bavaria's a big place. Do you know how to find it?"

Wulf gave him an odd look. "I just have to ask, Otto."

Jesus save us! Even the whirlwind ride from Dobkov had not impressed Otto as much as those simple words. What had his baby brother become? Marek might have exactly the same powers, but Marek was a peace-loving scholar. Wulf had more of the warrior Magnus blood in him; a lightning-bolt temper hid behind his easygoing manner. Would his saints rein him in if he tried to use his powers too hastily?

"Then I don't even need to wish you safe journey, but I'll do it anyway. I'll see you at the Bacchus when we both get back there."

"And I wish you a safe return as well, Brother Baron. It was good to come home and be made welcome, even if it's only for a very short time." Wulf wheeled his horse and took off at a slow walk along the grand street.

Ottokar Magnus knew where the palace stabled visitors' mounts and how to find the bureaucrats' wing where the work of government was done. His title and the impressive document he bore were enough to gain him admittance to the cardinal's anteroom, which was already crowded with petitioners. Two years had passed since he last graced the royal palace with his presence, when he came to beg for a royal grant to help ransom Vlad. Then he had been one of many on the same quest, and he had gotten no farther than he was now; even Vlad's warrior reputation had failed to win a hearing from His Eminence. This time, Otto had come on behalf of the baby of the family, and his chances of being admitted were considerably better. He found that amusing, although Vlad would not.

He strolled across the marble floor, noting rustic aristocracy like himself in their shabby hand-me-downs amid lawyers, burghers, and courtiers flaunting the latest styles. The points on some of the shoes were so long that they had to be chained up to their wearers' knees. Liripipes, the stupid tails attached to men's hoods, had grown until they were wrapped around the head like turbans. There were no women present to compare, only men, some standing, some sitting, and all of them wanting something that they probably shouldn't get. How did Zdenek stand it, day after day for a lifetime? Did he just enjoy the power to grant or deny? Didn't it pall eventually, even on the son of a butcher, which is what he was?

The chancellor at the desk beside the door to the sanctum was a friar in Franciscan brown, and a flock of bored novices perched nearby, waiting to carry messages. The friar looked up at the visitor with a studied smile of welcome.

Otto introduced himself and the sender of the letter he bore.

The cleric's smile curdled. He held out an ink-stained hand for the letter.

Otto retained it. "I must deliver this personally to the cardinal."

Stalemate. "If Your Lordship would be so gracious as

to take a seat for just a few minutes, I am sure His Eminence will be happy to accord you an audience very promptly." That meant an hour or two.

"His Eminence is most gracious." Otto turned away and was annoyed to see two men obviously trying to catch his eye. Almost certainly they were comrade knights from his campaigning days, but for the life of him he couldn't remember their names or where he had met them. He smiled and began wandering in their direction. He did not get far before a treble voice spoke at his shoulder.

"Baron Magnus? His Eminence will see you right away."

The two knights were too far away to overhear, but they could guess at the words and were staring as if the last trump had just sounded. With a shrug to indicate how disappointed he was at not being able to chat with them, Otto turned and followed the novice to the door of the inner sanctum.

Twenty years ago the Scarlet Spider had been a mere clerk, reticent and obsequious, his working quarters cramped and dingy. Now the center of his web shone in an obscene display of gold and crystal to proclaim his greatness. So much opulence made Otto feel slightly ill. The years had taken their toll of the old man. His beard and eyebrows were white, his fingers knobbed, and his smile displayed long teeth when he offered his cardinal's ring for the visitor to kiss. If he were a garment, he would be regarded as threadbare. Nevertheless, he flaunted the red hat and robes of a prince of the Church and his chair was just high enough to register as a throne. Not bad for a butcher's son.

"My lord baron, it is good to see you again. You didn't heed my warning, I see."

Otto straightened up. "I recall no warning, Your Eminence."

"Did I not tell you that if you grew any bigger you would become a very easy target?" He laughed. "No, I do not remember our conversation either, but that's what I always say to oversized youths, and my notes tell me that it was twenty years ago when your father brought you to court."

"I remember you, Your Eminence."

"I was more of a foothill than an eminence then. You have a letter for me?"

"I have a letter from my brother the count addressed to His Majesty." Otto held it out. The only other person present, a plump, fussy little Franciscan with a patch over one eye, came around his shoulder and took it, broke the seal with a knife, and handed it to Zdenek. He then pulled over one of the lesser chairs for Otto.

"Bring a goblet of wine for the baron, Brother Daniel. You will give me your opinion of the vintage, my lord, and how it compares with your own renowned Dobkov reds. Pray excuse me while I read His Majesty's mail."

Brother Daniel brought Otto wine and then retired to a desk behind the door, not easily visible from where Otto had been seated.

The cardinal's throne put his back to the light, which helped his reading, no doubt, but also shadowed his expression. He lowered the letter. "Incredible! Your brothers have done far better than I ever dared hope. Blood will out, as they say. Your family has long been a bulwark of the Jorgarian throne, my lord."

"Your Eminence is kind." The Zdeneks had butchered cattle and the Magnuses had butchered men.

The cardinal leaned back in his chair and chewed his

lip for a moment. He had conspicuously not asked how a letter dated the day before had arrived so incredibly fast, and he had spoken of *brothers*, plural, not of a man-at-arms and his varlet. Normally a varlet would not be mentioned at all.

"Why did the *landsknechte* run away, do you suppose?"

"I do not know, Eminence. The person who brought that letter did not know either; he mentioned a possible disagreement over pay, which I find strange. Count Anton is young and inexperienced, but he is not an idiot. He needed those troops like he needs lungs."

Zdenek nodded. "You are experienced in military matters, my lord. Tell a humble cleric what happens next in this forthcoming attack." His pretense of humility might have been intended to amuse, but even without the mask of shadow, his face would never be readable unless he wanted it to be.

"If Castle Gallant is as good as its reputation, even a beginner like my brother should be able to hold off the foe for a month or two. That may be long enough, because the Wends will be sleeping in tents, in the mountains, in winter. Neither men nor horses prosper in snow. I would not expect them to dig in for a long siege, especially as the lake that is their way home will start freezing soon. They cannot bypass the fort to impose a true siege, so they cannot starve it out. Your Eminence's reinforcements will arrive . . . when?"

The old man shrugged resignedly. "I have been promised some lancers and mounted archers, not many, and they cannot be there for at least another month. Even forty days may be optimistic. Gallant has always been considered impregnable. Is it still?"

Otto's grandfathers would have said yes. Father might

have done. "No. When Constantinople fell, we learned that nowhere is impregnable anymore, and the years since have confirmed that. If this bombard they call the Dragon is as large as my informant thinks it is, then the only question is whether the Wends can wrestle it in over a mountain trail."

The cardinal nodded. "It was made by the gunsmiths of Sweden, the best in Christendom, and is reported to throw three-hundred-pound balls for more than a mile."

"Then Gallant will fall."

"If the Wends can get the monster emplaced." The old man raised white tufts of eyebrow inquiringly.

So began the bargaining. "Of course. But who is to stop them? The obvious defense is to sally and try to seize the bombard itself and spike it, but Anton does not have enough troops to do that."

The old man's eyelids drooped slyly. "You have other brothers. If His Majesty was so generous to one who had yet to achieve anything, do you doubt that he will richly reward another after he has saved the entire country from rapine?"

He meant Wulfgang, but Otto was not without experience in negotiating.

"Possibly Your Eminence refers to my brother Vladislav? He hates to be left out of a good fight."

Zdenek produced a cynical smile as easily as if he had pulled it out of a pocket. "I gambled a county because His Majesty was about to lose it anyway. I doubt if I can afford two more. Titles, yes. Stars and ribbons, by all means. I am sure Sir Vladislav has military experience that his younger brothers lack, but he can do little by himself and I see no practical means of bringing in effective reinforcements for him to direct."

Of course not. Wulf would certainly not transport

men he could not trust to keep his secret, so only Vlad could be brought in. Besides, other men would not fight for a man they must consider a servant of the devil. It was Vlad or nobody—except possibly Otto himself, but he need not decide that until he knew what Vlad was willing to do.

Now the cardinal was frowning and drumming fingers on the arm of his chair impatiently. "Brother Daniel, see how many more petitioners are waiting and warn the chancellor that we may have to take a recess."

The friar rose and departed without a word. The moment the door closed and the two men were alone, Zdenek leaned forward and spoke more urgently. "The following conversation will never happen."

"Of course not," Otto agreed.

"Then let us speak freely. You are a soldier. You can bring the Dragon within five miles or so of Cardice by water, but then you must transport the monster over a mountain trail—not steep, I am informed, but muddy and punctuated by bridges and sharp bends. How do you do it?"

"I employ a Speaker, likely the same Speaker who cursed Count Bukovany and his son."

"Quite. And this letter tells me that your brothers have identified him as Father Vilhelmas, an Orthodox priest. Without Satan's help, Duke Wartislaw cannot bring his bombard along that road in the time at his disposal."

"Satan's help, Your Eminence?"

"Certainly. All my enemies work for Satan."

Again Otto could not tell if the old man was serious or joking, but he refused to be intimidated. "Not an implication I want to hear near my family, Eminence. If you cannot send reinforcements to aid my brother the count, can you reinforce the other one? He has achieved wonders so far, but he is young and alone and without experience." Now there was no doubt whom they were discussing, or what his role was.

There was a pause.

"A reasonable request," Zdenek conceded. "It presents some difficulties that I cannot explain in the brief time we have available. Something might be achieved. Such matters should not be written down, so tell him that the password will be 'Greenwood.' He may trust anyone who comes with that word."

"Excellent! There remains the matter of reward."

The cardinal's glare was very gratifying. "Your youngest brother is a Speaker. We both know that, and he gave himself away at the hunt a week ago. Had I realized that he was eighteen, I might have approached him directly, but my records inexplicably indicated that he was only sixteen. Women mature younger, but male Speakers' powers are rarely properly developed at that age. Someone had been shielding him, I suspect. I could not appoint an unknown of sixteen to be a lord of the marches—my action in promoting his brother to the earldom was bizarre enough. I hoped that Wulfgang's aid would help speed his journey to his new post, but I honestly did not expect such a daunting display of power. Who has been training him?"

"No one, I am certain."

"He must have the endurance of a seasoned warrior."

"It is in his blood. He is a Magnus."

"So now he wants to hold His Majesty to ransom, does he? Will a dukedom suffice?"

"He would spurn it," Otto said quickly. "He enjoys

hunting, so a forest of his own might tempt him, but all the duties and responsibilities of a great landowner would not. That is not what he covets."

Younger sons of noble houses were always ravenous for land, honors, and titles. It was largely they who kept Europe roiling in a perpetual state of warfare. Yet the cardinal did not seem surprised to hear of an exception.

"Speakers are not as other men, my lord. Or as other women. The best thing I can offer your Wulfgang is my protection. It is limited. If he starts walking through walls or striking men dead, then the Church will have him and that will be the end of him. As long as he remains discreet, I may be able to persuade the archbishop to turn a blind eye. More than that I cannot promise."

"Your Eminence's assurance is most comforting, but there is more. The little god with the arrows has intervened."

"*Martyrs pity me!*" The old man rolled his eyes at the ceiling. "The daughter? Are you telling me that we may lose this war because of an outbreak of juvenile lust?"

"It would not be the first such mishap since Troy, Eminence."

"No, I suppose it would not." Zdenek leaned back in his chair. "You expect the king to reverse his edict? How bad is it?"

"In Wulfgang's case, life-threatening—and unprecedented. He has never acted like this before. According to his account, the lady returns his ardor. Anton does not know, and probably will not care as long as his claim to the earldom is preserved."

The door opened as Brother Daniel returned. The cardinal straightened up. "Well, they must be discreet. Certain acts are irrevocable, you understand?"

Marriage, for example. Otto nodded. What God had joined together stayed joined together.

"If the castle falls," the Spider said, "the point is moot. If he succeeds, then Jorgary will be deeply in his debt. Meanwhile, I shall report your good news to His Majesty, and you may be assured that the house of Magnus will stand even higher in his favor than it has ever done."

Hopefully that would be higher than where it had stood when it needed to ransom one of its sons.

Otto rose, then knelt to kiss the cardinal's ring. Brother Daniel opened a door for him, but not the one by which he had entered. He walked down a stair and left the palace.

CHAPTER 26

Riding through Mauvnik, Wulf was anxious to consult his Voices, but reluctant to let any of the vendors, pedestrians, or barrow-pullers see him talking to empty space. He had to wait until he was almost at the Bacchus before he found a gap in the traffic.

"Holy Saints, if I ask you, can you take me to Castle Orel, in Bavaria?"

The Light brightened the alley and St. Helena spoke.

—*No.*

"What! Why not?"

No answer, of course. That sort of question they never answered.

But the Light remained, so he tried again. "You took me to Koupel, and you took me to Cardice. And Dobkov, and now Mauvnik. What's different about Bavaria?"

Still no answer, meaning he had to work out the answer for himself. He knew Dobkov intimately and he had seen pictures of Castle Gallant. And the Voices had offered to take him to Marek, not to Koupel.

"Could you take me to my brother Vladislav?"

—*Yes.*

Success! "Thank you, but not right now. Can you tell me where he is and what he is doing?"

—*He is in bed*, Victorinus said.

—*Fornicating*, Helena added.

That did sound like Vlad, although the timing was odd. Nor was it a likely occupation while chained to a cellar wall.

"At this time of day? Has he nothing better to do?"

—*No, he is a captive. But his captor treats him well. He is allowed to abuse servant women.*

Did the girls regard it as abuse, or a welcome break in their working day?

Wulf thanked the Voices and rode into the innyard. He was starting to define limits to their powers. He felt that this must be significant, if he could just see how.

Copper would not be welcome in Vlad's bedroom. Wulf returned him to care of the stable hands, and remembered to take the bag of gold away with him, trying not to tilt sideways too conspicuously as he walked. Upstairs he found the hired boy sitting outside the room, cleaning a basketful of boots.

"You carry on with that," he said as he unlocked the door. "I don't want to be disturbed by anyone except Baron Magnus himself, understand?"

He locked himself in. The room was probably the best in the house, and even two good-sized beds did not clutter it much. Large windows let in plenty of sun, but they were securely barred and not overlooked by any others. Miracle-working should be safe enough here.

"Holy saints," he said very softly. "What is Vlad doing now?"

—*Vladislav has dismissed his companion and is asleep already.*

"Will you take me to him, please?"

A rectangular slice of reality disappeared into darkness. Stepping closer, he smelled different air. There was a door-sized hole there into somewhere else, a dimmer place, and a wind blowing in his face. Gingerly, he stretched out a hand. It did not fall off, but it was in deep shadow.

—*Step through, quickly!*

Wulf obeyed and was plunged into gloom as the doorway behind him closed. A roar of thunder shattered the silence. He ignored it, hoping that the boy in the Bacchus had not heard. Already his eyes had adapted enough to see chinks of light around a shutter. He made his way to it without tripping over anything and opened it, to find himself looking out a window high up in one tower of a many-towered castle, upon a crag surrounded by green forest. In the distance lay a small silver lake flanked by a road that might be the main approach. White mountains lined the skyline. So this was Bavaria, was it?

Another explosion of thunder . . .

He turned to survey a circular and drafty chamber. The four-poster bed in the center almost filled it, leaving only space for a chair, a chest, a commode, and of course the ladder connecting traps in floor and ceiling. A pleasant enough jail, if the supply of servant girls held up.

"Saints, can anyone hear us speak?" Or, Speak.

—*Not at present.*

"Thank you."

Another monstrous snore . . . Why didn't the curtains billow and the tower sway? Wulf took a firm grip on the bed curtain nearest the window and hauled it aside, thereby exposing a mound of quilt like a haystack under snow.

"Vlad! Vlad! Wake up! It's Wulf."

The next snore didn't happen. "Uh?" Vlad mumbled.

"Wake up! It's Wulfgang, your brother."

"Wha—?" The quilt surged up and dropped to expose the top half of Sir Vladislav Magnus, sitting up and blinking.

Wulf had forgotten just how huge the largest Magnus was, and how hairy. His shoulders were thatched. His jaw and brow were massive, and although his hairline was starting to recede, there was little bare skin visible anywhere on his face. Or anywhere else, for that matter. Very few young men wore beards, but his was as huge as everything else about him.

"God be with you, Brother."

"Fires of hell! How did you get here, Wolfcub?"

Wulf put a finger to his lips and whispered, "I Spoke."

His brother glowered ogrishly. "After they took Marek, you swore you'd never do that!"

"And I didn't—not until I had to stop Anton breaking his neck. Once you get started, it's hard to give it up. Like servant girls. Here, Anton sent you this." He dropped the bag on the foothills marking Vlad's thighs—close enough to his crotch to get his attention, but not close enough to damage.

"God's breath! Be careful, boy! What's this?"

"Two thousand florins."

Vlad drew a deep breath. "From *Anton*?"

Despite the forebodings Wulf had jokingly expressed to Otto, he was looking forward to this discussion. "The first installment on his wife's dowry. Baby Anton's been growing up while you've been lazing around here, Sir Vlad. At the moment he is keeper of Castle Gallant, in Cardice, guarding the Silver Road north." He watched the shaggy eyebrows fly up. An honor like that would satisfy Vlad as a worthy reward for a whole lifetime of cleaving and skewering the king's enemies.

"Unfortunately the Pomeranians are invading. Anton doesn't have forces to withstand a long siege and the king can't get reinforcements there before the Wends bring up their wall-smashing cannon. Anton needs your help, Brother. He needs a seasoned warrior like you. He needs you very much and very soon."

Vlad's always-ugly face twisted into something worse. "You are making this up. How did you get here, really?"

"Before God, every word I said is true."

The big man scowled as he thought it through. "And how do I get to Castle Gallant?"

"My Voices will take us."

Vlad crossed himself. "Satanism!"

"If my Voices are evil, why have they saved Anton's life twice in the last week? Anyway, I can tell you everything when we get to Dobkov."

Vlad laughed at him. "Just like that? Am I allowed to put on some clothes first? Emilian isn't here. He won't be back until tonight, probably late. All this money will have to be weighed."

"It's warranted by a Medici seal on the bag."

"Won't matter, sonny. And there's not just me. What about my lance—two squires, a sergeant, and a varlet. You planning to talk the devil into taking all of us?"

"Just you!" Wulf snapped.

"Thought so. Well, they'll have to follow. You brought the money they'll need on the road?"

"You sent them home two years ago." Wulf had forgotten how annoying this brother's twisted humor could be. He seemed to consider it some sort of hazing, and he would probably be doing it to his youngest brother when they were both in their dotage.

"So I did. Just wondering if you remembered. You have the money to cover my quarter the last two years?"

"How much more do you want?"

"About eighty florins ought to cover it."

"*Eighty?* I don't happen to have that much on me."

"You'll have to find it before I can leave here."

"Maybe Anton can get by without you."

"Maybe he'll have to."

Wulf reached out to take back the money bag and a hand the size of a steel gauntlet closed on his wrist; he was helpless in that grip. No matter how hard he tugged, the hand did not budge.

"Well, Wolfcub? You haven't answered my question."

For a moment the brothers just stared at each other. The big man had never been known for his courtly manners, and now that he was learning how two junior brothers had lapped him during his captivity he must be feeling especially vicious. Wulf wondered uneasily if Vlad was truly someone he should entrust with his big secret.

"Why don't you grow a beard, Wolfcub? Or can't you, yet?"

"Why don't you write a note for the rest of the money, or doesn't he trust you? Ow! That hurts!"

The big man released his wrist. "It was meant to. All right, I'll talk to Emilian tomorrow and see how much he wants."

"Otto added another sixty florins. What do the servant girls charge?"

Anger bristled the great beard. "You been spying on me?"

"No, but when I asked my Voices what you were doing a little while ago, they told me."

"That's a pretty handy trick. You going to stay the night?"

"No. What time tomorrow? Terce? Can you be up that early?"

Vlad scowled. "Could be ready then, or at least I'll know if I can't come."

"Then I'll ride up to the front door about terce. I don't want to meet anyone or see anyone. You ride out to meet me. If anyone else appears, then I'll be gone and you can stay here and rot."

"For a beardless brat, you give a lot of orders to your seniors."

"Victorinus, take me to the inn." Wulf spun around and stepped into a blaze of sunlight. The mystic doorway closed behind him. Screwing up his eyes against the brightness, he laughed. He wished he could see Vlad's face right then, but imagining it was almost as good.

Obviously Otto had not yet returned from the palace. That left Wulf the choice of wasting his appetite by eating his dinner in the inn, or stretching out on a bed to wait for him.

Hunger won. He went down to the dining room, which was dark and packed tight with plank tables and benches, but he was happily surprised to see how crowded the place was. The food might not be good, but it must be better than the Bacchus's competitors'. He found an empty space on a bench and paid the wench half a silver penny for water to wash his hands, a flagon of wine, and a trencher of four-day-old bread. He proceeded to heap the trencher with slices of salt pork, fresh boiled mutton, rye bread, and spoonfuls of onion sauce and beans. He had barely put his knife back in his belt before Otto squeezed in beside him.

"Much as expected," he said, smiling. "Promises, no more."

"Same with me. I have to go back for him at terce tomorrow."

There were too many other people at their table and directly behind them to say more about important matters. They could speak only in generalities.

"How long," Wulf asked, "until our other brother gets some company?"

Shrug. "My friend said maybe forty days."

"Why so *long*? The boy Gintaras rode here in eight days!"

Otto grinned in an affectionate, big-brotherly way. "First he has to find the money, and no king ever has enough money. Then find men. He won't send the regiments, because they have to stay and guard the capital. If he does, they have to be replaced here. Either he must find mercenaries or call up a feudal levy. September is the worst possible time to muster levies. Is the mutton as tough as it looks?"

"Tougher. The pork is good and lardy, though, and there's lots of honey and raisins in the frumenty."

Otto cut a slice of pork with his knife and spooned some of the thick wheat porridge onto his trencher. "It's not just time from here to there that counts. It's couriers from here to the countryside, then men from the countryside back to here, then on to where you need them. Mercenaries are moving into winter quarters, the lords are away hunting so they can have salt venison in the winter, and even when they get the summons, they don't want to take their men from the fields and vineyards.

"Meanwhile the quartermaster has to find horses and tack, oxen and wagons, victuals, fodder, tentage, bows and arrows, guns, powder and shot, horseshoes and nails, blacksmiths, farriers, saddlers, anvils, carters, and fletchers and bowyers. Some of these are certain to be almost impossible to find, but you never know which will be lacking this time. Officers want attendants, heralds, secretaries, and cooks; the men want women and priests, in that order. If Mauvnik can even get such a force moving within forty days, it'll be a miracle.

"And the journey itself will be a teeth-grinding business. Armies often make only three or four miles a day. Winter days are short; they can't start before dawn, and they need daylight to pitch camp. Trails can divide or disappear altogether in the forest, and if it rains they become mud pits. Rivers in flood wash away ferries and bridges; they drown the fords and turn the water meadows into marshlands for a mile on either side of them. Don't even think about snow—you damn nearly have to carry the horses then. Armies always have food and forage problems. The lords don't want them anywhere near their game parks. In enemy country it's easier, you just go where you please and take what you want, but if you try that in your own homeland, you're going to have barons running to the king, screaming rape and pillage."

Wulf licked his fingers. "I think my way of traveling is better."

"Oh, it is, lad, it is!"

Would Castle Gallant still be standing when the king's men finally arrived?

After dinner, Otto changed back into traveling clothes and settled with the landlord, who was happy to rent out the same room twice in one day. Once they had left the yard, heading for the city gate, the brothers could talk freely of war and Voices.

"Vlad is as cantankerous as ever, and even bigger, I

think," Wulf said. "I'm to meet him at the castle door tomorrow. I should take him straight to Cardice, shouldn't I?" Cardice and Madlenka! He must see her again, even if all he could do was admire her from afar, like the poet Petrarch adoring Laura.

Otto agreed. "We don't want to have to explain any more miracles than we must. The Spider admitted that he knew who put Anton over that jump at the hunt. He admitted he wanted you more than Anton, but had been told that you were only sixteen, too young for his purpose."

"I think Marek started that story. Which means the cardinal gets his information from the monastery."

"Wouldn't surprise me," Otto said. "And if Marek misinformed the monks about your age, he was probably trying to protect you. But Zdenek knows who and what you are, and he agrees you should be rewarded."

"Does he truly? If I survive, of course. Reward me for Speaking to the devil? Can I sue him if he doesn't keep his promise?"

Otto laughed. "You can probably scare him by threatening to turn him into a real spider. As far as your ladylove is concerned, he seemed quite sympathetic and certainly didn't rule out a change of bridegroom. That is, as long as she doesn't go and marry Anton first. And I told him that you need help just as much as Anton does. Again he didn't promise, but he did say he would try to send someone. The password will be 'Greenwood.'"

Wulf thought about all that and said nothing while they waited to clear the gate, where a jam of travelers was lined up to be inspected by the guards. Then a path was opened for the nobility. They were waved through and saluted.

The road was less busy outside, but the city had outgrown its walls, and was flanked by a wide sprawl of cottages. There were still too many people in view to risk a disappearance, but not so many that they could not talk freely.

"Password?" Wulf said. "Then Cardinal Zdenek regularly employs Speakers? Like the Church does?"

Otto was looking bleak. "Possible, but I got the impression that the archbishop helps out the cardinal every once in a while and Zdenek may ask for such a favor this time. Obviously he did not admit that."

"Lord love me! You mean he's going to borrow a Speaker from the archbishop?"

"Why not? You tell me the Wends are employing a Speaker, Father Vilhelmas. But how many more do they have? How many Speakers does it take to move a bombard along a mountain road? The archbishop won't want a war, and certainly not an invasion led by Orthodox priests."

"But the abbot . . ." Wulf wondered if the Church might even send Marek and then discarded the thought. "How do Speakers control other Speakers?"

"That question," Otto said sadly, "is your largest worry right now."

No, it wasn't. Madlenka was.

"Koupel is famous for its medicinal springs, Wulf. People go there to be cured of their ills. Rich ones give generous endowments."

That was heresy, saying that the pilgrims were cured by Satanists.

Wulf looked away to study the road. So many people! Arriving from Dobkov in the morning had been easy—the road had been empty—but now there was no gap big enough to disappear from.

His reverie was interrupted when Otto said, "Can you move two men through limbo, as you call it? Could you take both Vlad and me to Cardice?"

"I don't move anyone, but I can ask my Voices. That would be wonderful, if you would come. Wonderful!"

Otto smiled. "I may be needed as mediator. Anton will become insufferable pretty fast. Does he wear his coronet to bed yet? He needs Vlad, but Vlad having to take orders from Anton is likely to blow up Castle Gallant faster than the Wends' bombard."

Wulf laughed, but then he noticed a couple of sizable barns near the road. "See those? If we ride between them, we should be out of sight long enough to enter limbo. Holy Saints, when my brother and I are out of public view behind that barn, will you please move both of us to Dobkov, to somewhere on the road where we won't be seen?"

—You are becoming very devious in your requests, Wulfgang, my son. Helena sounded amused, fortunately.

"I am wise to be devious, aren't I? I am very grateful for all your help."

His trick seemed to work. They ran the horses along the corridor at a fast pace and emerged on the Dobkov road. Again old Balaam was spooked, even making a game effort to buck. Copper merely flickered his ears in the equine equivalent of a shrug. Whether anyone back at Mauvnik was having hysterics about Satanism, Wulf could not know, but it seemed unlikely. Only someone deliberately watching the two riders would have noticed their failure to reappear, and who wouldn't sooner believe that their eyes were playing tricks?

As they rode into the bailey, the first thing Wulf

noticed was a groom rubbing down a chestnut stallion over by the stable door.

"We have company! That's Morningstar."

Otto frowned. "So it is. Where did you leave him—Mauvnik?"

"No," Wulf said. "Koupel."

CHAPTER 27

Thinking furiously, Wulf rode after Otto, over to the house door. By the time he had dismounted, Achim had come running from the stable to take charge of their mounts. He saluted the baron, looking up at the big man with a huge smile. "Brother Marek is here, my lord! Just came for a visit, he says."

"Alone?"

The stableman flinched at the sharp tone. "Yes, my lord."

"How is Morningstar? Has he been ridden far?"

"No, he's fresh, my lord. Still frisky."

"You're certain Brother Marek came alone?"

"Yes, my lord."

As the brothers ran up the steps, Otto put into words what Wulf had thought at first and then rejected: "Marek may be the help the cardinal promised."

"So soon?"

"Well . . . If Zdenek had a Speaker within call in the palace and sent him straight to Abbot Bohdan it would work. No, you're right. The abbot would want to consider the request, then summon Marek, and so on. It's too fast."

Hating himself for even thinking it, Wulf said, "So his visit may be bad news."

"You want to disappear while I find out?"

"If he had brought company I would," Wulf admitted. He attempted a smile, although he suspected it wasn't a very good one. "But I'd feel terrible running away from anyone his size."

As the brothers entered the lesser hall, three excited people shouted that Brother Marek was back. He had come on a visit. He was upstairs, in the solar with the baroness, meeting his nephews and nieces.

"Let me talk with him first," Otto said as they clanked up the spiral staircase. "You go and change."

Deeply troubled, Wulf headed for the guest room. All through his childhood he had been told that Magnuses were allowed to feel fear but were expected to ignore it. He was feeling fear now and it refused to be ignored. Had Marek brought a warning from the Church? Would his Voices be able to bind Wulf in some sort of obedience? Had he been so distressed by seeing Anton and Wulf that he had renounced his vows and fled the cloister? If that were the case, surely he would have hounds on his heels very quickly—Dominican friars, likely. It had been Dominicans who came for him five years ago. Not for nothing were the Dominicans known as *domini canes*, the Lord's dogs.

He threw open the door and went in.

A man was standing in the window alcove, leaning out and staring at something below. Apparently he had not heard the door open, and had been interrupted in the process of changing, for he wore only a breechcloth. His back was a hell of partly healed black and purple stripes, grooves of torn and crushed flesh. Wulf had seen men flogged, but never as savagely as that. A bulky monkish habit lay discarded on the floor nearby, close to a saddlebag like the one Morningstar had worn to Koupel.

In the deep window alcove, with his head almost outside, Marek had not heard Wulf's arrival. He could not see the bailey from there, but was it possible to creep up on a Speaker? Wulf slammed the door.

Marek jumped, spun around, and tried to cover his nudity with his arms, in a curiously feminine gesture. Many of the cuts wrapped around his ribs to his chest.

"Wulfgang!"

"Marek. What brings you here?"

"Cowardice." Marek reached for his discarded black habit, squatting rather than bending, as if trying not to expose his back. Or perhaps bending hurt.

Wulf shot the bolt. He removed his gloves and threw them angrily on the bed. "Never heard that word in this house before." His cloak followed, then his hat.

"You saw my stripes?" Marek was clutching the habit in front of himself as a shield, not moving to put it on.

"I caught a glimpse." As he was meant to? "I'd rather not see any more. Who did that to you?"

"Brother Lodnicka." Marek smiled thinly. "He has a mighty arm. Fifty lashes on Monday and another fifty next Monday. I couldn't face the thought of more, so I ran away."

"*Merciful Heaven!* I don't blame you. What sin requires that sort of penance?"

Marek smiled thinly. "I disobeyed orders. I was told to take you and Anton to the scriptorium so the abbot and the master of discipline could eavesdrop on you. I failed."

"Because we saw through you and refused? You were flogged for that? That's insane!"

"I had been given permission to seek aid from my Voices. I could have compelled Anton, as long as I was close to him. I was warned that it might not work on you."

Wulf thought a silent prayer of thanks. "I am grateful to you. But just for that they tied you up and gave you—"

"Not tied up. I had to stand for the strokes. It is a test of commitment and obedience."

It certainly would be. Wulf shuddered. "To prove that you wouldn't call on your Voices? And today, how did you get away?"

Marek hung his head. "I slipped away in the dark, after matins. I went to the stable. I recognized Morningstar, of course. Then, when I had saddled him, I asked my Voices, St. Methodius and St. Uriel, to bring me to Dobkov. I have broken my oaths, Wulf. I am an apostate, a damned soul."

Lies! Wulf felt ill.

"Why haven't you asked the Voices to heal your back?"

Marek whispered. "I swore that I would not."

"Then why don't I ask my Voices to do it?"

"No!"

"Why not?" Wulf asked, wondering if his brother had been driven insane.

Marek gave him a sheepish little smile. "I'll explain later."

"I know nothing about Speaking. I expect you to teach me, now that you're here."

Marek crouched to rummage in the saddlebag. "Did you call on your Voices when you were at Koupel?"

"Only after we left you. Why?"

"Do you notice a strange glow when you call on your Voices, a light you can see even with your eyes closed?"

"Yes."

"Other Speakers can see it too, did you know?"

Wulf's heart skipped a beat as he hastily thought back over the last few days, to times when he had called on Helena and Victorinus. Had he ever done so when he might have been observed by strangers? "No, I didn't. Thanks for the warning."

Marek had produced another habit, but was making no move to put it on. "You decided not to go to the northern marches? I'm glad."

"Yes, we did go. And I have to go back there."

Someone rattled the door. Wulf walked over to it.

"We're all right," he said loudly. "We're chewing over old times."

"Sure?" asked Otto's voice.

"Quite sure. We'll come and join you shortly."

Wulf sat on the stool and removed his spurs.

Smiling, Marek came over to help him with his boots. "And where is Anton? Even the baroness says she doesn't know."

"Anton is currently holding a castle that the Wends are likely to attack with cannon and Satanism any day now. He can't withstand them with the men he's got. I'm his resident miracle worker."

"False miracles," Marek murmured. "Witchcraft."

"We'll talk about that, too. Tomorrow Vlad's going to join us. In effect, King Konrad's chief minister has appointed the Magnus brothers defenders of the kingdom. And now that you've arrived, it will be four against the Wends."

Marek was just standing, watching him with wide eyes. "Four of us? Two men-at-arms and two Speakers?"

"Correct. And maybe Otto as our counsel and liaison with the court."

"I was not sent to join you, Wulf! I ran away, I told you."

He had not produced the Greenwood password.

Wulf stood up to remove his doublet and shirt. Standing close, he could look down on Marek even more than Anton looked down on him; the difference was that he tried not to. "Brother—and I call you that because we are of one blood, not because you were forced into a monastery against your will—Brother, you have been lying to me. You said you saddled Morningstar after matins, which is twelve hours ago now, but he arrived here so fresh that Achim says he's still frisky. Tell me the real reason you will not cure your tattered back."

Marek dropped his eyes and said nothing.

"And why you thought I had not been to the northern marches. Was that because I asked about your back?"

The smaller man looked up, surprised. "Yes. You know this? The Voices cannot hurt me when I am already in pain. One pain cancels out the other and pays for the false miracles. Without that, I could not have endured the agony of my journey through limbo."

Why was he just standing there holding the habit, instead of dressing?

"If that's what they teach you, they're lying. I suffered for my journey from Koupel to Castle Gallant, yes. My Voices told me that pain was the price I chose, so the next time I asked them for a miracle, I refused that price. I don't feel pain now when I Speak."

"Oh, Brother, what worse pain are you saving up for eternity?"

"I'll worry about that later." Wulf reached out a hand.

Marek stepped back. Wulf followed until his brother

was backed against the wall. Then he gripped his bare shoulders. "Holy St. Helena and St. Victorinus?"

The Light flooded the room. Marek's eyes widened.

"Please will you cure these wounds on my brother?"

—Of course, since you ask.

"And tell me if his superiors at Koupel have been lying to him?"

—Of course they have.

"Thank you."

The Light faded.

Wulf turned Marek around. The skin of his back was whole, unscarred.

Marek sighed. "Thank you, Brother. That does feel better. What did they tell you?"

"They said of course you've been lied to! But my Voices would say that whether they were angels or devils, wouldn't they?" Wulf went to the chest where he had put his meager wardrobe. "Can you and I share the truth now, as we know it?"

Wrapping himself in his gown, Marek said, "You're asking me to pit one loyalty against another, but the abbot did that first, and it's clear that he's been deceiving me. You have almost convinced me that the Voices are who they say they are." He went over to the empty hearth and sat on the hob. "I don't know much, but ask me what you want to know. No more lies, I swear."

Wulf started lacing his trunk hose to his shirt. The brothers stared at each other. It was not a time for smiles.

"You were sent here?"

Nod.

"To do what?"

"To locate you so that we . . . so that they could come

and apprehend you before you do any more of the devil's work."

"How do you 'apprehend' a Speaker?"

"Just by numbers," Marek said simply. "Physically, two or three men can usually pin another, and the same is true of Speaking. Then they put a bridle on you, an iron gag with a tongue piece, so that you cannot Speak."

"You honestly believe that the Voices come from the devil?"

Another nod. "I saved that boy's life—Hans. But you tell me he committed a terrible crime."

"Your thinking has been warped!" Wulf said angrily. "If I see a child drowning and rescue that child, am I responsible for every sin that child commits thereafter? How can you reconcile that idea with the doctrine that God gave us all free will?"

"Doctrine is a matter for the Church to determine, Brother."

"And lie about?"

Marek hesitated. "No. The Holy Father would not lie about that. But small lies . . . Sometimes the Church is forced to employ things that are otherwise evil in order to do God's work."

"Like attracting rich sick people to Koupel and having Speakers cure them so that they will enrich the monastery?"

"We have to pay the abbot's grocery bill somehow."

"That remark ought to earn you another dozen lashes."

"Or a forty-day fast." The little man's eyes twinkled, so perhaps they were drawing closer to the truth at last. "You have no idea how good it feels to be able to say things like that again!"

But he still wasn't saying all he knew.

"When we came to see you, you talked about a first

sin and a second sin. There are steps to Speaking, aren't there? How many?" If his brother's repentance was genuine, then Wulf might now learn some of the hidden lore of Speaking. If Marek was still playing false, of course, then he would just be pelted with more lies.

The monk wrung his hands. "I don't know. We are only taught as much as we need to know. The first sin, or first step, as I told you, is hearing the Voices at all. That temptation comes to very few people. The second sin is to listen to them and come to understand what they are saying. Many who are tempted manage to resist that step, so Speakers are very rare. I knew of five in Jorgary—two Dominicans plus three in Koupel, including me. You are the only other one I know of, and you were just starting when I left here, so I wasn't sure about you until you came to Koupel on Sunday. You make six. There may be more. The third step is to ask the Voices for their help. Just in little things, at first—to find a lost coin, to cure a baby's colic. It seems so harmless! Then comes the fourth step, undeniable false miracles and acceptance of the pain that is their price."

"That's where you are now?"

For the first time, the monk looked truly abashed. "Don't you remember how sick I was after I healed the boy, Hans? No, you probably don't, but for two days I felt that there was a thunderstorm going on inside my head. It was the worst pain I have ever known—until Brother Lodnicka's chastisement yesterday. I might never have Spoken again after what healing the boy cost me. As it was, of course, the Dominicans came for me and made me swear not to. And I never did until today. On Monday I was released from my oath for the purpose of locating you. I was offered a lighter penance if I promised to redress my sin in letting you escape. I had to find you and then fetch the, um . . . we call them missionaries."

Wulf suppressed a shiver, remembering the day his brother had been taken away. "The Lord's hounds?"

"They get called that, too. The first part of my penance remained the same."

"To stand for fifty lashes?"

"Forty-two that day, the other eight on Tuesday. I had to ask for a rest. Today I was judged fit enough to start looking, so I came to Dobkov as the best place to begin. And it worked! The pain in my back kept the other pain away."

"Or they were lying and I was right. You accepted pain that you could have refused altogether. They want you to believe the pain is inevitable so you will not call on your Voices without permission." Receiving no answer, Wulf said, "Try it now if you don't believe me. Walk through limbo to Koupel and then back here. Refuse the price, and you will be given the power as a gift."

Marek grimaced. "I will believe you. After all these years in Koupel being fed lies, I will believe you." He sighed. "I thought my search was over almost before it began. The moment I arrived here at Dobkov I was told that you had been here and were expected to return soon. My orders were to wait until dark and then go back and tell the abbot where you could be found." He paused and looked away. "Except that I knew I couldn't. Even before you walked in just now, I knew I wouldn't. I am sorry, Brother! I was wrong even to think of it. Please believe me. It is so good to be home," he added wistfully.

The first story had been a lie; was the second true? Lies could qualify as "things otherwise evil" that might be employed to do the Lord's work. Wulf donned a fresh tunic and a short cloak.

"So what's the fifth step in Speaking?"

Marek shook his head. "I'm not sure. I once overheard someone saying that there are eight ranks or grades in all. When you were able to refuse the cost and feel no pain, then that may have been when you reached the fifth level. I do know about the sixth, and now you have reached that."

"Which is?" Wulf asked uneasily.

"The sixth step is when you start believing in the saints—truly believing what the Voices tell you, rejecting the Church's teaching that they are devils. That's when the nimbus appears."

"Nimbus?"

"Well, you didn't have it when you came to Koupel."

Wulf crossed the room in two bounds to peer in the mirror. Light of no color and all colors glowed around his head as if he were a saint in an icon. He was still staring at it in horror when a concerned Marek appeared in the reflection.

"You didn't know?" he said.

"No! It wasn't there when I shaved this morning."

"Then it must have just come. Only other Speakers can see it."

"All other Speakers will see me like this now?"

"Perhaps not those with very low rank, but when the Dominican missionaries came here to Dobkov for me, the main reason I went with them so readily was that I saw them glowing like images of Christ."

This was appalling! Wulf was literally a marked man, branded like a thief. "Will it fade if I stop Speaking to my Voices?"

"I don't think so." Marek was looking genuinely sympathetic.

"Abbot Bohdan doesn't have a halo, not that I could see."

"I don't think Bohdan is a Speaker. If he was, he wouldn't have needed my help to eavesdrop on you. But there must be higher steps that I don't know. Higher ranks may be able to hide their nimbus."

"They don't need you to track me down now, do they?" Wulf wailed. "Any Speaker I meet will see me glowing like a bonfire."

"Most of them will be equally visible to you, though," Marek said. "Some won't be, like me, but those ones are probably not dangerous to you."

"So you still believe your Voices are sent by the devil? And mine?"

Marek bowed his head. "I suppose I must. Maybe, when I have had a few days away from the monastery and have practiced Speaking again, I will come to agree with your view. But, Wulf, I swear I will not betray you to the missionaries! By my immortal soul, I swear! Now I see myself through your eyes and know that no Magnus should ever betray another the way I was going to betray you. I won't go back to Koupel . . . willingly."

"I am glad," Wulf said. Glad but not convinced. He ran fingers through his hair and pulled on his flowerpot-shaped hat to hide it. "You can't go around in a Benedictine habit, though. We'll see if Branka's seamstresses can turn you into a Franciscan. Monk to friar, black to brown."

"You'll forgive me?"

"Nothing to forgive!" Wulf hugged him. "They had you for five years. They preached at you night and day, I suppose? Half starved you? Beat you? Kept you short of sleep? Their message was all you ever heard. You wouldn't be human if you could withstand such treatment. But you must do one thing to prove that you're truly repentant."

"What's that?"

"Join Otto and me in getting roaring drunk tonight and singing disgusting bawdy songs till dawn."

Marek started to laugh, but stopped abruptly, looking surprised. "You know, that's the first time I've made that vulgar noise in five years?"

CHAPTER 28

The weather in Bavaria had changed overnight. Under heavily overcast skies, an unfriendly wind wailed pitilessly around Castle Orel, promising rain to follow. Wulf had asked his Voices to deliver Otto, Marek, and himself to the road alongside the lake that he had seen the previous day. They had consented without argument. Clearly they would take him only to people he knew or places with which he had some previous connection, but as usual they refused to explain why.

Marek had tried a short journey through limbo on his own and had returned doubled over with pain, which Wulf had cured for him. By his reckoning, he was still only a Four. Wulf could only advise him to keep trying.

Seen from the lake, Baron Emilian's Castle Orel was a spectacular affair of towers, turrets and many windows, balanced on a rock like an osprey plume on a hat. Even to Wulf's uncritical eye it looked more like decoration than a practical machine of warfare. Otto laughed at it and asked what it was supposed to be guarding in the middle of a forest. It was only a glorified hunting lodge, he said. Indeed, the land around the lake was an open beech wood that lacked the close-cropped grass that indicated pasture. It was surely a lord's game park, and a moment's search turned up both old pellets of summer deer droppings near the lake and the ruts made by wild boar.

The brothers rode off up the hill. Roughly halfway to the castle, Otto and Marek found a secluded spot to wait, and Wulf rode on alone.

He reined in Copper at the front edge of the drawbridge. The moat was a dry trench, of course, up there on top of the crag, but it was deep, steep-sided, and floored with sharp rocks.

With the drawbridge down and the portcullis raised, he could have ridden all the way into the bailey if he wished, but dangers lurked there that he would rather avoid. The baron might want to know how his hostage had obtained that weighty bag of gold yesterday. Worse, Emilian might be hosting a squad of Dominicans, lying in wait for the Satanist. Wulf still did not trust Marek's change of allegiance and protests of family loyalty; it would have been easy for him to step through limbo to Koupel in the middle of the night and report what his devil-worshiping brother was up to. This suspicion and gnawing dread would be the pattern of Wulf's life from now on, aware always of the glowing nimbus that marked him as a Speaker and made him blatantly visible to any other Speaker, who might or might not be equally visible to him. He shivered as the wind sank claws through his cloak and tried to bluster him over the edge of the moat.

"Holy Saints, what is Vlad doing?"

—*Watching his sumpter being laden,* Victorinus said. —*His mount is saddled and ready to go.*

"Thank you." The Light faded.

He drew his dagger and inspected his blurred reflection in the shiny blade. The nimbus still shone around his head. Several times in the night he had dreamed that he was on a battlefield, all alone, facing the entire Pomeranian army. The army had charged and he had called on his Voices to aid him—and they had not been there. He had awakened shaking and sweating, and he must have called out in his sleep, because he had awakened Marek once.

If Vlad did not come soon he was going to find his youngest brother tragically frozen. Copper neighed in complaint and stamped a foot.

Last night had been a wonderful family reunion with Marek, all the better for not having Anton and Vlad there, although that was a shameful thing to think of one's brothers. Anton had very little humor and Vlad had far too much, of his own bruising kind. Otto had included Branka, who was entitled to be there as hostess and mother of the next generation of Magnuses. She had assured the family's Speakers that she believed they remained in a state of grace, and had not only joined in the singing, but had supplied some bawdy verses that even Otto had not heard before.

Vlad appeared in the archway, astride one horse and leading another. He wore a sword but no armor, having forfeited his when he yielded to Emilian.

Wulf had not counted on an extra horse. He would have to ask his Voices if they could transport it, or if he would have to come back for it. He backed Copper out of the way and doffed his hat in salute. "God bless, Sir Vlad, and welcome to liberty."

Vlad just scowled. His horses were nondescript nags, his hat and cloak a fair match for them. Baron Emilian had not quite thrown him out naked, but he had not been generous with parting gifts.

"I hope that you don't expect me to ride far on this pig. Or be seen in these rags."

"You won't be riding far. Just down this trail a ways."

"And then what?"

"Otto is waiting there."

Vlad looked surprised at that and fell silent. As they rode, Wulf outlined the events of the last few days, from Anton's craziness at the hunt to Otto's meeting with Cardinal Zdenek. He was just short of explaining Marek's defection before they turned off the trail and around a thicket, to a secluded dell where Otto and Marek were waiting. Vlad greeted Otto with a humility suitable to a shamed warrior who had put his family to considerable trouble and expense. He was always respectful to his older brother, even formal.

He had a personal name for the each of the others. "God's blood! If it isn't Midge! And a friar now? Koupel threw you out?"

Marek smiled with good humor. "They couldn't afford to feed me."

Anton, had he been there, would have pointed out that Marek hadn't needed to be ransomed.

Vlad snorted. "So what are you doing here with these devil spawn?" he asked Otto.

"Enjoying their company and admiring their astonishing success. They have generously offered to let me accompany them to Castle Gallant, so we can have a joyful family reunion and celebrate our brother's advancement."

"I have to go to Dobkov first. I can't go anywhere in these rags and riding this spavined bone rack." Vlad was probably right about the horse, which looked incapable of carrying his weight very far.

"We are not going to Dobkov," Wulf said. "Marek and I are being hunted and that is the first place our enemies will look for us. They may track us down at Castle Gallant, but that risk we must take."

"Dobkov first!" the big man insisted.

"Your choice—Cardice, or stay here and eat weeds?"

Vlad's face flushed above his great beard. He looked to Otto. "You let this brat speak to you like that?"

Otto smiled. "He never needs to speak to me like that. Tell him which you choose."

"Gallant, then." Vlad's glare at Wulf suggested that he might bring up the matter again in the future, in private. "Except that I don't want to be accused of being in league with the devil. You left there only two days ago, you say, to deliver a report to the king and bring my ransom here, in Bavaria. Today you ride back with me? You'll be denounced. We all will be! The Magnuses are Satanists!"

In fact, the miracle of Anton's recovery might already be causing that sort of trouble, but all the fires of hell were not going to keep Wulf away from Cardice and Madlenka.

Otto said. "We've made up a story. We don't have to deceive many people. Servants and the townsfolk don't ask nobility impertinent questions. The daughter, Madlenka Bukovany . . . Wulf thinks she's already guessed."

Wulf said, "She's a smart girl, smart enough not to tell anyone. Her mother was still hiding under bedclothes when I left. I can't see the constable or the seneschal or any of the senior staff questioning the odd small miracle that helps save the castle from the Wends. The bishop is the problem. If he will overlook our little ways, we'll be all right. If he doesn't, nobody will."

Vlad pouted. Bishops were unpredictable and often lacking in respect for secular nobility.

Otto said, "Now listen carefully! Tell him the story, Wulf."

Wulf said, "Anton is the best liar in the family, so we built on the hints he's been dropping. And we decided to stick as close to the truth as we could. Cardinal Zdenek was warned about the Wends months ago. He ordered Petr Bukovany to hire *landsknechte*. He didn't trust Havel Vranov. All true so far! Now comes the invention—Zdenek set up a secret command post somewhere near the border, to keep an eye on all the northern marches."

"In Gistov," Otto said. "It's the next county to the east. We have a distant cousin there, Sir Bedrich Magnus of Rovny. Met him once."

"So did I," said Vlad. "He can't ever be distant enough."

"But he fits nicely in the plan," Otto continued. "Zdenek decided you were a good man to put in charge, Vlad, so he secretly loaned me the money to ransom you from Bavaria, and you chose Rovny as your headquarters. You got there not long before the count of Cardice died."

"Why didn't Anton know all this?" Otto said suspiciously.

"He did, but it's a state secret. If we get caught lying, we say we were told to lie. At Rovny, you organized border patrols and one of them intercepted Gintaras, the boy carrying news of Bukovany's death. Rovny pigeons took the news directly to Mauvnik. The murders were totally unexpected, but the Spider improvised and sent Anton north to take the count's place."

"Why not me?" Vlad demanded. "I was in the area, you said."

"Because of Madlenka. You're already married."

"I didn't know that."

The others laughed, which was often unwise around Vlad.

"Well you do now," Wulf said. "Congratulations. Be fruitful and multiply. Besides, you're the overall commander, isn't that enough? Anton's title was signed by the king on the day of the old count's funeral. Of course when I left yesterday, I went straight to you, at Rovny—remember? Once you read Anton's report, you knew that Cardice was where the Wends would strike, so today you've come to take a personal look. Makes sense," Wulf said, hoping that was the case.

"How many pigeons would you need to carry Vlad?" Marek murmured.

Vlad glowered. "How long have I been skulking at Rovny?"

"A month?" Wulf suggested.

Otto said, "What sort of man is this bishop? Wouldn't it be simplest just to confide in him? Count Vranov started the Satanism by murdering Count Stepan and his son. Cardinal Zdenek responded by sending Wulf. If the bishop's at all reasonable, he'll agree to turn a blind eye, surely?"

"It would make our next confessions easier," remarked Vlad, who was not as stupid as he often seemed.

Marek smiled shyly. "He who speaks with the devil needs a glib tongue."

"I haven't met the bishop," Wulf said. "But Madlenka says he owes his miter to being the son and brother of a duke. He's pompous, she says, and not likely to approve of a mere baron's brother being promoted to an earldom."

"Then let's hope he never suspects anything more,"

Otto said. "It's a good story, very good! But, Vlad, remember that we made it up. If you march into Castle Gallant and announce that the commander-in-chief has arrived, Anton will throw you in a dungeon."

"Think I'm stupid?" Vlad growled. "I'll grovel to the kid if I must. Now let's move out before I freeze."

Wulf still had to deal with the packhorse, and he could not ask Marek to help. Five horses, four riders, two Speakers? How could he keep them together? The sumpter would certainly panic when it found itself in limbo. He spoke to his Voices. "Can we take the packhorse with us to Cardice?"

The Light shone around him. *—There are ways you could do that.*

That was Victorinus dropping hints again. Marek was quietly talking to Saints Uriel and Methodius.

Wulf said, "Can you open a doorway, as you did when I went to speak with Vlad in the castle?"

—You are progressing, my son, Helena said. *—We can.*

"Marek, let's do it this way. The saints will open a gate for us. I'll ride through first, with Otto next. Then Vlad follows with the packhorse. You bring up the rear and ask your Voices to close the gate. You can do that?"

Marek asked someone on his left, "Will that work?," then added, "No pain, you promise?" He nodded. "All right."

"Merciful Mother!" Otto said. "When they both do it, it makes my hair stand on end."

"It shrinks my balls to acorns," Vlad said. "I smell sulfur."

Wulf said, "Saints, please open a door to the road below Castle Gallant. As long as there's nobody there to see," he added.

A gap like a church door appeared in front of him. It was a hole in the world, so that where his view of the trees should be he saw instead the road up from High Meadows to the south barbican. Wind hurled rain in his face, but he nudged Copper through, much against the courser's will. He turned to see Otto making the sign of the cross as he followed, from dry forest glade to muddy mountain trail. Vlad was loudly praying to St. Stanislaus of Cracow, patron of soldiers in battle.

In a moment Marek brought up the rear and the hole in the sky disappeared behind him. He smiled at Wulf's inquiring glance and made a thumbs-up sign to show that he had not been smitten by sudden agony.

Cowering against the weather, they urged their mounts up the trail. As they rounded a sharp bend, the long line of cliff came in sight, topped by its curtain wall of red stone. Vlad and Otto whooped in approval. They also liked the barbican, when that appeared.

The gate was closed. The riders huddled in the archway, but there was too little overhang to shelter them from the rain. Wulf banged on the postern shutter until the grille opened. An unfamiliar face peered out.

"Squire Wulfgang, the count's brother, bringing three honored guests."

"Got orders to admit no one." His dialect sounded like rocks in a bucket.

"Bring me the captain of the watch."

"I am the captain of the watch. Come back at nones."

Nones was hours off. Wulf would freeze to death before then.

"I am Count Magnus's brother. I left here two days ago. Don't you recognize this horse?"

"No. Told you—no visitors before nones."

Wulf felt a surge of anger and a nudge of warning

from his conscience. His Voices could almost certainly change the man's mind, but to call on their help just to escape from the discomfort of rain and the embarrassment of having Vlad laugh at him would be an abuse of power. He was convinced now that his gift came from God and must be used for worthy purposes. Denying other men their free will would be contrary to God's plan.

"Holy St. Christopher!" Marek proclaimed loudly, "St. Joseph, St. Melchior, St. Anthony of Padua, and all other blessed saints who protect travelers, *St. Methodius* and *St. Uriel*, I pray you to soften this man's heart so that he will admit us poor wayfarers."

Marek was completely hidden inside his hooded Franciscan habit, but for a moment as he named his Voices, Wulf saw a nimbus glow around him.

"Hellfire!" the guard said. "You look harmless enough, and it's a pig of a day. Herkus, open the sally port."

"*Harmless?*" Vlad repeated incredulously. "Me?"

Marek flashed Wulf a triumphant wink. Either he saw nothing wrong in Speaking for minor personal advantage, or he was just eager to help and prove his loyalty. Inside the barbican, the guards stared in surprise at seeing a friar on a horse. Otto and Vlad continued to enthuse about the defenses.

Wulf could hear a band playing in the distance.

"What's the occasion?" he demanded. "Why no visitors?"

"Holiday," the captain of the guard explained. "New count declared a one-day break in the mourning. Festival to celebrate his taking over."

Taking over what? Or *whom*?

"This way!" Wulf shouted. "Move!"

He urged Copper forward, through the inner gate. That put him on the road that wound between the curtain wall and the cliffs to the west, and he had to pass through a third gate to enter the city. The festival was in full romp already, with flags and colored cloths hung from windows, bands competing, young men showing off their juggling and acrobatic skills, boys on stilts. People dancing in the streets hastily cleared out of the horsemen's way, cheering them good-naturedly as they went by. An odor of free beer hung over the town.

Had Anton thought this up all by himself? A party to cheer everyone up after all the bad news was probably a good idea, admittedly, yet it seemed a little out of character for Anton to be so perceptive. What was in it for him, personally?

The horses clattered into the palace yard. Fortunately, not all of the stable hands had been given the day off, and one of them knew Wulf.

"Have the bags sent to the Orchard Room," he ordered, and took off at a near run. Three other Magnuses followed, Vlad demanding to know what all the hurry was.

Again Wulf's luck held, for the porter on the door remembered him. He said he thought they would find the count in the hall, supervising the arrangements for the banquet.

Otto's heavy hand descended on Wulf's shoulder. "Take your time," he whispered. "What are you afraid of?"

Wulf pulled free of the hand, but forced himself to walk calmly to the ramp. "Nothing." But he had thought of a reason why Anton might want to hold a party.

Otto stayed close. "Perhaps you should be. Don't do anything rash."

"Me? Rash? What do you think I am, a Magnus?"

"You're very much a Magnus, and I don't want any of my brothers turned into a toad."

What if that brother was a toad already?

The hall was a turmoil of harassed servants. Tables and benches stood around three sides of the long room, and Anton towered in the middle, resplendent in scarlet robe and golden coronet. Around him fussed a group including old Seneschal Jurbarkas, Arturas the herald, Secretary Radim, and four or five unknowns. No doubt they were arguing problems of precedence. Whether one was seated above or below one's favorite enemy would be a matter of scandal and gossip in the town for months. Anton looked up and caught sight of the newcomers.

"*Vlad!*" he roared, startling his companions. "Vladislav Magnus!" He pushed out of the group and came striding forward to greet Vlad with an embrace and much back-slapping. "I have never been so glad to see you, Brother!"

"Were you ever glad to see me at all?"

"Of course not, but I certainly am now!" Laughing, they hugged again.

"And *Marek*! Brother-Brother Marek!" Again brother embraced brother, although Marek's head did not reach Anton's shoulder. "I did not expect you to rally to the cause, too. Wonderful to see you after all these years. And . . . oh, no!"

He stared at Otto in inexplicable dismay. "I did not expect *you*."

"All the greater your pleasure, I hope?" Otto opened his arms for a hug.

"Well, yes . . . of course!" Anton made a fast recovery and they embraced. "You didn't bring Branka, did you?"

"No," Otto said, frowning at Anton's peculiar reaction to him.

"And Wulf." This time, Anton offered a mere smile—a very thin smile. "You waste no time on your missions, squire. But then, neither do I. Madlenka and I are handfasted, so confine your attentions to the kitchen sluts from now on."

He was wide open. A fist like a mallet rammed into his solar plexus, doubling him over; then its partner struck his jaw hard enough to straighten him out again. He landed full length, and his coronet rolled off across the floor. A very satisfying start!

The spectators all screamed.

Wulf planted a boot on Anton's outstretched hand. "You will apologize from down there," he said loudly. "Do it now, because if you get up first I will knock you down again. And again. And—*arrgh*!"

Vlad's great arms wrapped around him and lifted him clear off the prostrate count. "You're even faster than you used to be, lad. Nice one-two, but not the best of manners."

Anton surged to his feet and found himself nose-to-nose with Otto.

"You offended first," Otto said quietly. "So you apologize first."

Anton snarled wordlessly and tried to dodge around him.

Otto grabbed a handful of fur-trimmed robe. "You first!" he insisted.

"Or what?"

"Or we all go home and leave you."

The coin spun . . . There was honor involved. There was a new count's dignity before his servants and vassals. Anton was lord of justice and could certainly order his brother jailed or flogged. But that raised the problem of how Wulf's saints or demons might react, and there was the need for their help against a Wend army practically on the doorstep.

The coin came down showing peace.

Anton whispered, "Sorry. Wulfgang. I ought. Not. To have. Said. That."

Wulf, with his arms clamped to his sides by Vlad's great hands, said, "Your apology should not be addressed to me."

"I certainly did not mean my joke to refer to anyone else."

Wulf considered that, then nodded. "My mistake, then . . . Sorry."

Vlad released him. Otto told them to shake hands, which they did.

"My little brother a count!" Vlad boomed, bringing the audience into the conversation. "A lord of the marches must certainly be a knight, and the traditional start of a dubbing is the *collée*. That's a light blow delivered by a priest, and since we don't have a priest handy, we asked Squire Wulfgang to do the honors. He was perhaps a little too enthusiastic, but the lad is excited and got carried away by the solemnity of the occasion." He turned to Otto. "Draw your sword, Brother, and do the honors."

Otto smiled to acknowledge this nimble effort to divert the audience's bewilderment and drew his sword. Anton knelt. Otto touched the blade to his shoulder and dubbed him a member of the international brotherhood of knights. Vlad removed his own spurs and attached them to Anton's heels. Then Otto belted the sword on him and the deed was done. The audience cheered.

"Well, you're obviously busy here, my lord count," Otto said. "Why don't we go off and change? I assume we are invited to the banquet?"

"You are more than welcome," Anton said. With a sidelong glance at Wulf he added, "All of you."

Wulf said, "Thank you," very clearly, but as the visitors headed for the door, he muttered, "Knighthood? Toadhood would be too good for him."

CHAPTER 29

"Do try to smile!" snapped Dowager Countess Edita. "You look as if you're dressing for a funeral, not a banquet."

"I wonder why?" Madlenka murmured. With her father and brother not ten days in the family vault, a funeral face would be much more appropriate.

Yet here she was, robed in virginal white, being primped and tugged and adjusted by her mother and Ivana, Mother's crony and personal seamstress. Ivana was all bone and angles, with ears sharper than razors and a tongue to match. Today she was a-tut-tut at this unexpected festivity, shocked by its timing, so soon after the late count's death. It was officially a recognition of the new count's accession and a chance for the town dignitaries to meet him, but no one within the castle doubted that it was a wedding feast.

"Mm," Edita remarked, surveying their masterpiece. "You really are quite beautiful, my dear. In a sylphlike way."

"Scrawny, you mean." The hat wasn't helping. They had insisted she wear a hennin, a steeple hat about two feet high, trailing white lace—the latest fashion from

France, they said. She would tower over even Anton. It was totally wrong for her, making her feel like a lance.

"Well, most men do prefer their partners plump, but fortunately the count seems content with the match. Now it is up to you to accept it as equitably as he does and make the best of it. It is the king's decision and we all owe our duty to His Majesty. By Our Lady, you're shivering! It isn't cold in here. You're not catching a fever, are you?"

Madlenka considered blaming her chill on lack of sleep, caused by two nights of instruction from Anton in how to please him. But there were no laurels to be won in battles with her mother anymore. At the moment she was nothing—no longer a marriageable heiress, not yet a countess. The Church might regard her as Anton's wife, but in the eyes of the world she was just the count's bawd. Once she was properly married, she would be able to displace her mother as head of the household and become a somebody, but until then, she was powerless. And by spring she would be hugely gravid.

The door opened and in scuttled Neomi, another of Mother's gossips. She was fat where Ivana was thin, all butter and smarm.

"Have you heard what happened?" she exclaimed, rubbing fat hands gleefully.

The dowager countess said no she hadn't, frowning at Neomi's yellow-fanged leer. Whatever the news was, it must be bad.

"The count's brother is back! Squire Whatshisname. And several other brothers, with him!"

Madlenka guessed from the sideways glances that the trouble concerned her, and schooled herself to the stoicism of a tombstone effigy. She did not even shrug. What was he to her?

"The count said something to the squire," Neomi gushed. "Nobody seems to know what . . . but the squire knocked him flat on his back! Right in the middle of the hall, in front of everybody. Then the other brothers pulled them apart and made them shake hands."

Mother was looking colder than Mount Naproti in midwinter. "How loutish!" Those two words would be the text for a future three-hour sermon on the theme of *See What I Saved You From?*

"He was probably upset that he didn't get invited to the wedding," Madlenka said sweetly, quite certain she was not blushing the tiniest bit. Wulf was back already! Her heart sang.

Stupid, stupid heart.

Standing at the end of the hall with Anton, Madlenka remembered to add a beaming smile to her appearance. She could gripe at Mother in private, but for outsiders *noblesse* must *oblige*. The guests waiting to be welcomed and pay their respects were mostly residents of the town—priests, doctors, a couple of notaries, the wealthier merchants, plus some knights from the backwoods. The day after his accession, Anton had called in his able-bodied vassals to do homage to him and to defend Castle Gallant against the Pomeranian attack. Very few of them had arrived yet, and there had been no time for anyone else to make the journey in the rain, or even be notified. Men greatly outnumbered women.

Give him his due, Anton looked striking in Father's scarlet, ermine-trimmed robe. Even the absurd upturned mustache seemed less presumptuous when worn under an earl's coronet, and the golden baldric placed him in the highest ranks of Jorgarian nobility. Life was not turning out as Madlenka had imagined it would, but the unexpected usurper was a more attractive husband than she could have realistically hoped for. So she told herself. She ought to be wonderfully happy by now, and might well have believed she was, had she never met Wulf.

She must not stare too often or too admiringly at the beautiful swelling developing on the count's jaw. Why on earth had Wulf knocked him down in public? Anton would never tell her, but he would certainly have to banish his brother, so she would never see him again. The scandal would echo around the town for months.

The arrival of more brothers had forced Arturas to tear up two days' work to rearrange the protocol and seating arrangements. Bishop Ugne still took precedence, of course, pompous popinjay in his glorious robes. After the count and future countess had kissed his ring, he took his place beside them to bless the guests as they came by.

After him came Baron Magnus of Dobkov, future brother-in-law Ottokar, who was a very large man in his thirties with a friendly smile on a tough-looking face. His words were conventional, but she suspected that his eyes saw more than most people's.

Then Sir Vladislav, the largest man she had ever seen, as tall as Anton and twice as wide. His bristling black beard prickled as he kissed her.

"Understand you're handfasted with Beanpole," he boomed. "That's what we always called him. You'll find him quite a handful in bed. He's a terrible rascal with the girls."

Face flaming crimson, Anton said, "Don't believe a word of what he says, my dear. Not now, nor ever."

"Ah, that reminds me—is your ankle all better now, lad?"

"Move along, Vlad," Anton said resignedly. "The bishop is waiting to hear your confession. This is another brother, Brother Marek of the . . . um . . . Well, he was all our mother could manage after producing Vlad."

Marek was tiny compared with the others, but he had Wulf's happy smile and the same twinkle in his eyes. Another clever one, she decided. So those were the four brothers senior, and the youngest did not appear. Of course Wulf should not be presented, for he had already met her and was one of the count's servants, not a guest. Or possibly he had already been kicked out of the castle gate forever.

The banquet began late, but banquets always began late, and the food was always cold. As was customary, the tables had been arranged in a U with everyone backed against a wall, facing inward. Of course the host presided at the end of the room with his noble guests. Lesser folk sat along the sides of the awkwardly narrow hall, men with their backs to the windows, women facing them. In this case there were enough men to take over half the women's table also, so the women had to be relegated to the far end, beyond the door, as if they were attending another banquet altogether.

Arturas had completed a frenzy of rearranging. Now the lineup along the head table was Sir Vladislav, Dowager Countess Edita, Bishop Ugne, Count Magnus, Madlenka, Baron Magnus, and then the fireplace. The dais being too short to take more people, Arturas had been forced to improvise even more. Anxious not to insult brothers of the count, he had put Marek at the high end of the men's table, ahead of the six priests of the town, who were shocked at being thus upstaged by a friar. Wulfgang was directly opposite, next to the corner fireplace, similarly offending the constable and the knights.

Madlenka had endured ghastly banquets before, but never one where she was pinned between a new husband—to whom she must be devotedly attentive—and a brother-in-law she had never even heard of until now, who asked the most extraordinary questions.

Like, "Why did the *landsknechte* leave, my lady?"

What sort of dinner conversation was that? She rummaged through several possible names—Anton, the count—before settling on the unfamiliar, the unbelievable, "My *husband* . . . says that they wanted more money than he could afford to pay."

"Odd. What does everyone else say?"

"Everyone else was happy to see them go, my lord."

And so on.

Bishop Ugne kept asking Anton questions he clearly did not want to answer, so he tried to stay in conversation with Madlenka by asking her to name and discuss particular people. She helped prolong the conversation as much as she could by inquiring about his childhood home at Dobkov.

But then the bishop would snatch him away with another question and Baron Magnus—"Do please call me Otto"—would grab his chance again. He was charming, cultured, and wonderful company. He told a few amusing stories about Anton, but otherwise praised him highly, as was to be expected under the circumstances. He spoke affectionately but solemnly of Brother Marek, hinting that he might be having misgivings about his calling. He even apologized for Sir Vladislav's rough manners, which he blamed on ten years' campaigning, but he was obviously proud of his brother's military reputation.

"What did Sir Vladislav mean when he met Anton and asked if his ankle was 'all better'?" she asked.

The baron rolled his eyes. "That is typical. When Vlad rode off to the Bavarian war two years ago, Anton was going to go with him as one of his squires. The day before they were due to leave, he broke his ankle, so he couldn't go. Vlad found it amusing to imply that he'd done it deliberately, out of cowardice. That isn't funny even among family members, all of whom know that Anton is anything but a coward. He nearly went out of his mind because he had to stay home."

But what had that to do with her? "And how did he break his ankle?"

Otto sighed. "Just remember that I didn't bring this up, all right? He slipped while climbing up to a window."

No doubt it had been a lady's window and that was why Vladislav had mentioned the matter in front of her. Very funny.

Wulf was at the head of the adjoining table, on the other side of the fireplace, not ten feet away from Ottokar. The brothers could speak to each other quite easily if they wished, but Wulf never once glanced that way, because he would have to acknowledge Madlenka also. The fact that Ottokar likewise did not address him showed that he understood the lovers' problem.

Indeed, he never even mentioned Wulf to Madlenka except to say that their mother had died bearing him and their father had never remarried. So Wulf, Anton, and even Marek must have been reared by servants. Ottokar was obviously head of the family in more than name. The others clearly deferred to him, so much so that she suspected even Anton might still heed his orders, at least until Anton had grown into his new duties as a feudal landowner. She liked Ottokar.

The first course was removed and the second brought in—swan and roast piglets, beans and a spicy sauce, sweetmeats and fall fruits. The baron and Sir Vladislav went to work again, but she could not face another mouthful. Anton nibbled. The poor would do well out of today's leftovers.

The wine still flowed. The hall became very noisy, with everyone shouting over the musicians who strolled around. Two boys performed acrobatics; jugglers juggled. As each act ended, Anton dispatched gifts to the performers.

Then the entertainers departed and the servants withdrew to the far end of the hall. Madlenka braced herself for the highlight of the feast.

"My lord?" she murmured.

Anton turned and smiled. "My wife?"

"Have you met Jurgen?"

"Remind me."

"Your fool. He's a dwarf, about half your height. He can be very funny, but he'll certainly be making comments about height and, um, related matters."

His smiled broadened. "Are you worried that I can't take jokes, or that I have something to be ashamed of? You know you need not worry about either."

"That's reassuring," she said, although she had serious doubts about the way Anton took jokes. "I just wanted to warn you. The bugler will give him a fanfare and he'll enter in a cart pulled by two old hounds. He may be dressed as a Moor or Julius Caesar or the Emperor Barbarossa. You never know what—"

Her voice was drowned out by the shriek of a trumpet from outside the door. The fanfare, played extremely badly, ended in a very vulgar noise that died away into merciful silence. Thus all eyes were on the doorway as Havel Vranov limped into the hall.

CHAPTER 30

For a moment Madlenka's mind refused to accept what her eyes were seeing—the hooked nose, the burly physique, the bushy dark brows—but there was no doubt that he was the count of Pelrelm. He was not alone, of course. Right on his heels came young Leonas, excitedly clutching something to his chest. Then followed the sinister Father Vilhelmas in his bushy beard and oddly wrong priest's robes, and, lastly, Marijus, the soldier son whom she would have made keeper of Castle Gallant four days ago, had Anton not appeared so magically in the cathedral.

Surprisingly, the first person to react was Brother Marek. Even before all the visitors were inside the hall, he leapt to his feet, yelling, "No! No! Stop them!" He dodged between the ends of the side table and the high table and ran forward, waving his arms and shouting at the newcomers.

The next was Anton, who may have started at the same time, but had a lot more *up* to leap. He was even louder, "*Stay where you are!*" And then, "Constable, knights! Block them!"

The worthy knights of the county were no-nonsense country lads who welcomed any chance for a rumble.

As if they had drilled for it, they overthrew their table, trestles and all, spilling an avalanche of food, drink, and dishes across the floor, and went charging forward over the debris to form a human wall between the visitors and their liege. No one came armed to a feast, of course, but the Pelrelmians were not armed either. Having no choice in the matter, they stopped.

In a comically delayed reaction, all the women then screamed, including the dowager countess. The only exception was Madlenka, who was wondering where Wulf was. He had been sitting beside the constable just moments ago, but now he was nowhere in sight. The way these Magnuses came and went was eerie to the point of bloodcurdling.

Brother Marek spun around and went back to his place, grinning sheepishly at Anton as if he had just made a complete fool of himself. Madlenka did not know what had provoked his outburst, but she did not think that Marek was foolish at all. Why had the diminutive friar been included in this family invasion of Castle Gallant? Just to enjoy a family reunion? Or for the same reason the squire had been included? Could there be two Speakers among five Magnus brothers? The idea seemed absurd and cruel, but she could not put it out of her mind.

"How dare you enter this house without an invitation?" Anton boomed. High on the dais, in red robes and coronet, arms folded, he dominated the hall so completely that no one else dared to make a sound. "I ordered you out of here four days ago, Pelrelm. Who let you back in?"

Vranov smiled, unabashed. "I'm so sorry we can't stay longer."

"I asked how you got in!"

"We just dropped by to offer you our best wishes on your latest concubinage, lad. May it be fruitful! And also, of course, on your amazingly fast recovery from the wound that so nearly killed you on Tuesday."

"Your wishes are as unwelcome as you are," Anton retorted. "That heretic priest beside you was leading a troop of Wendish invaders and should be beheaded for treason if he is a Jorgarian, or as an enemy combatant if he is not."

Vranov looked at the priest in mock surprise. "It would seem he does not want your prayers either, Father."

Vilhelmas mumbled a reply, but he seemed to be scanning the hall for somebody or something. With eyes askew, he ought to be able to see in two directions at once, unless one eye was good only for casting evil spells on people.

"However," Vranov continued, "and ignoring your rudeness, we have brought a gift for your lady, a bolt of fine silk from distant Cathay. Marijus?"

The warrior raised his hands to show that he was holding a package that looked the right size to be fabric. Madlenka could almost drool at the thought of such a gift.

"We want none of your trash," Anton said, speaking strictly for himself. "Constable, escort—"

"I brought the lady a puppy!" Leonas squealed in his childish treble. "I wanna give the puppy to the lady!"

"And no puppies!"

But the boy marched forward and the knights let him through instead of just straightarming him back. Anton drew breath for another bellow.

Madlenka gripped his arm. "Wait! Let him give me

the puppy." He turned to her in anger, but she stood up. "Let me deal with it, I beg you."

"Woman!" he whispered. "You do not question my authority!"

"It's a trap to make you look foolish. I've seen Vranov do this before. Trust me."

For a moment, she thought he would yell at her to stay out of men's business, but then he relented. "All right, the puppy." He spoke between clenched teeth.

By then the simpleton had reached the dais and was beaming at her.

She held out her hands. "That's a lovely puppy, Leonas."

She was on the dais, and the table was between them, but he was tall enough and rangy enough to thrust the smelly, furry morsel right into her waiting hands. It was very young, eyes barely open, and about the same ginger-gold color as he was. It stank.

"Oh, he's very cute!" she said, wondering how Mother was taking this, because Mother knew her dislike of dogs. "What's his name?"

The youth's face fell. "Hasn't got one."

"Then we must give him one. Would you mind if I called him Leonas, to remind me of who gave him to me?"

He uttered a single, discordant laugh. "Leonas is my name."

"Yes, I know. Well, I'll call him Honey, because he's honey-colored. Do you like honey cakes, Leonas?"

He nodded vigorously.

"Well have one of these. Take the whole basket and go share them with your Da."

As Leonas happily went off with the cakes, Anton

muttered, "I hope you don't expect that rat to sleep with us?"

"I hate dogs."

"Likewise, except for hunting hounds." Anton returned his attention to the visitors and the human fence watching them. "Constable Notivova, escort Count Vranov to the gate and see him and his friends off." He sat down.

"Do not trouble yourself, constable," Vranov said. "A pox on you and yours, Anton Magnus. May this fortress crumble to dust and all who live within it be consumed by worms and torment. May you all burn in hell forever."

He and his companions vanished from where they stood. For an instant there was absolute silence as the witnesses came to grips with what they had just seen. Then the hall erupted in terror and screaming.

"What charming neighbors you have!" said Ottokar Magnus. "May I refill your wineglass, Countess?"

CHAPTER 31

Until the Pelrelmians crashed the party, Brother Marek had enjoyed the banquet very much, simply because he was left alone. He helped himself to each dish, poured his own wine, and no one paid any attention to him. On his right the affronted priests diligently ignored him, while Vlad, seated at the high table to his left, relentlessly bored Countess Edita with accounts of his youthful military exploits in Burgundy. The only remark he had addressed to Marek had been to ask if this food was better than the monastery's. The countess had raised an eyebrow at that, no doubt wondering what a friar had to do with a monastery, but she probably assumed that Vlad was drunk, which he wasn't. Even as a stripling he had always been able to hold more wine than any two other men Marek had ever met. The food was pathetic, but one must make allowances for the banquet having been ordered at very short notice.

He welcomed this neglect because he had not been alone in the last five years. He had slept in a dormitory, eaten in a refectory, studied in classrooms, and worshiped eight times a day in church. Even weeding the herb garden, he had been under the raptorial eye of Brother Lodnicka. Now he was free to do as he pleased.

Yes, he must try to help his brothers defeat the Wends; and yes, the missionaries from Koupel would hunt him down eventually, but just at that moment no one would care if he turned cartwheels or opened a stall and started selling indulgences. It was heaven.

His enjoyment was further increased by the presence of women. Only the dowager countess and countess elect were anywhere close to him, the rest of the female guests being at the far side and beyond the doorway, but there were lithesome servant girls hurrying to and fro. For five years, until yesterday, Marek had not set eyes on a woman. He might be doomed to return to Koupel quite soon, but he might commit a sin or two first.

Wulf, directly across the hall from him, had been seated above Constable Notivova and the knights. They might have snubbed him as the priests were snubbing Marek, but Wulf possessed almost as much native charm as Otto, and soon he and the constable were laughing together, drinking toasts, and sharing jokes with men farther along the table. Wulf and Madlenka were ignoring each other so obviously that they must be either deadly enemies or secret lovers. That should be funny, but it was tragic.

The entertainment was clumsy and crude compared to some acts Marek remembered at Dobkov, but it was a treat after five years of ironclad piety. Then the floor was cleared and a fanfare sounded to proclaim the star of the show, whoever that might be. All eyes turned to the door as a man entered.

There was a Speaker following right behind him. Marek could see the nimbus because he was facing the door and the dark corridor beyond it. Wulf's halo glowed just as brightly, but Wulf was on the other side of the hall and would not see the newcomer until its wearer had entered the room. Wulf must be warned! Almost before he had time to think, Marek ran around the end of the table and into the center, screaming and waving his hands. Many people cheered, thinking he was part of the act.

He had often been tempted to try something like this in Koupel, and it was a satisfying outrage while it lasted. Then Anton bellowed orders to the knights, they overturned the boards, and the banquet collapsed into a near riot. Wulf was nowhere in sight. Chuckling and satisfied that he had done his part, Marek headed back to his place. He took a celebratory draft of wine. What would Abbot Bohdan say?

The nimbus glorified a walleyed Orthodox priest, who must be the Father Vilhelmas that Wulf had mentioned. None of the intruders was armed, so only the Speaker was dangerous. For the next few minutes Marek watched him like a cat at a birdcage. Vilhelmas might have caught a glimpse of light as Wulf departed, because he kept glancing around suspiciously.

Although Vranov's departing curse was mere playacting, the intruders' disappearance was a genuine display of sorcery, quite convincing enough to start a panic. A mob of guests charged to the doorway. Vlad, with a warrior's fast reactions, vaulted the table and raced over there, bellowing, in an effort to restore order and rescue those who were being crushed. The bishop and Anton jumped to their feet, shouting for calm. The countess had disappeared under the table. At the far end of the table, Otto caught Marek's eye and smiled cynically, as if to say that it was turning out to be an interesting evening.

Marek went to help Madlenka deal with her mother, who was not truly unconscious, but mumbling nonsense. Between them they raised her to a sitting position.

"Just the shock, I think," he said. "Holy St. Uriel, I

humbly beseech you to aid this poor woman." He made the sign of the cross, and the dowager countess opened her eyes.

—*Why was this woman stricken, Marek?* Uriel asked inside his head. —*It is important that you understand this.*

Anton's betrothed was staring at him. "St. Uriel the archangel?"

"Certainly. He stands in the presence of God. Let us help the lady to a seat."

The two of them raised Countess Edita and set her on a stool. She stared around at the disaster, then began to weep. Madlenka knelt to comfort her, although Marek thought that a good cry might help better than anything. Most of the guests had gone now, but at least a dozen people had been seriously hurt in the panic, and others with lesser injuries were being helped away by family or friends. The bishop was conferring with his black-robed minions. This bizarre happening would have to be reported to Archbishop Svaty and probably the pope himself.

Suddenly aware of someone towering over him, Marek looked up to find Anton glaring down at Madlenka.

"Wife," he said. "Who was that boy who gave you the odious animal?"

She stood up. "Leonas Vranov, my lord, one of Havel's many sons. He's an imbecile. Despite his size, he thinks like a two-year-old. If you're nice to him, he's usually very sweet."

"I've seen him before. The day I arrived, when I was hurrying to the cathedral, he was sitting in the street outside, playing with a stray dog. Men-at-arms were guarding him."

She nodded. "Vranov wouldn't let him go inside. Marijus told me he gets upset by the way sounds reverberate in churches. He's just a baby in a youth's body, but Vranov takes him everywhere. He says if he leaves Leonas at home, the others boys pick on him. I suspect he's more concerned about protecting them than him. Leonas might be dangerous to small children."

"He couldn't hurt me, so why did you contradict my orders about the puppy?"

"It was a trap, my lord," the girl said, being servile to an unpredictable husband. "When Vranov came visiting last month, Father got into a shouting match with the boy. He wouldn't let Leonas sit at the high table and Leonas went crazy, screaming, throwing things, foaming at the mouth. Havel just sat there and watched as if it was all a big joke, or else Father's fault. Petr got involved. Mother tried to reason with Leonas, but nothing worked. Eventually he broke down and lay on the floor, weeping. I didn't want to see you involved in another scene like that."

"Thank you," Anton said stiffly. "I apologize for doubting you. See your mother to bed. The celebration seems to be over."

"Does anyone have any idea," asked Otto, who had been watching all this in silence, "what Count Vranov hoped to gain by that harebrained performance? He frightened a lot of people, but all he really did was confirm the stories that he is in league with the devil. What good can that do him?"

"If I may make a suggestion," Vlad remarked diffidently to Anton, "you are liable to have half the population of the town streaming out the gates before sunset. I suggest you give orders that no one is to leave."

Anton nodded uncertainly.

"Anton—my lord!" Wulf said loudly. Marek had not noticed him at the back of the group, but he must have arrived there by conventional means, for he was carrying a lantern. He had lost his hat and his hair was disheveled like storm-flattened barley. His eyes were wild. "A private word!" He grabbed Anton by the arm. "You come, too, Marek."

Anton angrily broke loose of his grip, but he let Wulf lead him over to the fireplace and Marek followed. What was making Wulf so excited? He was positively jumpy. Where had he been and how had he left the hall?

Wulf said, "You're lord of the marches. I ask for your approval of a sortie!"

"A what?"

Wulf turned to Marek. "The priest was the Speaker, right? Not Vranov. Only the squinty priest; no one else?"

Marek nodded.

Anton frowned. "How do you know this?"

"We can tell," Wulf insisted. "Trust us. So Father Vilhelmas was the one who nearly killed you at Long Valley and almost certainly the one who murdered the last count and his son. I know where he is right now. I want to go there and kill him. Have I your permission?"

Anton stiffened in astonishment. "Are you drunk?"

"I am sober as a nun. If I can take out Vranov's Speaker, I'll have drawn his teeth. It's the best contribution I can make to your cause right now, Count Magnus of Cardice. *Do I have your permission?*"

Anton looked to Marek, probably thinking the same thing as he was: this sounded like another Wulfgang out-of-the-blue thunderbolt, like the attack that had laid Anton flat on his back that morning. Warfare needed more planning than a bare-knuckle brawl, but to kill the enemies' Speaker would be a masterstroke like capturing an opponent's queen in a chess game.

"Lord Anton!" Bishop Ugne had arrived with a couple of priests. "It is imperative that we perform a ritual of exorcism to cleanse this hall of the Satanic taint left by the devil worshipers."

"Um, yes." For a moment Anton dithered. Then he dealt with Wulf first. "Permission granted. Be careful. My lord bishop . . ."

"Wait!" Marek cried, running after him. "Wait, Wulf."

Wulf did not seem to hear. He went past Otto without a glance, totally intent on whatever he was planning.

"Follow him," Otto said to Marek. "Don't let him do anything too crazy."

Marek almost caught up with Wulfgang at the door, but got stuck behind some of the injured and the priests and others trying to help them. The corridor outside was dark now, for the sun had gone behind clouds or mountains. Fortunately Marek could see Wulf's nimbus glowing as bright as his lantern. They arrived at the stairs together.

"I want to help," Marek said.

Wulf went up two steps at a time. "No you don't. What I'm going to do is nasty, not honorable. But I thank you very much for the warning you gave me when Vranov and his gang came into the hall." He was bubbling like a brewer's vat. "That was brilliant! And fast! Very well done." He reached the landing, turned right. He seemed to know where he was going in this labyrinth.

Marek stayed close. "Glad to help. Tell me how you got out of there."

"The same way Vlad taught me to swim—he threw me in the moat." Wulf threw open a door and went in.

Marek followed and recognized the Orchard Room,

where they had changed out of their traveling clothes that morning. The floor was still littered with boots, swords, daggers, saddlebags, and wet cloaks, and scattered clothing covered the bed. It was slightly brighter than the corridor, but still dim and cold. Wulf set the lantern on the mantel above the empty grate. Marek closed the door.

"You didn't swim out of the hall, Brother, and you didn't have time to call on your Voices. You just vanished."

"Yes." Wulf went over to the bed. He located his own boots in the heap and set them upright. Holding a bedpost to steady himself, he slid a foot into a boot. "I seem to have advanced another grade. Now I'm at least a Seven, maybe an Eight. It's incredible!"

"Tell me."

He smiled diffidently. "I won't. And I'm not saying that just to vex you. I think I know now why the Voices won't answer questions and the monks wouldn't teach you much. There's a good reason why Speakers don't talk about Speaking. Telling you would do more harm than good. And listen, Marek, you honestly don't want to be involved in an assassination. No chivalry, no challenge or warning, just cold-blooded murder. This is not for you."

"Execution," Marek said stubbornly. "Did Vilhelmas give the Bukovanys a formal challenge? Did the Wends warn us that they were going to attack Long Valley and murder the garrison? This is war, not a tilting yard. I want to help!"

Wulf pulled an unhappy expression. "We do trust you. You don't have to prove whose side you're on."

The problem was worse than that. Marek didn't trust himself. After five years of enforced piety, he wasn't sure if there was any sort of real man left in him at all. He felt like a wet rag compared with his brothers, especially young Wulf, for some reason.

"Please?" he said. "It matters a lot to me. Give me a sword and I'll stick it in Father Vilhelmas myself."

"A crossbow is what I have in mind, but I'll find you a sword."

Wulf buckled on sword and dagger, took a candle off the mantel and lit it from the lamp. At the door he stopped, looking at Marek. "This is horrible, I agree, but if the Wends have no Speaker to help them, they'll have to give up and go home. Then the war will be over for this year. I will have done my duty and I'll be free to go far, far away. Tonight, even." He reached for the latch.

"Wulf!"

Wulf turned.

"I'm sorry about you and Madlenka," Marek said. He had meant it as a comfort, but knew at once that he had only increased the hurt.

Wulf froze, his face twisted in pain. "So am I. But the king has commanded and she has consented. So now she sleeps in Anton's bed and I have to get out of here and far away before I do something crazy. That's another reason to kill Father Vilhelmas."

"You can't be serious!"

"Not about the reason, but I am about killing him. Once that's done, I'll have won the war and won't be needed here anymore. I'm going downstairs now to get a crossbow. If you're serious about wanting to come with me, then I'll be very happy to have you along. I suggest you change into more appropriate clothes."

He closed the door quietly behind him.

Lord have mercy! Killing priests? How had Marek gotten himself into this? But what sort of priest led men-at-arms on a raid to kill other men?

He wandered to the bed and looked over the heap of clothes. Branka's needlewomen had made him his Franciscan robe, which he thought of as his friar disguise, and also a set of garments suitable for an esquire. He planned to be a friar until his tonsure grew in, but that was hardly a suitable guise for a swordsman assassin. Preparing to strip, he untied the first of the three knots that bound a friar's girdle, symbolizing poverty, chastity, and obedience.

A voice behind him said, "May the Lord be with you, Brother."

He turned so fast that he lost his balance, tripped on a discarded boot, and toppled back onto the bed. Sunk in the mattress, he stared up in horror at the two men standing over him, their heads wreathed in the shining nimbus of sanctity. One was Brother Lodnicka, his master from Koupel. The other, even worse, was a tall, skeletal man of around fifty, with a silver fringe around his tonsure; he wore the Dominican garb of a black cloak over a white habit. Even after five years he was easily remembered as Father Azuolas.

Marek opened his mouth to scream. His tongue was seized by invisible fingers and dragged out between his teeth, as if he were a horse being immobilized by a farrier. He could not call on his Voices for help.

Azuolas had a smile to breed nightmares. "We grew tired of waiting for your return, my son."

"You were supposed to come back and tell us when you found Wulfgang." Lodnicka was shorter and older, but massive and still immensely powerful, as Marek had learned under the lash. He had been a quarryman until the Church detected his talent and recruited him.

"Did you find him, Marek?" the monk asked.

Marek shook his head and then nodded.

"He seems a little confused, Brother," Azuolas said. "Does this bother you, my son?"

Marek's tongue was yanked painfully hard. He nodded and made urgent noises.

"Of course we are not permitted to use violence except in self-defense, but gentle restraint is permissible. Indeed, I seem to recall that you had to be restrained a few times when we first met, some years ago. Ah, you remember also. I must warn you that resistance may be dangerous, although hurting you is not my desire or intent. So I shall give you back your tongue, but you must promise not to call on your Voices. Agreed?"

Marek nodded, having no choice. His tongue was released.

"Now, who was that young man who left here a few moments ago, the one you addressed as 'Wulf'?"

Marek swallowed a few times. Standing, or even sitting upright, he would not feel so vulnerable as he did engulfed in the soft feather mattress, helplessly tipped back on his elbows. "My brother Wulfgang, Father."

Any minute Wulf would walk in and be taken by surprise. He would be rendered powerless and dragged off to be tried for Satanism.

"And you and your brother were planning to go and murder a certain Father Vilhelmas. How would you rate this as a sin, my son? Venial or mortal?"

How did they know this? Marek had been a fool to think he could outwit the Church. "Justice, Father. He is a Speaker and a traitor to his king. He murdered the previous count and—"

"But this is not your concern. If you have reason to suspect him of wrongdoing, then your correct course is to report him to Brother Lodnicka. Instead you plot murder? You see how quickly you are perverted when you speak with the devil, Marek?"

"Vilhelmas is a schismatic, of the Orthodox Rite!"

Azuolas barely shrugged. "He is misguided, then, but that will be charged against his soul, not yours. We may have arrived just in time to save you from an eternity in the fires of hell, my son. Brother, you brought the bridles?"

"Yes, Father." The monk produced two iron contraptions he had been holding behind his back.

The friar held up a hand to stay him. "Some more questions first. When Wulfgang came to Koupel on Sunday, Marek, I understand that he did not display a nimbus. Is that correct?"

"Yes, Father." Marek struggled off the bed so he could stand erect, but he still had to look up to the two men. Azuolas moved closer to the door, as if to cut off any attempt to escape.

"And does he now? Have a nimbus, I mean?"

Marek said. "No, Father."

"You are certain of that?" the Dominican demanded suspiciously. "I have your oath on it?"

How much had he seen?

"Yes, Father. He glows when he calls on Satan to perform his black arts, that is all. Not otherwise." Now Marek was a perjurer, but they couldn't do anything to him much worse than what they were planning already.

"So he is still no more than a Four or Five, as that listing was explained to you?"

"Yes, Father." Fours or Fives were obviously much less dangerous than whatever Wulf was now.

"So why did you not come back to Koupel and report?" the monk asked angrily. "As you were instructed to do and swore you would?"

The longer Marek could spin out the conversation, the better the chance that he would still be able to do some good in the struggle when Wulf returned. "When I got here my brother healed my back, and I couldn't face the pain that the journey would cause me."

Lodnicka smiled, showing long yellow teeth. "You have worse to face than that now, Brother Marek. I may gag him, Father?"

"Go ahead. And hurry. We must be ready for the other child of Satan when he returns."

Lodnicka dropped one of the iron bridles on the floor and held out the other. "Put it on, Brother. You know how. It isn't hard."

Yes, Marek knew how. On occasion he had spent days at a time locked in one of the horrible things, for penance, unable to call on his Voices for help. He had nightmares about them sometimes.

"No!" he said. "Please not. I promise I won't Speak."

But the monk just smiled, and Marek's hands took the contraption and raised it to his face without any instructions from him. Even when the metal pressed against his lips he did not resist, for then there would be a struggle for control and the bridle might break his teeth. He opened his mouth to accept the clumsy and foul-tasting tongue plate. He was a puppet, being moved by Lodnicka. His hands pulled the clasps around to the back of his head, and his feet turned him around so that the monk could close the hasp.

The click of the padlock was followed at once by a stunning explosion. Father Azuolas hurled himself onto the bed, facedown. Marek stared in bewilderment at the red foam spurting from a hole in the Dominican's back, the surging bloodstain spreading over his clothes. Brother Lodnicka uttered a roar of fury and whirled around to meet Wulf's attack.

CHAPTER 32

Wulf had worked hard to seem to enjoy the banquet. To sulk or mope would have been unthinkable, giving Anton cause to gloat and increasing Madlenka's distress. He had shared one wistful smile with her at the beginning to show that he felt no bitterness, and since then he never once looked at her, or even at Otto, who was sitting between them.

Dali Notivova proved to be good company, once he had been tactfully assured that none of the Magnuses would try to take his new title away from him. He had a couple of years' mercenary experience, which he was willing to share in exchange for some well-edited stories of the new count's youth. So the talk was good, with a bit of effort. The food was indifferent. The beer was weak and had absolutely no effect on a man whose beloved had been forced into marriage with another. Wulf thought he could have drunk a barrel of it and stayed both sober and somber.

That he was still capable of swift decisions proved to be good fortune when the trumpet sounded and Marek ran screaming across the floor. Wulf saw a man with a limp enter and caught just a glimpse of a nimbus on the one behind him. The Church's enforcers had found him; he was trapped. Go! Go where?

—Just go!

Then he had gone, into darkness in a cold, silent place. Unbalanced by the sudden move, he staggered, banged his leg on the edge of a stool, and steadied himself before he fell. His eyes adapted and found a faint light from barred windows, enough to show that he was in the seneschal's counting room, which had flashed into his mind as a safe and private refuge. He had made the transition so fast that he wasn't sure just what he had done, and had to think back and analyze it. He had gotten there by . . . how, exactly? Not by calling on his Voices. There had been no time for that.

"Holy St. Helena, hear my prayer."

Silence.

Alarmed, he tried again. "Holy St. Victorinus, answer me, I beg you."

Still silence. No Light.

Again he tried, and again there was no response. Were the Voices angry at him? Would they return after he had worried a while, or would he would never hear from them again?

He could worry about that later. Meanwhile, what was happening upstairs in the hall with enemy Speakers on the loose? If they came from the Church, then Marek was in danger, and if they were Wends, then his brothers were. Moving cautiously in the gloom, he made his way to the door, and was not surprised to find it locked. Could he repeat his miracle entry and magic himself back to the hall? Was it safe? What was going on? He needed to *see*!

Then he recalled that strange vision of Dobkov that he had been granted just two days ago.

—*Look.*

He could see! He saw just as if he were up in the hall. He felt as if he were peering through a peephole, as he had in the earlier vision, and his view was strangely jumpy. He was standing, apparently, above the high table, looking at four intruders standing in the center, facing in his direction but blocked from coming any closer by a line of young men, the knights of Cardice. One of the four wore a nimbus; his black gown and hat and his oversized pectoral cross showing that he was a cleric of some kind.

The peephole shifted, to show Marek back at his seat. It kept shifting: right, left, right, up, down. Then it switched completely, showing Wulf the hall from the side, looking across to where he had been sitting a minute ago. The tables there had been overturned since he left, and the floor was a midden of food, dishes, spilled wine, and happily scavenging dogs. Again, his view was restricted and would never keep still, as the owner of the eyes he was looking through kept moving them. His peephole was also much lower than it had been, so it might belong to Marek. He was seeing through Marek's eyes. And hearing through his ears.

". . . your rudeness," one of the intruders said, "we have brought a gift for your lady, a bolt of fine silk from distant Cathay. Marijus?"

Madlenka had mentioned Sir Marijus Vranov, one of the Hound's sons. The leader of this invasion must be the count himself. Again a shift, back up to the vantage point at the head table. There were the rest of his brothers, towering over the bishop and the dowager countess. Fair Madlenka in her steeple hat was the tallest of all.

Another lurch in viewpoint. Very high, so now he must be seeing through Anton's eyes. He tried to look at where he felt he had just come from—almost certainly from

Marek's vantage point—but still could not control what he was seeing and hearing. The eyes reported to him as well as to their rightful owner, but they took only their owner's orders. Wulf felt as if he were speaking, but the voice he heard was Anton's.

Flip! again, and now he was one of the visitors, looking past the glowering knights. Much of this leapfrogging would soon nauseate him, but any new skill needed practice. If all high-rank Speakers could do this, that explained how these Pelrelmians had known that there was a banquet in progress and exactly when to intrude. It explained all sorts of things.

One of the the intruders slipped past the knights and headed for the high table—a youth, carrying something. He spoke with Madlenka, under Anton's glare, and gave her a squirming puppy. She gave him a basket of cakes in exchange.

Wulf was inside Marek again when Vilhelmas's aura blazed extra bright and the four uninvited guests vanished.

Ha! So the invasion was over, leaving the question of what its purpose had been. It might have been an admission of weakness. If Vranov had gone to all that trouble just to utter a fake curse and frighten the townsfolk of Gallant, then perhaps he and his Wend friends were having more difficulty than they had expected in bringing in their Dragon. The castle's defenses would be weakened if most of the population fled. Or the intention might been something worse, which Anton's quick action in blocking their approach had prevented.

So Vilhelmas did not need to Speak aloud to work his miracles or witchcraft, and now Wulf did not either. He must have moved up another rank. He wondered how far this new Seeing talent could reach. Could he consciously control it and peer out of anyone's eyes? Branka's, say, down in Dobkov? That would feel like the worst form of snooping. How about Count Vranov's? *Yes!* He was looking straight at Vilhelmas, who was leering triumphantly through his beard and raising a beer stein as if about to propose a toast.

Wulf withdrew quickly in case his spying was detected, back to the silent dark of the counting room. But now his duty was obvious—he must use his new skills to track down that Pelrelmian Speaker and kill him. That move alone might win the war, if the Wends did not have another Speaker handy. And it ought to be done quickly. He would have to ask for Anton's approval, though.

He knelt and said a formal prayer to his Voices. As before, there was no response at all. Had he offended them in some way? They had moved him out of the hall to safety, but he had not asked them for that blessing, nor had he spoken aloud. He had . . . he had thought a command, or a wish. He had better try it again, for if they would not help him somehow, he would be locked in until morning, at which time he would have a lot of explaining to do.

—*Limbo!* Wulf stepped through where the door ought to be. Fortunately the corridor was deserted and a bronze lantern on a hook cast enough light for him to see where he was going. His first attempt to free the lamp from its captivity burned his fingers, so he used his hat as a glove. Then he hurried off, back to the hall to find Anton.

He heard the riot before he reached it. A torrent of people was flowing down the staircase he needed, all heading to the castle door. From upstairs came weeping and cries of pain and occasional bellows from Vlad and others trying to impose order.

Wulf stood back against the wall and sought out Count Vranov again. Now he was sitting in a circle of men around a crackling fire in some sort of timber building, lit by lanterns, reeking of smoke and men and beer. His son Marijus was there, and Father Vilhelmas, the glow of his nimbus apparently invisible to everyone else. Someone was singing a song and the rest were joining in the chorus. The Wends seemed to be celebrating.

Back in Castle Gallant, the tumult was dying as order was restored. Wulf started up the stairs.

Receiving Anton's permission to proceed was no surprise. Many leaders would have refused to dabble in Satanism, but Anton had taken that plunge days ago, at the royal hunt. Others might have maintained that a priest must be treated as a noncombatant, and sacrosanct, but Vilhelmas had cast away that defense when he led the attack on Long Valley.

Wulf had not expected Marek to want to join in. At first he pretended not to hear, but Marek was persistent and followed him all the way to the Orchard Room. The idea of a monk or friar helping to bushwhack a priest was bizarre, unthinkable; which raised the question of why such a deed would be any more forgivable when done by a layman. Had Wulf already been perverted by the devil's voices? Had his saints fled from him because of that? He needed time to think about this; he was starting to regret his impetuous offer to Anton.

Even worse, if possible, was being questioned by Marek about his mysterious disappearance from the hall. How could he explain it when he didn't know the answer himself? He was so far ahead of Marek now that even to describe his new powers must seem like hurtful bragging. Whatever the monks had done to Marek at Koupel, they seemed to have stunted his ability to Speak. He had managed a couple of minor miracles, but none of Wulf's encouragements had helped him progress beyond the level he had reached before he left Dobkov, five years ago. Was it possible that people could only advance up the ranks by their own efforts? Was that why both the Voices and the monks declined to answer questions?

So Wulf refused to answer questions.

He began calculating what he would need. Outdoor clothes, a sword, a dagger. Assassination was always less risky when done from a distance and Vilhelmas's current companions were almost certainly men-at-arms. A quick trip through limbo, a point-blank shot, and an even faster escape . . . Yes, a crossbow would be the best weapon.

He knew where the armory was. He promised to find Marek a sword, and made his way there.

The armory was locked, of course, but no light showed under the door and locks were no longer a problem. The windows, although protected by massive iron bars, were large; he could see reasonably well by the lights in the bailey.

The racks held a bewildering choice of crossbows: wood, bone, or steel; old and new, small and large. He chose the best he could see, a full-sized military bow of shiny steel with a hand crank. Locating the stores of strings, quivers, and quarrels took longer. Then he had to string the bow, setting the tiller vertical and putting a foot in the stirrup to hold it steady on the floor. Spanning the bow with the crank required a few minutes' hard work, but not the monstrous strength needed to draw a longbow. He hooked the string over the nut and fastened it with the pin so it would be safe to carry it like that. He dropped four quarrels in a quiver, although there was little chance that he would have time to reload.

His own sword was upstairs. He chose a shorter one for Marek and slung it on a baldric.

Carrying a spanned bow indoors was antisocial behavior that would invite questions. He took a quick glance through Marek's eyes to make sure that he was still alone and saw two men with halos looming over him. Wulf had always sympathized with his brother's lack of stature, but experiencing it directly like this was a shock. It must be like living in a world of Vlads and Antons.

". . . still no more than a Four or Five, as that listing was explained to you?"

"Yes, Father."

Right! —*Limbo* . . . Wulf emerged in the corridor outside the door of the Orchard room, took a bolt from his quiver, and loaded it into the groove of the bow. He pulled out the safety pin. Before he could open the door, one of the men backed away from Marek so that he stood directly on the other side of it. Wulf squeezed the trigger.

The noise made by the crossbow being struck by its string was very nearly as loud as an arquebus being fired, and the crash of the bolt going through the planks doubled it. There was no time to reload. He dropped the bow and stepped through limbo into the room.

The friar sprawled facedown on the bed, half on and half off, bleeding copiously and twitching so violently that he might soon slide to the floor. His nimbus flared erratically, as if he might be trying to heal himself.

Marek was struggling to remove his iron gag.

The third person was an elderly Benedictine monk, with a lined face and sparse white hair around his tonsure. He was not tall, but the bulky habit did not hide the outlines of a massive torso. He might be three times Wulf's age, but he would still be a dangerous opponent to wrestle.

And he must have many times Wulf's experience as a Speaker. Invisible hands tightened around Wulf's throat, forcing his head back and downward until he thought his neck would snap. Then his combat training snapped in. He countered with an imaginary punch to the monk's solar plexus that hurled the man back against the fireplace.

That broke his grip, and Wulf gulped in air.

"Stop this! We must heal your friend!"

"You think I am a fool to be snared by such lies?" The monk clamped Wulf's neck again, tighter than ever, choking and bending, forcing him down to his knees.

Men of God should not use force. They certainly should not tangle with trained warriors. *—Kick!* An imaginary boot slammed into the monk's groin. He screamed and crumpled to the floor. Some contests were not governed by the laws of chivalry.

Wulf rushed to the bed, where the Dominican had fallen still. Before he could even think about healing, the same giant hands closed around his head again, thumbs pressing on his eyeballs.

—Kick!

This time the monk either blocked the kick or cured his hurt instantly, for Wulf's reprieve was momentary. Marek was still struggling with the gag, unable to call on his Voices for help. The fight continued, two contestants half a room apart trading blows, kicks, and holds that were invisible but felt just as effective as their counterparts in an all-out physical brawl.

Fighter or not, Wulf was outclassed. His opponent knew far more psychic tricks than he did. His feet flew out from under him even as a noose tightened around his throat. He hit the floor and was kicked on both sides of his chest simultaneously. The light was fading. There was no air . . .

And then there was. His opponent was flat on the floor, and Marek stood over him clutching the poker from the fireplace.

Wulf scrambled dizzily to his feet. "Thanks! I was starting to get worried there." He turned to the prostrate friar, but Marek came to him, making urgent noises.

Wulf said, "Sorry," and examined the padlock on the metal gag. He had no time to waste looking for the key. —*Open!* It opened and he lifted it out of the hasp. "There," he said. "If you will keep an eye on your prisoner, I will see what I can do here."

He knelt beside the Dominican and took his hand. He searched inside for that flicker he had seen in the dying Anton. This time he had no trouble finding what he sought—the friar's soul blazing like a bonfire, about to depart. Quickly Wulf visualized kicking dirt over it, mortal clay. After a moment he even visualized a shovel to bury the blaze. —*Live!* —*Live!* It was a strange way to conceive of healing, and it might have worked if he had started sooner, but the friar's soul broke loose and flew up and away, leaving only a swirl of ash behind, without as much as an ember.

"He's dead," Wulf said. He said a hasty prayer, crossed himself, and stood up. He had killed a man, shooting him in the back from cover. It had never been a fair fight and there was no honor in it. He felt sick and shaky.

The monk was sitting up, showing no sign of a distress, so either he or Marek had healed his headache. Marek stood behind him holding the poker, ready to hit him again. Both were murmuring prayers.

When they had finished, Wulf said, "Wasn't he one of the Dominicans who came to Dobkov for you, five years ago?"

"Yes. Father Azuolas. And this is Brother Lodnicka, who was my master at Koupel." Marek looked at least as shaken as Wulf felt.

"And who will be again," Lodnicka said tartly. "So you have murdered a priest, Wulfgang Magnus. You are doomed to the pit!"

What to do with the body? What to do with Lodnicka? Both physically and magically, he was enormously powerful. Killing him would be the simplest solution. Otherwise he would return with an army. But a friar and a monk . . . Who would ever believe Wulf had slain them in self-defense?

"Brother Marek, you lied to me," the monk continued. "You told me that Wulfgang was still only a Four."

"And you lied to him," Wulf roared. "You told him you were sending him out to find me and then go back to report where I was, but that wasn't true, was it? Because you knew him, you could watch through his eyes. You could also go to him, anywhere, as you just did. You didn't know me, because I had kept my face hidden when I came to Koupel. And the abbot's attempts to eavesdrop on us prove that he didn't have any Speakers handy just then anyway. So you sent Marek to find me and open the way to me."

The monk sneered. "We did not lie to him. Telling partial truth in a good cause is a minor sin compared with murdering a priest!"

"But kidnapping is both a breach of the king's peace and violence forbidden by canon law. We are fighting a war here in Cardice. Pomerania has invaded Jorgary. Your interference is treason and I doubt if King Konrad will pay much attention to benefit of clergy if he learns of it. Do you understand?"

"We fight the greater war of Christ against the armies of Satan!"

"Then fight it in your cloisters and leave this one to us. Take that corpse away and give it Christian burial, because if you don't . . . disposing of two bodies in these mountains can't be much harder than disposing of one. The wolves and the bears will be happy to assist. And stay away from here in future!"

Wulf was now so furious that he could barely restrain himself. Perhaps that showed, for the Benedictine stopped arguing. Scowling, he rose and went to the friar's body. In an impressive show of strength—physical or psychical—he lifted it and draped it over one shoulder. Red with rage, he said, "You will regret this sin for all eternity."

"So you keep saying. Last chance—take that cadaver and go!"

CHAPTER 33

The murderer sank down on a stool, disgusted at himself. It had been a terrible day, and was likely to get worse. Now the Church had a lot more reason to arrest him. He couldn't imagine an army of Dominicans openly invading Castle Gallant to get him, but they would surely do something. The blood-soaked bedding where Azuolas had died would have to be explained. Vilhelmas was another Speaker who had to be killed, another shot in the back. Was this how Brutus had felt when he came home with Caesar's blood on his knife?

Marek was examining the two metal bridles, which the intruders had left behind. "These wouldn't hold you, would they?" he said. "You weren't calling on your Voices when you were fighting Lodnicka. Neither was he."

"No, they wouldn't hold me now," Wulf said, but without explaining more. Not even cutting out his tongue would disable him now. How had the English managed to burn Joan of Arc? How had they even managed to keep her in jail?

Marek looked at him disbelievingly, then closed his eyes. His lips moved silently, but he remained stubbornly solid. He opened his eyes again.

"Nothing."

"It will come in time," Wulf said firmly. "You've been held back for five years, so you need to practice. Bear with me a moment."

He closed his own eyes and searched for Vranov's to make sure he still had a chance to get at Vilhelmas. *Too late!* The Hound was leaving the party—on his feet and walking. Images flashed in nauseating jitter as the man's attention flickered from one angle to another: men's faces grinning up at him as he passed, calling out incomprehensible jokes; rough-cut plank walls and the door he was approaching; eye-stinging smoke from the fire; the youth Leonas on the floor in a corner, playing with puppies. That was a good sign, because if his father wasn't taking him he must be planning to return. No sign of Vilhelmas. An open door, a gust of cool, wet night wind bringing scents of trees and swamp. A sickening lurch as he went down two steps to the muddy ground. No rain penetrated the heavy tree cover, but water fell in heavy drops from the branches.

Then wet tree bark, very close.

Wulf squirmed with embarrassment as his host, unaware that he was being observed, fumbled with laces and pulled down the front of his trunk hose. But once Vranov had himself in position and was enjoying what he came to do, he turned his head to study his surroundings. Through a sparse forest of conifer trunks, Wulf saw cooking fires and a camp of leather tents. He saw horses and heard men singing, oxen lowing. Then the Hound turned his attention to the opposite direction. About a hundred yards away, beyond the trees, stood half a dozen wagons, including one especially massive dray with a large, anonymous package chained to it. Four great campfires surrounded the wagon encampment and at least a dozen pickets were patrolling it. There slept the

Dragon! Now Wulf knew he was at Long Valley, which Dali Notivova had described to him.

His business complete, Havel Vranov laced up his hose and headed back to the barracks shed, giving Wulf a good view of it. It was about fifty feet long, built of pine logs and roofed with shingles. There were no sentries posted around it, there in the middle of the Wend army, and almost certainly it was Castle Gallant's advance post, whose garrison had been murdered two days ago. That crime was about to be avenged.

Vranov stamped his feet on the steps to shake mud off his boots and went inside, where the same nine or ten men still sat in a loose arc before the hearth, arguing in an impenetrable dialect. Father Vilhelmas had the place of honor in the middle, directly facing the fieldstone fireplace. Vranov went back to the stool he had vacated. Wulf opened his eyes and returned to reality and Gallant.

Marek had already changed into layman's clothes. "Well?"

"They're at Long Valley. Vilhelmas is still there. It should be easy."

"Those are ominous words, Brother!" Marek said, with an almost-convincing grin.

"True. But I can open a gate through limbo. Step One: emerge right behind him. Step Two: pull trigger. Three: leave, closing gate."

Marek nodded. "Let me do it. You'll have to take us there, but I want to pull the trigger."

Wulf eyed him doubtfully. "Why? There's no honor in this. It's craven butchery."

Marek pouted. "Chivalry died a long time ago. I remember Grandsire complaining of that. It was only ever a set of rules agreed between Christian gentlemen, and the poor pikemen never got the benefit of it. Did you ever hear Otto tell about the man who tried to steal Balaam? Otto picked up a crossbow, armed it, and shot him dead before he had ridden out of range. Balaam turned around and came back to let his master unload the corpse on his back. Same justice here. Vilhelmas killed the count and his son. You need a cleric to kill a cleric."

That was the weirdest logic Wulf had ever heard. "I killed Azuolas. They can hang me if they catch me, but they can't hang me twice."

They had burned Joan of Arc three times.

"But five years of singing psalms is enough. I'd much rather dance on the gibbet beside you than go back to that. Please, Brother?"

This belligerence was unexpected. Of the brothers, Marek had always been the least interested in martial exercises. What was he trying to prove, and was he proving it to himself or to the others? Wulf had brought only one bow, and if Marek botched the shot, the results might be disastrous. To go back to the armory for another bow would be heartless, showing a complete lack of faith in him.

"If you wish. Let's do it, then."

Marek took the bow and tried to span it, but after five years as a monk, he lacked the necessary muscle. He handed it to Wulf to do it for him. Wulf did.

"Ready?" he asked, conscious that his own heart was racing fit to burst. "Tuck it under your cloak to keep the string dry."

"Ready."

—*Limbo.*

Wulf did not feel confident enough in his powers yet to try opening a gate right into the cabin at Long Valley.

Instead he put it outside in the glade, facing the door but a few feet away from it, relying on the view that Vranov himself had so kindly provided. The air smelled of wood smoke and trees. Heavy drips from the branches were at least as unpleasant as the rain itself would have been, but at least there was no one close. He stepped through the gate and closed it when Marek followed. Together they ran around to the side of the building in case someone came out for the same reason Vranov had. Sounds of drunken singing showed that the party was still in progress inside.

Wulf pointed out the sentries guarding the shrouded shape of the bombard on the dray. "That must be the Dragon. Nothing else would be so well guarded."

Marek nodded, and then suddenly gripped Wulf's arm as he was turning away.

"Look there!" he whispered. "Is that him? Beside that wagon on the right?"

The pickets were too far away to make out any details, not even whether they were wearing armor, but Marek was indicating a group of three men standing in apparent conversation. One of them had a nimbus. Could it be Father Vilhelmas?

"Not enough time," Wulf said. "He couldn't have got there since . . ." Of course he could, because he was a Speaker.

He looked through Vilhelmas's eyes and was instantly back in the party inside the log building: lamplight, wood smoke, strident laughter. So Vilhelmas was Count Vranov's Speaker and the Wends had at least one of their own. A Speaker to guard the Dragon was hardly unexpected, but even one must make Wulf's task of destroying it very much harder. Any more than one would make it impossible.

"No, he's still inside." Wulf handed Marek a quarrel. "Tell me when to open the gate. Don't give them time to react."

"Ready."

—Open a gate just behind Vilhelmas and at the same level.

The gate opened. Firelight blazed out with a sound of music, someone strumming a lute out of the assassins' view. It stopped abruptly as men cried out in alarm. Just on the far side of the hole in the world sat the Speaker priest, with his back turned to it, and a glow around his head. For a moment that seemed to last forever, nothing happened—or at least nothing that was supposed to happen. *Marek! Shoot!* The Wends started leaping to their feet. Father Vilhelmas turned his head, one eye glaring just above his massive beard. *Do it now!*

At long last, Marek's crossbow loosed with a crack like a cannon. As the Speaker fell off his stool with the bolt half-buried in his skull, Wulf closed the gate.

Then the two of them were alone in the dark, with only the wind and the rush of steadily increasing rain overhead. Wulf caught Marek in his arms for a congratulatory hug. The little man dragged a couple of hard sobs, then twisted out of Wulf's grasp, leaned against a tree trunk, and threw up.

"Well done, Brother!" Wulf said. "You have avenged two foul murders and probably won the war."

Marek heaved again.

"He deserved to die."

The second Speaker was still among the guards around the Dragon.

Firelight poured out of the cabin as the door flew open. Wulf grabbed his brother and dragged him back to their room in Castle Gallant.

CHAPTER 34

Vlad was leaning over the bed, examining the drying blood. He straightened up with an oath and reached for his sword. Then he recognized the newcomers and scowled. Vlad always scowled.

"I've been looking everywhere for you two. What happened here?"

"I killed a priest," Wulf said callously. He would not pretend to mourn Father Azuolas. No doubt the man had been sincere in his beliefs, but kidnapping boys and locking them up for being Speakers when he was a Speaker himself had been contemptible hypocrisy.

"That's a relief. If this were a wedding bed, I would fear for the bride's health. What happened to the door?"

"Woodpeckers."

"So where have you been?" The big man took a hard look at Marek. "And what's wrong with Midge?"

Marek was still leaning on Wulf. Their boots had splattered mud and water on the tiles, and a reek of forest filled the little room.

"Buck fever," Marek muttered. He pulled free and wiped his eyes with the back of his hand. "I just killed another. Another priest, I mean. It's a family weakness." He attempted a smile. "But we did it, didn't we, Wulfie?"

"We did. And what's wrong with you?" Wulf asked Vlad.

"Well, I'm happy to report that the bishop has finished exorcising the hall and gone home to write a long, gossipy letter to Archbishop Svaty. I'm unhappy to report that Anton has just spilled some very bad news. Otto's in the solar, drinking up the castle's wine supply."

"Anton and Madlenka?"

"They're both with Otto. I don't think Anton trusts his lady out of his sight."

Wulf sighed. The events of the evening had left him emotionally numb, which was a sort of blessing. "Let's go and join them."

Castle Gallant's solar was of modest size, hard-put to hold even five chairs, and the Magnus family filled it tighter than a meal sack. No one had thought to order a fire in the dreary little hearth, so Wulf perched on the hob, leaning his forearms on his knees and staring glumly at the tiled floor. Once in a while he would glance at Anton and Madlenka holding hands, just to make his wounds bleed more. He also drank. He had decided that what he needed was the world's worst hangover. A dozen or so spare flagons of wine stood ready on a table beside Vlad's chair. It beat the insipid beer that had been served at the meal.

No one spoke as Marek recounted the Speakers' adventures since the end of the banquet. No one suggested that Madlenka should be excluded and she must have been warned what to expect, for she seemed unsurprised by a discussion of Satanism. She was carefully displaying no emotion at all.

At the end, Vlad said, "Well, now you're both blooded!

A Magnus isn't a real man until he's killed someone. That just leaves Anton."

"I hanged a man on Monday," Anton said coldly. "Does that count?"

"Not unless you whipped the horse yourself. Count us four bull's-eyes and a blue, then." The big man took a drink.

Madlenka's lip curled slightly.

"Vladislav," Otto said, "you have the grace of a hog and should not be allowed indoors. Marek, Wulfgang, I approve of the way you went after Vilhelmas. Priest or not, he was leading troops and doing nonclerical things. A combatant cannot claim benefit of clergy. Well done, both of you!" He raised a glass in approval. The others joined in the toast.

Wulf smiled across at Marek and raised his own glass to him. He cared nothing for Vlad's opinions, but approval from Otto was welcome.

Marek smiled and responded, raising his glass. "*Omnia audere!*"

They all shouted approval and drank again. Jollity reigned: it was five years since the brothers had last been united. Wulf might not be the only one heading for a Magnus-sized hangover.

It was Otto who brought them back into the shadows. "But, Brothers—and new Sister—the Dominican's death is going to bring real trouble. You said they were using Voices to force you to put on that iron bit, Marek. But a bystander wouldn't have seen that, would he? It would look like you were doing it voluntarily."

"Not 'Voices,' " Marek said. "Lodnicka doesn't need to Speak aloud. Nor does Wulf, now. They're both top-rank, um, Speakers. But I know what you mean."

Otto nodded. "A court of law would say that Wulf

was the aggressor. I don't think that, but the law will. He heard the priest speak behind the door and shot him through it in cold blood."

"They'll have trouble making a case at all," Marek protested. "How can they explain these events without revealing the Church's own use of Satanism? I expect they'll think up something, but it'll take time."

"Yesterday Cardinal Zdenek told me he could protect Wulf from the Church, but it was a very conditional offer. Wulf must defend Castle Gallant against the Wends without Speaking so anybody can notice. Killing friars was not discussed. The Church will now be howling for Wulf's blood."

"It was an accident," Wulf said innocently. "I didn't mean to shoot the quarrel at the door."

"My lords?" Madlenka murmured and five pairs of eyes swung toward her.

"Yes, my dear?" Anton frowned, as if he hadn't known she was capable of speech.

"Havel Vranov has been a Wend-killer all his life; he hunted them down like vermin. Then a few months ago he started consorting with this Orthodox priest who's supposed to be a distant cousin, but is certainly on the Wends' side. Do you suppose that Vilhelmas was an evil genius, bewitching him? Now that he's dead, will Vranov come back to his senses and repent?"

They all looked to Marek, the expert on Speaking, but he looked blank. "I can't tell you. But let's hope so!"

After a moment Otto said, "Day before yesterday, Wulf, you told me that you had to Speak aloud to your Voices. Now Marek says you don't."

"No, I don't." Wulf did not want to admit that his Voices would not answer him now. "So what I can do is not Speaking, strictly speaking. I don't know what it is. It's not witchcraft!"

"Can you prove that?" Vlad demanded. Incredibly, he still sounded almost sober.

"God hears if we pray to him in silence."

Even Otto was looking doubtful now. "Joan of Arc always insisted that her Voices came from God."

"So will I, if the Church ever puts me on trial. I'm telling you all this because you're my brothers and sister-in-law and I trust you. If you don't want me here, just say so and I'll be gone in a flash." He did not look at Madlenka.

"Have you worked out why Joan could lift a siege of a city and yet couldn't rescue herself from a jail?"

"No," Wulf said unhappily. "Maybe it's like all the fairy tales, and we only get so many wishes." Last night again he had dreamt of fighting the Pomeranian army single-handed and his powers disappearing in the middle of the battle.

"So you can work miracles?" Vlad said. "Show us."

A wine flagon rose from the table beside his chair and floated across to Wulf. He refilled his goblet from it and sent it back. There was a long silence while the others stared at one another. Finally the big warrior laughed and raised his wine in a toast. "To St. Wolfcub!"

Wulf wiped his mouth. The wine was not as good as Dobkov's. "So, Brother," he told Otto, "if you've enjoyed your visit to Castle Gallant and would like to return to the arms of your loving wife, I'd be happy to arrange the journey for you."

"*Ha!*" Vlad roared. "He can't go! Tell them the news, Brother Baron."

Otto scowled at him in disgust. "Vladislav, you're a

blabbering bone-skull." From him, that was a stinging rebuke.

"It's long past bedtime," Anton said, rising to his full height. "Sufficient unto the day is the evil thereof, as Father Czcibor always says." He held out a hand to Madlenka.

Evidently she could be trusted with Satanism but not with whatever the other news was. The rest of the men rose also.

"Don't run away yet, Beanpole," Vlad said. "You still have some explaining to do."

"You go ahead, my love. I'll be there in a few minutes."

Just for a moment, Wulf saw a flicker in Madlenka's eyes, but then she accepted the dismissal with a humility that he was certain must be costing her dearly. Anton's Madlenka might be a kitten, but the one Wulf knew was not. She curtseyed to the company and departed.

Anton closed the door he had held for her, then leaned back against it.

"You great blabbering ox!" he snapped. "I do not want panic in the town!" He was being Count Magnus of Cardice, lord of the marches, clad in awesome authority.

Unimpressed, Vlad just chuckled. "But our miracle workers have a right to know. Listen, little brothers. Here's the worst news yet. Before our noble count could carry his bride off to the conjugal chamber, Otto and I backed him into a corner and threatened to break his legs if he didn't tell us the real reason the *landsknechte* left town."

"Plague," Marek said softly. He smiled his wan little smile at them.

Appalled, Wulf flopped down on the hob again. Lord have mercy! *Pestilence?* Then no one was safe. Even Madlenka.

"Midge is calling you a liar, Beanpole," Vlad said angrily. "You told us you hadn't told anyone at all before we got it out of you!"

"Knowing Marek," Otto said, "I expect he worked it out with Aristotelean logic. Father always warned us that he was the smart one."

Marek smiled at the compliment. "Why else would a mercenary band run away from certain money? The *landsknechte* wouldn't even have been in serious danger in a siege, because Gallant's a unique stronghold in that it always has an escape hatch on the other side. A threat of plague was the only possible explanation."

"Bribery would be another," Vlad grumbled.

"But the way Wulf described it, they made no attempt to bargain and play one side off against another. And when we arrived this morning, Anton was pleased to see all of us except Otto. He has a family. The rest of us can take our chances, but if he takes pestilence back to Dobkov the whole Magnus line could be wiped out."

"Why?" Wulf snapped. "Why did you keep this news quiet?"

Anton shrugged. "I was told of one woman with a lump in her armpit. She died. That doesn't make an epidemic. I don't want my people fleeing out into the moors with winter coming on."

"Was she by any chance in the infirmary while I was there?"

"I don't know. We must pray to Our Lady that it was a false alarm and we shall be spared that horror."

"Amen to that," Otto said, "but meanwhile I can't go home. I don't even dare write a letter and ask Wulf to deliver it. Anything a pestilence victim has touched or breathed on can spread the disease."

"I don't believe it!" Vlad proclaimed. "If the trollop really died of plague, half the town would be sick by now. Half the town might be *dead* by now!"

"Possible," Marek said, still quietly—he had learned long ago not to contradict his biggest brother directly. "But they say a town can't be certain the pestilence has ended until forty days have passed without a new case. We have thirty-seven days to wait. After that you can go home, Otto."

"A lot of people have left town already," Anton said. "Scared away by Count Bukovany's death, the threat of war, the *landsknechte*'s flight. If even one of them is carrying the pestilence, it'll be all over Jorgary by spring."

"Don't forget that stupid curse tonight!" Vlad boomed. He was showing the effects of the wine at last.

"Right. On Vlad's advice," Anton said. "I've ordered the gates locked. Nobody's leaving now."

Heads nodded in approval.

Vlad explained. "I don't believe for a moment that Havel Vranov came here to play with puppies. He came here to frighten everyone. He brought the silk and the puppy along as gifts in case he was made welcome, but his real reason was to make that spectacular exit. It was simple terrorism."

"It's possible," Marek agreed again. "But I think Vranov came for Wulf. Vilhelmas had seen how badly Anton was wounded. He spied on him later and saw him alive and restored to health, so he knew there must be a Speaker in Gallant. That changed the odds! A war must be much easier to win if you have Speakers and your opponents don't. That was why he had Vranov crash the banquet, and why he kept peering around, looking for another Speaker. If he'd seen Wulf, he might have done to him what Wulf and I just did to him."

Vlad completed a long drink from a wine flask. "Faugh! Sometimes you just try to take on your foes one at a time and hope they never get to combine against you. If Vranov risked appearing here tonight, even for a few moments, then he doesn't believe in the pestilence. I'm with Beanpole. Let's deal with the Wends first and worry about plague later, if ever."

Anton said, "Thank you. I'm going to bed." He glanced momentarily at Wulf, without expression, and then he was closing the door behind him.

Wulf took a brief look out of Anton's eyes to make sure he was going away and not lurking outside the door, then through Madlenka's to make sure she was alone. Then he stood up and stepped through limbo to her room.

CHAPTER 35

Madlenka was seated at her dressing board, taking pins out of her hair. The room was dim, with only a single lamp to scare away the shadows. She felt wrung dry by the events of the day, shattered by Wulf's expected return, and nauseated at the thought of another interminable night with Anton. He wasn't an evil man. If he saved the castle from the Wends, he might eventually make a good count and lord of the marches. At the moment, he was just an arrogant and insensitive youth. Perhaps few men of that age were much better, and Wulfgang was an extreme exception. She suspected that she might now be quite content with her lot if she had never met her husband's brother.

There were two reflections in the glass.

She spun around. "Wulf! Idiot! Go away. I rang for my maid."

"She'll knock." He was standing well away from her, his face grave.

"Anton—"

"Is on his way. We have a moment, that's all. Oh, Madlenka! I just came to tell you that it was my fault and I am—"

She jumped up. "No, it was mine!"

"I told you I would be forty days and—"

"And I betrayed you in forty minutes."

He shook his head and came a step closer. "I should have told Anton about us when I cured his wound."

"Told him you wanted me as your share of the spoils?"

He smiled wanly. "Would you have minded if I'd called you that?"

"No. I would happily be your loot. Pillage me now and take me far, far away. I will never complain."

He shook his head. "There's no escape. That would make you a fugitive, a felon, an adulteress, and God knows what else. Even an accomplice to Satanism. We would be outside the law and condemned by the Church. Our children would be bastards, nobodies."

She knew all that. She thought about it in bed a lot. "I don't want you to reproach yourself. It was my fault for being so weak."

"Mine!" he insisted.

"Your only mistake was healing Mother. If she'd not been there I could have stood up to them. But she threatened to lock me up in the Poor Claires' convent until the king could decide what to do with me. Anton would never have done that. But she would! And the bishop . . ."

They had been moving closer. Now they were close enough to touch, but neither made the move. In the gloom his eyes were not golden, they were silver, like moonlight reflected in water.

"Forget all that," he said. "It's done, and you could never have found happiness with me. I am a Satanist. I've killed a priest and helped kill another. The Church will hunt me down and order me burned at the stake. I will love you forever, but you must forget me and love Anton. And pray that none of his children are Speakers, because Speaking is the curse of our line."

Knuckles tapped softly on the door.

"My love," he said, "always." Then he vanished.

"If you keep doing things like that, I think I'll burn you at the stake myself," Vlad said.

Wulf resumed his place on the hob and filled his goblet. No one had moved in his absence: Marek was seated in the center facing him, Vlad to his right, Otto to his left.

Getting no answer, Vlad said, "Even if Anton dies, of the plague or anything else, a man cannot marry his brother's widow."

Wulf drank and picked up the flagon for a refill.

Vlad tried again. "Well at least you were quick. Did she enjoy it, too?"

Wulf stared at him coldly. "One more joke like that," he said softly, "and I will burn your balls off, so help me God." He put the goblet to his lips and drained it.

Silence.

"You are a dangerous combination, Brother," Otto said. "The family chronicle begins almost two hundred years ago, in the time of the fourth baron. It names six Speaker daughters and hints at another, but only two Speaker sons before Marek. Meaning no disrespect to him, he has always been more of a scholar than a warrior. He would rather settle a dispute with law and reason than with sword or fist." He glanced at Marek, who smiled to show he was not offended. "But you, Brother Wolfgang, wield your powers audaciously. You have a hair-trigger temper and you fear nothing, true to the Magnus motto."

Wulf did not reply. He wished he had not threatened Vlad, but he would not withdraw his words.

"You are probably the most dangerous man in Jorgary," Otto persisted.

"What I think," Marek announced solemnly, "is that I'm going to get catastrophically drunk for the first time in my life." He took a long draft, straight from a flagon. "Foul stuff! I'll say this for Koupel—it does have grand wine . . . Brothers, one thing still puzzles me. Tonight, when I asked my Voices to restore the old countess, St. Uriel told me that it was important for me to know why she had been affected. I have asked him since to explain, but he will not. My saints have never volunteered advice before. Any helpful suggestions?"

He was looking at Wulf, who made an effort to think about it. "Vilhelmas had cursed her before, so perhaps she was more susceptible and he could do it from farther away."

"Puppies make her sick?" Vlad suggested.

"I suppose . . . Mother of God!" Marek fell back in his chair, gaping up at the chimney above Wulf's head. The room filled with a swirl of wood smoke and the sounds of voices and a crackling fire.

Otto and Vlad both spoke at once, demanding to know what was wrong.

"You killed my friend!" cried a shrill voice.

Marek made croaking noises. His brothers stared at one another in bewilderment. Just as Wulf realized that there must be an open gate in front of Marek that was only visible from that side, Leonas Vranov stepped from nowhere into the space between them. He was clutching a puppy. His always-pale face was white with fury, his fair hair stuck up in spikes, and he was slobbering.

Vlad roared an oath and started out of his chair. He drew his sword.

Otto shouted, "Wait! Careful!"

Leonas shook his free fist in Marek's face. *"You killed my friend and I HATE you!"*

"That'll do, Leonas," his father's voice said.

"I want you to die too!"

Wulf leaped past him and turned to view the gap, the same timber barracks, faces watching, Havel Vranov with a sword in his hand . . .

"Come back here, Leonas!"

The youth spat, turned around, and disappeared back into nowhere. The gate through limbo vanished.

Otto muttered a prayer and made the sign of the cross. "Gone! So now we know how it was done. But who opened the gate for him, if you killed Vilhelmas? The Wends have more Speakers?"

"Or Leonas himself is one!" Wulf said. "He was close to Countess Edita tonight. Could that be why your Voice told you . . . Marek? *Marek!*"

Marek was leaning back in his chair, eyes glazed over. Otto and Wulf lunged across simultaneously and knelt on either side of him.

"No! Marek!" Wulf grabbed his brother's hand. "St. Victorinus! Holy St. Helena! No! No! No!"

He could find no fire, only ash. Like Azuolas, Marek had gone.

"No pulse. He's dead." Otto reached out and closed their brother's eyes.

The three stared at one another in dismay, struggling to believe it.

One by one they bent their heads in prayer.

Marek, oh, Marek! You never wanted to hurt anyone until tonight. Five years locked up in Koupel, two days' liberty, and now this! Why didn't you let me kill Vilhelmas?

Eventually Wulf spoke. "He warned me. He told me when Anton and I went to the monastery, 'Anything the Voices do for you will turn to evil eventually!' "

Otto and Vlad just nodded.

Leonas! Who could have imagined that an imbecile could be a Speaker? They should have noticed that the knights didn't stop him when he went to Madlenka in the hall. Why hadn't they? Probably because they suddenly didn't want to. Leonas had not deliberately done anything to them or to the countess. Like a small child, he just wanted things and expected them to happen. And in his case, they did. He had no nimbus, because that came with understanding, and he would never understand.

Otto had his hands clasped as if he were still praying. "No wonder his father keeps close watch on him. He threw a tantrum at Count Stepan and his son and they died—when? A few days later, a couple of weeks later? Is that possible?"

"You know as much as I do," Wulf said. He felt as if he were standing inside a block of ice. *Marek! Oh, Marek!* "Seems anything's possible."

Vilhelmas had certainly been a Speaker with a nimbus, but he might not have killed Stepan and Petr Bukovany. He was a distant cousin, so Satanism ran in the Vranov family also.

Wulf put it in words. "Maybe Leonas's curses took time to act. Or one day his father said, 'Remember those two bad men who shouted at you at Cardice? You don't like them, do you?' Madlenka was kind to him, so she wasn't affected. Leonas doesn't like the old countess and he was close to her tonight. He doesn't even know what he's doing—but his father knows! Vranov uses him as a weapon, a puppet Speaker."

Otto shook his head in despair. "You mean that just now Vranov said, 'Do you remember that funny little man with the shaved head who ran around in the banquet hall, shouting at us? He was the one who killed Father Vilhelmas. Go and tell him how much you hate him'?"

Wulf nodded, tasting vomit. "The boy can't be trusted in churches because the voices echo and sound like his Voices. He probably doesn't understand what his Voices are saying."

"He scares the piss out of me," Vlad said. "We'd better tell Anton."

"Tomorrow," Otto said. "Right now we need a priest."

"What do you want me to do about this, Brothers?" Wulf demanded. "A Magnus lies dead. Do I avenge him? Go and kill that half-wit boy?"

"No!" Vlad bellowed. "No, not now. It's a trap. They'll be waiting for you."

"Not ever, I think," Otto said.

"Why not? I'm damned already. Obviously my Voices came from Satan. I've killed two priests and now my brother has died because of what I did."

Vlad and Otto exchange shocked looks.

"No!" Vlad boomed. "Never, never think that way! Your intentions were good."

Otto said, "But now you understand the dangers your Voices warned you against. To civic rulers like Anton you are a killer who can strike anyone, at any time. To the Church you're Heresy Incarnate. You're the Antichrist. You could start a great heretical movement like Jan Huss did, or overthrow the pope. Duke Wartislaw may not know about you yet, but you'll certainly be his prime target as soon as he does. Even Cardinal Zdenek must disown you now. You could supplant him, or depose King Konrad and take the crown. You're more dangerous than the Ottoman Sultan or the Great Pestilence. Can anybody or anything control you now, boy?"

"Another Speaker," Wulf said. "Azuolas would have beaten me tonight if Marek hadn't come to my aid. A gang of them certainly could."

"You must leave Castle Gallant," Otto persisted. "Tonight! Go far away and make a new life under a new name."

Wulf shook his head and reached for wine. "No."

"Remember what I told you about Joan of Arc being burned? Remember Julius Caesar, stabbed? Alexander the Great, poisoned? You're a danger to *everybody*, Wulf! All power is unpopular but absolute power will turn every man's hand against you."

"You must go, Wolfcub." Vlad looked genuinely concerned.

Wulf desperately wanted to do that, to be far away from Madlenka and the torment of seeing her as Anton's wife. Now that he knew that the Wends had at least one Speaker guarding their great bombard, the chances that he could save Castle Gallant had dropped from slim to very close to zero. But there was no place to hide from Speakers. Brother Lodnicka knew his face now, so he could come to Wulf anywhere, at any time. He might be watching through his eyes right now, listening with his ears.

"You're absolutely right," he said. "I don't have to stay here and die. It's Anton's pissy castle. Let him defend it! So where shall we go?"

"*We?*" his brothers barked in perfect unison.

That seemed so funny that Wulf almost laughed, until he remembered that Marek's corpse lay sprawled in the chair beside him. *Oh, Marek, Marek!* How were they going to explain this death to a priest?

"Everything you said about me applies to both of you. Cardice is none of our business. So where shall I take us?"

"Magnuses do not run away!" Vlad roared.

"No, we don't," Wulf said. Of course, when the castle was about to fall, he would rescue Madlenka and move her to somewhere safe. But then he would come back and stand with his brothers. It was the Magnus way. He raised his glass. The other two saw what was coming and raised theirs.

They proclaimed the toast together: *"Omnia audere!"*

Before the wine touched their lips, a fist banged on the door. Vlad hurtled across the room to open it, using his bulk to block the newcomer's view of Marek. He also hid Wulf's view of the newcomer, but Wulf recognized the voice of Dalibor Notivova.

"Campfires, Sir Vladislav! Down at High Meadows. The lookouts spotted a couple just after dark and now there's at least a score of them. Seems an army's moving in, pitching camp!"

"High Meadows?" Vlad said. "You mean *south* of us? Not the Wends, then?"

"No, sir. Pelrelmians, maybe. Can't be king's men, or they'd come to the gate."

"Vranov!"

"Seems likely, sir. But a lot more men than he had there last weekend."

Vlad boomed out a laugh. "Well, Dali my lad, that's good news! Excellent news! I am exactly in the mood to head out and *kill* somebody! Let's find me a warm cloak and you and I will go have a look." He glanced over his shoulder. "You two clean up here." He chivvied Dali out ahead of him and closed the door.

HISTORICAL NOTE

Jorgary is entirely imaginary. Outside its borders I used real place names, but you will not be able to fit them to any atlas, modern or historical.

The story takes place around 1475. The Middle Ages had ended. The Reformation was still almost fifty years in the future.

Michelangelo was born that year. His future patron, Lorenzo the Magnificent, ruled Florence, and Pope Sixtus IV was building the Sistine Chapel. England was embroiled in the Wars of the Roses. Ferdinand and Isabella had not yet driven the Moors from Spain. Louis XI (known as the Spider) was ruling France, while his archenemy, Charles the Bold—duke of Burgundy from 1467 to 1477, was changing the nature of warfare forever.

As late as the Battle of Agincourt, in 1415, the cream of French chivalry attempted cavalry charges against English bowmen, with results even more disastrous than those their ancestors had suffered doing the same thing at Crécy two generations earlier. In fact, the days of the armored knight on horseback had been waning since 1314, when lowly Scottish infantry clobbered English cavalry in the Battle of Bannockburn.

The fighting horse had become too vulnerable and too expensive. The whole concept of knighthood was fading, so that commoners and aristocrats became lumped together as men-at-arms. They were usually grouped in "lances," consisting of two men in armor to wield the actual lance and a youth to look after the horses. Both infantry and archers would ride to battle, but fight on foot. Cavalry could be used to raid the enemy's baggage train or ride down the fugitives when his forces tried to flee the field.

The old feudal levies, where a vassal owed his liege forty days' knight's service a year, were already largely replaced by taxation, which the king could use to hire mercenaries. In the fifteenth century the mercenaries began to give way to full-time professional national armies with their own uniforms and insignia—the first standing armies since Roman times. The new system was largely introduced by Charles the Bold, but the changes did not happen at the same time everywhere. My fictional King Konrad employs regular cavalry troops but hires mercenaries as well. Out in the sticks, at Cardice, the landowners are still calling up feudal levies.

Pomerania was a duchy occupying parts of modern Poland and Germany. It was ruled by many successive dukes named Wartislaw, a name I could never invent. Wends was a name applied to various peoples of Slavic descent.

Guns were first used in battle in Europe in the fourteenth century, but they were primitive, and often more dangerous to the gunners than the targets. Only in the fifteenth century did they become effective. Henry V of England took several hundred guns with him when he invaded France in 1415. He used them in his siege of Harfleur, but they appear to have been of limited help. In 1453 French cannons devastated English bowmen at the Battle of Castillon, and that same year the Ottoman Turks used guns to breach the ancient walls of Constantinople. Handguns followed later. In 1498 the senate of

Venice decreed that in future its forces would be armed with firearms instead of crossbows. Modern warfare had arrived.

The "Dragon" gun in this book is based on the giant bombard Mons Meg, still on display in Edinburgh Castle, Scotland. According to Wikipedia, it was made in about 1452 and fired 400-pound, 22-inch stone balls for up to two miles. Notably, the barrel has no trunnions to fit it to a gun carriage. It would have been transported on a cart and then "emplaced" on the battlefield.

For an account of the change in warfare, see: *A Brief History of Medieval Warfare: The Rise and Fall of English Supremacy at Arms, 1314–1485* by Peter Reid, Running Press, 2008.

And, finally: horses have to be trained to trot, and in those days they mostly ambled or ran.